BLASTED THINGS

BLASTED THINGS

Lesley Glaister

SANDSTONE PRESS

First published in Great Britain by
Sandstone Press Ltd
Willow House
Stoneyfield Business Park
Inverness
IV2 7PA
Scotland

www.sandstonepress.com

ISBN: 978-1-913207-12-0
ISBNe: 978-1-913207-13-7

Cover design by Rose Cooper
Typeset by Biblichor Ltd, Edinburgh
Printed and bound by CPI Group (UK) Ltd, Croydon, CR0 4YY

To Jill Glaister with much love.

1920

*D*ARLING, WE HAVE A SON.
    The voice echoed from somewhere far away. There seemed no connection between this news and she.

'A *son*, my darling, a beautiful boy.'

After a period of drifting she registered that it was Dennis's voice. That it was light. That it was over. The child was born and it was a male.

She turned her face to the wall, which was pitted, the paint a sickly green to match the smell of ether. *A boy.* Cannon fodder. Imagine pushing that paint into all those little pits, the sticky brush, the claggy pigment, the chilly smell of it. But perhaps it would be a soothing occupation?

Later they put the boy, shawl-wrapped, into her arms and he snuffled his face towards her breast. She gazed down at his black-wisped head. It seemed that he had been bathed. His eyelids opened to reveal dark slits of shine. She put the vast tip of her forefinger against his open palm and as the fingers closed around it, her heart was crushed.

Before

I

October 1917

A T T H E E N D of a shift that had seemed endless, Clem stood yawning and shivering in the grey dawn light. Inhaling the bitter smoke of a Red Cross ciggie, she listened to the cheeping of some poor bird. An officer, a doctor, loomed beside her. He was one of the Canadians, a lanky thing.

'How do?' He lit one of his own superior cigarettes.

'Perfectly fine,' she said, rather stiffly. Small talk was the last thing she required.

'Where are you from?' he asked.

'Suffolk.'

'A Suffolk girl. Bit hazy about British geography.'

'East Anglia,' she snipped.

'East Anglia,' he mimicked in a prissy tone.

'Sorry, asleep on my feet.' She glanced up at him. She'd never met a Canadian, was rather vague about their distinction from Americans.

'Powell Bonneville.' He clicked his heels ridiculously. 'At your service, ma'am.'

'No service required, thank you,' she said, thinking she ought to wash her hair, a dreaded task in the draughty ablutions tent. She realised he was inclining his head, waiting for her name.

'Clementine Armstrong.'

They each pinched their cigarettes between their lips to perform a perfunctory and rather ridiculous handshake, and resumed smoking in silence until he said, 'I wonder where are you? In there?' He tapped his own brow and studied her – rather impertinently – with his cool grey eyes. The lashes were dark and distinct, the hair was fair, greying, but his skin, now she looked closer, was fresh. He had a long, elegant face, perhaps a touch fey.

'Nowhere thrilling. Sorry to disappoint.' She took a last puff of her gasper, dropping the end into the mud between the slatted duckboards.

'Well, Miss Armstrong,' he said, 'you go and get yourself some shut-eye directly. Doctor's orders.'

She blinked at him wearily and plodded away, aware of his eyes following her, but too tired to be either flattered or irritated, though she was reminded that she really must write to Dennis. How many weeks? She'd lost track.

In the ablutions tent she heated water, added it to cold to make a tolerably tepid mixture, and then, shivering behind a skimpy curtain, stripped off her clothes and washed every bit of her body with carbolic soap. There were bites around her waist and at the top of her legs, bedbugs probably, or lice. They got everywhere; the men carried them on their bodies, in their clothes, in their equipment, and there was no getting rid of them despite the bonfires of lousy clothes with their palls of khaki smoke. A mosquito buzzed around her wet body. She smacked at it and dried herself, too tired to wash her hair after all – goodness knows what might be living in *it* – and hurried back to her hut, head down, avoiding eyes – *please, no one speak to me and waste a precious moment of my rest.* Back in her hut she kicked off her shoes, dropped her outer clothes, clambered up the ladder into her narrow bunk and plummeted straight into proper, marvellous, profound sleep.

Something startled her awake – gone by the time she opened her eyes – cat or rat or dream? She blinked at the wooden wall, the wavery slivers of light between the boards. On the wall some wag had pinned a calendar, open at last June: hollyhocks and thatch, a duck pond and a weeping willow on a village green. A wag, or a hopeless nostalgic. Grief regrouped inside her during sleep, and only when she was awake enough to be fully cognisant of where she was did the burden lift. At least here she was busy; there was hardly time to think. Busy, *useful* and so tired she actually slept – in fact could never get enough of it.

Now, she allowed herself an extra two minutes of wallowing before she climbed down the ladder and shivered into her clammy clothes. She felt a little triumph for having achieved the first uninterrupted rest for days. Only two bunks in this little hut, and sometimes a mattress on the floor, but not at present, so there was the luxury of floor space. She felt lucky to be in here, and sharing with Iris too, rather than in the great khaki dorm tent with most of the girls. In this small place one could at least have the occasional, enormous luxury of being on one's tod.

There was a mirror tacked to the wall, and in its cheap glass her face appeared pale and somewhat warped – and that seemed right. There was a look of Ralph – *no, don't think, don't* – but it was irresistible. Holding her breath, she allowed him into her mind. An experiment. *Ralph.* Her beautiful, funny, clever little brother. And yes, it hurt, but it didn't destroy her, didn't barge her off her feet as it had done at first. She felt closer to him now; helping boys like him was helping her through her grief. But of course it still hurt like hell and it always would. Always should.

She began to brush her wretched hair – *get on, get on, don't dwell*.

Iris pushed through the door and, without removing her shoes, sank down onto her lower bunk. She took off her specs, rubbed her eyes and lay prone, staring at the underside of the top bunk.

'Take your cap off at least,' said Clem, pinning her own over the coiled greasiness of her hair.

'Forster's gone,' Iris said.

'Well—'

'Don't,' said Iris fiercely. 'Don't *dare* say he's better off out of it. He was seventeen. *Seventeen!* Never had a sweetheart, he was telling me at the end. Wasn't stupid, knew he'd bought it. Never even kissed a girl.'

Ralph had never kissed a girl either, Clem thought, not as far as she knew. And he'd only just turned eighteen. 'Actually I wasn't going to say that,' she said, 'I was going to say I'm so very sorry.'

Iris harrumphed.

The boys were never in the Clearing Station for long. The task was to patch them up for their journey to the Base Hospital, but this depended on the transport convoys getting through unscathed. Even in a short time, though, it was possible to become attached, and there were some with whom it struck home more. Forster had been so young; younger even than seventeen, Clem guessed, or certainly seemed it. His bowel blown out, he'd never stood a chance. Furtively she'd sketched him: a hasty line, the shape of his nose and soft young chin. The sketch was never finished as Sister had come along and she'd had to stuff the sketchbook under her cape.

'I kissed him.' Iris sounded oddly triumphant. She touched her lips. 'So he *did* kiss a girl.'

Clem gazed at the reflected flame from the Tilley lamp dancing minutely in the burnished leather of Iris's shoes. Though she was slapdash about her appearance – always a drooping hem, a wrinkled stocking, a wisp escaping her cap – Iris took real pride in her shoes and polished them daily. Clem's were scuffed. She'd never been in charge of cleaning her own shoes before; someone else had always done it, and till now she'd never even noticed.

Clem stepped out into the drizzle. She could hardly think what time of day it was, but of course it was late afternoon. Darkness gathering; about this time at home they'd be drawing the curtains, stoking the fire, buttering scones, pouring tea.

Iris kissing the lips of a dying boy. Imagine! So very kind, so killingly funny! Cross-eyed Iris in her specs, whatever did the poor boy think?

'Hey,' barked Gwen. 'You're needed.' She was standing at the door of the theatre hut sucking on a cigarette.

'But I'm on dressings.'

'Well, we need another pair of hands. Pronto. Cleared it with Sister, don't fret.'

Gwen was tall, angular, with cropped hair and sharp critical eyes; beside her Clem always felt weak, inadequate, a flibbertigibbet. They'd met when Clem joined the Red Cross in Felixstowe in the run-up to the war. It was Gwen who'd encouraged Clem to join the Voluntary Aid Detachment and, once Ralph was killed, to serve in France. Gwen had proved to be a staunch friend, though an abrasive one, always goading, pushing, always testing.

'Do I have a choice?' Clem asked.

Gwen shook her head.

Clem glanced towards the dressings tent where the casualties waited to be assessed by a doctor and for their wounds to be dressed. After all these months she was swift and neat, although there were some shocking injuries where one had to use all one's ingenuity to work out how on earth to cover the area, how to hold the wound – and one's expression – together. One must never reveal to the patient the horror one felt.

The boys were so brave, most of them, as parts that should never have seen the light of day were swabbed with Lysol, dabbed and squeezed, had picked from them morsels of shrapnel, gravel, bone, insects, slivers of uniform and skin; finally to be pressed tight and neat under clean gauze.

For her first few weeks at the station, Clem had done nothing but wash heaps of blood- and pus-stained bandages and had done it in furious resentment, weeping into the steam, wanting, needing to do something more important, but now she understood how utterly vital it was that the dressings were clean and rolled and ready for a reaching hand.

She turned her back on the dressings tent and followed Gwen reluctantly to the theatre hut. She had not yet assisted at an operation. There was nothing minor here. All operations were emergencies, wounds that couldn't wait. Anything that could be safely left for a few days, they cleaned and patched up the best they could and the men were sent off down the line. She'd heard the cries and groans and awful sudden silences that came from here and always scuttled past, dreading being called upon to enter.

'Get a move on,' Gwen said. 'Scrub up.' She pointed to a basin of water, a cake of carbolic soap.

'I won't be much cop,' Clem said.

'Fit of the squeams?' Gwen said. 'Pull yourself together.'

The skin round Clem's nails was cracked and split, and the carbolic stung. The first operation was, as she'd feared, an amputation. The patient was unconscious, the mask on his face delivering a mixture of ether and air. The light over the table was dim and flickering; the leg, white and hairless, extended from beneath a green tarpaulin, the foot an unrecognisable mash of flesh, hanging toes, shreds of knitted sock and delicate broken bones. She swallowed against a surge of nausea, tears standing in her eyes as she steeled herself to look. It was her job to hold the upper limb firm. Despite the ether it was sometimes possible for a patient to wake, or partially wake, and struggle. Behind the group huddled round this operating table there was another and then another two. Four tables, four operations in train.

Dr Lennox, a big, frowning surgeon, bristly black eyebrows jutting between his mask and cap, conducted the amputation. Just think of the sound of the saw going through the tibia and fibula as if it's a saw in wood, think of it like that, just one thing cutting another thing, think of something clean, a tree perhaps, but the catch of the saw teeth in the flesh and in the ragged leaking tube of a vein, made it impossible to conjure anything else. The unconscious leg twitched and bucked, and she clung on tight. The air reeked of blood, flesh, sweat, Lysol.

'Catch it,' Gwen said. She handed Clem a galvanised bucket, and Clem found herself able to let go of the limb and catch, as it fell – hanging for a moment on a thread of skin – the foot, the weight of a kitten, with a soft thud. Lennox sutured the arterial and venous rags, stretched down the skin and fastened it like a sausage casing, and then, without pause, scrubbed up ready for the next case.

There'd been a recent push at Cambrai and it had taken days for the convoy of ambulances to arrive. One ambulance had been hit and the surviving injured had had to wait it out, allowing gangrene to set in. Not safe to send any of these amputations down the line; there were twenty or thirty operations to be done and no one would sleep till they were finished.

By the time she was granted a break she'd carried three feet, an arm above the elbow, a mash of genitals, a hand and countless fingers to the crematory, from which leaked endless, meaty smoke.

'You did well,' Gwen remarked later. They were in the ablutions hut, and Clem was scrubbing her raw and stinging hands. The knuckles and fingers were swollen, nails clipped to the quick. Once so smooth and pretty, now they were ugly hands. She looked at the finger where the sapphire and diamond engagement ring, slipped off before her surreptitious departure, should sit. Would it even fit her thickened finger now?

Gwen offered Clem a cigarette, lit it from her own. The smoke bit into Clem's throat, curiously clean, helping to clear the sickly stench of gangrene that seemed to cling to her clothes and hair, even her skin.

'You held your nerve,' Gwen said. 'Admit I had my doubts.'

'Why ask me to, then?'

'Needs must.' Gwen smirked as she blew out smoke. 'Anyway it was Sister Fitch, not me.'

'But you could have persuaded her not to.'

Gwen yawned. She looked done in, but so did they all. Clem was spun back to those days in the Scout Hut in Felixstowe, the day she met Gwen, this older, intimidating, rather mannish woman teaching her to tie a sling, making her take it off and put it on, over and over again until she got it right – could probably do it in her sleep. Oh, sleep, yes.

Ida and Ada, middle-aged twins, came in. 'I say, do you have to smoke in here?' they said in unison. They were a thin pair with narrow faces and hooked chins, the two of them together added up to about the bulk of an average-sized woman. Qualified civilian nurses, they barely tolerated the amateurs with whom they were increasingly surrounded.

Gwen and Clem donned their overcoats and stepped outside. It was the middle of the night now, foggy, no moon or stars. It was as if they were in a chill cloud, stained with the light that leaked from huts and tents. They stood and smoked and added to the smog.

'Any news of anyone?' Gwen said.

'Haven't been writing,' Clem said. 'Too bally tired.'

'Not even to your *fiancé*?' Gwen always gave the word a sarcastic twist. Though she'd never met Dennis, she'd made her disapproval of him clear. And when she'd learned that Dennis had forbidden Clem to serve overseas, Gwen had encouraged her defiance, facilitated her escape.

Clem ground out her cigarette, and immediately wished she hadn't. It had felt like something live she could hold on to. A comfort. She thought of the dead limbs and digits burning. A mushy smear of penis. All that sticky ash.

'Better get some grub before the next lot,' said Gwen. She held the minute remains of her cigarette between finger and thumb to draw out the very last of it before she threw it down between the duckboards.

'I'll go back to dressings, I suppose.'

'Now you've passed the test, you're on theatre duty till it calms down. Another convoy due.'

It was the *sound* of the disembodied body parts, Clem thought, the independent weight of them. A body should not come apart.

How cruel the law of physics was to give a sawn-off limb its own mass. One hand had been perfect, only the arm smashed beyond possible repair. A hand with brown hairs on its back, dirty of course, the fingernails cut neat and square, a sensible hand. One you might like to hold. She never saw its owner's face.

2

November 1917

SHELLS CRUMPED IN the distance and the darkness tasted of cinders. Relieved of the theatre for a three-hour break, Clem stretched, rotated her neck. The duckboards creaked with the movement, or was it her own joints? Half dead with lack of sleep, she was reluctant to take a single step. To be able to stand idle was enough. Her fingers rolled the tiny pencil she kept in her pocket. The pencil was taken from the spine of a diary – slim enough to be undetectable in a pocket. Though there was rarely time to draw, just feeling it between her fingers was a comfort, the muscle memory reminding her of the soothing immersion of sketching.

But then came a volley of fire that sounded nearer. Wounds were happening out there, she could hear them: skulls shattering, shrapnel tearing into flesh. In a day or two's time she'd be seeing them. One never got used to the variety of injuries. There were still some that caused one to reel, but at the same time, gaping flesh, visible bones, intestines, gleams of brain were becoming queerly quotidian. One thanked God for a normal fracture without gangrene, or a wound with fleshy suturable lips.

The cat that had turned up at the field station wound around her legs. It had been starving, probably the abandoned pet of some fleeing family from the bombed-out village, a skinny ginger thing that someone in a fit of punning had dubbed Mange, because of the state of its skin and because it never stopped begging for food. Opinion was divided between drowning the creature and making a pet of it. Sometimes it crept in and curled up with a patient, providing a scrap of comfort – it would certainly be despatched if Sister Fitch got wind of this.

There was a creak of board, a light touch on her shoulder. She turned to see Dr Bonneville smiling down at her. 'Hi there,' he said. 'Taking a breather?' He crouched to stroke Mange, who arched against his hand, purring fiercely.

'Someone's easily pleased,' Clem remarked. 'How divinely simple to be a cat.'

Dr Bonneville straightened, hands in the small of his back.

'Smoke?' He lit two cigarettes and gave one to her. Her lips met the papery tube where his had been.

They stood smoking in contemplative silence. Over the weeks she'd tried to avoid him because he was so damnably, *dangerously* nice. Difficult to ignore a person like him though – due to his height he was often visible and his expression consistently pleasant. It was his manner – the amused set of his mouth, his accent, his kindness, the way she could be comfortably quiet with him – that made him dangerous.

'If you could have one wish, Clementine?' he said. 'No, don't think, just say.'

'No need to think,' she said. 'I'd have a long hot bath with sweet soap and endless water and I'd wash my hair. Honestly, I'd commit bally murder to have clean hair. Some days, I feel like shaving it all off.' It was true. Often she was tasked with shaving the chests or bellies or limbs of men in preparation for surgery, rasping the razor-blade as near to the wound as possible, through curling body hair, or scalp hair, and had thought how tremendous it would be to take the razor to her own head, be shot of the greasy, crawling mass.

'You?' she said.

'*Filet mignon*, French fries, green beans, a slice of cherry pie, a Coca-Cola, a coffee and a shot of Jack Daniel's followed by a long nap – and I mean several days – on a soft bed with clean sheets.'

'You've obviously put a lot of thought into that.' She smiled, watching the smoke plume from his lips. 'I've never tasted Coca-Cola. What's it like?'

'Sweet, fizzy, gives you a lift.'

'You can't get it in England. Not that I know of.'

'Hey,' he said suddenly. 'Wait there.' He dashed off towards the officers' quarters and returned with a bag under his arm – containing Coca-Cola perhaps? But no. 'Now,' he said, 'come along with me and don't say a word.'

'Where are we going?'

'To make your dream come true.'

'Don't talk rot!'

'Shh. Keep schtum or no dice.'

He was leading her to the officers' ablutions hut. This could not be! Reaching the door, he looked both ways like a comical thief, peered inside, then dragged her after him into a blast of warmth and flickering lamplight. There was a potbellied stove with water heating above it, and cubicles with actual wooden doors rather than the limp curtains in the nurses' equivalent. From behind one of them, the sound of someone in the bath, a squeak of buttock on cast iron, a slosh of moving water.

'Don't say a word,' he whispered, 'or we'll be busted.' He pulled her into a cubicle, where there was a tin basin and jug on a wash-stand. From his bag he pulled a towel, soap and a hairbrush.

He mimed that she should remove her coat, took off his own and rolled up the sleeves of his tunic. He gestured to the chair and shoved it against the back of her knees so that she had no choice but to sit. He removed her cap and hairpins and, ashamed, she felt the grimy tumble of hair down her back. He pushed his thumbs up under her skull and she tipped her head back, heard him move the washstand behind her and fill the jug with hot water.

She gasped at the sensation of heat.

'No need to commit bally murder,' he whispered, warm breath in her ear. Clem closed her eyes and let the weight of wet hair stretch her neck backwards, realising with delight that the soap was not carbolic but scented with something flowery and fresh – freesia perhaps. He began to massage her scalp, fingers firm in the sweet lather.

And then he rinsed, pouring mugfuls of water through and fetching more, gloriously clean and hot.

'Divine,' she breathed.

'Shh.'

Another mugful sluiced over her scalp – utter heaven – but then there was a long bubbling expulsion of wind from the officer in the bath, followed by a satisfied sigh, and she felt a laugh coming on and had to sit up straight so as not to choke.

The water ran down her neck and soaked her blouse as irresistible hilarity surged through her. Powell clamped his hand hard over her mouth, so hard that it made her bite the inside of her cheek, but still she shuddered with laughter and tears spurted from her eyes. He pulled her up and against him and held her tight, hand still on her mouth. 'Shut up,' he hissed. She shook in what seemed as much hysteria as hilarity as they listened to the mystery bather haul himself up. As his bath water drained away, the laugh drained from her too. Powell felt it and wiped her wet face on the towel though the tears kept flowing and then he was supporting her as her legs went soft.

It was Ralph of course, but it was also all the other deaths. It was the lies, it was the truth, it was the war, it was Dennis, it was lice and blood and rot and filth, it was tenderness, it was chaos. It was the dark and the dark and the dark.

After a time, he sat her down again and brushed her wet hair, untangling as he went, gentle and deft with his surgeon's fingers. Again she let her head fall back as he brushed, feeling the tears dry itchily on her cheeks. She could hear his breath, rapt, catching as he paused to unsnarl a knot; sometimes he hummed beneath his breath, the tune to – how it made her smile – 'Oh my darling, oh my darling, oh my darling, Clementine'.

Someone else came into the hut, whistling, and banged a cubicle door. Her hair was smooth now and he indicated that she should stand and handed over her coat and cap. Finger to his lips, he opened the door, checked that there was no one in sight, and ejected her into the night. The door closed with him behind it, shutting out the light and warmth.

As she walked away the cold air chilled her damp hair against her scalp. He'd said nothing, hadn't even smiled as she left. She'd not even had a chance to thank him, and, oh heavens, what a frightful, idiotic goose she'd made of herself, after such enormous kindness.

Walking back in the lamp-stained dark, the duckboards greasy and glittering with frost, she wanted to sing, she wanted to scream, she wanted to make love to him, she wanted to die.

Kneeling before the stove, she dried her hair, smelling the sweet scent as the heat dried it, and separating a few stiff strands where the soap was imperfectly rinsed. What tenderness in her diaphragm, the end of the storm, a few sore hiccups as she calmed down. The way he'd touched her hair and her scalp, so gentle and deft. Surgeon's fingers. Did he play an instrument? Piano, perhaps? *Oh my darling, oh my darling, oh my darling, Clementine.* A yawn stretched right through her. If only now she could sleep sweetly in the clean cloud of her hair but she had another half-shift first. She pressed a hank of hair to her nose to breathe in the soapy scent again before she coiled and pinned it, replaced her cap, tightened the belt of her coat and went to find coffee and bread to sustain her for the night.

Three times she saw Dr Bonneville and he didn't utter a word to her, or only in passing when it was necessary. The line had moved and they were now much closer to the Front, the thunder of ammunition shaking the floor of the hut so that there was a constant shifting and rattling, a flickering of lights. Shifts had become so random now, they scarcely merited the name; if you were on your feet you were working, with the torrent of shattered men pouring in on their way to the base hospitals. 'Germs don't sleep' was Sister Fitch's motto and she was right, of course.

One morning Clem happened to be assisting Dr Bonneville on a severe abdominal, which necessitated the removal of a couple of feet of intestine. She watched his confident, adept fingers as she held her breath against the stench. The only notice of her he appeared to take was to snap when she wasn't quick enough in passing him a swab.

Later the same day she came upon him outside the officers' mess. He was standing on the duckboards smoking and staring up at the khaki sky; in that light he looked utterly fatigued, with deep shadows under his eyes and in the hollows of his cheekbones. She stood beside him for a moment before he acknowledged her.

'Smoke?' He shook out a cigarette and lit it for her.

Gratefully she inhaled, blinked through the rush of giddiness. 'I never thanked you,' she said.

He didn't reply at once, but looked down at her speculatively. She did like his height; few men were tall enough to have to look down at her like that. He must have four or five inches on Dennis.

'I wash my sister's hair,' he said at last. 'Used to.'

'Really?' She hesitated. 'That's . . . unusual.'

There was a long pause, in which he finished one cigarette, ground out the stub, toed it over the duckboard into the mud. She was afraid he'd go, but he took out another and lit it, and took a puff before he said, 'Thrown by a horse when she was twelve. Broke her neck.'

'Oh Lord.' Clem's hand flew to her own nape. 'How ghastly.'

'Paralysed below the fifth cervical vertebrae. She'd been riding since she was . . .' He put his hand down to indicate a tiny child. 'Just one of those tricks our merciful Lord likes to play.'

'Like this lot,' said Clem, waving her arm. As she spoke, there was a crunch as a shell exploded, uncomfortably close, and he snorted in agreement.

'She was fair too – hair not as thick as yours, not quite so pale. Wavier. She couldn't wash it herself and Mom was pretty slapdash.'

'How enormously kind of you,' Clem said.

He shrugged. 'No, I liked to do it.'

'Little sister?'

'Big sister, coupla years older. Lou. Lives in a home for the handicapped now. Folks visit on Sundays. That soap, gardenia, she has them send it out here.'

'I thought it was freesia.' She hesitated before she said, 'My little brother, Ralph, was killed. Ypres. He'd just turned eighteen.' Her voice cracked and she stopped.

He put a hand on her arm. 'So sorry for your loss,' he said. 'That why you're here?'

'Yes, you see . . .' she began, but there was another, closer explosion, and they both involuntarily ducked and straightened. Sister Fitch hurried past, flicking Clem a stern look. Once they were alone again, all in a rush Dr Bonneville grasped her hand and said, 'Hey, Clementine, marry me?'

Clem choked on her smoke.

'And come home with me to Vancouver?'

The boards beneath her feet were quaking and underneath was mud and worms and fag ends and mud and mud and mud. Drizzle spangled the smog. Her heart thudded. Someone from somewhere, some poor soul, gave an agonised bellow.

'I can't.'

'No such word,' he said. 'Heck, I know it's not much of a courtship, but look at you. You're perfect. You'd love Canada. My folks would love you. I—'

'Don't, Dr Bonneville.'

'Powell, for pity's sake!'

'Powell,' she repeated, loving the rounded, pillowy sound.

He cleared his throat. 'Hey, I . . . I know it's crazy soon to ask but the moment I set eyes on you I knew you were the girl for me.'

She darted a look at the side of his face. 'You've barely even looked at me for days!'

'Been plucking up my courage. This the quickest proposal you've ever had?'

She swallowed, unable to speak. Oh, if it wasn't for Dennis . . . she should say, she should tell him about Dennis. Now. She took a preparatory breath. *I'm engaged* – just say it, say it and put an end to this nonsense.

'I've a month's furlough coming up,' he said. 'I'm going home. Don't know if I'll get sent back here. Don't wanna lose you.'

Canada. She had never even thought of Canada. She had only the slightest notion of what it was like. Except for mountains and snow and bears perhaps, and, oh yes, she'd heard there were giant maples that bled delicious syrup.

'You could drink Coca-Cola every day,' he coaxed. 'Vancouver's a great city, and there's the folks' place on the weekends – horses. Do you ride?'

Clem shook her head. 'Not more than once or twice.'

'What do you say?'

'We haven't even kissed!'

'Let's put that right.' With a finger under her chin he lifted her face and there was the soft brush of his lips on hers.

'So?'

She shook her head, speechless.

'If it's definitely no-go, then okay, just say it and I'm done. But if there's a possibility you might consider . . .'

She stopped gaping and found her voice. 'Well, they say nothing is impossible.'

He put his arm around her shoulder and she leant her weight against him for a moment.

'Okay, I can go with that for now,' he said. And then he released her and strode away. The boards creaked under his feet, the back of his greatcoat glistened in the smirry rain.

3

December 1917

MID-AFTERNOON, GWEN BARGED into the hut, waking Clem from a snatched doze. 'For you.' She brandished an envelope, but Clem could not make herself move. She was trying to draw together the dissolving threads of dream – what was it, what was it? Oh, the hand, an elegant hand, long straight fingers, its back satiny brown. She squeezed shut her eyes for a last try and the hand padded silently away.

'Snap out of it,' Gwen said, 'or you'll be late.' The dank cold air she was letting in sent Clem further beneath her blankets. It was dark in the hut and Gwen lit the Tilley lamp, slapped the envelope down on the shelf out of Clem's reach and went off, banging shut the door behind her.

Clem lay blinking at the fluttering light. She felt a warm vibration at her feet and realised that Mange was curled up, purring. When did he, with all his fleas, creep in? But his warmth was nice, and his throaty purr. Something was different – and then with a sharp little shock it came back to her: this morning she and Powell had made love. She hadn't been a virgin; once she'd allowed Dennis to instruct her and had recoiled, startled by his angry red ramrod and it had hardly been *pleasure*. Sex was overrated, she'd decided then, something a wife must put up with but this morning . . . *oh, oh*.

They'd wangled a break between shifts at the same time and wandered together between the row of poplars that lined the road and down into a forest. Once they were out of sight they'd held hands, feet crunching on the frozen grass. The trees sparkled with hoar frost. The sounds of war had seemed irrelevant as, entranced, they'd moved through avenues of shining beeches and found a copse where fir trees huddled and the ground was padded with soft needles, and here Powell had spread his coat and they'd lain down side by side.

'Oh, honey,' he said when they kissed, and what a kiss – their mouths, their bodies melting. 'Oh, baby.' And it would not have been possible to pull away when his hand, warm from its glove, found her breasts, and found the place between her legs that melted, ached; never had she known a feeling like it and with his fingers he brought her to the moment and then she understood what it was that drove men and women to madness and found her bold hands inside his clothes, and wondering at the beauty of him and when he entered her – only holding back for a moment, eyes questioning – it was imperative that he should be inside and she pulled him, arching and jutting her body in a shockingly animal way till they were one and there was no choice. She cried out and he yelled and she lay stunned on the outspread wings of his coat and knew, *knew,* in every sinew of her being that this was right, that this was meant, that this was love, her love, her love.

And then it was so very cold of course, and shivering and with kisses and laughs and endearments they'd pulled together their clothing and hurried back to wash and to work. And after her shift, she'd climbed the ladder to her bunk, buzzing with tired-ness, with excitement and guilt, not expecting to sleep, perhaps never in her life again, but she did of course, she slept and, oh, the hand – Powell's hand? – scuttled crablike in her dream to hold her own.

She lay a moment longer. Oh, it was so queer; she was *ignited*. Now she understood it. *Love*. And she was changed. The corner of the envelope protruded over the edge of the shelf. Dennis, it would be. At first she'd written to him at reasonable intervals but there had only been two or three terse notes in reply; he was angry and disappointed in her, of course, for 'running off' as he put it, against his 'express wish'. But he would wait. Of course his pride had been dented. Perhaps this would be a longer, more considered missive; perhaps it would be forgiveness? But did she want that now? I'm in love, she thought, now I know what love is; oh, she *did* hope it wasn't Dennis being decent and forgiving. For what, now, could she reply?

She swung her legs round, climbed down the icy rungs of the ladder and sat on the edge of Iris's bunk. Mange jumped from the top bunk and stretched, rubbing himself against her shins. The stove was out. She pulled a blanket up round her shoulders and reached for the letter.

Darling Clem,

Since my brother is too pig-headed, I will take it upon myself to write. First, the biggest news – I've had the babies, girls (a fortnight ago), both safe and surprisingly hefty. And mixed with the joy, of course, is the sadness that my Stan will never see them. They have such a look of him – his eyes both of them. They are an enormous comfort to me, greedy great guzzlers that they are, just like their poor daddy!

Dennis wants to hire a nursemaid and have me return to the Beeches, but I am happy in the cottage, near Stan's family, who are a marvellous help. I know Dennis considers the Burkes utterly *déclassé* but he can go and soak his head.

He's terrifically hurt, you know. He's been in the most colossal sulk since you ran off. He must still be thoroughly gone on you – after all, he's an eligible type and there are plenty of eligible types around . . . Don't worry though. He may be sowing a few wild oats but he still very much expects you to return to the fold.

Perhaps you could write soothingly to him, a few words of love would go a long way – or better still come back for a visit? Surely you must have leave now and again? This request is also selfish, of course – you know me! I miss you most frightfully. I understand what you're doing and applaud you for it, but I did miss you in the first terrible weeks after I got the telegram. And I want you to meet the girls. After all, as soon as you're married you will be their <u>favourite</u> aunt. I have called them Phyllis and Claris, both names from Stan's family – I think that would have pleased him and it's certainly a great comfort to his mother who has taken to grandmotherhood with enormous gusto!

Till soon, I hope.

How I do look forward to calling you sister!

Affectionate wishes,

Harri

Clem folded and unfolded the letter. How disappointed Harri was going to be. Before the war, she'd been sweet on Stanley, a joiner, much to the disapproval of her father – and of Dennis. In 1916, when Stanley was home on leave from Africa, defiant against her family's snobbishness, she'd eloped with him. And now here she was, a widow, mother of *twins*.

Clem put the letter between the pages of her sketchbook, unable to resist as she did so the temptation to gaze at the last few pages: Powell, Powell, Powell, done not from life but memory. There had not yet been time for him to sit for her. One day would come that enormous luxury. Here was the angle of his head as he bent over a patient; the tight intensity of his brow above the mask; a serious expression, the pale eyes wide, the sudden comical width of his grin.

Naturally she must write to Dennis and to Harri. After this shift, she resolved. Although she burned with love, the thought of what she must write was a terrible blast of cold and she stood up quickly, reaching for her overcoat.

On that shift two boys in succession died on the operating table. Both high femur amputations, both with smashed pelvises. One lost his genitals and part of his large intestine. Better off dead, of course. Some part of her must have become cauterised because behind the immediate horror and sorrow, revulsion and compassion, there nagged the knowledge that after this, and somehow *harder* than this, there were the words she must write to Dennis. And even behind that, a tiny spark stayed lit, a tiny point of excitement. She thought of peat fires that for years burn invisibly underground, minute filaments of conflagration.

Later she went to seek out Powell, but he was working and there was no chance to speak to or – what she really craved – to touch him. She watched him from the door of the theatre hut, back bent, profile intent, over the table under the weak, guttering light. She could see the feet of the patient, white and loose, the wide hips of a nurse whose name she didn't know.

*

The walls of the canteen tent flapped in the breeze and any warmth generated by the stove wisped away. An orderly was doling out greyish lumps of scrambled egg.

'Only a little of that, please, with bread and coffee.' Clem stretched out her plate.

'You've blood on your forehead, pet,' the orderly said.

Clem felt a crusty patch on her brow and picked at it with her nail.

'You look dead beat,' he said and offered her the box of Red Cross cigarettes. Thin, mean ciggies made of sweepings, but better than nothing. Clem put a few in her coat pocket. The scrambled egg was grim but necessary, and she forced it down and smoked a cigarette before taking out paper and pen. But half an hour later, with head nodding and eyes closing, she had got no further than *Dearest Dennis* on one sheet and *Darling Harri* on another.

4

January 1918

DAWN, AND THE incongruously fresh sound of a blackbird nearby, and through chinks round the door, a gleam of primrose. Clem woke sandy-eyed, tipped from a cloud of dream into the sound of birdsong and then shelling. She lay listening, rather detached. There was no fear, or not much of it, though today it was closer than ever. Where was the fear? She searched herself as she listened: sometimes the rat-tat-tat of gunfire, rapid and snippy like the keys of two vast, duelling typewriters battering out threats to each other on a paper sky; crumpings like oil drums being crushed by massive fists; a whistling followed by the soft whoomph of a missile striking, then virtual silence, then the battering of the typewriters again.

She forced herself out of the blanket, stood in the cold damp, stretched and yawned. She opened the door and looked up at the sky, half expecting to see it full of flying words – English, French, Walloon and German – but there were only distant wisps of smoke smudging the creamy yellow.

The Front was shifting north; the Clearing Station would soon be moved in accordance. Clem shivered through washing and dressing, and hurried to get to her coffee. She sat deliberately alone at a rickety table in the canteen, dipping stale baguette in sweet black coffee and sucking the stimulating mush. She lit one of the Red Cross gaspers, longing for one of Powell's Lucky Strikes. But still, this moment was luxury and she would take a few moments over it, blocking from her mind what she might see and do today, what she saw and did yesterday. Thinking of nothing but the taste of the coffee and stale crumbs, noticing the way the bread's structure broke down immediately so that you had to rush the sopping, darkened stuff to your mouth before it disintegrated.

Iris stomped over and indicated the chair opposite. 'Mind?' She sat down, crunching an apple. Her knuckles were swollen and rough, specs smudged and askew, complexion grey with fatigue, but still there was the cheery, snaggle-toothed smile.

'Just up?' she said. 'Me, I'm off to kip for a bit. Quieter now.' As she spoke a shell whistled and exploded, and they both ducked involuntarily, then grinned.

'Getting too close for comfort,' Iris remarked, biting into the withered little apple.

'*Comfort!*' said Clem.

'Take your point.' Iris took another crunch. 'Right, that's me off to the Land of Nod.' She hauled herself up.

'Wait,' said Clem.

Iris sat again, tilting her head quizzically.

'Had a letter lately?' Clem asked. 'How's Sidney?'

'So-so.' Iris wobbled her hand. 'Poor old stick. He's got his problems and he wants me home. And I want to be with him, of course, but . . .'

'I know.'

'This is what I have to do.'

'I know.'

They shrugged at each other.

'Eh, this'll sound queer,' Iris's face crinkled mischievously, 'but do you know, I just want to *smell* him. Just bury my nose in him and smell and smell and smell.'

Clem blinked.

Iris was watching her face. 'I expect you feel the same about your Dennis,' she said. 'Barmy, isn't it!'

'Sounds like true love to me, proper love,' Clem said. A morsel of bread sank into the murk in her cup and she tried to fish it out with a spoon but it dissolved to nothing.

'Proper love?' Iris inclined her head. 'Funny way of putting it. But yes, proper all right, except when it's being improper – but then, you need a bit of spice, don't you?'

Clem tried to imagine Iris's husband, a big-bellied whiskery professor twenty years her senior, being improper. Rather a queasy picture it made, but if Iris was happy . . . It really does take all sorts.

'I'm thinking of ending things with Dennis,' came out of Clem's mouth.

'Oh, my dear.' Iris gulped and grasped her hand. 'Oh, I'm so sorry, gushing away like that. Did you get a letter?'

'No . . . I simply feel different.'

'Well, your feelings might change again once you're home. I shouldn't be hasty if I were you.'

'Iris,' Clem leaned towards her. 'Don't tell Gwen, will you? Don't tell anyone, but there's someone here.'

'Here?'

'Oh, I shouldn't say.' Clem hid her face in her hands.

'Who?' Iris took off her specs, polished them on her apron, as if for a better look. 'A doctor I'm guessing?'

'Please don't tease,' Clem said.

'Why *not* tell Gwen?'

'Oh, I don't know! She's always so sarcastic about everything I do. She mocked me for getting engaged . . . and now . . .'

Iris smothered another yawn as she stood. 'Sorry. Beddy-byes for me.' She patted Clem's shoulder before she left. 'Good luck to you.'

Clem sat a moment longer, eyes closed, wishing she hadn't spoken. How indiscreet exhaustion rendered one. But still, how *lovely* to say it. To bring it out into the light of day.

Her shift was starting but still she sat there, eyes closed, thinking of the lovely whiff of Powell's neck, his hair, even the fabric of his greatcoat. He still awaited her answer – but she couldn't, in good conscience, say yes until she'd written to Dennis.

At Christmas she'd dropped him a line in a card, but that had hardly been the occasion. And he'd sent a parcel with ridiculously dainty handkerchiefs, silk stockings and violet creams, and included a hand-painted card from Harri with a photograph of her chubby-faced twins. When she'd opened these, Clem's heart had flailed guiltily and her resolve had wavered. After all, there *was* a life back home, a safe, respectable life, waiting for her. A fine home, a handsome and devoted husband. Did she really have the strength to turn her back on all of that?

5

March 1918

CLEM BEGAN TO drift off over her coffee. Her back ached from bending awkwardly for more than an hour to assist a severe cranial – who bought it anyway. The atmosphere, always tense but sometimes laced with a febrile humour, had darkened when the chap, a captain, died. The surgeon, Lennox in this case, turned away in despair at this failure, the others tasked with a sketchy sewing-up before the body was wheeled away. Lennox, Clem had come to respect enormously. He was a man of few words, his ferocious frown a sign of concentration, of how much he cared, rather than of bad temper.

Death was so commonplace it had become almost banal. She had to remind herself that each one would cause devastation in the hearts of some, ripple through the lives of many. Someone had given birth to each of these men and boys, cradled his newborn head against her breast, wanting only to keep him safe and warm.

She noticed with mild interest that the hand was on the table, a gold ring winking on one finger, pale clicking nails . . . Her head dropped forward and she woke with a start. Must stand, must put one foot in front of the other, must . . . a paler hand now, smaller – was it a child, was it female?

'Armstrong!' Clem jerked her head up and blinked. It was Sister Fitch's hand. 'Get to bed now. You're no use to man nor beast in that state. Up, now...' She pointed to the door and Clem stood. Shellfire – rattety-tattety.

'Sorry, Sister.' She dragged herself outside where it was surprisingly light. What time of day was it? She'd lost track. And then Powell was there, dear man: pale, dark rings under his eyes, an angry spot on his chin; they all had them, bites and pimples, cold sores, red chapped patches.

He raised his hand in a weary salute.

'Hello,' she said, and as the corners of her mouth lifted, something seemed to lift inside her and she felt a quickening despite her exhaustion. 'Dead on my feet.'

'Any progress?' he asked. He tapped his wedding finger. A sudden wide hopeful grin, big healthy teeth. He needed a shave; she could see the bristles peppery on his chin.

'Oh . . . that.' She paused, still half in a dream. 'Yes, of course,' she said, amazed as the words floated from her mouth. 'I'll come to Canada. I'll marry you.'

He blinked. 'That, baby, is entirely the right answer!' He pressed his lips against her brow and her eyes clicked shut like a doll's. 'Now, go get some sleep.' He shoved her gently towards her hut.

Clem skidded on the slippery boards, regained her balance and went on, looking over her shoulder at his retreating back. She kicked off her shoes, climbed the ladder to her bunk and plummeted into a pit of deep, astonishing sleep.

From which she was woken, only minutes later, by Iris. 'Up, you're wanted,' she said.

Must move, though it was dark and every atom of her mind and being clung to sleep. She dragged herself up, stumbled through her ablutions; something niggled, something from a dream or . . . She dropped her hairbrush on the soggy wooden floor of the wash tent – no, not a dream. That long pale serious face, those silvery eyes. She had, hadn't she? She had said yes.

Orders had come through and it was official. Casualty Clearing Station 94 was to be moved five miles north-east. In the meantime, the nurses and volunteers would be employed in treating patients at stations along the roads and railways. Powell had been granted furlough, as he called it, but Clem, though she applied, was unable to get leave until the new station had been established, after which she was promised three weeks. Then, she'd go home and break the news to Dennis. Better that way. How cowardly, after all, to do it by letter.

The move was underway; they'd ceased receiving casualties. Most of the medical staff had been shifted to their temporary postings and teams of British and French volunteers had begun the process of dismantling the huts and tents. Clem, Iris and Gwen, with three other VADs under the command of Sister Fitch, were left behind to disinfect and pack medical and surgical equipment in preparation for transport. They did this to an accompaniment of rumbles and shellfire that had become so normal now they scarcely flinched.

Clem and Iris were finishing up in the theatre, hurried intermittently by Sister Fitch who kept coming in – 'The Hun won't wait till you finish larking and gossiping' – though in fact there was no 'larking' and they worked mostly in silence. Iris was a rare person, Clem thought, with whom one could be comfortable without the need for constant chatter. Clem watched her friend's busy fingers. She'd developed some kind of arthritis in them and had chilblains too;

they looked awfully bent and sore. Clem examined her own – not much better, though at least her chilblains were limited to her toes.

Iris never complained about anything. The Professor was lucky, really very lucky. There was a beauty in Iris, not obvious at first, with her sturdy shape, her specs and snaggled teeth. One had to know her to see how she shone with a soft steady brightness. A child's hymn came to mind – *Like a little candle burning in the night* – and with it a deep squirm of memory. Maybe her mother had leant over her cot and sung it? If ever I have a child I will too, she decided; such a pretty tune. *You in your small corner, and me in mine.* And with the thought of a child, the suspicion she'd been suppressing for the past two weeks returned and she paused to rest her hand on her hollow, hungry belly.

'Hello! Anyone at home?' Clem realised Iris was laughing and clicking her fingers. 'Look at her! Miles away! You've a visitor,' she said, lifting a pair of forceps from the steriliser. And there was Powell. Iris lifted her eyebrows with a look of amused comprehension. 'Get on with you then,' she said.

'Just two minutes. If Sister comes back, tell her a call of nature or something.' Clem followed Powell out into the frostiness of late morning. She was groping for something to say, something about the relative peace of the day now that the camp was almost deserted when a shell exploded nearby, shaking the duckboards. He put his arms around her and they clung for the moment it took to realise they were still standing.

'I'm all packed,' he said. 'Won't be seeing you again for who knows how long. Who knows where they'll send me.'

'We can write.'

'Well, of course!' He looked at her thirstily as if he wished to drink her with his eyes. 'Will you say it again?' he said.

'What?'

'That you'll marry me.'

A shadow flitted across her heart as she smiled and said, 'I will.'

'Don't look so worried, baby.' How she loved it when he called her baby.

'Actually, I might *have* to marry you,' she said and watched his expression change as he grasped her meaning.

'I'm not *sure*,' she said.

He blinked, shook his head, a slow grin stretching his lips. 'Oh, Clem.'

She looked around, no sign of Sister. There was activity at the far side, the dismantling of huts and tents, but no one was taking a blind bit of notice of them. She tilted up her chin and they kissed, just a cool brush of dry lips but it set up a detonation inside her and inside him too, judging by the flaring of his pupils, the way his breath came harder.

'Can we be alone, just for a minute, before I go?' he breathed against her neck.

'I don't know. I really shouldn't.' Legs gone soft, she leant against him. 'I'll try to sort something out.'

'Armstrong!' shouted Sister, coming round a corner. 'Haven't you got enough to do?'

Clem hurried back into the hut.

Iris raised her eyebrows and grinned. 'Well, he's certainly a dish. Is it serious?'

'Yes, it is. Actually, he's proposed.'

'No!' Iris dropped a pair of sterilised tweezers. 'Damn, now I'll have to do them again.' She stooped to retrieve them. 'And?'

'I've accepted!' Clem laughed, a little incredulous herself.

'Oh, my word! Oh, goodness me!' Iris threw the tweezers into the steriliser and they hugged, hands held out for hygiene's sake so that the embrace was a bosomy apron rub. A shell whistled overhead and they ducked and waited for the explosion, which rattled the corrugated roof, shaking down a shower of dust.

Iris waved her hands to indicate the dusty air. 'Oh, the *bally* Hun. We'll have to start again now.'

Sister Fitch came back in, frowning. 'Pack those as they are,' she said. 'We'll sterilise at the other end – just be sure to mark the box. Be ready by three.' She checked her watch. 'That'll be the last transport. You'll have to squeeze those in the back with the other boxes.'

Iris flopped down onto her stripped bunk. 'Oh, my poor feet,' she groaned. 'I've got to put them up, just for a bit.' She propped them, in their shiny shoes, up on the wall. Sister Fitch would have a fit if she saw; they both looked at the door and, catching each other in the same thought, grinned.

Sister Fitch and Gwen were finishing up the linen supplies. Of the Red Cross they were all that remained now; the rest of the activity was soldiers and orderlies dismantling this home, this place of rest, of sustenance and death. Most of the doctors had gone but there was still a small Canadian contingent, Powell amongst them, preparing to leave at any moment.

Clem opened her case and began folding inside it her belongings: spare collars and cap, letters, a hairbrush. She took down the calendar with its thatched cottage, weeping willow, duck pond, hollyhocks. Funny to think that this enclosed space, this box of air, which had been home for months, would soon be gone, the air just any air, the space just any space. Perhaps they might dig a trench right through it.

She ached to run to Powell but best not. They'd write. She had his address in Canada where he'd be on furlough for a month. They'd be together soon. No messy goodbyes. Best that way. Just go.

Vehicles, motor and horse-drawn, had been arriving and departing with their loads of people and equipment all day, and now it was afternoon and only half an hour before their transport. She almost hoped he'd already gone. Best not to see him, though the thought caused a ghastly plummeting sensation in her belly.

Heart quickening, she turned to the door as a shadow complicated the brightness.

'Hi there.' He nodded to Iris and widened his eyes at Clem. *So?* they said.

Iris removed her feet from the wall, swivelled herself into a sitting position. Clem grimaced at her pleadingly.

'Two minutes.' Iris stood up. 'I might even stretch it to three. No wish to play gooseberry.'

'Thank you, nurse,' Powell said.

'I'm not a proper nurse, as you well know,' Iris said. She belted her coat, saying before she closed the door, 'But I don't object to being called it.'

'Good sport,' Powell remarked as she left.

'She's kind,' Clem said. 'Isn't it so important to be kind?'

Powell opened his coat and drew her into its warm folds. 'Let's not waste time,' he said and they began to kiss, deep and slow, coffee and mint, fire spreading from her mouth and throat right down through her till her legs began to melt and he was holding her up. Together they moved towards Iris's bunk, gravity drawing them to the horizontal. Clem's whole self was turning irresistibly, terrifyingly molten and Powell had to stifle her mouth with his hands, and then she lay, damp and amazed, listening to a great rat-a-tat-tat, a thunderous rumble of explosions.

'I love you,' she said into the skin of his neck. 'I *really* love you.'

'Really?' he said.

'Really.'

'Just as well,' he said and put his hand on her belly. 'A kid, huh! We better get hitched then. P.D.Q.' He stood to pull up his trousers and she watched his elegant fingers buckle his belt. 'Hey, baby,' he said, 'come back home with me? We can get hitched somewhere along the way and I can take you home as my wife.'

'But it's so fast, I . . .'

Her mind was spinning. She could, she *could*, and then she never need face Dennis or his family; she could simply vanish off to Canada and marry and then write to them from there. Cleaner that way, perhaps? Kinder? Easier for everyone?

'I wonder if it's a little guy, or a little girl?' Powell was gazing at her belly.

Clem sat up, pulled down her skirt, reached for her hairbrush. 'It *might* not be either,' she reminded him.

'If it's a girl, can we call her Aida?' he said. 'Always thought that was the cutest name for a girl.'

'Aida?' she said. 'As in the opera?'

'It's a family name,' he said. 'My great-great-grandmother was part Arabian. Means "one who returns".'

Aida, she thought – strange, but he might as well have said Lemon or Bookend and she would have agreed, agreed to anything.

'Aida then?' He was kneeling to tie his shoelaces, glancing up at her through a flop of hair that had fallen across his brow. This could be the face she saw every day, the father of her child, of her children: her husband.

'Aida. Yes, I rather like it.' She put her hand on her belly, and felt a warm and sudden blooming of joy. 'And if it's a boy?'

'You pick,' he said and she began to think

and then   the world   broke

ear-warp of noise . . . blood bead trickle like a wheeee   and things rising

falling

which way up is upside down?

maybe nothing for a bit and

a patter of something   breaking up and coming

loose

inside is outside

squeeze out from under a dead man

legs lift her

Powell grey and grainy but for the red, the stove pipe torn and planted in his back

in his back like a twisted arm

his spine his ribs

smoke   choke

a blinding stink

gasp stagger

                    stagger gasp

by the hut the remains of it   a crater

men running now   silent

silent men running

                              NO

there is a foot   a foot all alone . . .

torn stocking and blue bone

wearing Iris's shoe

She reaches down, a long way it seems, a long time for her hand to travel down through the shimmer to wipe the dust from the toe of Iris' shoe

Gwen standing across the crater   grey   silent   open mouthed

Sister Fitch her arms wide turning turning turning like a girl in a dream silent men running

all the holdings fixings guy ropes all the barricades

all the things that keep it together

gone

During

6

1920

THE INFANT'S EYES were as black as if night were trapped behind his lids, and when he opened them she feared she'd be consumed. She focused instead on Dennis, his face infused with love, voice thickened by it, as he gazed at her and the baby in her arms.

'He's perfect, darling. Sterling job. Well done.' He kissed her brow, and her lips lifted at the corners as if on strings. Together they regarded the tiny pink face, dark wispy hair, smooth lids shut tight now, pale blinds against the night.

An innocent newborn.

But he was the wrong baby.

She wanted to ask them to take him away and give her the right one. But she could not say it; of course she could not. Instead she pressed a kiss against the queer soft pulsing of his fontanelle.

The wrong baby.

After the Clearing Station had been hit, she, Gwen and Sister Fitch had been transported to a hospital in Boulogne to recover. In the bathroom there, a few days later, Powell's child, small enough to curl into a walnut shell, had slid away from her onto the white floor. On her knees, she'd watched blood ooze into a gaudy chequered grid between the tiles until Gwen had found her and come to her aid, asking no questions, withholding all judgement, and afterwards, recognising that Clem was fit for nothing, had her packed off home.

And home meant Dennis, innocent of everything, his ring back on her finger, flashing sapphires and diamonds, once his mother's, once his grandmother's. Too numb to object, she'd gone along with it, allowed the wedding, allowed this other child to come.

This black-haired boy.

The wrong baby.

From the window of her room in the convalescent home, you could see the empty branches of trees, the colourless sky and the mud-brown flow of the river. Barges sailed across the window during the day. From her pillow she watched the sails, and when the nurses opened the windows to air the room, she could hear clanking and the mew of gulls, and the smell of the river, like a wet animal, padded in to shake its fur.

Dennis brought roses – extortionate in January – stiff, red, scentless. He brought chocolates, hothouse grapes with tight green shiny skins. He was proud, exuberant, *normal*. He'd slipped paternal love on as easily as an overcoat, and she envied him.

Old Dr Everett had tears in his eyes as he held the baby, his full grey beard spread bib-like over his chest. 'Violet should be here to see him,' he murmured. 'Your image, Dennis, your dead spitting image.'

Harri, red-faced and slapdash, paint in her hair and a twin on each arm, had come and enthused, bestowed wet kisses and a strange green matinee jacket she'd crocheted out of twine.

Once visiting hour was over and a nurse had removed the infant from her arms and drawn the curtains for her afternoon nap, Clem lay startlingly awake, trying not to think but thinking, thinking.

This was a mistake, like having got on the wrong bus and arrived at the wrong destination, only, of course, a million times worse.

She should be in Canada with Powell and the little girl. When she shut her eyes she was there, on a sunlit prairie, watching the child, Aida – marvellous name – toddling, pale-haired, silver eyes so like her father's. Powell was crouching and holding his hands out to her as she took those first wobbly steps, such a glow of pride on his face!

But no, here she was in a convalescent home on a dank English January afternoon, the wrong baby sleeping in his crib, the wrong man feeling proud. She should be glad, she should be grateful, yes, she *was*. How lucky to have landed, as Harri put it, on her feet. After all, her life was perfect now, *enviable*: married to robust Dennis, not a scar on him – the war seemed barely even to have dented his optimism. He hadn't volunteered – medicine a reserved occupation, of course – and he had done wonders here, everyone said so, and it was true. He'd supervised the conversion of Middlesham Hall into a military hospital and worked there, while still keeping up the family practice. He was marvellous. She was lucky. And now a healthy son. Lucky. Lucky.

A seagull glided past in a ray of orange, its shadow on the wall. She turned over in bed, feeling the empty fold of belly flesh where the baby had been, and she thought of Powell about whom no one – except Gwen – even knew. What would have been the point of telling them? She'd wondered if, being a doctor, Dennis might have been able to tell what her body had been through: but no.

On the prairie the wind blows and the palominos toss their manes, kick up their heels.

*

Clem fed the baby when he was presented, gazing down at his stern working face. The chin moved up and down, the cheeks pulsed as he suckled, pulling threads of milk that curled her toes. His eyebrows were rows of invisible stitching, eyelids bruisy, irises gradually resolving from black to smoky damson to chestnut, a little clearer every day. She held her palm beneath his marching feet.

But most of the time she kept her eyes on the book she made a pretence of reading.

'Mother!' She jumped. 'Mother! Whatever do you think you're doing?'

This nurse was younger than she; only the uniform lent the authority for such impertinence. 'We should concentrate on baby as we feed him!' She plucked the book from Clem's hand, slapping it shut, losing her place. That scarcely mattered, the page had only been a place to rest her eyes. The nurse's face was pertly cross, complexion smooth under her starched cap. She would have been a child in the war – the few years that separated her from Clem a filthy great gulf of understanding.

'First baby too!' she went on, clucking her tongue. 'Whatever next!' She lifted the infant from Clem's arms and held him against her shoulder. 'Now then, little chap, is your mummy a naughty girl? We'll have to give her what for!'

Clem's face twisted in a kind of smile as anger rose in her and fell again like a wave unbroken. This girl did not know. Why should she? To her generation the war was nothing but a bore. Old hat. And that's the world Clem wanted for her son after all. His greatest challenges would be in sport, examinations, commerce, romance. So she forgave the nurse, but somehow Dennis she could not forgive.

Stop it, stop it, that's not fair.

Not forgive him for what?

Not being Powell.

Not divining what she'd been through.

Trampling so cheerfully on her grief.

Ramming his great red thing in where it wasn't wanted.

Not having been to the Front.

Not that he was a coward – *was not, was not, was not, was not, was not*. He had done wonders.

But still . . . but still.

They were at home on a cold February afternoon, darkness eating at the windows. Mrs Hale wheeled in the trolley with its tea and toasted crumpets and her blasted seed cake.

'Shall I?' she asked, indicating the curtains.

'Please,' Clem said. The velvet shushed along its rails. The baby, Edgar Leonard Dennis Everett, was nearly three weeks old. On his shawl danced shadows from the flames.

Mrs Hale seemed to be waiting for something.

'Thank you,' Clem said. 'That'll be all.'

It had become their routine since Clem came home, that Dinah, the nursemaid, would bring Edgar into the drawing room at teatime while she took her hour off. Dennis would come up from the surgery for his tea, and if it was especially busy, old Dr Everett would take a turn down there although he really wasn't up to it any more; he was half deaf and 'not so quick on the uptake' as Dennis put it (Clem thought doolally was closer to the mark).

Today Clem's nerves were raw. She hoped Dennis would not come, that no one would come, that she could simply be quiet and drink her tea and that the baby would not cry. Mrs Hale was still hovering. Why did she not go? Her eyes were on Edgar on the rug before the hearth. The firelight flickered on his face and he seemed entranced.

'Is he safe there, madam?' ventured Mrs Hale. 'A stray spark . . .'

'He's quite all right,' Clem said though the housekeeper's words stung like sparks themselves. 'That'll be all,' she said again, when Mrs Hale seemed about to object further. At last, unwillingly, the woman retreated. The noise from the fire was mice scurrying amongst the coals. Dennis came in with a concerned expression, having been bothered by Mrs Hale no doubt.

'He's all right,' Clem said, but she dropped to her knees and dragged the shawl and Edgar with it further from the flames.

'Why not hold him, old thing?' Dennis said.

'I'm about to pour the tea.'

Dennis sighed, and sat.

Clem sipped tea, insufficiently brewed, and gazed blankly at a book, perhaps the same book as in the hospital ward, she didn't know. A book is a defence, a paper fence. She supposed it was cosy; the lamps lit, the flames crackling and flapping, the baby making little effortful grunts as he squirmed on his shawl.

'Darling,' Dennis said abruptly, 'buck yourself up, do!'

He meant no harm. How could he know how far her spirits had dropped when he'd entered the room, spirits that had in any case been hovering only just above the carpet. Her lips lifted to think of them down below the floorboards now, depressing the earwigs and spiders.

'That's the ticket,' he said. 'Such a pretty smile.'

'More tea?' she said. 'Cake?'

He peered at the trolley. 'Seed cake, scrummy.'

She pushed the knife through the pale disc. The seeds were like mouse droppings speckled through the pale sponge. Just looking at it made the insides of her cheeks contract. Mrs Hale's cakes were like blotting paper though Dennis enjoyed them. The taste of his childhood. She handed him the plate.

'What have you been up to?' he said.

'The usual.' The page she was on had one paragraph at the top.

. . . was stationed at the edge. Mariella crushed the satin between her fingers before she turned to leave.

And all the rest was blank. It was her favourite page. Of course there were empty end pages, but one could not seem to be reading those. Anagrams from the first phrase: *detain, sedge, satin, sewing, snowing*. Each day she saw another. *Gestation*.

She tore her eyes away. More tea. Positioning the cups, she lifted the snooty spouted pot.

'And how's our little soldier today?' said Dennis through his cake.

The tea kept pouring, running over into the saucer. She put down the teapot. Inside the spout the white china was tarry from years of tea. Her hand shook as she poured the slops from the saucer into the hot-water jug. She dropped two lumps of sugar into his tea and stirred and breathed, watching the minute fizz of dissolving sugar, wincing at the deafening chink of silver against bone china.

Dennis took the tea. 'Busy day,' he said. 'The world and his wife have got this bally impetigo. Ripping through the Clarks like wild-fire, of course.'

She poured her own tea, sat down, took a sip. 'Please.' She strove for equanimity. 'Please, dear, don't call him that.'

'Beg pardon?' There was a crumb of cake caught in his moustache, a caraway seed, lodged like a mouse dropping between the bristles.

She put down her cup. '*Little soldier*. Please, not that.'

Dennis guffawed. 'Don't be absurd, you silly child! I call all the nippers "little soldier" – it means nothing.'

Her hands were birds flapping to escape her wrists.

'Not my son,' came a version of her voice.

Dennis was frowning, and her heart went fathoms deep, actually left her entirely, at his doctorly expression: serious, reasonable, a mite amused. Poor heart throbbing loose. 'Are you quite all right, Clem? Here, let me feel . . .' He got up and approached her to put his hand against her brow but she shrank back into the chair. His face floated over her like a balloon.

'Quite well. Don't touch.'

Maroon balloon buffoon. Dirigible. Is that a word?

He stood for a moment, considering, then shrugged, cut another slice of cake, sat down, picked up and flapped open *The Times*. She could smell the ink and the paper and his scrubbed coal tar hands. Those coal tar fingers went inside her sometimes as if he was fishing for something lost.

The infant began to mewl and she scooped him up, cupped her hand round the vulnerable curve of his skull, held him against her chest as if protecting him, or herself, from the enemy, his brain in soft skull-bone against her heart. All the insides packed in tight. Outrageous anger blasted through her, a series of detonations in her mind.

Dennis put down the paper, stood. 'Here, let me take him.' He reached out but she could not put the child in those fishing hands.

'Don't ever again call him "soldier".' It came from somewhere in a scream.

Her feet took her from the room, climbed her up the stairs – oh, so cold after the hot room – up towards the nursery, Dinah's realm.

Her knitting – the start of a sock – lay abandoned on the floor beside a rattle. But Dinah was out. Clem lay on the nursery daybed with Edgar squirming in her arms. *Not a soldier, not a soldier, not a soldier, not a soldier, you will never be a soldier.* The infant was deafening now. *Never be a soldier. Never.* There was a pillow. Oh yes, of course. She got up and laid him on the bed and one hand went onto his chest and the other held the pillow just above, not touching, just above, a soft, smotherly, motherly way . . . surely better than war?

Dennis stood white-faced in the doorway, the black of his moustache comical against the chalky skin, a trick moustache cut out of felt. Clem stepped back, held the pillow against her chest like an easier, more pliant child. Dennis lifted Edgar just as Mrs Hale came in. He handed the infant to her, removed the pillow from Clem's arms, which had gone like raw pastry now; he could easily have torn them off.

> *Of course she wouldn't have done it.*
> *Of course she wouldn't have done it.*
> *Of course she wouldn't have done it.*
> *Of course she wouldn't.*

7

No NEED TO call a doctor; this was a house of doctors though old Dr Everett barely ventured from his room any more. Dennis knew what to give her to make things right.

Months, months after months, a blur. Fingers on the arm, a steel shaft in a vein, sparkle of drug in blood, limbs loose, child cries, someone always looking in. Hands between legs, smell of coal tar, another injection, wetness, after all, only reasonable, *wife*. Light all night it seems, birdsong, child sound outside, stale nightdress, sweet slop, white food, white drink. Sometimes a face in the mirror, pale, all that hair, should have it bobbed, one day. Write to Harri, where have they all gone, the people in her life? A magpie in the gutter cranes down to peer in; one can hear the scritch-scritch of claws. The hand roams, Powell's hand she's almost sure, clutching, clutching at the air. Sometimes it rains, sometimes it moans, sometimes it shines; ponies and carriages, motorcars drive by. A leaf sticks to the glass, sycamore, mottled like an old hand, and a feather drifts past, dirty white. Don't they say angel? Murmurings in the chimney, chinkings from under the floor, feet on stairs, doors banging, telephone ringing and smells of food. Sometimes a wisp of appetite, a sudden longing for lamb chops or an apple. Mrs Hale is hale and hearty; Dennis all solicitation, moustache and fingers. Old Dr Everett looks in now and then, and she overhears an argument about medication. *Speak up*, he roars as always, *speak up, you blithering idiot*. Such a very handsome man is Dennis, or so they say. Keep your voice down. Funny how it gets so hard to tell. One day Harri's there, is she? But not like Harri, her face askew; she says nothing. Sometimes a child appears, not Edgar but a shining insubstantial child who reaches out her hand, retreats and vanishes. Light at the end of tunnels one never seems to reach. Sun setting earlier now, rust in the sky, fog pressing its mushy face against the glass. Mrs Hale brings nourishment, soft things, mashed like baby food and milky sweet. Dennis lies with her now and then; arms giving a shape to her body. Coming back to herself, they say, coming back.

Rain beat on the windows and shadows of the drops ran down the pale hills of her knees. Her hands were soft and clean, so clean, from doing nothing, the nails long and sharp – a stranger's hands.

Dennis came in. 'Darling.' His face broke and he was crying, *crying. Dennis* crying. 'It's Father,' he said.

He'd had a stroke so another invalid in the house. But the new one did it properly; he overtook her and died. People came and went. Harri, dressed in black, the squeals of her twins winding up the stairs. How many hearts beating in the house all at once? A complicated syncopation like the clocks in different rooms, the chimes and booms. *Pull yourself together, darling. Best foot forward.* Dennis the man of the house now, taken over the whole of the practice. The smell of tears. A reaching hand. Regaining edges, coming back to herself at last, they said, becoming bored. *Canada, Canada*. Now, don't allow that. Stuff and nonsense. Tommy rot. Here we are now. Here.

They brought in the infant – big and strong, all fight and bluster, black hair like Dennis and already the eyebrows darkening. And bright brown eyes like conkers. A perfect baby stranger.

And then she was up. Finding her feet. A daily stroll in the garden where it was spring, it seemed; crocuses ached mauvely among the drifts of last year's beech leaves, green sparked on twig tips, the last huddles of snowdrops hung their creamy heads.

She was allowed an hour a day with Edgar, supervised by Dennis. They resumed their habit of afternoon tea, Dennis up from the surgery carrying his smell of coal tar, bay rum on his cheeks, hands scrubbed red, knuckles like something from the butcher's shop.

'Watch him walk,' Dennis said, one afternoon. 'Come on, Eddie . . .' He was on his knees on the hearthrug holding out his hands and the child managed to stagger a step or two before he tumbled back and sat grinning on the rug, flames flickering on his white woollen suit, his rosy cheeks.

'He'll be running around in no time,' remarked Clem. 'We shall have to get him some shoes.' She switched her eyes to her needlework. She was hemming a handkerchief, a singularly useless occupation, attempting a picot edge. It was destined for Harri's birthday.

'Such a clever little s—' Dennis stopped himself. 'Er, fellow,' he finished. Clem was grateful to him for refraining from the appellation. No warlike words near Edgar, please. Her skull's interior was a house with an upstairs room and a basement; the basement locked with a long, serious key; Edgar and teatime and picot-edged handkerchiefs stayed upstairs. As long as that was the case, one was safe.

Dennis returned to his chair and his cup of tea. 'You're looking more chipper,' he said, and Clem relaxed a little in the sun of his approval, realised how tightly her fingers had been pinching the needle.

'I am chipper,' she said with a little smile.

'Good show,' Dennis said. 'Have a macaroon. We want a bit more flesh on those bones, please, Mrs Everett.'

Clem stretched out her hand, twisting it and admiring the thinness of her wrist.

'You know I can't stick macaroons,' she said. 'But I'll take a piece of bread and butter.'

She began to get up, but Dennis rose instead. He put a finger of bread and butter on her plate, leaned in to kiss her head. 'Tell you what,' he said. 'Why don't we visit Harri on Sunday? About time you saw the hovel she chooses to live in. Perhaps *you* can help bring her to her senses.'

A spear of excitement shot through Clem, followed by a clutch of alarm. The limp buttery bread drooped between her fingers, and she returned it to her plate. She hadn't been further than the garden for such an age. 'Perhaps,' she said and unthinkingly wiped her buttery fingers on the handkerchief.

'That's the ticket.' Dennis flopped down in his armchair. 'And look!' he said. Edgar had balanced on his feet and managed two steps towards Clem before falling onto his bottom and reverting to the greater efficiency of hands and knees.

'Oh, I've ruined it.' She held up the greasy scrap of cotton lawn with its uneven edging. She could stitch skin together, it seemed, but not make a tidy handkerchief. 'Please excuse me a moment,' she said, and fled.

The cottage was in Malton, one of a row that slumped damply beside a boat yard, low by the river. The lane was untarmacked and the car jolted horribly over the ruts. The air smelled of the river, of cinders and cats; a bramble caught in the hem of Clem's coat as they unlatched the rickety gate.

'See what I mean?' Dennis said. He rapped at the door and flakes fell from the rusty elfin knocker.

Harri opened the door. 'You wretch,' she said to Clem, hugging her, 'you utter wretch, not coming for such an age.'

'What ho, Harriet,' said Dennis. 'Foot in your mouth before we're over the threshold. Top marks.'

Harri swooped Edgar from his arms and buried her face in him. 'Oh, the divine odour of an infant!'

In the tiny hallway, Clem tried not to stare as she removed her jacket and hat, found room for them on the cluttered pegs. Harri, always a messy girl with a singular taste in clothes, looked odder than ever in a shapeless rayon thing – could you even call it a dress? A scarlet comb haphazardly stuck in her bundled hair. She'd grown stouter and there were no stays, nothing to hide her loose fleshy figure, from which Edgar was struggling to escape.

'Now, you must meet the girls properly *at last*. Do step in.' She swept her arm in an ironically grand gesture of welcome. The hot, poky room into which they followed her was a-scatter with skittles and piles of clothes. As they entered, a thin, dark-complexioned girl with a twin in each hand came through the opposite door.

'Thanks, Mildred,' Harri said. 'This is my sister-in-law, Mrs Everett. And you know my brother – we're still not speaking to him.'

'Pleasure, I'm sure.' Mildred flashed Dennis a confused look. She had a missing tooth in the front, the tip of her tongue probing the gap, the pits of old blemishes on her rather fine cheekbones.

'Mildred helps with the girls and her mother does for me twice a week. Does a marvellous job, they both do.'

Mildred turned dark red. 'Ta very much.'

'And this is Edgar.' Harri plonked him down on the floor.

By now, a girl had wrapped herself round each of Dennis's legs. They were a sturdy pair, identical, with floating white hair, round faces and clear hazel eyes. One had a flaming rash on her cheeks. Harri squatted down to their level. 'Now, this is your auntie Clem, who's been so poorly. Say hello.'

''Lo,' they both said, regarding Clem shyly from under white lashes.

'This is Phyllis. Dennis, you may as well look at her rash since you're here. And this is Claris.'

Claris was hugging Edgar roughly round his head.

'Hello, girls,' Clem said. 'How on earth do you tell the difference?'

'Not sure that I can,' Harri said. 'Mildred, could you get the tea, please? Do sit down, Clemmie, before you fall down.'

Clem moved a golliwog from the sofa before she sat, noticing the grubbiness of the old chintz and a low frieze of smudges on the walls and woodwork. The smell of smoke and grime was sweetened by that of a bowl of hyacinths, lolling their blue heads against the window. The room was bewilderingly strewn with books, paintings, jars, brushes, a vase of dead roses, twigs that dangled ribbons, apples and painted fir cones. A goldfish lurked sadly in a murky bowl.

Harri rescued Edgar from the twins, and sat with him on her lap. 'Now then,' she said. 'Let's have a proper look at this little chap.'

Edgar reached out for her amber beads. 'Of course you shall have them, my darling.' Harri unlooped them from her neck and let Edgar put them in his mouth. 'Imagine – he's teething on a prehistoric fly!'

One of the twins came and stood before Clem, regarding her curiously.

'Have you been playing skittles?' Clem asked.

'Not skittles, *farms*,' the child replied.

'Rosacea,' Dennis pronounced, letting the other twin go. 'It'll clear up. No treatment required.'

'In the meantime it'll help me tell them apart,' said Harri. 'No, of course I can tell: Claris is bigger and her eyebrows are thicker. And Phyllis is the menace, aren't you?' The rashless one supplied a demonic grin.

'This is a pig,' said Claris seriously, 'and this is a bull, silly.' She put two identical skittles on Clem's lap.

'Don't be cheeky to your aunt,' Dennis said.

'Pretty name for an ailment! Rosacea. Is it catching?'

Dennis shook his head. He settled back into an armchair, regarded his sister through narrowed eyes. 'You look seedy,' he said.

'Your considered medical diagnosis? Seedy? How much should one have to pay for that?'

Dennis ignored her. 'Sleeping? Eating properly?'

'He's dropping off,' Harri remarked; Edgar was leaning against her bosom, sucking rhythmically on an amber bead.

'There's no need to manage all alone, as you perfectly well know,' Dennis said. 'Stanley's gone, his family would understand.'

'I'm not alone,' she said. 'They're marvellous.'

'Move back to the Beeches, just for the time being,' Dennis said. 'Clem would love it now she's better, wouldn't you, old thing? Why not come back with us today?'

Clem stared at the faceless skittles on her lap.

Mildred rattled in with a trolley of tea and cake.

'Shouldn't you like that, Clem?' Dennis insisted. 'A bit of company. Bring you out of yourself. You'd do each other good.'

'Could you take the twins out of the way?' Harri said, and Mildred took one in each hand down the passage to the kitchen. 'They'll have the trolley over,' Harri explained. Edgar was asleep on her lap now, clear drool spilling from his open mouth.

'Out of myself? What a ridiculous expression,' Clem said. 'Harri should live wherever she chooses.'

'See,' said Harri.

'You can hardly think this a suitable place to bring up children.'

'I've managed up to now!' said Harri. 'And people do, they manage in places worse than this.'

'Not people like us.'

'Dennis!' shrieked Harri, waking Edgar, who looked around with big startled eyes. '*People like us!* Great heavens above, if your patients could hear you!'

'You know perfectly well what I mean.'

'There's nothing wrong with it,' Clem said. 'It's . . . quaint.'

'Well, *you're* hardly in a position to judge,' Dennis said.

Harri snorted and Clem gaped at him. 'I *beg* your pardon?'

Dennis rubbed his chin; he did have the grace to look abashed. 'I only mean you haven't been yourself, old thing. Don't take on.' He braved the eyes of the two women for a moment. 'Look here, Harri, see sense. There's ample room at the Beeches and I don't mean for ever. This damp – not good for their chests.'

'Their chests are perfectly splendid, thank you,' said Harri. 'The whole world doesn't revolve around the Beeches, you know!' She turned to Clem. 'How *do* you stick him?'

Edgar wriggled down and staggered away.

'Now, you simply must try the cake,' she said. 'Stan's ma invented it; it was his favourite.' She removed the skittles from Clem's lap and replaced them with a wedge of yellow cake on a cracked plate. 'Guess the secret ingredient? Make yourself useful, Dennis, and pour the tea – if that's not beneath you.'

'Of course I'd rather no one suffered poor conditions,' he said as he stooped over the trolley.

'Well, how very civilised of you,' Harri said. 'You'll be joining the Fabians next.'

Scowling, Dennis reached for his tea.

Clem lifted the damp, heavy slab of cake to her mouth. It was sticky and so sweet it made her teeth ache.

'Marzipan?' she said.

'Isn't it killing? She drops bits of it in the mix. One can see the creativity in the family. Look at that darling stool.' Clem regarded the stubby three-legged object. 'We had a plan, you know, for after the war: Stan was to make furniture – stools and little tables and so on – and I was to decorate them.'

'God almighty,' said Dennis. 'And then you'd go hawking them from a gypsy caravan, I suppose?'

Clem put down her plate and stood, feeling a sudden longing to be outside, away from them.

'We shall all take a stroll, presently,' said Dennis.

'Clem?' Harri caught her hand. 'Are you quite all right, you look frightfully—'

'A breath of air.' Clem plucked her hand from Harri's and made for the door. She put on her jacket, repositioned her hat with its stupid curving ostrich feather. Old hat, she thought, and almost laughed. Dennis stood, and she managed to look him in the face, almost to meet his eyes in a normal manner. 'Really, I'll only be—'

'But, darling . . .' Dennis began.

'We'll come and find you,' said Harri.

'I'm not sure she should be out all alone, not yet.'

'Who's *she*, the cat's mother? Bolt, Clem, bolt!' Harri pushed Clem out of the door and stood barring it with her hands on her hips.

'Harriet! You're behaving like a chimney sweep!' came Dennis's voice.

Clem fled.

8

SHE HURRIED AWAY, threading through a warren of narrow lanes till she found herself on the riverbank. There, she stood inhaling the dank air, reeling in the bright openness. Mud flats, threaded with the silvery creep of the tide, reminded her of the stretch marks on her belly. Old posts sculpted thick with weed stood in the shallows like a gathering of stubby monks; the arched ribs of an ancient wreck provided a perch for a heron, which, as she approached, lumbered into the air and flapped away.

Any minute Dennis might catch her up. On an impulse, she cut up from the riverside, through a deserted boatyard, and along the muddy lanes, head down, not sure where she was going, needing only to be gone. Eventually she emerged on the main road that led to Seckford and continued to walk briskly past modest cottages with handkerchief gardens, larger houses enclosed by willows and poplars bending in the breeze. A white terrier on a rope bared its teeth as she passed but didn't bother to shift itself. Seagulls swooped over the road, finding something to shriek and squabble over. The breeze was cool with gusts of river smell and something sweetish she couldn't identify.

Filled with feverish energy, she strode and strode; her legs seemed something mechanical that did not know how to stop, and yet they became shaky with this unaccustomed exercise. It was the first time she'd been out alone, unshielded, since . . . she could not remember, and though she was warmly dressed, green velvet hat heavy and secure on her head, the bobbing tip of feather like an insect appearing at the edge of her vision now and then, still she felt naked, shivery, exposed. And quite abruptly the need to move left her, and with it the ability. She looked around for somewhere to sit and rest but there was nowhere. What was she doing? She should have waited, Dennis had been right, should have waited, needed now to sit, nowhere to sit. Out of herself now, like he said. Out.

She stumbled on, turned a corner where the lane went downhill; it was easier to let momentum propel her than to resist. It took her round a bend, the river smell gone now and replaced by the reek of flowering currant, and the sweet smell again, stronger, man-made; she knew it but couldn't quite identify it. She considered sitting on the front wall of a cottage, but no, there was the low stone parapet of a bridge and she sat there instead, listening to the flow of the stream beneath her, gazing at the slope back uphill, defeated by the thought of the slight ascent.

Breathe, she used to tell patients, those whose lungs weren't gas-burned, those who still had ribs and lungs intact, *breathe deeply in and out. It calms one, it really does*. Remember the look of a cage of ribs, bluish shine under the meniscus, the jerky spasms of gasped-in air. *No, don't*. Inhale. She took the outside in, and pushed it out again; so intimate, breathing is, taking in the same air that has been in other lungs, through trees and water, rabbits, herons, across lovers' bed sheets, across the fields of war. With her eyes closed, she felt the hoops of her nostrils expand, her lungs bloom foamy pink, in and out, in their elastic cage. When she opened her eyes again the world was in brighter colours. It was all right then, she was quite all right. But she must turn back uphill – Dennis would make such a devil of a fuss – and find her way back.

She must have stepped out into the road. She didn't even hear the motorbike as it veered round the bend approaching the bridge. The driver saw her, swerved and hit the wall, his machine flipping onto its side, skidding along the road. The crash sent starlings shrieking from a tree, a wheel turned in the air, flashing chrome. The engine stopped, the starlings vanished, and it was quiet again but for the buzz of a fly.

The rider's goggles had come off and lay broken on the road. His head was turned to the side: a long bony face, nose hooked, specs, eyes closed. A flash of electricity shocked her legs from beneath her. *Powell.*

No! It was too much, and she fainted. From far off came a shout, running feet . . . Smelling salts seared her nostrils. *Powell?* Now she was in a stranger's house and it smelled of hops, of brewing. Of course, she was near the maltings – that was the smell. She focused on the mantelpiece. At one end stood a china soldier with a gun against one shoulder, at the other a weeping china girl waved a handkerchief. A clock pecked laboriously at the seconds. *Powell?*

Mrs Court, the lady of the house, bade Clem sip sugary tea and take a morsel of burned rock cake. She was dressed in weary, well-worn black, her face dour and downy. She'd been bereaved, husband or son or sons or everyone; Clem could smell it on her, read it in the downward grooves of her face.

'Your husband's on his way,' she told Clem. 'You'll soon be right as rain. Wretched motorbikes. What's wrong with a pony and trap, I say?'

Clem remembered, dimly, saying who she was, where Dennis might be found.

'You're the colour of a tapioca pudding. Another sniff?' The woman held out the little bottle.

'I'm quite all right now, thank you.'

'You said another name too. Pole? Powers?'

Clem stared at the china girl, the stiff flag of her handkerchief.

When Dennis arrived Mrs Court looked at him with a kind of awe, and Clem herself, as his wife, with an increased respect. And he did look like *someone*, a solid citizen, uncommonly virile and handsome with his glossy eyes and natty moustache, his charming manner – and above all the life still in him. He *was* someone. It did make her proud, when others so clearly admired him, that he was hers. And she should be, would be, nicer to him. After all, he had been right in this case, and she had been wrong.

'Darling,' she said. 'Thank you for coming.'

'The idiot rider's in the cottage hospital,' said Dennis.

'I stepped out,' Clem said. 'My fault entirely.'

'Nonsense,' said Mrs Court.

'Nonsense,' echoed Dennis. 'He'd been drinking and going like the clappers no doubt. Wants stringing up.'

'It wasn't his fault.'

'Thank heavens you weren't hit, poor child.'

'I must go and see him, apologise.'

'Tosh!'

They extricated themselves from Mrs Court and drove back to Harriet's. Dennis insisted that Clem lie down and drink yet another cup of sweet tea before they drive home. Obediently she lay on Harriet's bed listening to the children down below – the bossy lisping of the girls, Edgar's excited shrieks. Martins nested in the eaves. She watched the parent birds flying in, beaks a-dangle with grubs, and out again in a speedy fluster, and she could just make out the squeaking of their chicks.

At first she averted her eyes from the nightstand where stood a framed photograph of Harri's Stanley in his uniform. In tiny increments she turned her head, and then seized the image to study it, with a sort of greed. Stanley's face, about the size of the tip of her index finger, his mouth, looked stern but perhaps on the verge of smiling. Beneath the brim of his cap, one eyebrow was higher than the other, and his ears stuck out comically. He looked exactly what he was: a decent, ordinary man got up in ridiculous fancy dress.

Of course the man on the motorbike wasn't Powell, she knew that. Powell was dead. She'd seen him dead, the stovepipe in his back. Curling her knees to her chest, she moaned as grief blasted through her again – grief for Powell, for his child, and for her brother, the pains competing. Ralph's face had almost vanished from her mind. She could list his features: thick fair hair, straight brown lashes, hyacinth eyes slightly downturned at their outer corners – but she couldn't really see him any more.

Dennis creaked upstairs to fetch her. 'Rested, darling? Shall we set off? We'll soon have you back in your own bed.'

Clem sat up. 'I'm perfectly all right,' she said. 'It's the poor rider I worry about. I shall visit him.'

'Absolute rot! Straight home for you, my girl.'

'It seems only polite.'

'Polite!' Dennis hooted.

'And decent,' Clem added.

Clem sat at Harri's dressing table to tidy her hair and replace her hat. She loathed the stupid thing. No one young wore such great feathery things any more. In the glass she caught an odd look of helplessness on Dennis's face, and paused, hatpin pinched between her fingers, feeling a surge of fondness.

'Decent like you, darling,' she added.

Harri came up the stairs and, puffing a little, poked her head into the room. 'Ominous silence!' she said. 'Mildred wants to know if she should give Eddie his tea.'

'We're about to leave,' Dennis said.

'He could have his tea, then we could fetch him after my visit,' Clem said.

'She's got a bee in her bonnet about visiting the blithering idiot who nearly ran her down!'

'Why not?' Harri said. 'Poor chap.'

'Poor chap!'

'*I* stepped out in front of *him*,' Clem said. It was the first time she'd felt any real spirit since when? It was a peculiar feeling, frizzling skeins of chemical in her blood. 'He might have been killed. I might at least pay him the courtesy . . .'

'Of course you must,' said Harri.

'Oh, thank you,' said Dennis.

'So that's settled. Mildred and I shall feed Eddie.' Harri went thumping downstairs.

Shrugging, Dennis turned to Clem. 'Well, we'll have to be bally quick then. I don't want to be driving after dark. You'll have to go in on your own – I've no wish to see him. And don't go blurting out that it was your fault, for pity's sake.'

Clem hesitated at the hospital threshold. Who might she meet at the bedside? Wife perhaps? Might she have to converse with strangers? Perhaps Dennis was right, perhaps there was no need. After all, how killingly awkward to approach a perfect stranger in such circumstances. What on earth could one say? She glanced back and caught the set of Dennis's jaw. He was leaning against the car smoking a cigarette; how gratified he'd be if she returned to the car and told him he was right.

No, it was the decent thing to do, and besides, she had to see that face again, to see whether the fellow did indeed resemble Powell.

Matron warned her that visiting time was almost over, looked at her askance when she said she didn't know the name of the chap she was visiting. Clem found him – alone, thank heavens – at the end of the ward beside a window, through which the pinkish sky cast him in an odd light: bony cheekbones, blade of nose, gold glint of wire-rimmed specs. Coming closer, she observed with a start that the upper left quarter of his face was prosthetic; a painted eye and brow, and a cheekbone that fitted snugly to the side of his long, handsome nose. The glass in the spectacles that held the prosthesis to his face was broken; that side had been on the ground, concealed from her. His hands lay on top of the green blanket, thin and elegant, the fingers long, the nails tapered.

'Good afternoon,' she said.

He turned his eyes towards her, showing no sign of recognition.

'It was myself you swerved to avoid,' she prompted.

For a moment his expression did not change, then, 'Hah,' he said, focusing his real eye on her with more interest. 'Yes, I see it now.' His voice was common, local. A tradesman of some sort, or perhaps in the clerical line. 'That hat,' he added, with something of a smirk.

The iris of his good eye was a curious pale grey, almost silver; the edges were darker, as if tarnished like a coin, and the artist had made a brave attempt to paint the other eye to match. The eyebrow had been finely painted, with the most miniature of brushes, the most delicate of strokes, but it was a shade too yellow. The blank eye gazed beyond her.

Sucking in a breath, Clem said, 'I wanted to call and . . . well . . .' The words dried up in her mouth and she felt foolish, but also weakened by a feeling both strong and strange for there really was a strong, almost *uncanny*, resemblance.

He began to haul himself up, and it came naturally to her to move forward, plump the pillow, settle him comfortably back.

'Concussion,' he said. 'I'll be out tomorrow. I've had worse.' He tapped a fingernail on his tin cheekbone.

She smiled weakly.

'But my Norton – motorcycle – wrecked,' he said.

'I can't apologise enough,' Clem said. 'So careless of me to step out like that.'

'I won't contradict you there.' Had his voice refined itself? He seemed harder to place now. Tearing her eyes from his face, she noticed the ridges of his collarbones under lilac pyjamas and a scar on the side of his neck – thick raised tissue, healed but angry, the same side as his mask. That must still hurt, she guessed, nerves tangled in the clumsily healed and thickened epidermis.

'Please feel free to stare,' he said.

Heat rose in her face. 'I do apologise. I'm not, I . . . Heavens above, I haven't even introduced myself!' She held out her hand. 'Clementine Everett, Mrs, that is I'm married.'

He lowered his head in a single nod, the corners of his mouth quirking with amusement. Like Powell's mouth, though wider, the lips narrower. Languidly he held out a hand. 'Pleased to meet you, Mrs Married Clementine Everett,' he said. 'Oh, by the way, are you, by any chance, married?'

The nerve of him! But to her own amazement she found herself laughing. A bell drilled out the end of visiting time.

'Well, I . . . might I offer to pay for repairs to your motorcycle?' she said, taking his hand. 'It seems the least I can do.'

He hesitated; his natural instinct was to refuse the offer, she could tell.

'In fact I insist,' she said. 'I shall chain myself to your bed if you refuse!'

His real eyebrow rose. 'Well, now, *that* sounds rather tempting!' His sudden wide full smile spread to the eye on the intact side of his face, the white pinked by capillaries, the pupil inking larger in the silver.

'What I mean is—'

'I know what you mean!'

They looked at each other for a moment, and now she squirmed under *his* scrutiny, in which there seemed a kind of challenge. A stranger, he had teased her and made her laugh! Beside his eye was a spray of lines, deeper, she guessed, than his years deserved, painted much more faintly on the other side. She longed to ask him about himself, about his war, but seeing the nurse approach she took a pencil and notebook from her bag. 'My address,' she said, jotting it down. 'I shall leave the matter in your hands.'

'Come on now,' the nurse said. 'No shilly-shallying, if you please.'

Clem pressed the piece of paper into the man's hand. 'You haven't introduced *your*self,' she added.

'Fortune,' he said, 'Vincent. Sergeant, as was.'

Ah, she thought, an NCO, and down on his luck. 'Well, good-bye, Mr . . . Sergeant . . . Fortune. May you recover swiftly.'

She walked down the corridor and through the hospital door to where the air was shrill with birdsong, sharp in the greenish spring dusk.

Dennis was leaning against the car door. 'Duty done?' he said, grinding out his cigarette end with his foot. 'Satisfied?'

'Thank you, darling,' Clem said, touching his hand before she climbed into her seat and waited for him to crank the engine.

9

LEANING ON THE bar watching Doll, Vince finds himself
grinning – that involuntary stretch of lip and hoick of cheek a
rare sensation. It stretches the tight scar, the skin sliding itchily
behind the tin. Doll bends over, checking a barrel; she's got hips on
her under that skirt, sturdy, bovine, though she'd kill him if he said
as much. His cheek yearns for her lap, for her stroking hands, for
her fantastically common reek of beer and ham and Parma Violets.
No stays for her, not today. She's like a big old flower blooming her
heart out, a big old cow flower; now he actually laughs and drains
his glass, bangs it down on the bar.

'Same again?' she says, face pink from exertion, hair springing
free of its pins. Not a natural blonde he knows, and you can see the
roots and her dark brows but he likes that about her; natural is
overrated in his opinion. She's his age or older, pushing forty and
with a kid; he doesn't mind kiddies. Her old man Dick copped it at
the Marne right at the start of war, poor sod.

Doll fills his tankard, and another pint of Adnams slips down a
treat. Her capable hands on the pumps, on his pump too! 'Marry
me' is in his reckless mind to say, but someone else is calling her – a
stranger in a trilby. Vince watches her flirt, those bosoms swelling
out from under the blossoms on her blouse, buttons straining.
Huge nipples she has; great pink saucers. She'd always be flirting,

and who knows how many men she's had after closing time, in the bar, a quick, hot, wet one, beery and bleared with smoke, a happy, dazed, *lucky* bastard staggering out into the cold. In need of a husband to keep her on the straight and narrow. Not too straight or too narrow though; you wouldn't want to squash the life out of her, only to rein it in, save her from herself – and reap the benefit.

Now she hands bread and cheese and one of her famous pickled onions that make your eyes run to a travelling salesman – sharp moustache, lust in his eyes as they stray to her chest. He'll eat his ploughman's, swallow his half of light and be off, weaselling his way into some housewife's bed with a demonstration of his wares. Encyclopedias? Brooms? Those were the days.

And in any case, Vince isn't budging. He's been in her bed more than once, her *sanctuary*, and that makes him different, not just a fly-by-night. The second time when they were only just finished, the boy came through, rubbing his eyes – 'Mum, I dreamt a robber was here' – and Doll was up and out of that bed, soothing and petting and gone an hour or so.

'You still here?' she'd said when she returned, sounding quite taken aback.

'Kept the bed warm for you.'

'Kind of you, I'm sure, but you'd best be wending your way.'

'Come on, Doll, can't I stay?'

But she'd only folded her arms and waited for him to leave, to climb up that ladder to his room in the loft.

Nearly closing. Then there's an hour before Kenny gets back from school and in the meantime . . . Sun gleams through the stained-glass tops of the windows onto the optics and the brass bar fittings. The beer is pure gold. He lights a cheroot, sups his ale – home from home, this is.

'A sight for sore eyes,' says some chancer, and as she fills his glass Doll raises her eyebrows at Vince. He likes it when she gives him a special look like that, conspiratorial, like they're in it together. Ridiculous, but he more or less *would* marry her if it meant he could spend his life right here, like this, leaning on the bar, watching her serve other men, knowing she was his, whetting his appetite for all those later-ons.

Is it so ridiculous?

Ten to two, last orders, but most have gone by then. Only Amos left; he has a seat in the corner where he catches punters unaware and winds them into his endless yarns. No takers today, so he mutters to himself, clacking dominos in some form of solitaire. Too old for service this time, but served his time at Mafeking, won that war single-handed if you credit a word he comes out with. Doll knows how to handle him, kind but stern, and he's like a lamb, trots off home without a murmur.

Once Doll's locked the door, Vince straightens up and drains his glass. The leg's got its old shudder again, but she'll soon soothe that out of him.

'And you,' she says. 'Come on, dearie, shift yourself.'

'Doll,' he says, opening his arms to her.

'No, Vince, you can't go expecting that,' she says. 'Anyhow, I've other fish to fry. Help me with the glasses if you can't tear yourself away.'

He keeps up a piteous expression but she isn't falling for it.

'What fish?' he says. 'I'll harpoon that bloody fish.'

'Stop your nonsense!'

The sun dims and the colours fall away; scummy glasses on the bar that needs a wipe. In fact she's already got her cloth, mopping the splashes off the tables, straightening beermats, emptying ashtrays.

He goes up behind her, hands full of her glorious chest, nuzzles into her hair, but she pulls away.

'Now, now,' she says, and her voice has taken on the strict, patient tone she uses with Amos and the other barflies. He could go up to his camp bed in the loft and sleep till opening. But he's needled, so he says toodle-oo, and goes out, surprised at how he bangs against the table on his way. Not as if he's had that much.

Outside is bright, cold. As he knots his scarf he notices the window boxes, her pride and joy. She's put tiny mauve blooms in with the greenery, really artistic. 'What I long for is a garden,' she told him once. 'Somewhere for Kenny to play. Trees and that, a garden pond. Goldfish.'

On his Norton he roars down the lanes towards Seckford. He might have a pint at the Crown, or maybe call at the teashop see what that little Dora's up to. Though it's Doll he's committed to, *committed to* – yes, like an asylum! He snorts. Drinking helps keep his mind away from all the hell. No, don't think it: feeble sun on mud, caked in mud, rifle like a muddy branch, the stench. *No!* Two years since and here he is, and, Vincey, you've landed on your bloody feet. Stop thinking. But those plank roads at Passchendaele, mud knee-deep, poor bloody mules and horses, hooves sliding, screaming, frothing at their mouths, whites of their eyes.

He swerves his mind away, hits a bend, grips the throttle tighter. Speed helps. Drive through the memory out the other side. Narrow bridge – oh Christ, someone in the road, a woman – pulls the wheel sharp right and

10

H E'S ALL RIGHT. Knocked out for a bit, mild concussion. But what about the Norton? What's the damage? She's the only thing he owns. Can't imagine life without her now. His hand goes to his tin plate, scraped on the road; specs are smashed and some of the electroplated lashes snapped off. Doll's never seen him with it off – no one has since it was fitted – and nor does he look himself in the mirror without it. The wires from the specs can his cut ears like buggery, specially when he's tired.

Visiting time, and if she comes it will go to show. Go to show she cares. A caring type she is, motherly. No better than she ought to be, but he can put a stop to that. Get a ring on that finger. Look after her like every woman needs, whatever they might say. She's not a suffragette type – not his Doll, no such rot.

And she comes, she actually bloody well comes, bustling down between the beds, bless her heart, in her best coat and vile black straw hat, more fit for a funeral than anything. He'll get her another, whatever she wants, the best money can buy. He's so pleased to see her he could nearly bloody cry.

'You poor sausage,' is what she says and gives him a peck on the cheek. He grabs her, tries to keep her close a moment; she's got her Parma Violet scent on and her cheeks are powdered. 'That's what you get for riding off with a drink inside you,' she scolds, like any wife would. 'You'll have to get them specs fixed.'

'It's the bike I'm worried about,' he says as she pulls away.

'You and your never-ending motorcycle! Now, I'm only here for a tick. Pub won't open itself.' She brings a tiny bunch of grapes out of her bag. 'I could have done without this to-do.'

'Sorry, Dolly.'

'I'll sorry Dolly you!' she says.

'Where's Kenny?'

'I've had to get Mum to pick him up and you know what a carry-on that'll be, what with her feet. Oh, she send her regards.'

'Like hell she does!'

He pops a grape in his mouth, bites the skin, and the sour juice puckers his cheeks. Doll's ma, Edie, doesn't have much time for him. She hasn't cottoned on yet that he isn't just any old barfly. He's here for the duration. But give her time; he'll win her over. He spits pips into his palm.

'Bet you're giving the nurses a right old run around.' Doll raises her eyebrows as a pretty one walks past and he grins, but truth be told he's had enough of nurses, enough of hospitals, to last him a lifetime. More than a year of it he had. Not just the face and the headaches, but the *nerves*. Truth is, when he came round on the road this afternoon he thought he was back at the Front. Lay there petrified, expecting mud and shells and torn-off bits of his mates to meet his eyes when all there was was quiet, the sound of a bird, a woman's thin ankles, the cutting into his cheek of the tin. Shook his nerves up good and proper. They warned him that could happen, that a shock could set him back. But he won't bloody let it. He won't.

'What about your family?' she's saying. 'Want me to telephone someone for you?'

'No one to speak of.'

'You never do speak of anyone,' she agrees, frowning. 'But there must be *someone*, dear?'

He thinks of his ex-wife Ethel; she's not family any more and good riddance to the frigid bitch. His folks were old when they had him and long gone now. There's a fleeting sadness as he remembers Mum's hand in his; he'd kept a hold of it when she passed over. Dad had gone years before.

'You're a sight for sore eyes anyway,' he says, aware of the lameness. There can't be a day goes by when someone doesn't say that to her.

'Well, dear, I'll have to love you and leave you.' She tucks a stray curl under the brim of her hat.

'Home tomorrow, all being well,' he says. Does she flinch at the word 'home'? It is his home for now at least, that's all he means.

'Thanks for coming in, Dolly,' he says.

'Don't mention it.' She blows a kiss as she walks off. He watches her go, along with all the other men in the ward, then shuffles himself down and stares at the ceiling. It's painted thick shiny cream with cracks like roads; he follows them with his eyes as if he's riding along them: junctions, choices. *Poor sausage*, he likes that! He'll give her poor sausage! He'd give it to her now if she'd come back and they could draw the curtain round. He told the cops he couldn't remember a thing and it's more or less the truth. Unless someone else presses charges, that's the end of the matter. He got ticked off for having a drink, of course, but he hasn't broken any law. It was only one for the road, or thereabouts. What's the world coming to if a bloke can't have one for the road?

He'll have to have the Norton fixed – that's the worry. Can't do without her, not living out in the sticks, not any way. My better half, he thinks, my better, shinier half. All his savings went into her – couldn't resist when she came up for sale, sitting there in the sun like a queen. He'll have her fetched to the garage near Ipswich where his mate works, find out the damage. And he'll have to have his face fixed up again.

His fingers travel over the tin plate; you can feel the scrape, the stubs of the bust lashes. It's cash that's the problem; there's a bit of a war pension but not enough. Not disabled enough, it seems. They can turn you into a gargoyle but as long as you've got four working limbs . . . He can't expect Doll to pay him for his help in the pub, what with the free board and lodgings, but he does need cash. He finds his empty fingers rubbing.

Not expecting another visit, he ignores the footsteps that stop at his bed. He's in a dream, why not? No harm in it. Christmas morning, and there's himself and Doll behind the bar, which they've got all decked out with holly and tinsel, the locals coming in for a beer, wives for a sherry. He could mix festive punch, don a paper crown – the very spirit of Christmas. All morning, warm and flushed, Doll'd be popping in and out between bar and kitchen, smell of a roasting goose drifting through. Then they'd shut up shop, shouting, 'Merry Christmas'. Maybe mistletoe kisses for anyone eligible – yes, hang a bunch above the door. After he'd locked it, the day would be theirs, a slap-up dinner of goose and pudding and . . .

There's a tall woman standing at the end of the bed: smart, pale, a curling feather in her hat.

'Good afternoon,' she says.

He stares at her, rifling his memory, but she's not there. Not his type anyway – thin, insipid, tense. Looks like she'd shatter if you touched her. Silvery flakes float in his vision; one of his heads coming on, hardly a surprise.

'This afternoon,' she says, in a colourless voice, 'it was myself you swerved to avoid.'

Interest snagged, he begins to sit up, dizzy with the movement, and she's there plumping the pillow for him to lean back on. He sees the recoil as she clocks the tin plate with its scratch and bust lens. You get used to it. Everyone does it, even Doll did at first. You steel yourself – ha, a joke there – steel yourself to get it out of the way.

He pretends recognition. 'I see it now, the hat.' His voice takes on the chill of hers, the intonation of her class. Ethel used to call him a chameleon, the way he changed when he met a person. Comes naturally, can't hardly help it. It's not a hat you'd forget, the feather curling over from the back as if craning to see. 'Concussion,' he says. 'Out tomorrow. I've had worse.' He taps a fingernail on his plate, and her pale face gets paler still.

She apologises for wandering into the road. The flakes drift like glitter in a kiddies' snow globe as he struggles to remember. It wasn't her that caused it. He's about to say as much, but she looks like someone with a bob or two and he does need to get his Norton fixed. The way she's studying him, a little frown on her face.

'Feel free to stare,' he says, and she looks away, blushing.

'I'm sorry,' she says. 'Oh, good heavens, I haven't even introduced myself.' She holds out a creamy glove. 'Clementine Everett,' she says, 'Mrs. That is, I'm married.'

He squeezes shut his eyes to try to clear the interference before he looks at her again. She's younger than he'd thought – too young for that hat – fair, smooth-skinned, a certain sort of perfect. He takes her hand and squeezes it a mite too hard. When the bell for the end of the visiting hour goes she starts, jumpy as a sack of frogs.

'Look,' she says, 'might I offer to pay for repairs to your motor-cycle? It's the least I can do.'

Ha! A perfect catch, just needs to reel it in. Must not seem too eager though. Softly, softly, catchee monkey.

'In fact I insist!' she says. 'I shall chain myself to your bed if you refuse!'

He gapes at this unexpectedness; there's even a bit of a twitch below the blanket. 'Well, now, *that* sounds rather tempting,' he says.

She's gone scarlet now. Of course she was thinking of the suffragette lot, nothing more spicy than that. Priceless, though, the expression on her face! From her bag she pulls a notebook and pencil and jots down her details.

A nurse comes over to shoo her out – she's the last visitor on the ward – then she's gone and he lies down flat again, the bloody flecks swarming in his vision. He sees them even in the eye that isn't there. The eye he left in France. Gone by now, rotted away. Or been eaten by a rat, a fat French rat.

But Mrs Married Clementine Everett now! Doll will split her sides when he tells her the tale; she'll say he has the luck of the devil. He'll stand Sid, the mechanic, a few pints, get him to add a bit on the bill, all between friends. Mrs Married won't know the difference.

But his head is throbbing. He'll ask Nurse for something when she comes round again. A gin'd do it; he'd like to see her face if he ordered one of those.

Christmas day, then: after lunch, a lovely drowsy boozy crawl between the sheets. Would they open up in the evening? A few quiet drinkers dropping by, all full of festive cheer – they might have carol singers in the bar to round things off – him the landlord in his paper crown. Sergeant Fortune as was – still worthy of respect.

11

No LETTER FOR days, and then at breakfast an envelope beside her plate, carelessly upside down. Mrs Hale talking, talking, asking something – the pork chops looking a little off, might she substitute lamb?

'Splendid,' Clem said distractedly. 'Whatever you think best.'

The new kitchen maid, Linda, a great-niece and protégé of Mrs Hale, trotted in with the toast. The smell from Dennis's kipper hung in the air. His place had already been cleared. One could hear the murmur of voices in the surgery below, a woman's high-pitched complaint and the deeper rumble of his professional reassurance.

'Thank you, Linda,' Mrs Hale said, adding, 'She's a treasure this one – you want to appreciate her, Mrs Everett.'

'I do.'

Linda, a pillow-shaped girl with a constellation of gingery freckles, turned an unbecoming shade of crimson as her aunt boasted on. 'A useful girl all round. Lays a good fire and quiet as a mouse, seen and not heard, just as she should be.'

Clem's fingers inched towards the envelope.

'And a nice apple charlotte, I thought?'

'Yes,' Clem said. 'That'll be all now. Thank you.'

As soon as the door had clicked shut she picked up the letter – and sagged with disappointment. It was only Harriet's wild scrawl.

She buttered a slice of toast and spread it with comb honey, squashing with the side of her knife the intricate wax cells. She took a bite before slitting the envelope with a paperknife, fashioned like the weapon of a savage.

Dearest Clem,

What a pleasure to see you on Tuesday, and looking so much better too, despite the unfortunate mishap in the afternoon. Hope the shock of it hasn't set you back?

The girls loved playing with their little cousin and Mildred really took to him –how could one not? Such a divine little manikin never crawled this earth.

Do come again. Without Dennis! I mean – goodness, how disagreeable is it possible for one person to be? How <u>do</u> you stick him? I'll come and see you in good time but still feel uncomfortable *chez vous*, even now poor Daddy's gone.

I suspect Dennis has a scheme to 'bring me back into the fold', probably marry me off to one of his stuffed-shirt doctor pals. No, thank you. So you see why I stay away, but now that you're so recovered I do hope we can become closer friends?

Indeed sisters!

Do come soon.

Love and fondest regards,

Harriet.

Clem licked honey off her fingers; a smudge of butter was rendering a corner of the paper transparent. Why had Mr Fortune not sent the bill? *I'm bored*, she thought. There's not *enough* – though enough of what she was not clear. Perhaps she might take Edgar for a walk. She really ought to have more to do with him – sometimes he seemed more Dinah's child than her own.

Upstairs in the dim green bathroom she stared at her reflection: so pale, the skin glassy, the hair and eyes without colour; it reminded her of the faces she'd sketched at the Front. The one sketchbook she'd brought back, Dennis had asked her to burn, and she meant to one day, but for now it remained concealed. Morbid to dwell on the past, best foot forward, darling, skeletons in the closet and all that.

She unearthed the sketchbook. Oh, the times Sister Fitch had scolded her for drawing, but she'd never done it on duty, only in quieter times when she was free to sit with one of the men, try to provide the comfort she hoped someone had given Ralph in his last hours. No spare time in those last few months though, hardly a gap between shifts, and . . . *Oh, don't think, don't. Dennis so right, don't look.*

But still, she carried the book to the morning room and sat under the window leafing through, breath gripped as she turned the pages. Here, the sweet expression of a boy just dead; here the shattered face of one who couldn't die, would live on as a monstrosity. Worse, far worse than Mr Fortune: nose gone, half the jaw. Here, a German boy she could not understand though he spoke to her earnestly as he faded. She'd put her pencil down to hold his hand. Only his last word did she understand: *Mutter.* Here, a French boy who had flirted with her even as he died, a fingerprint of blood smudging the edge of that page. The stink of gangrene, Lysol and all the worst that the human body can produce seemed to rise from between the grimy pages. Filthy thing. Really *should* be burned.

The last few pages she could not bear to open. Not yet. And now her mind strayed to Mr Fortune, *Sergeant,* as he'd made rather pathetically plain. But he was only Mr now. Fortune – rather an unfortunate name in the circumstances. How *familiar* he'd seemed, like Powell,

yes. Her fingers itched to turn the pages, but no. Perhaps the familiarity might mean something more than a chance likeness? Perhaps
Fortune had been amongst the hundreds, thousands perhaps, of boys
and men – and occasional females – she'd helped to treat. With such
wounds he would have been deemed a bad case; he might well have
passed through the Clearing Station, the wound swiftly cleaned and
dressed before he was sent down the line. Perhaps her own hasty, in-
expert care had resulted in the untidy scar on his neck, and who knows
what under the prosthesis? Or perhaps she'd never seen him at all.

As Mrs Hale entered, Clem hid the sketchbook under some
embroidery patterns on her knee, pretended to be scrutinising one.
Mrs Hale looked at it curiously and then meaningfully towards
Clem's abdomen; it was a layette for a newborn. Of course they
would all be wondering when the next would make its appearance.
She flicked to a tray set, examining the ridiculously intricate border.

'Another letter for you,' Mrs Hale said. 'Got mixed up with the
doctor's post. Are you quite all right, madam? Ready for your
coffee, I dare say?'

Clem took the envelope. Thin and cheap; the writing bold, slop-
ing and unfamiliar.

'And perhaps a biscuit?'

Clem nodded and smiled in a hard and possibly quite demented
way until Mrs Hale had taken her leave.

The Wild Man,
Gipswick Road

Dear Mrs Everett,

    It was nice of you to visit me on Sunday afternoon after the
accident and very nice to make your acquaintance.

You might remember that you offered to cover the expense of repairing my motorcycle. In case you are still of this mind, I enclose the bill for repairs. You can send it to me c/o above address.

It occurred to me only after you'd gone that I failed to enquire about your health. I hope you weren't too upset by the experience. I apologise for my bad manners. I was not at my best.

Thank you again for visiting me, and your kind offer to pay for repairs.

Yours truly,

Mr V. S. Fortune (Esquire)

She read the letter thrice. Esquire indeed! The Wild Man, Gipswick Road. The landlord perhaps? But 'care of'? Perhaps he was merely passing through? The bill came to £8 10s 6d. Of course she'd pay. Though it would mean asking Dennis, who was sure to be disagreeable, he could hardly deny her. During her indisposition, he'd paid the housekeeping directly to Mrs Hale and that arrangement had not yet been changed. If she needed a dress or hat, naturally she had only to ask. But it would be useful to have a fund of her own to use in whichever way she chose. Her father, who, with his new American wife, had moved to California before the war, might help if she reminded him of her existence . . . There was a trust fund, her mother's money, due to her at twenty-five but that was more than two years away.

Mrs Hale returned with the coffee and a plate of fresh ginger snaps. Clem sugared her tea and, since no one was looking, dipped the biscuit, sucking the sweet, melting crumbs into her mouth. She re-read the letter before folding and hiding it in the base of her sewing box.

*

Chewing the woody end of a pencil, she studied the lemons in their green lustre bowl. How to capture the skin, with its slight sheen and porousness? When to ask Dennis? Over dinner perhaps? The end of the lemons, little snouts, the gleam of the bowl, shadows and reflections and borrowed light. Ask him breezily: oh, darling, by the way . . . Perhaps she should slice one and attempt those wet, packed-in filaments of juice?

Dinah was in the hall, chattering to Edgar – there was his giggle. Perhaps she was tickling him. *One step, two steps, tickly under there.* Why not get up and wave them off on their walk? Why not accompany them? She listened to Dinah's heels, the creak of the pram, the sounds of the door till it was too late. But later she'd play with Edgar – *Round and round the garden,* yes. And she'd sketch him as he played and as he slept.

The telephone rang and was answered. From the surgery below voices carried – Dennis had a particularly loud jocular tone with which he greeted his patients, settling into the low grumble of the consultation. And there came the ding of the bell summoning the next patient, sometimes a cough or a baby's cry, and the intermittent banging of the door. Stop listening and concentrate on the lemons. The carriage clock began its tinkle, followed by the slow *doi-ing* of the grandfather clock in the hall.

Mrs Hale came in. 'There's a person on the telephone for you, madam.'

'For me?' Clem stood. She rarely used the telephone; it seemed the official property of 'the Doctor' and Mrs Hale, as his agent and gatekeeper.

She grasped the receiver from its tall stand.

'Clementine?' Through a crackle came a gruff female voice.

'Gwen!' In the hallstand mirror, Clem witnessed her own surprise. 'It's been so long.'

'Well, whose fault is that?'

Clem closed her eyes against herself. It was true. There had been more than one letter in Gwen's huge bold hand since the war but they'd gone unanswered. Perhaps she'd even flung them on the fire – but that was back in the vague time when she was ill and not responsible. The letters had seemed too dangerous a connection with all she'd been through in France. And hadn't she also feared Gwen's scorn that, after everything, she'd fled straight back to Dennis?

'Thought we might call on you tomorrow,' Gwen was saying. 'Will you be at home?'

Clem opened her eyes, smiled at the mirror. 'Of course! You must come to tea.'

'Rightio.'

'Who's we?'

'Avis, friend, and Captain, dog, but he needn't come in.'

'Of course he can come in! We usually have tea at four, but come whenever you like.'

'Toodle-oo then,' Gwen said, and her voice cut off.

'Hello, caller?' said the operator after a stretch of crackle.

'Thank you. That will be all.' Clem replaced the receiver, intrigued by the thought of seeing Gwen again, though a shadow dragged itself after the pleasure because of the last time she'd seen Gwen and because she couldn't recall what had been said, how they'd left each other. And if Gwen were to mention Powell in front of Dennis? Surely she'd have the tact, the decency, not to do so? One never did quite know what Gwen might do or say.

She returned to her drawing to find her composition disturbed, one of the lemons gone. She slapped shut her drawing pad and stood by the piano, pressing and pressing Middle C. The leaves of the aspidistra, which lived upon it, shivered.

Mrs Hale came in. 'Everything all right, madam,' she said. 'Not bad news?'

'Did you take a lemon?'

'Oh!' Mrs Hale's hand flew to her mouth. 'For the Dover sole,' she said. 'You know how the doctor likes his fish of a Friday.'

'Please don't interfere with my still lifes in future.'

'Oh, I do apologise, madam,' said Mrs Hale. Her forehead crimped but she didn't quite lose her smile. 'I hadn't realised it was a *still life*.' Her emphasis was surely teetering on the edge of mockery. 'I'll fetch it back, shall I?'

'It's no good. Once something's moved, it's ruined. I can't go back to it. Do you see?'

'Won't happen again, madam, I assure you.'

'Well then, tomorrow a friend will be joining us for tea,' Clem said. 'Two friends in fact and possibly a dog.' It was so rare for Clem to be offering such a direct instruction that the two of them had to pause to adjust.

'Of course,' said Mrs Hale. 'Will you be wanting anything particular?'

'Anchovy toast,' said Clem, remembering Gwen's preference for savoury over sweet.

'And how about a nice seed cake?'

'Do you know, Mrs Hale?' Clem struck B-flat and let it ring before she spoke. 'I'm really not all that partial to seed cake. Perhaps something else for a change?'

Mrs Hale's expression suggested she was sucking the absent lemon.

'Now, that will be all.'

Once the door had clicked shut behind the housekeeper, Clem hugged herself and snorted. It was time she asserted herself, and it was satisfying to do so. Hard sometimes to grasp that *she* was the lady of the house. A lady with visitors coming. *Flowers*. Tulips. Oh, Gwen. She knitted her fingers together. Gwen *would* have the tact, wouldn't she? Why not speak to her first, telephone perhaps? But Mrs Hale might hear. A letter, then, or telegram – but wouldn't that be most fearfully crass?

Too fidgety now for drawing, she was filled with sudden resolve. Hale must drive her into town where she'd walk about the shops, stretch her legs, select the most perfect tulips for tomorrow.

12

T HE FOLLOWING AFTERNOON, she changed into a straight, slim dress, pale silk stockings, left off her stays. Her hair she unbraided and brushed, bored with the sheer burden of the heavy stuff. It made her arms ache. Perhaps she would have it cut, despite the ructions Dennis created whenever she broached the notion. Make it a *fait accompli* rather than discuss. For now, she rebraided and wound it round her head, a thick crown.

At three, she tapped on the nursery door. Dinah opened it, finger to her lips. 'His nibs has just dropped off,' she said. 'He's a proper grumpy-grogs today so I thought it best. Come and see, madam. Isn't he a picture?'

Together they gazed into the cot at the sleeping child who lay sprawled on his back, rosy and gleaming, palms open like padded satin shells. Clem looked sideways at Dinah's adoring face. She loves him, she thought, and it was a little shock to remember that other people's feelings were going on around her all the time.

'He does look a picture,' she agreed. 'Bring him down as soon as he wakes, won't you?'

She gazed round the nursery, where she felt rather like an intruder. But it's *my* house, she reminded herself, he's *my* child. Wooden blocks were scattered on the floor alongside painted animals from the new Noah's Ark, beached on the hearthrug. On the dresser waited a pile of small, ironed clothes. A tidy fire burned behind a fortress of a fireguard. Dinah's knitting, a scarf, lay on the floor.

'Is it safe? The needles?' Clem asked.

'I only get that out when he's asleep.' Dinah sounded dented.

'Of course.' Clem put her hand on Dinah's sleeve. 'You do so well with him. Where would we be without you?' She indicated the knitting – clearly a man's scarf in the making, thick brown wool. 'Who's it for?

'Dad,' said Dinah. 'His birthday's coming up.'

'How kind,' Clem said.

When Dinah smiled her plain face shone. Or was it really plain? She was a sallow, foxy little thing, but her eyes were unexpectedly blue and there was a deep dimple in one cheek. Clem remembered her mentioning going out to meet a chap last Sunday.

'I never asked you how you got on with . . . I'm afraid I can't recall his name?'

Dinah wrinkled her nose. 'Not my cup of tea as it turned out.'

Clem went downstairs to wait for Gwen. Far too restless to sketch or read, she opened the piano stool, unearthed some dog-eared Chopin studies, and had a go. Years since she'd tried to play, she kept her foot on the soft pedal. She played so stumblingly it must have maddened any musical patient downstairs. In the glossy wood of the piano lid hung the ghost of her face, framed by its ridge of plaited hair.

I love Edgar too, she thought, and felt it like a stab.

Her eyes went to her sewing box, at the bottom of which were concealed the letter and the bill. She simply must present the bill to Dennis once Gwen's visit was over. *You've been corresponding with the blighter!* Oh yes, he'd be sure to make a fuss but he would pay.

Oh, soon Gwen would be here, and how queer to see her. Last time . . . Clem paced around the room, a dampness growing under her arms, a little staleness. Her suspenders felt twisted. She would go upstairs for some Eau de Cologne, refresh, untwist and redo her hair perhaps out of this stupid tight plait. Perhaps a different frock?

The doorbell rang and she jumped up, heart pounding. The palms of her hands were wet. She held her breath – but there came Mrs Hale's voice, pitched to address a tradesman.

Oh, please, let Dennis be called out. Lately he'd been busy, a plethora of spring colds and fevers lodging in a plethora of chests. Let there be an emergency. *Please*. She didn't want him there, didn't really wanting him meeting Gwen at all. She'd told him only that an old friend was coming to tea . . . Oh, let there be a heart attack, a car crash, a sudden birth.

From the stairs Edgar's voice came loud and clear. 'Babababaa!' he cried. Clem jumped up, met Dinah in the hall. 'Thank you,' she said, taking the child from her arms, sensing a reluctance in his body to be transferred. 'You've made him look smart.'

Dinah flushed. 'I do my best.'

'You do beautifully,' Clem said.

She carried Edgar, in his white knitted suit, into the sitting room, where the afternoon sunshine flowed through the window onto the vase of pink tulips, primly pursed when she'd bought them, beginning to yawn open in the heat. She bent her face to breathe their hothouse smell. This was the first time since she'd been in the house that she'd had a visitor of her own. Edgar made a grab for a bloom.

She put him down and he tottered to the toys on the hearthrug, reached for the kaleidoscope – an old one of Dennis and Harri's. He was far too young to understand how to look into it, of course, but he liked to shake it and listen to the silky sifting of the particles.

Dennis came in looking expectant, moustache freshly waxed. 'Oh,' he said, 'not here yet?'

'Rather obviously.' Clem's voice grated with disappointment. One would feel a proper booby if they didn't turn up – but wouldn't that be just like Gwen? There would be a telephone call or note later, an excuse without apology.

'Shall I bring in the tea?' Mrs Hale asked from the doorway.

'Must we wait?' Dennis adopted his little boy face and rubbed his stomach. 'I'm famished.'

'Yes, we must,' Clem said firmly.

Dennis bent down to scoop up Edgar, to throw him into the air and make him shriek.

Mrs Hale left the room and Dennis flopped down on his chair with Edgar, who stood on his lap and tugged his moustache. 'Ouch! Steady on!' The doorbell drilled out its sound and Dennis rose to his feet, Edgar on his hip. 'Here we are at last,' he said.

Clem smoothed her skirt and took a deep breath. Ridiculous to be so nervous! Her eyes darted round the room, cosy with the fire, the tulips, the rug scattered in a homely way with toys. Voices in the hall – oh yes, the rough timbre of Gwen. The door opened, and in she strode dressed in a costume of thick green tweed as if she was off shooting, shoes stout, stockings thick cocoa-coloured lisle, hair cropped short as a man's.

A massive dog, a deerhound perhaps, loped in and stood beside Gwen, head as high as her waist. Edgar shrieked with excitement and craned towards it.

'Doggy,' Clem said, eyeing the huge creature warily. 'Is he good with children?'

'Haven't the faintest,' said Gwen. 'Hello, there.'

Clem approached and kissed her cheek. 'Feels like an age,' she said.

'Because it *is*.'

'Pleased to meet you.' Dennis shifted Edgar onto his other hip and stepped towards her, extending his hand.

'Likewise.' She shook it, looking speculatively between him and the child. 'Spitting images, aren't they?' she remarked to Clem. Edgar hid his face in Dennis's shoulder.

'Avis?' Clem asked.

'Washing her hands,' Gwen said and mimed someone primping her hair.

Clem was aware that Dennis was trying to give her a meaningful look, but she would not play.

'Hello.' Avis entered, extending a long white hand. She was younger than Gwen, with red hair cut into a bob; a sharp red fish hook curled on one cheek like a streak of blood. She was tall, as tall as Dennis, strongly perfumed, with harsh vermilion lips.

'Charmed,' Dennis said, taking the extended fingers. Edgar shrank against him.

'Do come in and sit down. How lovely to meet you,' Clem said. Stiff and false, acting the hostess in front of Dennis, sensing his amusement. 'Lovely day, isn't it?'

Avis sank elegantly onto the pale sofa. Gwen was standing with her back to the fireplace. The dog sighed and stretched out before the hearth as if terminally bored. Dennis sat down with Edgar, who wriggled and yearned towards the creature.

'At bally last!' Dennis released Edgar as Mrs Hale arrived with the tea trolley, followed by a blushing Linda with the hot water. Clem poured the tea and offered anchovy toast; Mrs Hale had taken notice of her request, it seemed – the cake was not seed but coconut. The talk turned to the weather, the countryside, the touring plans of Gwen and Avis, and was abruptly broken by a snarl and snap, and then a huge gape of silence from Edgar who, too shocked to scream, had gone rigid, his mouth a huge O. Clem jumped up and snatched him away from the dog.

'Oh Lord,' said Gwen mildly. 'Bad boy, Captain.'

Edgar was turning blue with his stuck scream, but there was no blood, no puncture, Dennis ascertained, just a little pink indentation from the teeth on the back of his hand. The scream emerged at last, and Mrs Hale was there like a genie, reaching out her arms to spirit the boy away.

Once his cries had trailed off up the stairs, they settled back to their tea, trying to catch the threads of the almost successful conversation – all but Avis, who found it unnecessary to participate much bar the odd flick of her foot. Gwen sat beside Avis on the sofa now, tweed knees beside silky blue ones.

'Do you work, Gwen?' Dennis asked, munching a piece of toast.

Captain rose and padded over to sink his great head on Gwen's lap.

'I've got a place in an old folks' home,' she said. 'Never was a qualified nurse. All that experience counts for nothing, it seems. Auxiliary,' she added.

'All what experience?' asked Dennis, looking towards the cake. Clem jumped up to cut it and to hide her face.

Gwen drew her head back in surprise. 'Didn't Clem say? She didn't say? Really, Clem! Red Cross. We were at the Front together.'

Dennis received his piece of cake, face expressionless. 'Ah, *that* Gwen,' he said.

'And Avis is a stenographer,' Gwen said.

'I can speak for myself, darling. Really!' Avis raised her well-shaped eyebrows at no one in particular. Her face was viciously beautiful, though lined – she was older than she had at first appeared. Her perfume, mixed now with the smell of dog, rather ruined one's appetite.

'I'm gasping, if I may?' she said, waving an absurdly long holder.

'Of course.' There was a relieved flurry of offering and lighting of Players.

Clem took one to steady herself.

'Well, in any case' – Gwen gave a Clem a curious look and puffed out a smoky breath – 'she came up trumps out there. Not such a delicate flower as she looks.'

'Whilst Dennis worked wonders at Middlesham Hall,' said Clem. 'He supervised the conversion to a hospital and worked himself to the bone there, as well as almost single-handedly keeping the surgery going here.'

Gwen said nothing, her silence eloquent.

'Oh, let it go, Gwendolyn,' Avis drawled, tipping back her head to allow a plume of smoke to unfurl from between her scarlet lips. 'Anyone who didn't sign up's still a shirker in her eyes,' she explained unnecessarily.

'Dennis wasn't a shirker,' Clem said hotly. 'We still needed doctors at home.'

'Of course,' said Gwen. 'Avis does talk tommyrot. She likes to stir – don't you, darling?' She revolved a finger in the air.

Avis smiled lazily and waggled one foot in its pointed white brogue. Her ankle bone looked sharp enough for murder.

Dennis stood suddenly and Captain turned his head, curled back his lip and snarled.

'Captain,' Gwen said fondly. 'Down. He means no harm.'

The dog loped back to the hearthrug, circled several times and collapsed, sighing, in a heap.

'Well,' said Dennis, 'if you'll excuse me. Jolly as this has been' – he shot a look at Clem – 'I've patients waiting.'

'*Enchanté*,' said Avis as he closed the door.

'Really!' Gwen glared at her.

Avis tilted back her chin, lips twitching with amusement.

'He did his bit,' Clem said.

'No one denies it,' said Avis.

Clem got up to poke the fire, edging round Captain who moved not a muscle except for his eyes.

'Would you have married the Canadian?' said Gwen. 'Or were you planning all the time to return to *this*?'

Clem steadied herself on the mantelpiece, staring at the crazed old face of the clock between its pair of rearing bronze stallions.

'You're very well set up here, I must say,' added Gwen. 'Wouldn't blame you in the least.'

Clem turned. 'Cake?' she offered, and when they declined, cut an entirely unwanted slice for herself.

Captain gazed meaningfully at the trolley.

'Have we finished with the savoury?' Gwen said, reaching for the plate. She began posting the anchovy toasts one by one into the dog's jaws. 'He likes a little something when we have our tea.'

'Isn't the weather simply heavenly?' said Clem and saw Avis raise her eyebrows.

'Divine,' she said.

The mantel clock chimed its tuneless quarter and from the hall came the dreary echo of the grandfather.

'Do you think much about it?' asked Gwen, making Clem flinch.

'Oh, yawn,' said Avis.

'Stuff your ears with cake, darling,' Gwen said, 'or go and do a piddle.'

Avis sniffed and lit herself another cigarette.

Clem sat with a morsel of cake in her mouth, feeling her tongue shrivel and dry. This was what she'd dreaded: dredging, Dennis called it. *Don't go dredging up the past.* But still . . . there was a flicker of temptation, like that of poking a stick into an ants' nest.

A crackle from the grate.

'Naturally,' she said, 'from time to time, although I try not to . . . It doesn't do one any good, does it?'

Gwen kept her pond-coloured eyes on Clem's face as she continued, thrusting the sharp point of the stick right into her centre. 'Do you think about Iris?' she said.

Clem received the jab, keeping her expression pleasant though the effort was tremendous. 'Of course.' Stretching her lips into a smile, she injected lightness into her voice. 'But we must let bygones be bygones.'

Gwen stretched out her legs and folded her arms. 'If only that were possible,' she said.

'Oh, don't be such an old bore,' Avis said. 'In any case' – she made a show of consulting her wristwatch though the clock had plainly chimed out the time – 'aren't we meeting those people for drinks?'

Those people. It sounded like a code. It sounded like, 'Darling, this is too ghastly for words – rescue me.'

'And I must go up and see to Edgar,' Clem said. 'I hope he won't be scared of dogs for life!'

Gwen stood, Captain by her side, and Avis unfolded herself from the sofa. They managed a few awkward pleasantries before Clem was able to usher them into the hall.

'Delighted to meet you,' Avis said, holding out her hand, clad now in milky chamois. Rather to Clem's surprise, Gwen caught her in a hug, rough with tweed and smoke. 'Glad you've found peace,' she muttered into her ear, 'and that you've had a child after . . .'

Clem pulled away and they looked into each other's eyes.

Once they'd gone Clem curled up on the sofa, knees to her chest. Against the door in her mind came a battering, and from beneath it, onto cracked white tiles, seeped watery blood. Deep in her belly dragged the cramping pain of loss; she pressed her fist there and groaned.

But here came Linda, blushing through her freckles, to clear away the things and she must sit up, pull herself together, hold herself together, seal the doors.

13

THE WATER, SILKILY scummed with soap and Epsom salts, sloshed as she settled back in the bath and regarded her body: belly hollow but crumpled, scored with silver – not from the first, from Edgar. Calm now, yes. After a glass of Wincarnis in warm milk to settle her nerves she'd slept, waking befuddled for a lone dinner. Dennis was dining at the golf club, angry no doubt, and she could hardly blame him. The impertinence and revolting beauty of Avis, Gwen's increased mannishness – there had even been a few whiskers on her chin. Surely she could at least employ some tweezers!

Lord knows what Dennis thought, but she would find out soon enough. And, of course, there would be the inevitable topic of her 'running off to war'. How that made it sound like a fanciful spree, like running off to join the circus. Well, she'd simply have to put up with it. Tonight she was resolved to broach the question of the money, which she'd deliver personally to Mr Fortune. Surely that must be better, safer, than the post?

Distantly she heard the door as Dennis came in, his footsteps on the stairs. She lay until her fingers and toes were white prunes and the water so cool she was goose-pimpled and shivery. Slowly, she dried and powdered her body, put on her most forbidding night-dress, a stronghold of complicated ties and buttons.

As soon as she entered the bedroom, Dennis – already in his pyjamas, hair brushed back, that sickly Bay Rum smell that made her heart sink with the opposite of anticipation – said, 'You *do* know what they are, I suppose?'

Clem regarded him wearily. 'What what are?'

'Your *friends*.'

'Of course.' Sitting at the dressing table, she began to brush her dampened hair.

'And you didn't think to warn me?'

She put down the brush. '*Warn you?*'

'By God, Clem!' In the mirror she watched his hands fly out in a pantomime of bewilderment.

Detached, she watched amusement twist her own reflection. How Harri would snigger if she were here.

'A man likes to be prepared for what he's about to face in his own sitting room.'

'Heavens, Dennis!'

'Speaking to one like that, in one's own home!' he said. 'I ask you!'

'Yes,' she turned and met his eye. 'That was unfair and unfortunate. I'm sorry.'

'And you might have said that it was *that* Gwen you'd invited, the one who dragged you off—'

'She rather invited herself. And no one "dragged me off" anywhere.'

'I dare say she put the idea into your head.'

'It was *my* idea. And you know why.'

She picked up her brush again, hair damp and snarled, fingers trembling. Oh, how fed up with it she was; thousands of filaments of history growing from her scalp. How old was it? Had it been at the Front? Had Powell washed and brushed, had he touched, any of these same strands? She grasped a hank in her hand, tugged till it hurt.

'How long does a single hair last?' she said.

'Beg pardon?'

'From emerging from its follicle to dropping naturally.'

'That will depend on countless factors. You *did* go against my express will, Clementine, and just after we were engaged too.'

'You ask *me* not to go dredging—'

'And then you bring those inverted creatures into our home to mock me!'

She pressed her lips together, felt the breath rise and fall in her diaphragm. Abruptly he removed the brush from her hand and she flinched, but, 'Here let me,' was all he said. Standing behind her, he untangled the snarls with his deft, doctorly fingers and brushed smoothly. *No, no, no.* Her mind flailed against memory – oh, the battering, the battering against the door. *Stay here, stay here, stay here now.* In the glass she could not see his face, only his pyjama'd middle. Navy blue paisley, a neatly knotted white cord.

Suddenly he guffawed. 'But I mean, honestly, darling! Lesbians for tea!'

She took the brush back from him and began plaiting her hair. She caught his eye in the mirror and smiled. 'By the way, I could do with a little money. I—'

'Got your eye on a hat?'

She opened her mouth to tell him about the bill – and closed it again. Simpler this way.

At the foot of the stairs, the grandfather began wheezily working itself up to strike midnight.

'Just bits and bobs,' she said. 'Little treats for Eddie and the twins and so on.' She finished her plait and threw the long tail over her shoulder, patted Ponds cold cream over her cheeks and chin, smoothed it into her neck.

'Of course, old thing,' Dennis said. He was sitting on the bed now and had commenced clipping his toenails. Snip, snip, snip as the clippers went through the thin horn that would scatter on the carpet, no doubt. 'You shall have your bits and bobs,' he said, 'but no need to go spending it on the twins. Harri has a reasonable settlement from Daddy – and the less we give her, the more she might consider her position.'

He got up to put the scissors on the dressing table, and as Clem stood, he caught her to him, spoke into her hair. 'Listen, darling.' His voice was husky with sudden emotion. 'I realise I don't know the worst of it. I've never asked you about your war – not good for you to remember, eh? Best foot forward and all that. That's the spirit, yes?' He held her away from him by the tops of her arms. 'Eh?'

'Of course,' she murmured. 'Thank you.'

Oh, she did feel fond of him for his generosity, his clumsy attempt to communicate, even if it was only to open the door a chink, then slam it shut and lock it. He was right to lock it.

They climbed into bed, and she reached for her book, *The Old Wife's Tale*, found her page, but: 'So, what do you suppose they do?' he said.

She blinked at him.

'Your Sapphic friends?'

'Haven't the slightest inkling,' she said.

He took away her book and slapped it shut, then pushed back the bedclothes and stretched himself out beside her.

'It's cold,' she said, pulling back the covers.

'Do you suppose they rub themselves together down there?' His hand went to her groin.

'Dennis!' She pushed him off. 'Really!'

'And bring themselves off like that?'

'I'm not listening to this.' She put her hands over her ears, noticing an alarming tenting in his pyjamas. Of course the question had crossed her own mind, but for a man to think of it was sleazy, prurient even? Either way she was in for it, she could see.

'Disgusting . . . unnatural,' he breathed, reaching for her, 'and four breasts squashed together, imagine that!'

'Fetch a thing then.' She sighed. Better to get it over with than to object. But this time with those thoughts, *his* thoughts in her head now, prurient, yes, and unworthy, and a confusion of other faces in her mind, an ease came to her, a naturalness she'd never felt before with Dennis, and with her eyes tight shut against him, an onrush of intensity, of achy wantonness, that caused him to draw back when it was over and regard her. 'Oh, Clementine,' he said hoarsely, cupping her sex and squeezing. 'My own, my darling little harlot.'

14

V INCE WATCHES DOLL shoo out the last few drinkers; a devil of a job to shift them today – madness in the air, spring madness brought on by the heat.

'Thank heavens above.' At last she's able to slam the door, draw the bolt across with a satisfying clunk. She turns and gives an extravagant yawn, stretching her arms so that her bosoms lift. 'Rightio then,' she says, surveying the bar.

'Stop a minute, Dolly, put your trotters up,' says Vince.

She stands with her hands on her hips, gazing at him with her big, heavy-lidded eyes, and it could tip either way; he can see she's got things on her mind, but then she puffs and shrugs. 'Just a tick then.' Plumping down on one of the leather seats, she eases off her shoes.

He shifts a stool so she can put her feet up, pours them both a gin and lime, then sits down, taking a foot in its thick, darned stocking into his lap. Breathing in the smell of sweaty rayon, he squeezes and kneads the sole, pulls the toes, until she groans with pleasure. Her skirt is caught up in her lap, and surely, even with her eyes shut, she must know he can see up to where her stockings end, the tops of solid white thighs and the rubbery pink suspender nubbins.

Encouraged, he lifts the other foot, circles his thumbs in the arches, parting the legs a little for a better look. Been a while since he's been in her bed, she's so busy and taken up with Kenny, who always comes first, such a soft touch she is, but does he complain? No, he knows which side his bread is buttered. A cosy gaff, this. He can see himself as landlord on a sunny afternoon like this, shooing out the last few customers with a 'Haven't you got homes to go to?', and then settling down with Doll in the bar for a quiet drink and a foot rub – oh, how she loves it – before a bit of afternoon delight. She'll be Mrs Fortune by then and he'll be prouder than any punch to have this big soft creature for his own, the warmth, the comfort of her, the luxury. More he thinks about it, the more sheer bloody common sense it makes.

Funny he's never thought of it before, being a landlord; just his line after all, with his interest in drink – and it puts a roof over your head, a congenial roof too. You're never lacking for a bit of company. You have to have a line of banter, but he's got that from selling brooms and linctus and kiddies' books and, lastly, mustard door to door. Used to get a bonus every Christmas for exceptional sales – ice to Eskimos they said. The way he could flog that mustard! But that memory is like the sting of it in a wound. No, not that, not now.

'Got to pay a visit,' Doll says, removing her feet, hauling herself up and smoothing down her skirt. He lights up a cheroot, leans back on his chair, stretches out his legs. Mostyn's Mustard. Every time he sees a van it riles him up good and proper. That livid yellow. *Pep up Your Ham, Chops and Sausages with Mostyn's Mustards.* He'd been in on that. There was a long wrangle about the final 's' as Mostyn's did different strengths, mild to blazing hot. He convinced them of the 's', proving the influence he had. It's a chief selling point, he'd said at a sales meeting, speaking up for the first time. 'See, when people think mustard they think hot. I tell them our mildest is suitable for the most delicate palate.' He had his spiel off pat: 'Mild enough for a suckling babe. But if you want your socks blown off, you go for the top of the range, see? Not just one taste but a whole spectrum.' Oh, he was persuasive to housewives, and branching into restaurants too, that was his speciality. He'd had Lyons Tea Rooms in his sights. Before the war he was Mostyn's Number One Salesman – not once but twice, beating all records.

Then came the war and off he went to do his bit – with Sir Mostyn's personal blessing and a promise that he'd be hired as soon as he was back in Blighty. And so, once he was out of hospital, once he'd got rid of the shakes and the stutter, got used to facing the world with his tin plate, he'd gone to get his old job back. Invited into the inner sanctum, Sir Mostyn's office, no less. He was shown in by a girl he'd never seen before, baby sweet with rolls of strawberry blonde hair, who, to give her credit, never batted an eyelid at his face, which was better than Sir Mostyn managed.

'Come in, Fortune. Sorry to have kept you waiting, old chap.'

There was that split second as he extended his hand, that flinch, and his eyes skidded off the mask quick sharp before he braced himself to look straight into Vince's face. 'Can't tell you what a pleasure it is to see you back safe and well . . . The lady wife must be . . .'

Vince allowed his hand to be wrung, and sat in the proffered chair. He'd only been in Sir Mostyn's office once or twice before, the last time when he set off for the Front. Framed photographs of Mostyn's Mustards, the fleet of vans, the sales force and the factory workers lined the walls. The carpet was thick, red-and-blue pattern, Turkish most like, and the desk gleamed, smelled of pipe smoke and beeswax. Money.

'Wife no more,' Vince said. A year since Ethel left him, good riddance. She'd never come to terms with his face and there was someone else; of course there was. The minute his back was turned, Irish navvy he'd heard. But she never said that. 'Differences' is what she came up with. 'We never really loved each other, did we, Vince?' And to her credit she was right. It'd been a hasty wedding, babes in the wood they were. On his side it'd been based on lust but he soon discovered he'd been sold a pup – the way she winced her way through the act. Oh, she usually let him, but made it clear it was a bother and a chore, something on a par with beating carpets. She never made a bloody sound except for *ouch* and *mind*. In the end he gave it up as a bad job. Travelling in mustard the length and breadth of Britain, he'd had his dalliances. He'd like to put a map on the wall, stick a pin in all the places he'd had his end away. That'd be a sight to behold!

Mostyn was expressing his sympathy. 'Wretched business, wreaked havoc on family life one way and another. Still, you don't have children, I believe?'

'Not that I know of.'

They chortled man to man, then there was a pause as Sir Mostyn picked up and perused Vince's letter, lips working.

'Sergeant, I see. Congratulations in order, Fortune'

Vince nodded, heart swelling at the praise. Yes, it had been his finest hour. He had risen through the ranks and proved himself, and they could never take that away from him. Never. He'd proved himself, *bettered* himself. And was about to reap the reward. They talked about the war, almost on an equal level, Vince thought, Sir Mostyn bringing up his own last service at Mafeking. And then he returned to the letter.

'I understand you're hoping to return to your old position?'

Vince nodded.

'But surely . . .' Mr Mostyn stuck out his bulbous underlip. 'Surely you can see, Fortune, that a salesman, face to face with the public, well . . .'

Vince counted to three. All right. Of course, he had half antici-
pated this; he wasn't stupid.

'As much for *your* sake as ours.'

'Number One Salesman twice,' Vince pointed out.

'True, true, true,' said Sir Mostyn. 'Look, old chap, can I offer
you a snifter?' Mostyn pushed himself up with the flats of his hands
and turned to pour two stingy measures of brandy.

Vince sipped his drink. 'I'll take any other suitable position
that's more out of the public eye,' he said, as rehearsed. 'Something
clerical, bookkeeping perhaps. I'm a dab hand with arithmetic.'
This was in fact preferable; it was where he'd been aiming, a quiet
regular job in the office. The other staff would soon get used to his
appearance. As an officer, he would be sure to rise; mustn't set his
hopes too high, not at first, but something managerial eventually.
After all, it's only what he deserved.

Sir Mostyn had consumed his drink in one swallow and was
now looking longingly at the pipe balanced on a cut-glass ashtray.
'Here we arrive at the problem,' he said. 'You see, there are no clerical vacancies at present.' His teeth and the ends of his drooping
grey moustache were stained yellow-brown. 'If there were something, old chap, I'd offer it to you like a shot, of course, goes without
saying – man like you, loyal to the firm, to King and Country.'

Vincent stared at the old man, his swimmy bloodshot eyes, swollen nose and drooping jowls. Ugly as sin, yet no one recoiled from
his face, because it was *all there*. Because he was a sir who'd sat on
his fat arse throughout the war making money while younger men,
better men, were blown to smithereens.

'So there's nothing?' said Vincent.

'Ah.' Mostyn smiled with a sort of relief. He picked up the pipe.
'Now, I didn't say that, did I? Good Lord, employee of mine back

from serving King and Country, never let it be said that I would turn such a man away.'

Vincent waited, but he knew before it was said what he was about to be offered. Mostyn knocked the dottle from his pipe before he continued: 'There are no vacancies, times being what they are, but,' he paused, expression munificent, 'I'm sure I can conjure something up, something in the works, in the packaging line.'

'In the factory,' said Vincent. Snowstorm particles rose and swam.

'The packing line, a good regular position.'

'Manual work?'

'A good position. I dare say we could up the wage a notch as befits.'

Vince blinked, felt the tug of the scar, the twitch of muscles in the empty socket. 'Number One Salesman, twice,' he repeated.

'Well aware, old chap.' Mostyn had begun to fill his pipe now, rolling a bolus of dark shag in his palm.

'Sergeant. Life on the line more than once.'

Mostyn tamped the tobacco into the pipe's bowl. 'But with so many chaps returned,' he said, 'there simply isn't anything else to offer you.' He picked up an onyx lighter and lit a spill.

That onyx lighter could split a man's skull.

Vincent rose and walked out of the office, slamming the door behind him. He heard it open again. 'Wait a moment, old chap,' Sir Mostyn called, and the strawberry baby girl came swimming through the snow and tried to take his arm. 'Mr Fortune?' she said, heels dotting along behind him. 'Mr Fortune?'

'Let him go, poor fellow,' came Sir Mostyn's voice, and then Vince was out in the street where a brilliant yellow Mostyn's Mustards van was parked. *Pep up Your Ham, Chops and Sausages with Mostyn's Mustards*. His 's'. His fucking 's'. The road was busy with cabs and motors, horses, and an omnibus in front of which he stepped.

He imagines the news, the headline: *Tragic Death of Shunned War Hero*. But the bus stopped in time, a horn blared after the fact and someone shouted, 'Blithering idiot.' And at any rate, no one would have known what had just transpired; Mostyn was hardly likely to own up.

Vince felt calm on the surface but there was a roiling within him, like something happening in the earth, something geological. His head had begun to ache and more thickly the flakes tumbled across his vision. The specs were digging into the tops of his ears – twin, thin, insistent cuts. Lucky to have both ears to attach them to, that's what they said. Thought he looked rather good in the specs, would've befitted a clerical position.

He floated amidst the turmoil, found his way to a pub and drank till his money was gone. Another man might have gone under then, turned up begging, pathetic – plenty of them on the streets, tooting tin whistles, stretching out their palms – but not Vince. He had a bit of compensation coming to him, along with the money left by Mum when she went, and with it he bought himself some smart gear and the Norton. It's all in how you present your-self; he knew this from sales. You persuade people you're someone and they'll treat you as such. And he is someone. His exploits in the war – bloody heroics, you can't say less.

And in this state of mind he'd stopped off at the Wild Man for a snifter and first clapped eyes on Doll.

15

'WHAT WE WANT'S a good spring clean in here,' Doll says, bustling back into the bar. 'Take a mop to the floor this afternoon, could you? Give it a proper going over.'

'I'll give you a proper going over,' he says, but she frowns. He's overstepped the mark.

'Come and finish your drink, Dolly,' he says.

He feels a bit bleary, truth be told. He's been supping all lunch-time, helping himself to a nip here and there, perk of the job – not that it is a job exactly. She lets him have the loft and in return he helps out behind the bar at busy times and does the man's work, shifts the kegs and so on.

He resolves there and then to take the bull by the horns, pop the question. She's been sweet lately, all the little niceties you can't take for granted: smiles, touches on the arm, little signs that haven't been wasted on Vince, oh no. And giving him an eyeful up her skirt just then! Though she's not let him in her bed again. Playing hard to get, that's all that'll be, saving herself . . . maybe marriage has crossed *her* mind as well. She won't want him to think her loose.

He lights her a ciggie, a cheroot for himself, and takes his time over it. No need to go at it like a bull in a china shop, the very bull he's about to take by its horns. That makes him smile, so they chat for a bit about the weather, about the lunchtime trade today, laughing at something Amos said. He watches how she wriggles the tip of her tongue on her lip between puffs, an erotic little habit she doesn't even know she has.

'Well,' she says at last, stretching her arms back. The stitching's split under one of her sleeves and he can see a wisp of hair. 'Reckon I'd better get on. If you'll do the floor and the grate, I've vowed to get them skirtings over with this afternoon.'

And it is the moment. Sunshine on the optics turns the brown drinks gold, the clear ones sparkle, the smoke in the air seems cosy, almost solid. He balances his cheroot on an ashtray and reaches for her hand.

'Doll,' he says.

'Now then!' She laughs. 'You're looking serious.'

'I *am* serious,' he says. 'Doll, why don't we make this a permanent arrangement?'

'What?' She looks genuinely dumbstruck.

'You and me, dear. Doll, Dorothy, I'm asking you to marry me.'

Her eyes flick to the clock behind the bar.

'What do you say?'

'Enough of your nonsense!'

'You and me, we could make a go of it. Share the work. I'd be a father to Kenny – a boy needs a man about the place. You could have an afternoon off once in a while. Put your feet up while I take the strain.'

'Get on with you,' she says. 'And don't you go telling me that's not the drink talking because I know what drink talking sounds like and it sounds exactly like that.'

'You think about it,' he says.

She stands up, puts their glasses on the bar though they're not empty, and begins to collect the ashtrays. 'Filthy beasts,' she remarks, as ashy beer slops onto the floor.

'We could build up trade. Slap-up lunches for the travelling salesman – that was my line, remember; I've got the experience. Holidays by the sea. I could teach Kenny to swim.'

She snorts, tipping an ashtray over the bin.

'You were talking about decorating. We could close up for a day or two mid-week. Give it a lick of paint. Jazz the place right up.' He likes that expression and gets the impression that she does too, senses a prickle of interest. 'Get it jazzed up, keep up with the times.'

Having emptied and wiped all the ashtrays, she sits down again suddenly. 'Look, Vince,' she begins, but he stops her. He uses the power he has with women (except Ethel), doesn't know what it is but he's always had it, still has, even with his tin eye. He leans over and kisses her smack on the lips and she only pulls away a bit, doesn't really stop him. Her lips are full and cushiony, luxury lips, and he knows from experience they're just a sample of her luxury body. If she were a liner she'd be a Cunard that's for definite.

'How about it, a coat of paint – something a bit lighter and brighter?' he says.

'Now *that's* not such a bad idea,' she says.

He tries to kiss her again, but she shifts her head.

'No, Vince.' She sighs, but there's a pliancy about her that he knows just what to do with, and he stands and pulls her to her feet.

She gazes up at him, a frown between her dark brows, a tender boozy look. 'You poor dear,' she says, stroking his cheek just where the mask fits. He flinches away from her hand, then takes it and presses it against his groin, showing he means business. She gives a little laugh. 'Fine figure of a man, I'll give you that.' Her voice against his chest is muffled. 'Just a quickie, then. Better prospect than the skirtings at any rate.'

She pours them a gin apiece and they go up to her room, and it's a dream as per usual. You couldn't find better if you scoured the land, if you were a million-bleedin'-aire.

She goes and spoils it afterwards, though: 'This can't happen again, Vince. You understand? Vince?' She keeps going on like that till he nods, but they both know she doesn't mean it.

And then she gets up and pulls on her housecoat, turfs him out of her room and goes down to do her blessed skirtings.

From the kitchen where he's filling in his pools coupon, he hears the door – second post – hears her chatting, then she calls, 'Letter for you.' He goes through. Her housecoat's stained, hair covered in a kerchief, and neither do her any favours. Hard to believe this is the same body that he had stretched out, practically molten, not an hour ago. Of course she needs more help. When they're married she won't have to skivvy like this, they'll get a little girl in.

She hands him the letter, damp from her sudsy hands. 'A billy-doo?' she asks, jealous, he hopes.

'You know there's no one else for me,' he says.

She shakes her head at him. 'Pull the other one.'

'What other one?' Her widens his eye at her.

'You mucky blighter!'

'Might be a lady though,' he teases, sniffing the creamy envelope.

'Well, good luck to you,' she says, and kneels down to her skirt-ings – not the desired response.

He goes back to the kitchen. The kettle's coming to the boil and he empties the pot ready, then slides one finger under the flap to open the envelope – nice thick paper, quality; there's money here.

Dear Mr Fortune,

Thank you for your letter.

There is absolutely no need, let me assure you, to apologise. No harm done and my health is perfectly fine.

Thank you for forwarding the bill for your repairs. I am of an uneasy mind about entrusting money to the post and would rather hand it to you in person if this would suit?

I wonder if I might buy you tea in Seckford one afternoon and thus hand you the money in person? There is a tea shop in the High Street – the Copper Kettle. I could meet you there on almost any afternoon at 3 o'clock.

I shall look forward to hearing from you with a suitable date.

Sincerely yours,

Mrs Everett (Clementine)

Bingo! Better if she'd just sent the cash, of course. But bingo all the same. Promise, the promise of cash, it bucks a man right up. He can pay Sid back for fixing the bike – she's good as new, more or less if you don't look too hard – and have enough left to . . . He'll do it! He'll only bloody go and do it. Imagine Doll's face when she sees the paint, the ladder, the brushes. Him in overalls, all tooled up for the job.

In the dim back parlour, where they never go, he rifles through the sideboard for paper, pen and ink; pencil won't do. He looks at the calendar. How about Saturday? They're busy on a Saturday but Doll'll have to excuse him. Other fish to fry, he'll say, give her something to think about. She puts on a pose of not caring what he does but it's just her way, he knows it. Two can play at that game. So passionate when she's on her back, that's when the truth comes out. Like tipping over a tortoise, he sniggers at the thought; tip her on her back and she's helpless, defenceless – she's his. This time next year they'll be man and wife. He fingers the paper, looks at the elegant way Mrs Married writes – an educated hand, expensive paper. Didn't bat an eyelid at the bill, chances are he could get a bit more out of her if he plays his cards right.

Doll comes through with her bucket, tips the dirty water down the sink. She smells of Sunlight soap and sweat. He doesn't look at her, not wanting to see her like that, not fair to see a woman at her worst. She'll do herself up before opening – dab of scent, hair tidied, rouge and powder – and she'll be back to her old self.

She refills the bucket, grates soap into it. 'You all right sitting there?' she says. 'That floor wasn't doing itself last time I looked.'

'No need for your cheek. I'll see to it pronto.'

Once she's gone he uncovers his letter and checks it through. It's all right, sets the proper tone. He'll meet her on Saturday. Three o'clock, Copper Kettle, cash in – and see what else he can tap her for.

16

ASSIGNATION, ASSIGNATION, ASSIGNATION – her foot-steps beat the syllables on the pavement. Thin blue shoes, sun hot on the crown of her blue felt hat. *Assignation*, a word with such associations . . . but this was nothing like that, nothing. This was an innocent meeting. After all, did one not owe the poor soul recompense for one's carelessness?

As far as Dennis was concerned she was still walking by the river with Harri. After lunch, on his way to the golf club, he'd driven her there. She'd hoped he'd simply drop her off, but he'd insisted, since the afternoon was so clement, on accompanying them – Harri, Clem, Mildred and the children – on the first leg of their river walk.

There had been a breeze down there and the tide was in, the deep sludge-coloured water sliding along the muddy banks, moored boats nudging and scraping in the current.

'Shouldn't you be buzzing off, darling?' Clem had been vibrating with frustration. 'You don't want to hold up the tee.'

'No rush.' He was maddeningly content to stroll, petting his nieces and wrangling with Harri. Mildred pushed the perambulator, Edgar waving and crowing, excited by the swooping gulls, and the girls pelting about in their muddy boots. It was fully a quarter of an hour before Dennis took out his pocket watch and declared it time to dash.

'He's in good form,' Harri said as they watched him stride away. 'What wonders have you been performing?'

Clem made some sort of half-witted remark and hid her face by stopping to adjust Edgar's sun bonnet. She waited as long as she could bear and then exclaimed, 'Oh gosh, Harri, I must dash too! I've arranged to meet a friend – just remembered.'

Oh, obvious, obvious tissue-thin lie.

'Who is she?' said Harri. Phyllis had ripped up a daffodil and was trying to reach her chin with it.

'D'you like butter?'

'That's buttercups not daffodils, silly. Oh, all right then. Do I?'

'Yes. Now Auntie Clem?' Phyllis waved the daffodil at Clem and she stooped to feel the soft bat of the petals.

'Auntie Clem don't like butter,' Phyllis declared.

'Oh yes, I jolly well do!'

'Oh heavens, the daffodil is wrong!' Harri laughed. 'We'll have to wait for buttercups, darling, and try again. So, who is it, Clem? Anyone I know?'

'Red Cross, we were overseas together.'

'Golly. Bring her back for tea? Oh, do!'

'Best not.' Clem turned to watch a barge scythe through the water, its wake surging against the bank. 'She's rather sensitive about children,' she added. 'Lost one when her husband bought it. The shock . . .' Clem's hand went to her own belly. *Why say that, why that?*

'I suppose we would rather rub her nose in it with this brood!'

'Mummy, come see the baby ducks.' Phyllis tugged her mother's hand.

'They're moorhens, darling.' Harri allowed herself to be pulled away. Mildred was holding the back of Claris's coat as she hurled crusts into the water and Edgar strained against his harness to see.

'What's her name?' Harri asked.

Clem watched the minute dusty creatures bobbing on the current, dipping and disappearing only to bob up elsewhere. 'Look, Harri,' she said, 'the idiotic thing is, I haven't mentioned it to Dennis.' She brought her eyes, flinchingly, to meet Harri's. 'You know how he hates me to "live in the past"? It's all best foot forward and so on.'

Harri's expression was dubious. 'So, I'm your alibi?'

'It's not like that!' Clem blurted an unconvincing laugh. 'Just, well, you know what a fusspot he is. He worries about me.' The mother moorhen swam away now, her flotilla of weightless chicks fanning out behind her. 'But I *am* better. Truly. And the more people trust that I am better, the better I will be. *Please.*' She turned and caught Harri's arm. 'He made enough of a song and dance last week about *Gwen* coming to tea.'

'Did Gwen come? I *adore* Gwen.'

'You hardly know her!'

'I'd like to.'

Clem was momentarily confused – Harri and Gwen existed in such separate compartments of her head.

'Look, ma'am,' called Mildred, 'a heron.' They all watched the great scruffy thing haul itself into the air and flap away across the river.

'And after all, it's *nothing*,' Clem said, sounding rather piteous even to her own ears. 'A cup of tea with a friend. For old times' sake. It's not worth the fuss. I know it seems queer. But, *please*, Harri?'

'Has this mysterious person got a name?'

'Aida.' The name slid unbidden from Clem's mouth.

'Ha! Quaint. Like the opera?'

And Clem had bolted.

Assignation, assignation, assignation . . . how hot her feet, her head; hands moist inside her gloves. No breeze here in the streets leading upwards into Seckford. *Oh, why say Aida?*

It's a proper scorcher all right. Vince roars along the lanes, verges all frothed up with hogweed, and putters down into town. Riding past a girl with a white parasol brings to mind a butterfly, dainty and crushable – like Mrs Married herself. She's a different breed from his Doll, who's all fat and blood and hair and heat – and that's what you want, something to get hold of, to bury yourself in, to feel at home with, but she can get on your wick all the same.

Wasn't easy to get out of a Saturday afternoon. 'You don't do much for your keep,' she said, 'you could at least stop in while I take Kenny to his party.' He'd had to bite his tongue at that; but after all she wasn't to know what he had up his sleeve. Wait till she clocks him up that ladder, paintbrush in hand!

She's been nagging on about work, halfway to a wife already! 'Get yourself down that Labour Exchange, then you can start paying rent.' The cheek of it! All the graft he does for her, behind the bar of an evening, changing the kegs. He gave Kenny his tea last night, boiled him an egg, even did him some bloody conjuring tricks – vanishing penny, floating handkerchief, what have you.

And to get back on the right side of her this afternoon, he's got himself lumbered with fetching Kenny from his party though it means he'll be pushed for time.

There's sudden quiet when the motor stops, then a bird cheeping. Takes off his helmet and goggles – with them on, his face looks normal, you'd never tell. He pats the warm and shiny Norton, beautiful girl she is, good as gold, good as new. Straddling her, feeling that engine rev between his legs, feeling the speed of the world rush by, is when he feels like a proper man again, when he feels complete.

He puts on his hat and pulls down the brim. No one about so he can adjust the arms of his specs, get his face straight. Hot as summer and a stink coming off the river. Christ, he's sweltering in his best bib and tucker. The coat someone left in the pub and it's a good 'un – must have cost a fiver at least, grey stuff, fits like a glove, could have been made for him. Hat tilted over his tin eye, glint of gold spectacle rim, you'd take him for a gent all right.

Nearly there, and will he be waiting? What's the time? Damn Dennis and his dallying; she almost laughed out loud at the ridiculous alliteration. *Damn Dennis and his dallying, he will keep shilly-shallying.* So hot she could melt, ridiculously hot for spring. Aida, though, of all the names in the world, why that? Now Harri was bound to ask about the meeting and force Clem to hear that hurting name. Sun sharp on the windowpanes and the remnants of puddles stung her eyes.

Now the town: past the bank, the post office – after all that she was on time – turn left at the florist – blooms craning from galvanised buckets, daffodils, tulips, irises, her favourite flowers. Dennis always gave her irises for her birthday, but don't think about him. There's absolutely nothing irregular. Not Aida. No, Harri simply misheard; not Aida, but Ida – no, Ada. Of course! A commonplace, much more likely name.

She turned the corner and there it was, the words stencilled in gilt on the window: The Copper Kettle, Quality Bakery and Tea Room. A surging in her chest now, a slowing of her feet, the brass handle hot, the door opening with a startling ping. Her eyes flicked round the room; he had not yet arrived. Two tables remained free, one in the window, one further back where it was dim. When a small dumpling of a waitress approached, Clem declined the window, asked to be seated in the back. Cooler.

'Most of our ladies like to be sat with a view,' the girl said pertly, 'but you know best, I'm sure.'

'Tea only,' Clem said, waving away the menu. 'Darjeeling. And two cups, please, I'm expecting a friend.'

The tablecloth was a vivid shade of pink, a shiny stuff she hadn't seen before; the table wobbled on the uneven floor. She sat facing the door. Of course, he might not recognise her; it had been such a short visit, and there was his concussion. But she would recognise him, no question of that. Oh, she was quite damp with perspiration. She removed her gloves, surreptitiously ran a finger under the brim of her hat, wiped it on her skirt.

The tea arrived in a pink pot, which tried to match the cloth. The jug and sugar bowl were black. Clem picked up the sugar tongs, grasped a cube, dropped it, picked it up, dropped it. She did this three times between each look towards the door. Soon the cube began to erode, its corners softening. Each time the door opened, the ping tore right through her. The window table was taken now, two women with great wide hats, blocking the view.

And then a stooping little person came in – brown coat, brown hat, brown wicker basket. She peered round the teashop, waited by the door for a few moments and then, appearing let down, left. She looked like an Ada, Clem thought, feeling vaguely soothed; let's call her Ada. Now it was the truth that she'd seen Ada.

She set the teacups on their saucers, poured milk into both. Through the kitchen door came the soapy smell of washing-up.

What if he didn't come? Maybe that would be best, after all. One could simply send him the money. Pick up the sugar with the tongs and drop it. Pick up and drop, pick up and drop, pick up and drop.

He follows an old biddy with an arse like a tank through the door; can't see Mrs M. at first then clocks blue hat, pale face, down in the mouth. Gawd almighty, talk about droopy drawers. He straightens up, dignified as befits the officer class. And after all that is what he earned the right to be. The thought sparks a filament of anger through his veins. Sir Mostyn, Sir fucking Mostyn. He grinds his teeth, swallows hard, readies himself to speak with Mostyn's plummy voice.

'Devil of a job getting away,' he says, sitting down opposite her. She looks straight at him, eyes the colour of . . . what? Pale, like something breakable. Pretty, actually, you have to give her that, but in that thin, intense way that sets your teeth on edge.

'May I?' She lifts the pot.

He removes his coat, making sure to flash the deep blue silky lining. 'Fine day, what?' He estimates half an hour of chit-chat, cash in his pocket and then another ten minutes or so – can't grab and run. He quails when he notices the girl approaching them. It's Dora, forgot she worked here, little piece he had a dalliance with; she'll keep her mouth shut if she knows what's good for her.

She takes his hat and coat to hang them up and returns with a smile on her face. 'Would the gentleman like a cake?'

Poker-faced, he orders an almond tart; Dora looks about to detonate with glee.

'She seems rather familiar,' says Mrs M.

'Her pa's an old chum.'

She looks around her, lifts the sugar bowl as if amused. 'Trying frightfully hard to be modern, isn't it?'

What's she on about? He catches himself frowning and stops. 'This is most awfully sporting of you,' he says, striking, he thinks, just the right note.

'It's you doing me the favour,' she says. 'I'll feel so much better, you see.'

'Well, as I say, I'm very grateful.' His fingers are twitching. Hand it over then! But of course there must be more small talk, of the weather and what not, and he can spin that out till the cows come home if necessary. But she seems to have run out of things to say. He watches her wriggle, fidget with the sugar tongs.

A memory comes: Dad on his stool by the riverbank, twitching his fishing rod. 'Patience, lad, you have to have patience. You just line up things right and wait, and the blighter'll catch himself.' A grey squirm of maggots in a tobacco tin; a wriggle on his old man's hard brown palm.

The almond tart arrived, glacé cherry like a bubble of blood on its white skin. Stop it. Clem watched him cut the pastry with a fork and take a hefty mouthful.

'I do feel responsible, wandering about on the road like some kind of . . . twerp.' She laughed weakly.

'You don't strike me as a twerp.' He had a touching way of pushing back his hair, allowing his hand to hover, as if to shadow the prosthesis.

There followed a silence. Clem could not think of a single word to say. Enjoying the remainder of his pastry, he seemed quite relaxed. The wobbling of the table was getting on her nerves. Flakes

of almond like snipped fingernails scattered on the cloth around
his plate.

'I suppose you don't live locally, given the address?' she said
idiotically. *Oh, this was torture.* Suddenly she was impatient for it to
be over – after all what had she expected?

'It's a place to rest my head for the time being.' He bit into the
tart and the cherry disappeared. 'You a native of Seckford?'

'Not a native,' she said. 'My husband's home. But not far,
Felixstowe. I moved here when—'

'Oh yes, you're married. I remember you mentioning that you
were married.'

She flushed under this teasing and watched his lazy smile.
From the flange of each nostril, a deep groove ran down to below
the corners of his lips, scored longer and deeper on one side. His
skin was freshly shaved, with a tiny patch of fair bristle missed on
his jaw.

Flipping open a leather case, he extracted a cigarette. 'You?'

'Thank you.' She had no wish to smoke, but it was something to
do, better than this neurotic destruction of cubed sugar. She took
her jade holder from her bag and leant forward as he lit the cigarette. As her lips touched the cool stone, she recalled Powell lighting
her a Lucky Strike: the intimacy of putting her lips to the paper
where his had been, the tobacco taste of his kisses, his Canadian
voice, deep brown, like tobacco itself. The nicotine fizzed through
her blood. Yes, there really *was* something familiar in the shape of
Mr Fortune's face; it wasn't just her fancy. And oh . . . the light in
his fake eye, silvery behind its lens – she caught her breath at the
queer notion that Powell was looking out at her through Mr
Fortune's painted eye.

*

She puts her hand into her bag. That's where it is; she's getting it out. He keeps his gaze on her face though. A white oval, those eyes – ice on a puddle, that's it! He used to love stamping on frozen puddles, cracking them to smithereens. Her hand stays in her bag. *Bring it out, bring it out.* He's getting the jitters now, the start of a headache, warning specks at the edge of his vision. From her bag she draws something – a handkerchief. A bloody handkerchief!

She smokes nervously. Her hands white and smooth as a child's make him think of Doll's paws, all rough and veined. The wedding ring's gold, the engagement ring sparkles: diamonds and sapphires, worth a bob or two. Even her skin looks top notch.

He asks about children, surprised she's got one, looks too delicate to push out a sprog. He sneaks a look at his watch. Must get going; Doll'll have his guts for garters if he's late for Kenny.

'Oh, Dennis is alive and well!' she says when he asks about her hubby's war. She tells him that she was at the Front, a VAD. Well, surprising as that is, it does make sense; plenty of posh girls out there, do-gooders getting under the real nurses' feet. At least that's what that nice sister in Calais let on.

'Do you have family?' she asks.

He shakes his head. 'Wife couldn't cope with this.' He taps his face.

They smoke their cigarettes and talk, but his jitters are coming back, that warning tremble in his eyelid. He's tired, tired of the pose, of fucking Mostyn's voice, needs a proper drink.

'What ho,' he says, glancing meaningfully at his watch.

'Of course.' At long bleeding last she removes an envelope from her bag. He slips it inside his jacket; that's that then, done and dusted.

'I wish you luck, Mr Fortune.' She removes the end of her cigarette, replaces the green holder in her bag.

'Don't believe in it myself,' he says. 'You can't go trusting in luck. You have to make your own.'

'Hmm,' she says. 'But some people do seem luckier than others, don't they?' And then she adds, 'And with a name like yours too!'

He manages a smile; leg jumping under the table. *Come on, come on!* Christ, the way she's looking at him!

'I wonder if I might not have nursed you?' she comes out with. 'You seem most terribly familiar, it's almost as if . . . forgive me if this sounds forward, but as if I know you.'

'Absolutely not,' he goes, smooth as bloody butter. 'I could never have forgotten a face like yours.'

Miscalculation? Looks like she's about to slap him for a second, but no . . . her eyes widen and she leans forward as if she's seeing something in him. Christ, it makes his skin creep the way she's staring now – but he senses a chance here. Don't go looking a gift horse in the mouth, Vincey boy.

Worth a punt at least. 'Mrs Everett,' he says, 'might we meet again?'

A door slammed in her breast, her body stiffened. Whoever did he think he was? And what did he think *she* was? This was, after all, just what you'd expect from someone of his ilk. Abruptly, she stood. 'I really don't think that will be necessary, do you?'

His chair grated as he stood too.

'I'm relieved to have recompensed you. Goodbye, Mr Fortune.'

She fled the café, head down – flash of flowers, paving stones, puddles bright with sky, horse droppings. Oh, compose yourself, do, woman! Running harum-scarum through the town, gloves off! Compose yourself. Entering a churchyard, she found a bench in the deep shade of a yew, and there she sat, dabbing her face, her eyes, with her handkerchief. Tears! Oh, what was the matter with her?

Dennis maintained that she was still delicate, that she must take care of her nerves. Nerves: a tangle of wires fizzing and snarling and sparking. *Breathe. Smooth, smooth, soothe, soothe.* Once her hectic heart began to slow, she let her head hang back, gazed up into the prickity branches of the yew, the ancient wood, the smell so deeply green. A tree hundreds of years old perhaps; here before the war, here after; unmoved, calm, oblivious. And the thrush singing high in its branches knew nothing – only the moment, only the sunshine, only its song.

He dons the helmet and the goggles, revs the engine. He'll feel better for a ride. A sudden laugh yelps out of him as the wind hits his face – pushed it too far that time, Vincey. Priceless! You'd think he'd goosed her, the way she fled, leaving that little Dora in stitches.

Can't find the house, parks miles away, but still gets there in the nick of time, kiddies all spilling out. Kenny gives him a filthy look. 'Where's Mum?' he says. 'She never said *you* were coming for me.'

'Thought you'd like a ride on the pillion.'

Kenny's pleased as punch but won't let on. You can see him looking around, hoping his pals might see. 'Where is it, then?'

'Down the street.'

The kid slumps with disappointment. He's nine, a knock-kneed, calf-licked little brat who's not really taken to Vince, not yet, despite the conjuring tricks. Give him time though; once he sees Vince as a father figure and, you never know, he and Doll might have another. Yes, he likes that idea, his kid planted up in Doll's big warm belly. That'd seal the deal all right.

'Good party?' Vince says.

'All right.' Kenny picks up a stick and clatters it along the iron palings of a fence.

'Cling tight,' Vince tells him once they're on the bike. Perhaps he ought to get the lad a helmet if this is going to be a habit. He's only once given Doll a ride, her soft bulk pressed against his back, shrieking in his ear – scared the flipping life out of her!

'You drive slowly,' she said to Vince this afternoon. 'You harm a hair on his head and you'll have me to answer to.'

'I'll treat him like bone china,' he promised. And true to his word he drives at a snail's pace, so that the boy shouts, 'Faster, faster.' They roll up at the Wild Man safe and sound. A car's still parked out the front, he notices, though it's long gone closing. He rides round the back and they enter through the dim kitchen where all's quiet.

'Mum,' Kenny shouts, 'I'm back.'

Doll's probably upstairs, taking the weight off or having a bath. Kenny hammers up there. Not a word of thanks; he'll have to teach that boy some manners. Doll spoils him, lets him wind her round his little finger. Yes, a man's influence definitely needed here.

He takes out the envelope and counts the money – lovely fresh notes – a bit more than he asked for too. He tucks it into his wallet and, whistling, goes through to the bar for a stiffener.

As he enters he hears Doll's laugh and there she is, changed into a new blouse, sitting opposite someone, clouds of smoke and tumblers of gin on the table.

'What ho,' he says.

'Talk of the devil.' Doll looks up at him. 'Where's Kenny?'

'Gone up.'

'Well, that was good of you,' she says. 'Now, where's my manners! Teddy, this is Vince, Mr Fortune. He lodges here' – she gives Vince a warning look – 'in a manner of speaking. Vince, this is Ted, Edward Chamberlain, an old friend of Dick's.'

Mr Chamberlain, a hulk of a man, head like a great moustachioed spud, doesn't shift himself, but reaches out his hand.

'Any friend of Doll's,' says Vince, shaking it.

'And I bet she's a great many friends, eh? What?' says Ted.

'Now then!' Doll nudges his arm. She has that soft, blurred look from one too many in the afternoon; she'll suffer for it tonight and who'll be the one to have to listen to her moaning then? The claws of his headache tighten and he stretches his neck this way and that.

'Copped it, eh? Who were you with?' Ted indicates his face.

'First Suffolk Yeomanry. Sergeant.'

'Greenwich Light Infantry. Captain. Pull up a pew, Vince. Can I call you Vince?'

Vince nods. 'Don't mind if I do. I'll fetch myself a drink. Anyone else?' Gives him satisfaction this, acting the host.

'Not for me.' Doll gives him a look. 'And no war talk, please.'

'Sorry, Doll,' says Ted and touches her arm. She's getting that misty look that comes over her when she remembers her old man.

'Kenny enjoyed the ride home,' Vince says, as he refills Ted's glass and helps himself to a double as well as a pint while he's at it. 'Clinging like a limpet. We should get him a helmet if I'm to be ferrying him about.'

'We'll have to see about that.' Doll frowns at his two drinks.

'Motorcyclist, are you? What have you got?' Ted asks.

Vince launches into detail about the Norton but Doll interrupts: 'Remember you've still got to change them kegs, Vince, before opening.'

'I haven't forgotten.' Vince rolls his eyes at Ted. *Women!*

Ted grins, pipe stem clenched between his teeth, big damp moustache. 'What's your line now?' he asks.

Vince takes a swallow of Scotch, lights a cheroot. 'Considering my options. Helping Doll out in the meantime. You?'

'Motor trade,' says Ted.

'Ted's got a lovely motor, and tomorrow he's taking me and Kenny out for a drive,' says Doll. 'You won't mind closing up for me after dinnertime, will you?'

'Not a bit.' Vince's fingers crush his cheroot. 'Just passing through?' he asks.

'Firm's setting up a branch in Ipswich,' Ted says. 'So I reckon you can count me as a new regular.' He winks at Doll.

'Bit far to come for a regular,' says Vince.

'Well, I dare say he'll pop in now and then,' Doll says, and the way she beams at Ted, it turns Vince's stomach.

17

The Wild Man,
Gipswick Road

Dear Mrs Everett,

I hope this letter finds you well.

I am writing to thank you for payment of funds. My motorcycle is fixed now thanks to you. Most gratefully received.

Also sorry for causing you offence. When I suggested we meet again I wasn't meaning anything wrong by it, only that you might like to talk about your time at the Front. But why should you? Only I got a feeling. I do get feelings, but this time was a mistake and sorry to be so forward and put you out.

I also want to ask you something else. I reckon this letter will be on the fire by now at any rate, so I will dare. You see, there has been a hitch with my compensation as well as some other funds I'm due and so I find myself short, just temporary. I wonder if you might be able to lend me £10, which I will repay at 5% interest when my boat comes in, so to speak.

I do not expect you're still reading and won't contact you again unless you find it in the goodness of your heart to help.

You did strike me as the kind-hearted sort. If so, you can write
to me at the above address as before.

Yours sincerely,

Vincent Fortune, Esq.

The cheek of the fellow! Yes, it should certainly go straight into the
fire and let that be an end to it. But curiously, she found herself
smiling. 'Esq.' – really, that was pushing it! She looked at the fire.
Poor soul – to be reduced to cadging from a stranger. And what an
utter ninny she'd made of herself, fleeing like that! She folded the
letter and tucked it back into its flimsy envelope. His first was still
in her sewing box under the spools of thread. This one might just as
well join it.

She took up her sketchbook and gazed at her attempt to draw
him from memory. All wrong, she hadn't captured his essence.
How to depict the contrast between the living skin and the simulacrum? An idea came, audacious enough to send a thrill through
her veins. Might she suggest that he sit for her? She could offer to
pay him. *Yes*. But dare she ask? Of course, Dennis would have a
conniption if he knew. And Mr Fortune himself might well be
offended; presumably he liked to think he passed for normal.
And why not? He *was* normal. Damaged, yes, but half the popu-
lation of Europe was damaged in one way or another. It was
normal to be damaged these days, visibly or not. Except, of course,
for Dennis.

Who chose that moment to bluster cheerfully into the drawing
room. She slid the sketchbook beneath a pattern book, began to
flip the pages.

'Darling girl.' He bent to kiss her hair. 'What are you
scheming?'

She looked down at the page. 'A fancy tray cloth perhaps,' she said dryly. 'They always come in handy.'

'Quite. Good for you. Nice to see you occupied. I've asked Mrs Hale to bring us coffee together. Oddly slow surgery today, so I've got ten minutes.'

'How nice.'

'Oh, I expect a tidal wave presently.' He stretched and yawned sonorously. 'By the way, you haven't said much about Harri? The visit's clearly done you a power of good.'

Clem flicked through the pages: napkins, table cloths, samplers, antimacassars.

'Did you get anywhere with the question of her move back here?'

'But you argue all the time!'

He was looking in the mantel mirror now, pinching the waxed ends of his moustache. 'If only she wasn't so beastly stubborn.'

'It takes two, Dennis.'

'She's always been contrary. "Mary, Mary, quite contrary," Mother used to say.'

'Well, I couldn't stick living in the middle of a cat-and-dog fight.'

He turned from the mirror, went to the window. 'Oh Lord, here comes Mr Jones and his blasted "rhumaticks".' He sighed. 'It wouldn't be for ever, sugar plum. She's bound to remarry. Though she'll drive them away with that preposterous Bohemian pose she's striking in that hovel.' He hooted. 'Painted stools – I ask you!'

'I think it rather a sweet cottage. Cosy.'

'And as for those wretched Burts.'

'They *are* her in-laws.'

Harrumphing, he flung himself down on the sofa. From below came the sound of the waiting-room door. 'Oh, I'm sure they're good people, salt of the earth and so on, but it'd be a much better start for the girls growing up here.'

Pen wipers, needle books, jewellery cases, handkerchiefs. Clem put down the patterns, and the concealed sketchbook slid out. Dennis reached for it but she snatched it up first.

'Been sketching?'

She pinched the book tight shut.

'May I see?'

'I'd rather wait till I had something worth showing.'

He shrugged. 'Well, as long as you stick to cheery things. Flowers and what not. No more ugliness, eh? I take it you burned those horrid old war sketches?' He cracked his knuckles. 'And after all, Stanley's dead now, no use beating about the bush. She's one of us again.'

'Perhaps,' Clem said.

Mrs Hale came in with the coffee tray. 'Beef olives for luncheon, doctor?' she said.

'Scrumptious,' said Dennis.

'Don't you find beef a bit heavy at lunchtime?' Clem said, when the door had closed.

'Not after a morning's work. You should do more, get out and about, build up your appetite.' He stood to pour the coffee.

'That's exactly what I intend,' Clem said.

Dennis beamed.

'But, darling,' Clem dared, 'organise some pocket money for me, *do*. I don't like to have to ask every time I need a shilling or two . . . Oh, Eddie said "cat" yesterday,' she added swiftly, before his expression could sour. 'At his age! Most distinctly. Harri thinks him most awfully advanced.'

'Well, with parents like us what do you expect!' He lavished cream into the cups. 'I wonder . . .'

'What?'

'Whether he should prefer a brother or a sister?'

Her womb contracted sharply.

'Eh?'

'Not yet.'

'No' – he smiled – 'not absolutely *quite* yet.'

The coffee was far too creamy; it coated the roof of her mouth. Below them went the door again; any minute he would go.

'The money?' she said. 'I know it's frightful to go on about it but . . .'

He bit into a buttered half-scone, chewed and swallowed before he spoke. 'As a matter of fact I have been giving the matter some thought. What about taking back the housekeeping from Mrs Hale? Then you can do the budgeting, cuts of meat and so on.'

'But . . .' Clem put down her cup. 'Dennis, really, I'm not the least bit interested in the housekeeping. I just want a little spending money of my own. A little independence. And Mrs Hale manages so well. Mightn't she be insulted? We don't want to upset her.'

He helped himself to another piece of scone.

'Besides,' Clem teased, 'you might find yourself living on carrots whenever I fancy a new hat.'

Dennis laughed and shook a finger at her. 'So I should starve to keep you in fripperies!'

'Or' – she dipped her head and peeped up through her lashes – 'we could leave Mrs Hale in charge, and you simply give me an allowance of my own. Anyway,' she added, 'every girl needs a frippery from time to time.'

He snorted. 'I'll mull it over,' he said. 'No rush is there? By the way, what did you buy last time?'

She took a little breath; of course the question was expected. 'Oh . . . hat, gloves, things for the children – little bits and bobs.'

'Damnably expensive bits and bobs!'

The surgery door banged.

Dennis dabbed his mouth on a napkin, stood, checked his moustache before the mirror.

'It's rather demeaning, darling, to have to account for every penny,' she said, smiling though her jaw was tight as a trap.

'Doesn't grow on trees, you know.'

'Oh, honestly, Dennis, what a screaming cliché!' She nibbled the edge of a scone, picked out a sultana with her nail and squelched it with her teeth. 'Here's an idea: I could look for a little job.'

He gaped at her. 'You are surely not serious!'

'But—'

'Absolutely not!' he said. 'Preposterous. Out of the question. A job!' He puffed out an angry laugh. 'You're surely ribbing?' Shaking his head, he left the room and soon, floating up from below, came the important, doctory sound of his voice.

The Beeches,
Seckford

Dear Mr Fortune,

Thank you for your note of 23rd. I must assure you that I am not in the least offended, and indeed it is I who must apologise for the graceless way I ended our meeting. Abruptly, I remembered an appointment and had to dash – frightfully rude of me.

Perhaps you might allow me to buy you tea as an apology for such disagreeable behaviour? I could meet you at noon on Saturday 7th May, in the same place, if that suits?

As for your other request, leave the matter with me. I do have sympathy for veterans like yourself who, after such tremendous personal sacrifice for King and Country, find themselves through no fault of their own in financial straits.

Yours sincerely,
Mrs Clementine Everett

The Beeches,
Seckford

Dear Father,

I am ashamed at how long it has been since I have written. Though, if you will forgive my saying so, you haven't been much better! I do hope you are happy in California – all that sunshine must be good for your health and spirits, I am sure. The weather here has been divine lately, you'd think it summer already, and I have been getting out and about. You'll be glad to hear that I'm quite recovered. I shall enclose a photograph of your grandson. I do wish you could meet him. He's the image of Dennis, 'a little bruiser' they say, though I don't know what that means exactly and I'm not sure I like the sound of it!

Now, I know Mother left me some money in trust until I am 25. Although that is still more than two years hence, it would be useful for me to have a portion of it now, if you think it fitting. There are various things needed such as hats and art supplies, a summer coat, now that I am better, and I prefer not to have to ask Dennis for every penny. Not that he is mean, but it makes one feel so beholden. Since my illness he treats me with kid gloves rather, questions all my decisions and so on, and I have no control over the housekeeping. A little money of my own would make me feel more independent, more like the grown-up woman, indeed wife and mother, that I am.

Please send my regards to Joan. I do hope she is well.

Love always,

Your own daughter,

Clementine

18

H E SETS HIS clock for five a.m., but in the thin grey light of insomnia clicks off the ringer at half past four. Carrying his shoes, he descends the ladder and tiptoes past Doll's door, pauses to listen for her breath: all quiet. She's never once let him stop the night in there. Her bed's soft, deep and musky – she's not a great one for washing the sheets (not like Ethel who'd whisk them off at the least hint of a whiff). What's wrong with a bit of a whiff, specially if it's Doll's? Going up that ladder to his camp bed after they've done the deed makes him feel like a bloody alley cat. Though lately there's been none of that. What's up with her when it's so good and all? She can hardly make out she doesn't enjoy it. Just wait till she sees what he's got up his sleeve!

It's all planned out, a proper strategy. Monday's quiet; if they stay shut today they can be open by Tuesday dinner with hardly a dip in the takings. She might have a bit of a go at him – she hates to let her regulars down – but it'll be well worthwhile. If he sets to, he can get it done in a day, show her what he's made of. Man at work – oh yes, he likes the ring of that.

Because the scuttle makes a devil of a din, he kneels to put the coals in the kitchen stove one by one. He sets the kettle on and goes through into the bar, rubbing his hands. First things first, get them curtains down. He fetches the ladder from the cellar, climbs up and unhooks them, sneezing in the avalanche of dust, then takes the paintings and mirrors off the walls. By the time she's up and about, he'll have done the back wall so she'll clock it as soon as she walks in the bar – see what he's been up to. Glorious sunshine yellow, enough to make your heart sing.

Then he stands in the kitchen, purposeful, keyed-up, spreading dripping on bread, folding it up and shoving it into his mouth between sips of tea. When he's done, he opens the drum of Walpamur he sneaked in yesterday. Bought it on tick, money more or less promised. He puts on an old shirt of Doll's hubby's, fit only for rags, over his own undershirt. It's chilly, but he'll warm up once he gets going. The paint's thick, separated into layers, and takes a hell of a lot of stirring.

He hums to himself as he works. Bloody cobwebs in the corners, never noticed, and straight away they get on the brush. Should have washed the walls first, done a bit more prep, but too late now. Here he is making a difference to the place. Making his mark. Like one of them birds that build a fancy nest to attract a mate. Though, fair enough, it is her nest already, but he's bettering it, bringing it up a notch. Jazzing things up. Bits of web and wing, dust and detritus caught up on the picture rail get in the paint, but you won't be able to tell. Won't show when the curtains are back up, the mirrors and pictures rehung.

Painting over the dark green is harder than he thought and it'll want another coat. All the more reason to get on: do it fast, a quick first go over, and don't worry what it looks like. He thinks of a cat he had as a child, the way it would spray piss to mark its territory. No, it's not like that; he's not just making his mark, he's doing a good turn – a nice surprise for old Dolly, still in the Land of Nod up there, bless her heart. Drips run down his wrist and he wipes them on the shirt. It's not six yet. As a rule she's not down till half seven. If he can get the first coat done . . . but it's taking longer than he thought, with the fiddly bits round the windows and the picture rail and the complicated skirting. Really, it all needs doing, but just the walls today, just to get that fresh, spruced-up look, just to see the look on her face. Priceless, that'll be.

Half the wall done and he stands back to inspect it, heart sinking at the mess. Streaky and uneven, the dark green's glowering through. Something wrong with the paint? Can't do a second coat till the first one's dry and he's going to need more paint. Never occurred to him one great big drum wouldn't be enough.

Maybe, rather than have her come down and catch him at it, he'll head her off at the pass. The original plan was for her to find him perched up the ladder, brush in hand, look at the freshly painted wall and then at him, all starry-eyed. But rethink, regroup: instead, take her up a cup of tea and forbid – yes, be firm about it, who's wearing the trousers round here after all? – forbid her from setting foot in the bar till he's given her the say-so. Then he can get it shipshape.

By half seven he's got the first wall done, but there's paint on the floor and the bench. Back in the kitchen, he gets the kettle on again, looks anxiously at the stairs; ought to get those spills wiped up before they dry and there's painty footprints on her floor tiles. He fetches a bucket and rags and clears up, then he goes through into the bar to start in there but there's a creaking from up the stairs . . . Sod it, sod it, goes back to the kettle, not boiled. Don't come down, Doll, he pleads, don't come down yet.

Feet on the stairs, but they're light and quick and Kenny comes into the kitchen, does a double take and says, 'Whatever have you got all over you?' Vince puts his hand to his head – yes, paint in his hair, and all over the old shirt and one knee of his trousers where he knelt.

'Doing a surprise for your mum,' Vince says. 'Be a good boy and run upstairs and tell her not to come down yet.'

'Why?'

'I'll tell you later. Do it now, and there's thruppence in it for you if you can stop her coming down.'

'Sixpence?'

Vince gazes at the hard-nosed little toerag. 'Sixpence then.'

'Promise?'

Vince nods. 'Go on.'

Kenny hurtles back upstairs. The kettle boils and Vince makes a fresh pot, puts a biscuit in the saucer to keep her going. He'll have to clean himself up a bit or he'll give the game away. But, oh Christ, there's the heavy creak of her on the stairs and he cringes at the sound of her voice: 'Whatever do you mean, don't come down! Whatever next!'

She comes into the kitchen, gawping at him. 'What the hell?'

'You shouldn't have come down yet, Doll,' Vince says.

'It's a surprise, Mum. You've ruined it. Do I still get my sixpence, Mr Fortune?'

'Paint?' Doll says. She comes closer to examine him. 'All in your eye.' She peers at the eye that can see nothing. 'You want to get that cleaned off before it dries.' She looks him up and down, her face troubled, crumpled, sleep in the corners of her eyes. 'Is that Dick's?' She plucks at the old shirt, shakes her head, looks sorrowful; of all the reactions he thought she'd have, that wasn't one.

'Do I still get my sixpence?' Kenny asks again. 'Not my fault she came down, is it?'

Vince follows Doll through into the bar. He stands behind her watching the stillness of her back.

'My sixpence?'

'Put a sock in it, Kenny,' she snaps.

'Just needs another coat, Doll. You wait till it's finished.'

She turns to him, face a shade paler than usual, lips chalky. 'You'd better get on with it then, hadn't you?' That's all she says before she goes back into the kitchen and firmly shuts the door.

She goes out, as she does of a morning to drop Kenny at school, leaving by the back door without a word. Once he's heard the door bang he watches her from the window, plodding down the lane to the bus stop in her green coat and hat, Kenny running ahead. He puts down his brush, goes into the kitchen. In the mirror he sees spikes of paint in his hair and a yellow streak right across the lens of the specs and on the eye; underneath the muscles tug and panic, trying to blink the paint away. He locks the door, turns away from the mirror – never looks in the mirror when it's off – unhooks the specs from behind his ears and sits cradling that part of his face, good eye meeting the cool gaze of the fake. He wets a rag and cleans the lens, but rubbing over the open eye is almost impossible, and in his empty socket the muscles flail, the nerves severed and twitching, healed but raw with the memory of pain – no, not just memory, *sensation*, like a finger jabbing an eye that isn't there.

Not a word of thanks, not so much as a smile! He's a good mind to walk out, bags, baggage and all, and good luck to her with finishing off the bloody bar. She's an ungrateful old cow, that's what she is; no appreciation for all he does for her, not a scrap. Now the coast's clear he goes upstairs to her room – she wouldn't like it but he doesn't care – picks up a discarded stocking, sniffs it and runs it through his fingers. On the dressing table: Pond's cold cream, rouge, lipstick, a cheap little bottle of Parma Violets, a drum of Bronnley's talc, a hairbrush-and-mirror set with embroidery under a foggy film on their backs, tweezers, hair clips, a pot of Vaseline. Each item he fingers, sampling the different smells. In the brush a snarl of bleached hair; he pulls it out. Yes, she can be a right old cow, but still, there's no getting round it, he's smitten, good and proper. Even when he doesn't like her, he still loves her. Her precious L'Heure Bleue's nearly gone, just a few drops swilling there in the bottom of the bottle. He'll get her some more of that; his heart rises at the thought – *oh, Vince, you shouldn't have!*

Tired out, what with the early start, he lies down on the unmade bed, keeping his boots hanging off the edge. On the bedside table sits a picture of her hubby, Dick, standing by an aspidistra, dark-eyed, drooping moustache; it does put a man off his stride to have a picture of the dead hubby gawping right at him when he's on the job. Once they're married that'll have to go.

He gets up quick. Don't go dropping off now. *Marrying her –* that's the ticket, and to do that he'll have to get a bit more money in his pocket. More work in that direction required. A proper military strategy. But first he'll pull himself together, have a cup of tea, ride into town for more paint, and by the time Doll's back he'll be well into the second coat and then she'll see what she will see.

19

11 La Plata,
Santa Barbara

Dear Clementine,

Thank you for your letter. I'm relieved to learn that you've recovered your health and that my grandson thrives. He looks like a fine little chap and I do indeed see a distinct likeness to Dennis.

Things are much the same here. I continue to work hard at the Infirmary and even harder on the golf course! Joanie is a hospitable soul and we very often entertain, so it is a full and busy life. And yes, thank you, we are both in good health considering our advanced years.

Now, to answer what I deduce is the main purpose of your rare letter: I'm afraid there's no question of beginning your allowance early. I do hope you haven't come under the influence of the dreadful suffragette brigade? You really must follow your husband's guidance. I should have thought being treated with kid gloves would be rather agreeable. It would be impolitic of me to interfere between husband and wife, and I'm afraid that is my final word on the matter.

Keep well, dear girl, and do send me further pictures of Edgar. He resides in pride of place on our mantelpiece, rubbing shoulders with Joanie's charming granddaughter, Ella-May.

With affectionate wishes always,

Your Father.

Mr Fortune tipped his hat as she approached. 'Would you mind awfully,' he asked, 'if we went over there?' He nodded towards the Crown Hotel.

Clem glanced at the pub's façade with a shiver of alarm. A pub! In daylight hours!

'Had a bit of a jolt this morning, you see,' he went on. 'Could do with a stiffener.'

There was a tic in his jaw; she watched the tiny shadow pulsing in and out. Poor fellow. And after all, what harm could it do? So, she followed him across the road into the bar where the air was a hot, glittering fug. A pale, unnecessary fire sputtered in a shaft of umber light.

'Take a seat. What's your poison?'

Her eyes darted round, heart skittering with the daring of this. If Dennis could see her now! 'Sherry, please.'

She spotted a booth at the back and made for it, squeezing into the cramped space. Here she'd be unnoticeable should anyone she or Dennis knew came in, though that was unlikely. All the other customers were men but for one harshly rouged young woman with a purple hat, the ridges of her stays showing through her cheap, skimpy blouse. She was laughing with her husband or – perhaps more likely – not her husband. It was all rather racy and thrilling. And there was the landlady with piled-up black hair and a withered doll's face, who'd looked twice at Clem as she entered and continued to peer at her as Mr Fortune ordered the drinks.

He sat opposite Clem and raised his glass. 'Cheers!' His brandy looked mellow in its glass. After a sip of the sticky sherry she wished she'd ordered that instead.

'What happened?' she asked.

'Beg pardon?'

'You said you'd had a jolt?'

'Oh!' He waved a hand in the air. 'Something and nothing. Nothing this won't put right.' He lifted his glass and smiled over the rim. As he drank, she watched the movement of his prominent Adam's apple, noticed again the scar on his throat. Must have been a near miss. There was silence for a moment. Nothing came to her to say. As the alcohol began to leak into her bloodstream, a clammy heat spread through her.

'Well, here we are,' he said.

'I don't know why they think we need a fire!' she said, waving her fingers like a fan.

Without asking, he lit two cigarettes and, with staggering familiarity, put one between her fingers. To cover her confusion, she fumbled in her bag for the holder.

'How's the nipper?' he asked.

She fitted the cigarette, breathed in the cool smoke and exhaled. 'He's well, learning words . . . seems quite advanced.'

'Isn't it just like a mum to think so? And Doctor Everett?'

Clem focused on the darkly ridged table; sticky, needed a thorough scrub. A grubby establishment, this was. She'd rarely been in a pub before, certainly never a public bar like this. Stained beermats advertised Adnams Ale and the ashtrays were cheap, scorched tin; burn marks all around the table edges. 'My husband is perfectly well, thank you.'

She noticed a small, hunched woman enter the bar, brown tweed suit and hat: ah, again, it was Ada! Clem watched her search for someone – husband perhaps? Oh no, she would be a widow, of course – and scuttle out again. She felt a trickle of perspiration down the back of her neck as she watched her cigarette shrivel to ash. This was so awkward, clearly a mistake.

'Well?' he said.

She didn't quite like the familiar way he was regarding her. This was all wrong. 'I do apologise, Mr Fortune,' she said, 'but I shall have to go.' She gathered her gloves and began to rise.

'Finish your drink.' His voice was rough, but then he cleared his throat and softened it. 'And Vincent, please. Aren't we going to be friends?' He gazed up at her, the tic in his jaw still visible, a sad light in his true eye. 'Don't go rushing off again, please, or we'll end up in the same position as before.'

She lowered herself down, puzzled by him. Last time there'd been a façade of pomposity – rather heart-breaking in retrospect – but now he seemed more open, even vulnerable. Since he made no move to let her out she couldn't easily leave in any case, so she stayed – a few minutes would make no difference – watching him sip and smoke, with those long, elegant fingers so like Powell's. Were they really? She could almost resent him for reminding her of her love. It was hardly his fault, poor chap, that he made her think of Canada – where she should really be, with Powell and Aida, living a different life under a different sky. The thought of all that fresh Canadian air began to make her breathless.

'The same position?'

'Apologies, embarrassment.'

She fiddled with the cigarette holder: cool, soothing jade.

'And now you're here . . .'

'Can't think why!'

'It was your suggestion,' he reminded her, gently.

She returned the holder to her bag, preparing once again to leave.

'Look, Clementine,' he said earnestly, 'if I may?'

'Mrs Everett,' she said. Oh, why did she say that? She made herself sound ridiculous, like a stuffed shirt or would it be a stuffed blouse? She took her handkerchief from her bag, dabbed at the perspiration on her upper lip and made herself, for this last time, really examine his face: the mouth wider than Powell's, the skin coarser, though in truth it was hard to remember. Mr Fortune's nose was prominent and finely shaped; thank goodness that had escaped entire. It lent him an air of authority that played interestingly against the otherwise rather common cast of his face. Really, he wasn't a scrap like Powell! Was he? She was forgetting that face, the face of her true love, confusing it.

Look at him objectively. He can't help the likeness – if indeed it is a likeness. Is it only a chimera conjured by her own longing? Oh, curious the way the smoky light plays with his skin and with the painted plate of his eye; he really would make a fascinating subject to paint.

'Do you want to talk about your war?' he suggested.

She puffed in an imitation of Dennis, benignly exasperated. 'Best foot forward, don't you think?'

'Only with your hubby not having been there.'

Under the table her fingers twisted. *Hubby!* Oh, the sheer vulgarity of him! The sherry had fogged her brain, that and the last trace of last night's Veronal. Within the shimmying motes of dust, everything was becoming pleasantly insubstantial, dreamy. The sherry was finished and she was suddenly thirsty. The other woman in the bar was hyenaing with laughter, leaning forward to slap her companion on his arm.

'My husband was no shirker, I can assure you,' Clem said. Speaking of Dennis with this impertinent man seemed a betrayal.

Mr Fortune drew on his cigarette, exhaled a long plume of smoke. 'Not the same though, if one's not putting one's own neck on the line, is it?' Unconsciously perhaps, his hand strayed to his throat. 'Only those – like you and me – who've experienced it can really *know*.'

'Perhaps, but . . . excuse me.' She stood, began to squeeze inelegantly past him. A glove dropped to the ground and he stooped to retrieve it – head intimately close to her knees in that dark space.

'Don't go yet,' he said, rather pleadingly, as he emerged. 'One more drink?'

'No, really, I must . . .' she began, but the thought of a refreshing drink did appeal. And a few more minutes would surely make no difference. 'Lemonade, then,' she said. A cool drink and then, in a dignified manner, after giving him the money, she'd take her leave.

Back at the table, he lit two cigarettes. 'Tell you what,' he said. 'Now we're here, why don't I talk about *my* war? Break the ice, so to speak.'

She shrugged. If he wanted to. What did it matter? 'I can only stay five minutes.'

As he spoke, she sipped the cool lemonade, feeling the bubbles detonate in her throat, and watched his face; the real eye animate, narrowing and darkening with memory, the other staring into some distance, beyond anything in this world. Powell gazed out at her as Mr Fortune spoke of his regiment, battles, promotions, his final wounding at the Somme.

'My luck held out till then,' he said. 'Beginning to think I had a charmed life, things I survived. Then Jerry gets me in the neck.'

Grimly he smiled, fingers probing the ugly thickened scar. 'And one in the eye for good measure.' He tapped the prosthesis.

I want to see, thought Clem, and the notion clamoured through her, like a ripple through metal sheeting, bringing an electrical taste to her mouth.

'Sounds as if you were very brave,' she said, as if to a child.

Mr Fortune shrugged; he looked defeated now, diminished. It was shameful that he should go through all that and survive only to be reduced to begging. She put her hand into her bag for the envelope. Inside were two ten-shilling and three pound notes. 'It's not quite as much as you requested,' she said, as, swiftly, he pocketed it. This morning she'd taken the money from Mrs Hale's cash box. Absurd, that she, a doctor's wife, should be reduced to pilfering the housekeeping!

'Consider it a gift,' she said, wishing the words would spool back into her mouth as his expression changed.

'I'm not a charity case,' he said curtly as he stood. 'I will repay in full, with interest, as stated in my letter.'

She followed him out. 'Forgive me,' she said as they parted in the street. How wounded he looked, how dignified, as he turned and walked away.

From their buckets, the florist's flowers jeered and snapped at the hem of her skirt. The pavement was damp, must have rained; it felt like hours since she'd stepped inside the Crown. Now she must return to Harri's for tea and Edgar; the idea that she had a child seemed incongruous, as if that small person existed in another dimension altogether. His little face – no, she could not bring it to mind.

There was Ada ahead of her. If she spoke to the woman it would mean it was less of a lie; perhaps they could make friends and truly she could visit her? She followed the small stooped body, the threadbare coat. On her arm was a wicker basket and she leaned a little to that side. Catch her up and simply ask her directions to somewhere – where? And fall into conversation. But it seemed impossible to gain on her, and when she turned a corner Clem lost energy, paused to lean on a wall. Was she a little drunk? And look at her all awry and without her gloves! She began to put them on: one was missing. Dropped, of course; she should retrace her steps, perhaps to the Crown. But the thought of entering again . . . No. For heaven's sake, it was only a glove.

20

STOOLS UP ON the tables, he sweeps the floor, ready for dinnertime opening. Lost custom on Monday and Tuesday: painting took longer than he thought, cost more too, what with the extra paint and that. Money on tap now though, if he plays it right. You have to have a plan. Things don't just happen willy-nilly. They need helping along. Sergeant V. H. Fortune M.C.: a military man after all; strategy, strategy, all about strategy.

Still hints of the old paint showing through. Really needs a third coat but Doll put her foot down. Clear up and open up. Slave-driver, that's what she is. 'You brought it on yourself,' she said. 'If you'd've said what you was up to, we could've talked it through.'

The bit by the door's the worst – a long patch of green, like a stubborn streak of cowshit. He's gone over and over it but it creeps back when the paint dries. Like the dirty truth behind a lie. If only they could stick something there – a plant, a hatstand or a flaming great statue – but Doll says it would be a hazard near the door.

Floor swept, he gets the stools down, clatters ashtrays on the tables and the bar, deals out the beermats. She's upstairs doing her hair; she washed it while he was putting the curtains up last night, took the opportunity what with being closed. What a palaver. Good job she does it so seldom, puts her in a right old tizzy. There's a smell of burning hair coming down the stairs from her curling iron, and those sharp pins on the carpet up there, you have to mind your footing.

She *will* marry him. He *will* become landlord. Yesterday they had tea together – toad in the hole, gravy and a baked apple – the three of them sat round the kitchen table, just like a family, and later he'd entertained the boy with a few of his tricks. They're coming back to him now. As a kid he was quite the conjurer: card tricks to amaze, coins produced from ears, a dancing handkerchief. Kenny loved it, and Doll, oh, he could see she was entranced, even though she was trying to stay cross, the way her mouth opened in surprise and her great big warm smile breaking through at last, just like the sun from behind a cloud.

While Doll chased Kenny up to bed, Vince finished putting the bar back in order, then he poured drinks, insisted she sit down – quite masterful he was – and they'd sat together in the clean and empty paint-smelling bar, sipping gin and lime, and she'd leant forward and squeezed his arm and said, 'Thank you, dearie, for the thought. Of course, I shall have to have it done over properly one day, but I know you meant well.'

He said nothing, only fetched them a top-up; it was hardly thanks enough for two days' grafting dawn to dusk, but it was something. When they were married she'd show a bit more respect. Mind you, he rather likes a woman who wears the trousers now and then – as long as it *is* only now and then. He thought he was on a promise last night, but when he put his hand on her knee, she got up and stepped away.

He'd asked her what was up, but she'd gone upstairs to bed without even saying goodnight. Saving herself, he reckons, silly old cow; no need, no need at all. Could've done with a comfort too, after seeing Mrs M., all them memories spewing out like rotten mud across the table. He stirred himself up good and proper there. What did he want to go doing that for?

He passes a cloth over the optics, picks up and inspects a glass. What it will take to marry Doll is simple: money. This is the life he wants – what could be better? He'd be properly set up: his own business, his own family, ready-made. There's an earwig creeping out from under a jug; he knocks it to the floor and crushes it. There's Ted to think of, but since he took Doll and Kenny on their picnic the other week, she's not breathed another word about him. When he asked she only said, 'We had a nice tea, thank you,' mouth like a cat's arse, so he guesses that hurdle's fallen, but there'll be more. No time to sit on the fence. Decisive action required pronto: all he needs is the spondulix – and now he has a source.

After closing, Doll puts her hand on his arm. 'Vince, can I have a word, dear?' But she'll have to wait her turn; he's been hatching his plan all dinnertime as he pulled pints of mild and bitter and cider, chit-chatted with the regulars.

'Can it wait, Doll?' he says. 'Got to see a man about a dog.'

She gives him a look but, 'Of course,' she says, 'you run along.' Looking her age today, strained round the eyes. 'But we shall have to talk later,' she says, all serious.

What's that about? Vince adjusts the goggles, wraps his scarf round his mouth, revs up the Norton. No matter what sort of a funk he's in, the minute that engine fires up underneath him, he feels better, strong, entire. What's he done wrong now though? Or maybe, like him, Doll's thinking it's time they move things onto a more permanent footing? He's getting to know her little ways; always so stroppy first thing – you want to steer clear if you can – she gets better and better as the day wears on, till last thing at night she's in her full glory.

He drives down into Seckford, the wind in his face, parky for May. She has a way of wrinkling her nose when she's thinking, quite a rabbit twitch, which he loves, yes, loves, that's not putting it too strong. Of course there are things you ignore, pretend not to notice, like the soft way she gives into Kenny's every whim, or doesn't always empty the chamber pot, or wriggles her little finger in her ear when she's miles away.

Through Seckford and out along the Malton Road, he slows down. This is the vicinity. Surveillance, that's the key. Get a good look, see what he's dealing with here. The Beeches, named for the trees, bloody great things everywhere. He parks the motorcycle on the verge opposite and removes his helmet and goggles, taking in the size of the place. There are two gateways flanked by trees, stone balls on the gateposts, greened over with moss. There's a beech hedge between the gates, both of which are open so you could drive in one, out the other. Grand stone steps lead up to the front door and smaller ones down to – he puts on his hat before he risks crunching over the gravel to have a proper butcher's – the surgery door.

Up them steps comes a woman supporting an old bloke, faces white as chalk. Vince goes back to the road, stands so that he can see the comings and goings. The old man's in a wheelchair now and the woman's pushing him away; a bloke wheels his bicycle out onto the road, hawks in the gutter, then mounts the bike and clanks off up the road. And then there's nothing for a while but birds cheeping, the odd car, a pony and trap clopping by.

Five minutes of so of nothing and he's starting to twitch, then the door opens again and out comes . . . Must be the doctor himself – dark hair, swarthy type, smart coat, Homburg, doctor's bag. A geezer in a flat cap follows him and they have a word, then the doctor gets in the Ford, the other bloke cranks it till the engine turns over and the doctor drives out. Beautiful motor it is, shining black with flashing chrome.

Vince shivers. Cold out here despite the sun, nasty edge to that wind. Shame about last night, Doll going off without a word. It's not like they haven't done it before! Tonight, then. It warms him just to think about it; you could lose yourself altogether in that woman, dip your wick and lose your wits. He never knew a woman could go like that and he's hardly had a sheltered life!

Remember Ethel though, her dry, tight, pinchy little ways you had to be so grateful for. He's never gone short, not when he was a salesman on the road, and then at the Front there were girls for sale wherever you went – perk of the job – but you had to be careful what you caught, and once he did catch the clap. Got it sorted out but it taught him a lesson all right. Once he'd become an officer there was not so much of that anyway, you had to set an example. Some of those girls were fun; there was one he got quite sweet on, a little Turk at Gallipoli, a proper dusky maiden, lashes like chimney soot.

He's getting fed up with this surveillance. Where's it getting him? But then the front door opens and out comes a nursemaid and a bigger missus in a pinny; they help each other with a pram down the steps. And then the girl pushes the pram along – bumping over them blasted roots – and he can hear the kid crying. He crosses the road and follows, not too close but close enough to hear her singing away.

'Go to sleep, my baby, close your pretty eyes, angels up above you, peeping at you dearly from the skies.'

Gives him a pang: was that ever sung to him? Gives him an idea too. He follows her along the road. She turns down a lane where the trees arch over and between the trunks the bluebells spread like a flood, and there's white stuff too, a whiff of garlic.

'Great big moon is shining, stars begin to peep, time for Master Eddie Everett, to be asleep, time for Eddie boy to be asleep.'

Seems to have done the trick, the lullaby, no more crying. The girl looks round sharply, sensing him behind her in the lane.

'Excuse me, miss.' He catches her up. 'I'm looking for a family called Jefferson.' Where the hell did that come from? 'Wonder if you can help?'

'There's some cottages at the bottom.' She hasn't looked up at him. 'Don't know who lives there though.'

Falling into step beside her, Vince peers into the pram at a sleeping child in a white bonnet.

They walk along in silence for a minute then, 'I'm his nursemaid,' she says. 'First job. Fallen right on my feet.'

'Come up trumps, eh?' he says.

'He sleeps when he's meant to, eats when he's meant to. He's like blooming clockwork. Not like my little brothers, they was scallywags compared to him. They was all over the shop!' She gives a fond laugh. 'Though he was a bit grumpy this afternoon, so we're having an extra walk.'

'Done the job, hasn't it?'

'Soon as you get moving it sends him right off. I reckon it's a tooth.'

'What's the mother like?'

The girl hesitates before she says, 'Nice.'

'Treats you all right, does she?'

'What's it to you?'

She speeds up and he keeps pace with her.

'Nice bluebells, aren't they?' he says. And after a moment she softens and they walk along, talking about the flowers and the weather, just passing the time of the day.

Round a bend at the foot of the slope there's a row of cottages. 'Try here,' she says.

'I will, thanks.'

'Well, bye.' She continues pushing the pram.

'What's your name if you don't mind me asking?' he calls after her.

She turns, looks him in the face for the first time and does the usual double take. 'Dinah,' she says. 'Dinah Harris.'

'Harris?' he says and laughs. 'Well, I'll be . . . there's a coincidence. I'm Harris too. Johnny.'

'Really!' Her face lights up with amazement though it's not that surprising. If they were both called Fortune, now that'd be something to write home about.

'Think about it,' he says, 'When we're wed you won't even have to change your name.'

She giggles nervously.

'Only joking.' He grins, then hesitates. 'Look, this is a bit forward, Dinah, but I wonder if I might take you out for tea sometime?'

'Oh, I don't know about that,' she says. With the toe of her boot she stirs the grass. 'P'raps, p'raps not.'

'When's your day off?'

'I get Sunday afternoons.' She peeps at him again.

'Well' – he straightens up – 'I'd better let you get on and see if I can't find my friend, an old mate from the Front.'

'That where you got this?' Her hand goes to her eye.

He nods, gives a brave smile.

'Call on Sunday at noon,' she says. 'We could go for a stroll, p'raps?'

'That time's not so good for me,' he says. Doll'd have his guts for garters if he went AWOL of a Sunday dinnertime! 'Three o'clock?'

Dinah nods, smiles up at him. She's nothing but a skinny little kid, sweet though. She walks on with the pram, and as soon as she's out of sight he turns back to fetch his bike.

21

The Wild Man,
Gipswick Road

Dear Mrs Everett,

I am writing to thank you for the money. It was not right the way I took it without the proper thanks and we never discussed terms. As I said, I insist on paying back in full with interest when my boat comes in. If you was able to manage a further loan it would be most gratefully received, just a few extra pounds to tide me over. Flaming cheek of me to ask, you're most probably thinking, but you have a kind heart and they are few and far between these days.

I enjoyed our little chat. Did you realise you dropped a glove, which I can give back in person?

Perhaps you'll allow me to buy you a drink? Nothing improper intended. I'll be in the lounge bar of the Crown, as before, at three Friday coming. No offence taken if you're not there.

Yours sincerely,

Vincent Fortune, Esq.

The roof of the car was up against the rain and the wipers jerked from side to side. Hale was a man of few words but many effortful sounds to do with his digestion and respiration, which were aggravating, but at least didn't necessitate a reply.

At first she'd determined to ignore the letter. Enough of the wretched man! Repeatedly she'd crumpled it and then smoothed it out. The loss of a glove was no more than an irritation. She recalled dropping it and his head close to her knees in the dark space beneath the table – perhaps he'd pocketed it deliberately?

As the car jolted uphill towards town her stomach was tight and her fingers jittery. She would ask him to sit for her, refuse to make it a loan – 'interest' indeed! She'd offer him payment instead – an emollient for his pride.

Inside her bag she felt the envelope which contained the ten-pound note received from Dennis. Of course, there had been a frightful fuss about the money she'd purloined. She'd owned up and, in the bedroom, let him chide her and make love to her. She could get away with murder, she was beginning to realise, if she was willing to pay in that way. All she had to do was make the eager sounds he liked and afterwards lie rumpled and dazed and grateful and then the matter was over. Really, he was easy enough to manage when you got the trick of him.

Hale dropped her in Church Square and she waited till he'd driven away before she hurried towards the Crown, grateful in the rain for the camouflage of her umbrella.

The bar was almost empty, and dim; no sunshine came through the stained glass today. The fire burned sluggishly, and the floor was wet with drips and footprints. Mr Fortune was waiting at the bar.

'Mrs Everett.' He took her hand in his; today her gloves were chamois, punched with holes. 'Or Clementine if I may? I've taken the liberty . . .' He turned and lifted from the bar a glass of sherry.

Clem had decided this time to keep a clear head, to request a pot of tea. But still, she accepted the sherry. The audacity of the man! There was the landlady, straightening up behind the bar, a knowing look on her face.

'Shall we?' Vincent gestured towards the booth.

'I believe you have something for me?' she said as soon as they were seated.

With a mysterious smile he held out both hands, swivelled them so that she could see the empty palms, reached over – she quailed as he inserted a finger under the brim of her hat – and produced her glove.

'How!' The place he'd touched seemed to tingle: what tremendous nerve! The landlady, craning to watch, returned to polishing a glass as she caught Clem's eye.

'Magic,' Vincent said. His mobile eyebrow lifted as he grinned.

'You're a conjurer?'

Modestly he shook his head. 'A few parlour tricks, you know. Used to entertain the chaps at the Front in quiet moments.'

'Well, thank you.' She smoothed the blue glove and tucked it into her bag. 'They're particular favourites of mine.' He looked touchingly pleased with himself. Conjuring in the trenches? Surely not? She noticed his eyes lingering on her bag. Naturally he'd be wondering if there were anything inside for him. The sensible thing would be to make her offer of employment – artist to model – in a businesslike way. If he declined, then that would be that. She'd go straight home to Dennis and Edgar and never think of him again. No more money nonsense. No more nonsense at all.

He pulled out his cigarette case. Though she'd vowed neither to drink nor smoke this afternoon, she accepted one. There followed a prolonged silence.

'So,' he said, at last. 'Where were we?'

'Thank you for returning my glove, Mr Fortune, but I really can't stay. I only—'

'Oh, not this again.' His voice grated.

She sensed a change, a darkening, even anger, and, alarmed, stubbed out her cigarette and stood. 'Please allow me past.' But he sat motionless so that she could not get out of the booth.

The landlady, arms folded, was staring.

'*Please.*'

The insolent way he was regarding her and the feeling of being trapped and watched were making her feel panicky. Not this again, not this. Perspiration rose on her neck; her breath was trapped in her lungs. She tried to push past him, but the floor seemed to lurch. She clutched at the table to steady herself.

'Whatever's up with you?' he said. 'Sit down.'

'Would she like to lie down?' a voice said.

Oh, that wretched landlady. 'If there were somewhere, just for a moment.' Clem's voice was muffled even to her own ears. Had she spoken at all? She needed home, she needed quiet. Above all, she needed to be alone. If only she could breathe. It was the sort of panic she'd had before though not for months. She'd thought she was over it, the hectic beating in chest and neck like a flock of trapped birds, a throbbing in her limbs as if she might burst. Her nerves, her nerves, still delicate – Dennis, dear Dennis, quite right – frizzling and sparkling like electrical wires.

'Poor thing,' the landlady said. Her mouth was like a dark red moth squashed against her powdery face. 'Ooh, doesn't she look pale? Let's get you lying down, shall we, Mrs—? Shall I fetch a doctor?'

'No, no . . .' Clem's voice faded out. 'It's just a funny turn. I get them. So sorry for the trouble.'

'No call to be sorry, dear. Can you get her up them stairs, do you reckon?'

Vincent indicated that he could and, following the landlady, supported Clem up a staircase and along a poky, slant-floored corridor until they reached a door at the end. 'This one's free,' the landlady said. 'If you take your shoes off, you can lie on the bed till you come to. Can I send something up? A nice cup of sweet tea? Aspirin?'

'Brandy,' Vincent said. 'That usually brings her round.'

The landlady hesitated. 'I'll leave you two in peace then. Mr and Mrs—?'

'Fortune,' said Vincent.

The door closed on them.

'Well, this is a turn-up for the books!' Vincent sniggered as he removed his coat and hung it on the back of the door.

Clem looked round at the mean, cramped room with its dark furniture. The bay window was covered with a stuffy crumple of muslin. It reeked of stale pipe smoke, camphor and the feeble wisp of lavender from a bowl of sprigs on the mantel.

'I'll be all right in a moment.' The fit of nerves was passing already – what a fuss about nothing. What a frightful exhibition to make of oneself! Still, she felt obliged to go through with the charade. She removed her shoes and hat, lay stiffly on the shiny green counterpane and concentrated on breathing: count three in, count four out, three in, four out. And was the attack even genuine, she wondered now, or a ruse of her body's, which seemed so oddly drawn to this common man's because of a chance, freak likeness?

As her heart settled back into its customary rhythm, she watched Vincent moving about the room, lifting the curtains to peer out, adjusting the position of a chair.

A knock on the door made her jump, and she sat up straight, but it was only a boy delivering a tray with a brandy bottle and two glasses.

'There's smelling salts here for the lady what's come over queer,' he said, peering curiously at Clem before he withdrew.

Vincent put the tray on the bedside table, moved the chair nearer and sat. 'Feel like I'm visiting the sick,' he said. 'Want a sniff of the salts?'

Clem shook her head.

'You're not, are you?' He made a gesture towards her abdomen.

'Not what?'

'In the family way?'

'No!' she said. *Really!* 'By no means.'

'Well,' he said. 'You are *married*, I believe?' A touch of humour in his voice, a touch of warmth. 'Mrs Fortune indeed!' He grinned, and the skin slid beneath the tin patch.

Although the light was stifled by the muslin, it was still a good northern light; it emphasised the change of texture, the minute gradations of shade between the real skin and the fake. But do not stare.

She lay back on the pillow and gazed at the ceiling instead, smoke-yellowed, cracked. How many people had lain here before her, staring upwards like this? And what class of people? She shuddered to think. She could feel him close by, hear the creak as he shifted in the chair, him clearing his throat, the tiny click as he swallowed.

Really, this was an absurd situation. She must set it straight at once. She sat up, stiff against the pillows. 'I'm sorry for my fright-ful . . . My goodness, surely you can see how this would look? I should leave at once.' But somehow she could not move. His head had dropped. She gazed at his thin sandy hair, the neat swirl of the crown, the gold arms of the spectacles that held his prosthesis in place, the slight shadow by his nose where it fitted imperfectly. Poor man. When he looked up and caught her gaze, she was wrong-footed. Beside her on the bed, her hat, her gloves, her bag. In this stuffy room, still in her coat, she was too hot, but to take it off would seem overly familiar.

He poured brandy into the glasses.

'No.' She swung her feet to the floor.

'Have a nip now it's here.'

She sighed. Oh well. Perhaps it would help; buck her up as Dennis put it. If *he* could see her now! In certain moods he liked to call her his naughty girl, but *this*! This was so far beyond anything he might imagine. She experienced a rush of shame and of fondness for him, innocently busy in his surgery, earning the money that she was spending.

'I want to show you something.' She lifted her feet back onto the bed, sat against the pillows. From her bag she drew her sketch-books – the little old one and the new – wrapped in brown paper. 'Sit here.' She patted the space beside her and untied the string.

Vincent walked round to the other side of the bed and stooped to remove his shoes. He sat beside her, very close. What difference does it make, she told herself sternly, where he sits? There was an awful unwanted intimacy in the sight of his feet in worn grey socks, a ridge of big toenail visible. She opened the book, turned to the first page: a perfect eye in a ruined face, far more ruined than his. She told him about this boy, how he'd died with that one eye locked on hers until it glazed. Vincent said nothing though his hand went to his own face and she could hear a constriction in his breath. She continued to turn the pages and found herself telling him how crucial drawing had become while she was at the Front, how it seemed to keep her sane, as if it gave her some level of control. As she spoke, the ruined faces and bodies flipped by.

At last came the drawings of Powell, handsome, whole – oh, how they made her ache. Did Vincent see the likeness? She waited for him to remark upon it, but he did not. He said nothing, and there was an urge in her then to continue talking to him, to tell him things she hadn't been able to tell anyone, to speak the name she was never able to say.

As if he'd read her mind he said, 'Go on. Get it off your chest.' For an instant his hand rested on the back of hers, light as the brush of a wing; how it sizzled, that small place. She glanced down, half expecting to see a flush, but no, there was just the uniform white-ness of her skin. What fine fingers he had; she would love to draw those hands. Not quite clean, there was a nicotine stain between the tips of the index and middle finger on the right; his nails were unevenly cut; and there was a ridge of what appeared to be yellow paint under his thumbnail, but they were elegant, tapered hands.

Vincent lit two cigarettes. She did not bother with the holder but put hers between her own lips, tilted her head back and sucked the smoke right to the bottom of her lungs, held it for three and exhaled, enjoying the fuzziness it brought. And then she closed her eyes and began to speak, slowly at first and then in a rush. She told him everything, but really it was as if he wasn't there. She was hear-ing it herself, hearing her own voice saying the things that had been locked up, and, oh, the relief of letting it all out and, most of all, of saying Powell's name out loud.

When she stopped and opened her eyes it was as if the room had changed colour. Everything appeared magnified and bright. She took a sip of brandy, which, rather than making her drunk, caused her mind to shine bright and clear. A silvery spider dangled from a thread attached to the ceiling; from outside came the clop of a horse's hooves and a friendly cry of greeting.

Her voice came to a stop. Powell's face was there in the sketchbook, grey on white; her fingertip stroked the skin of his cheek and it felt warm. 'So he was killed and I survived and came back and married Dennis and had Edgar and that was that,' she finished flatly.

The spider was twizzling down close to their heads now. She sipped her brandy, shut her eyes.

'Quite a *that*,' Vincent remarked.

Clem shook her head, tasted the bitterness of her own smile. 'An everyday story of war, isn't it? Not half as bad as some.'

She had not told all though. She had not mentioned Aida. Why not? It would have made no difference to Vincent. But instead she pulled away her hand, swung her legs to the floor and reached for her shoes. Sensible brogues for a wet day, for a doctor's wife; her fingers trembled with the laces. And then she sat up again and took out her new sketchbook: 'There's something else I want you to see.' She flipped past pages of flowers and fruit to the sketches of Vincent.

He took the book from her hands, and as he looked she compared his face to that on the page, recognising at once that the dimensions were all wrong. She'd given him the flare of Powell's nostrils whereas his own were narrower, rather pinched, and she'd misremembered the angle of his jaw.

'Me?' he said. 'Why?'

'I have to draw,' she said. 'I have to draw what interests me.'

'Me?' He gave a little snort, tickled by the idea.

She took a breath. 'I wonder whether you might sit for me?'

'Sit?'

'As a model? Yes. Look, Vincent, how about this? I pay you to sit for me, then you'll be earning the money fair and square?'

Vincent was slipping his feet back into his shoes and she felt a twinge of disapproval that he did this without unlacing them. She returned the sketchbooks to her bag.

'Just *sit*?' he said.

She put on her own shoes, went to the mirror, stooped to adjust her hat. 'I'll give you the money now, as a gesture of trust, and then we'll meet and you shall sit and I shall sketch.'

He had his own coat on now, his own hat. They were two fully dressed strangers in a cramped little bedroom. 'Where?' he said.

'I'll write to you.'

She handed him the envelope, and this time he gazed at it thoughtfully before sliding it into his inside pocket.

There came a knocking on the door. 'Mr and Mrs Fortune? Are you all right in there?' called the landlady. 'If you don't come out soon I shall have to charge you for the room.'

Clem opened the door and in her frostiest voice said, 'Quite all right, thank you. Fully recovered. Most kind.'

'I shall have to charge you for the brandy in any case.' The landlady's narrowed eyes were darting between Vincent and Clem, the rumpled counterpane and the depleted bottle.

'Naturally,' said Clem. 'Mr Fortune will settle with you downstairs.'

22

'THREE PINTS OF best,' a bloke orders, a young regular, though the name escapes Vince as they natter about the weather, Ireland, Saturday's match. But he can hardly keep a straight face, can hardly contain himself. She's going to pay him to 'sit'? To 'sit'! Fancy being paid to sit! It's priceless – but that's the joke of it; it's precisely *not* priceless. Pricey's more like it, pricey for her. He takes the money, gives the change, nice satisfying ring of the till, rubs his hands. He can string it out – to kingdom come if need be. Her pale eyes come to him, how they pinked up when her story came out. Truth be told, he felt sorry for her: but she hardly needs pity, married to a doctor, living in that bloody great house. Talk about falling on your feet!

'And a port and lemon for the lady.' It's the butcher from Seckford, didn't catch what else he wanted. Concentrate, and go on about the weather again, Ireland, the match. He'd love to tell Doll about getting paid for sitting on his arse! But she might not like it in a man, might think it makes him sound like a right nancy boy; best keep it quiet.

She comes out with a plate of ham sandwiches and puts them on the bar. He takes the money for the butcher's drinks. Doll pulls a pint now, gives him a look, nods at a table of empty glasses.

It's mid-evening of a Friday, busiest night of the week, and she's got a navy gingham dress on, hair piled high, rouge on her cheeks, all corseted up. Why does she have to go and do that? It gives her a battleship shape instead of all that softness; still, it does make a man proud to be associated. They still haven't had their ' little talk'. Perhaps it's all blown over whatever it was, ten to one some tizzy about nothing.

'Just popping upstairs to see Kenny's in bed,' she says, hand brushing his arm. 'Ten minutes.'

He pulls a couple of pints of stout, laughs at a joke he's heard a hundred times, fishes some pickled onions from the jar; all the regulars in tonight plus some passing trade, and there's the thwack of darts, the rattle of dominos, but above all the babble and shout of the end of the week, there's Clarke who comes in of a Friday, regular as clockwork with his mates to play cards – all of them missing something, a leg or both or an arm or a hand, and that one, Ellis, is it? Missing both arms and an eye.

'Pint of Adnams, if you please, sir.' Vince turns, a greeting rising to his lips, and it's only bloody Ted Chamberlain after all these weeks. His heart plummets like a lead weight. Didn't expect to see him again, but here he is, large as life, moustache like a bloody great dead hamster on his lip.

'Coming up,' Vince says, holding a tankard, a little chipped, he sees too late – oh well, under the tap. He keeps his eyes on the froth as he puts it on the counter. 'Ninepence, if you please.'

'Keeping well?' Ted slaps down some coins and takes a swig.

'Tolerable,' Vince says. 'Yourself?'

'Tolerable.' Ted yawns, revealing yellow teeth, a chalky tongue. 'Where's the lady of the house?'

'She'll be down presently, just seeing to the kiddie.'

'Nice little chap, isn't he?' Ted says. 'Wants a father figure, I reckon though, twists her round his little finger.'

Every hair on Vince's head and body bristles. What right's he got to go talking about Kenny like that when he's only met him the once? Oh, you can see he's got ambitions.

'He's good as gold when it's just me, him and his mum,' he lies. 'Got any kiddies of your own?'

Ted looks down into his beer. 'As it happens I have a daughter, looked after by my sister since my good lady passed away.'

'I'm sorry to hear that,' Vince says, allowing a beat of sympathy. 'How old's she?'

'Twelve, lives in Cambridge. I see her every week or two. Happy enough with her auntie and cousins though.'

Vince nods, uneasy at the chink of sadness; that's something a soft heart like Doll's would take to. She likes an underdog, but an underdog with teeth. Yes, that's what Vince is, an underdog now, maybe, or so it seems. But he has that bite, that attack, that officer capacity that will see him through this campaign, and see him victorious.

Ted makes his way to an empty stool at the end of the bar. He perches his fat arse on it, and as he fills his pipe you can see his eyes going to the back of the bar, waiting for Doll to emerge. Stay up there, Vince thinks, stay up there. Put your feet up for half an hour.

It's plain what Ted's up to: seeing a ready-made mum in Doll, seeing them as a family unit – Mum, Dad, sister, brother. Oh, it's so bleeding obvious what he's after. And he's got the money to back it up too. But remember the picnic; that didn't go off as planned. Hang on to that, Vincey boy – something went awry that day.

When Doll comes down she's got fresh rouge on, a touch too much in his opinion, and she clocks Ted but doesn't go across at once. 'Little tinker didn't even have his jimjams on,' she says to

Vince. 'Said you'd be up in a tick and give him what for if he's not in bed.' Shame Ted didn't hear that – put that in his pipe and smoke it.

Doll takes a tray of drinks over to the amputees and stops to pass the time of day; she's always kind to them. One of them, Vince doesn't know the name, lights a fag and sticks it in Ellis's mouth, lifts the glass to his mouth so he can drink. Watching that makes Vince thank his lucky stars. Two legs, two arms – imagine not even being able to wipe your own arse.

As he serves drinks, Vince keeps an eye on Ted and on Doll. They're watching each other all right, even though she doesn't go up to him, and he just sits there biding his time, nursing his pint, puffing away at his pipe.

'Go up, dear,' Doll urges and he has no choice. Upstairs he finds Kenny kneeling on the hearthrug, still dressed, playing with a cotton-reel tank, trying to get it to climb a little pile of cinders he's built.

'Your mum sent me up to give you a rocket,' Vince says.

'Watch,' Kenny says. He picks the tank up and twists the matchstick round and round, winding the rubber band tight, and then sets it down and they watch the thing battering itself against a lump of clinker and finally starting to climb, then toppling off.

'That's too steep for it,' Vince says. 'Get your hands washed now and into your pyjamas.'

'Just one more try,' Kenny says. 'We could build a ramp.'

'Tomorrow,' Vince says. If it wasn't for Ted down there, he'd spend time with the boy now; whatever Kenny wants, Doll wants. Get him on side and half the battle's won. 'Tell you what, tomorrow we'll make another one, then we can have a race, make an obstacle course, eh?'

'No, *now*!' Kenny says. Under his shorts his little knees are rough with grazes, grimed with coal dust. His face and neck are smeared with dirt – and the state of his hands! What he wants is a proper scrub but no time for that.

'Bed,' Vince says. Yes. The boy needs a firm hand.

'Don't want to.' Kenny starts winding the matchstick again.

'School tomorrow.'

'So?' He sets the cotton reel climbing and Vince snatches it up.

'I'm telling Mum,' Kenny says, face gone red. 'Who are *you* anyway with your tin eye?'

Vince puts the toy on the mantelpiece. 'Never mind my tin eye. Any more of your lip and you'll get a tin ear.'

Kenny makes a farting sound and Vince's hand itches to carry out his threat.

'Mum reckons you're a sad sap,' Kenny says.

'And I reckon you're a cheeky little toerag,' Vince says. 'Into that bedroom with you. Now.'

The boy hesitates, peering at Vince's face to try to gauge how serious he is, but he does go, dragging his feet, slamming the door behind him. Vince breathes steadily and unclenches his fists. Kids! He gives the fire a vicious poke, shovels on more coal. The hearth is gritty with clinker and the chimney furred up. That wants a sweep; he'll see to that, get a sweep in tomorrow. *Sad sap*. She never said that, she never would've said that.

He gives the boy a minute or two and then he goes in. His clothes are in a heap on the floor and he's in his pyjamas. Not washed by the look of him, but you can't have everything.

'Goodnight,' he says. 'Sleep tight and that.'

Kenny glares at him.

Vince looks round at the mess: scattered bits of jigsaw, toy cars, a tin gorilla that clashes cymbals together when you wind it. He picks this up and together they watch it weakly stamp and clash a few times before it tips over sideways. 'You want a good tidy up in here,' he says. 'Done your homework?'

'It was only some sums.'

'What happened on the picnic?' Vince asks.

'What?'

'That picnic you went on with Mum and Mr Chamberlain.'

'Don't remember.'

Vince waits. Eventually Kenny says, 'We went in his motorcar. It's an Austin Seven. Seen it?'

'And?'

'He drove really fast till Mum got cross. Then we had sausage rolls and ginger beer and we was going to have an ice-cream, but Mum slapped him and we came straight home with no ice.'

'Why'd she slap him?' Vince asks.

Kenny shrugs.

'I'll get you an ice, next chance,' Vince promises.

'Promise?'

'Hop into bed now.'

'Will you do me a trick?'

'Tomorrow.'

'Teach me one?'

'Can't go giving my secrets away.' Vince taps his nose.

The boy climbs into bed and picks up his comic. 'Go on,' he says. 'I won't tell.'

'Night-night.' Vince closes the door. Job done. It's not so hard, is it? You just have to be firm. Christ, he was sergeant of a regiment, should be able to get one little kiddie into line!

Slapped Ted, eh? Interesting. Downstairs he finds the blighter propping up the bar, Doll leaning over, talking to him, serious faces.

'Little tyke,' Vince says, butting in. 'Took some doing but he's in bed now.'

Doll turns and gives him a vague smile. 'Oh, you're ever so good, dear,' she says and squeezes his arm. That doesn't go down well with Ted the look he gives him. 'Clear them glasses, will you?' Doll says, 'Just having a word with Teddy here.'

Closing at last. Ted had left soon after his talk with Doll. Vince, ears on stalks, had tried to get the gist, but picked up nothing – nothing but the way he squeezed her hand before he left, the way her eyes followed him to the door.

'Go easy, dear,' Doll said when Vince tried – a bit too force-fully – to eject Amos. But he couldn't help it. He felt jumpy. What was that bloody smarmy bastard after?

They cleared away the glasses, emptied the ashtrays. Doll always insisted on that of a night; the rest could wait till morning. She seemed distracted.

'Penny for them?' Vince said. 'Shall we have a nightcap?'

He hoped a nightcap might lead to more but she shook her head. 'Tell you the truth, I'd rather have a cuppa. Be a dear and make a pot, will you, and bring it up? My feet are killing me. Should never've worn these shoes.'

She'd stomped up the stairs and he'd stood twitching before the sluggish kettle. Come on. Come on. Could he just come straight out with it and ask what that was all about? It looked like a pact, that hand squeeze. Asking her out again, was he? Another crack at the picnic? Or something more than that, worse than that? Unease slithered in his gut, muscles twitched and tugged at the scar. What to do, what to do? Think like a soldier. Strategy – the best form of defence is attack.

Upstairs he finds Doll with her feet up on the arm of the sofa. She opens her eyes as he comes into the room with a tea tray.

'Nearly nodding off,' she says, and gives another great yawn. 'You are a dear,' she adds, clocking the tray.

'You want to get out of that corset.' Vince goes to the fire and stirs the embers.

'Blooming cheek!' She giggles tiredly. 'What do you know about corsets?'

'I know what's under them.'

She snorts and swings her legs round. 'You're the limit! Go on then, pour us a cuppa.' The gas lamp sputters; Vince turns it up, pours her tea, milky with two sugars the way she likes it.

She takes the cup, blows on it, then sips noisily. Some has slopped into the saucer and she tips it back into the cup, blows and sips again. Vince stands, leaning on the mantelpiece, lights a cig.

'Bit of a struggle to get Kenny down,' he says. 'But he went like a lamb in the end.'

She smiles tiredly, opens her mouth to speak, takes a preparatory breath, changes her mind, drinks more tea.

He picks up the tank from the mantelpiece, winds the matchstick and holds it while it twizzles round. 'Got an empty cotton reel going spare? We're making another tank so we can race. I said I'd teach him some tricks.'

'Listen, dear.' She hesitates. 'You know I wanted a word with you the other day?'

He nods, taps his ash into a saucer, scar tissue contracting.

'It's been nice having you to stay and help and all, and you've been lovely with my Kenny – I know he's not always the easiest of kiddies – but you know I have to make allowances. What with him losing his daddy and everything.'

'Exactly. What he wants is a man around the place.'

She sighs. 'Yes, dear, but I don't want you adding two and two and making five.'

'What does that mean? I can add up all right.' He tries to keep his voice light. He kneels down. 'Poor old trotters, let's have a go at them.' He knows she can't resist that. He's getting to know her so well; she's the type who takes the path of least resistance. He picks up one of her feet, flesh spongy and ridged where her shoes were digging in, lumpy little darns in the rayon. He pulls her toes the way she loves and she sighs. 'Ooh, that's lovely, that is.'

'How about,' he says and stops – an idea like a bloody great hothouse flower suddenly blooming in his mind. Get her right away from here, from bloody Chamberlain, woo her properly. He takes up her other foot. Here he is kneeling at a woman's feet! Who'd have thought it?

Her eyes have been shut in bliss but she opens them to look at him. 'How about what? Ooh, yes, squeeze like that.'

'A break, a little holiday. Walton-on-the-Naze.'

'If pigs could fly,' she murmurs.

'Maybe they can. Just think how Kenny would love it. We could get him a bucket and spade and a windmill and that.'

'Cost an arm and a leg though, wouldn't it? And I'd have to shut up shop.'

'You leave all that to me,' he says, squeezing the fleshy ends of her toes one at time. 'This little piggy went to market,' he says.

'You fool!'

'This little piggy stayed at home. This little piggy had roast beef.' He bites the end of the toe quite sharply and she shrieks. 'This little piggy had none – oh, poor piggy – but *this* little piggy' – he tugs her little toe – '*this* little piggy cried wee wee wee all the way home!' And he runs his hands right up her stocking under her skirt and she laughs and slaps, but she doesn't stop him. He reaches the naked flesh where the stocking ends – hasn't been this far since God knows when – and she begins to sigh as he burrows his finger-tips into the clammy place beneath her drawers.

'Vincey,' she whispers, 'you're a devil you are.'

23

THE LANDLADY GIVES him a very iffy look when he walks in, and jerks her chin towards the stairs. 'She's here, same room.' Can't blame her for thinking this a rum do. It's a rum do all right. And he's late and all.

After he parked the bike he got a fit of the jitters, crossed the bridge, smoked a cig on the riverbank, watching the water and the boats, a swan – vicious brutes, they are, have your eye out given half a chance. Ha! What a laugh! But the scar tugs and flinches just as if a beak was jabbing in.

Now he mounts the stairs. Doesn't mind admitting he's nervous. Is she going to want him to strip off? That's what life modelling means, everyone knows that. Does 'sit' mean sit or is he going to have to sprawl on the bed with a rose between his teeth? He sniggers at this as he makes his way along the corridor and knocks at the door.

'I thought we said ten?' says Mrs Married.

'I'm here now.'

She looks different, hat off, sleeves of her blouse rolled up, hair a messy bundle. She's pulled the curtains away from the windows so the room's brighter and she's all set up with her sketchbook, pencils, a little box of paints.

'What on earth did you say to *her*?' He points at the floor.

'Only the truth.'

'She'll be thinking all sorts!' he says.

'She can think what she likes. We have until one o'clock.'

'I'll have to be off before that.'

'Best get started directly, then. Hat and coat off, please.'

Vince turns his back on her to remove them, and to adjust the specs. 'All right. Where do you want me?'

She arranges him on a chair – literally sitting, and fully clothed, thank Christ – beside the window. Her plan, she tells him, is to sketch him quickly from different angles, only five minutes or so of stillness each time, and then she'll ask him to hold a position for half an hour while she goes into more detail.

It's all right. Hard to let someone stare at you like that at first though. For the past couple of years he's shied away from that kind of scrutiny, but she isn't looking at him like a person, more like a thing. It's not personal. Last time someone looked at him like that . . . A shudder right up his spine remembering the tin-nose shop. The physical memory returns and he grits his teeth. The woman artist standing so close, painting the prosthesis to match the other side of his face, her breath smelling of something sour as well as peppermints, a crumb of sleep in the corner of one eye. She did a bloody good job though, he had to give her that. That memory swims at him now as if through a snowstorm and he blinks to dispel it.

Mrs M. hums under her breath as she sketches, does she realise? Talk about easy money though! Think about the holiday, get that sorted before Ted pounces. Last night he remembers with a snort.

'Can you hold still, please?' she says.

He holds his neck stiff – needs to swallow, surely that's all right? Last night the bloody chancer turned up again, parked himself up at the end of the bar as if he owned the place, hanging around like a bad smell till Doll stopped for a chat. Left Vince run ragged.

'Could do with a hand here,' he called out in the end.

'Well, I could've done with a hand earlier,' she said in that dear grumpy way she had. Vince grinned and shrugged at Ted, man to man, quite the henpecked hubby!

'How's the boy?' Ted asked later and Doll started on about his poor school report.

'I could give him a hand with his sums,' Ted said. 'Got quite a way with numbers, me.'

'I bet you have!' Doll treated him to that special smile, and Vince, though he hadn't meant to make it definite till the money was in his pocket, blurted, 'Has Doll told you what we've got in store?'

Ted shook his head and Doll pulled a face, just like she'd been caught out in something.

'Two pints of light and bitter when you're ready,' called someone. There was a proper scrum building up at the bar.

'I'm taking Doll and Kenny on a holiday,' he said.

Ted's face when he heard that!

'Keep still, please,' says Mrs M.

'Nothing's decided,' Doll said.

'A holiday, eh?' Ted pulled his chin in, reached for his pipe, fingers worming in his tobacco pouch.

'We're dying of thirst over here,' called some wag.

'No rest for the wicked,' Doll said. 'Come on, Vince.' They set to pulling pints, leaving Ted to stew in his own juices.

Mrs M. sighs, tears out and screws up a sheet of paper. 'You've got rather a smirk – can you try to look more neutral?'

He obliges. Of course he'll have to bring in temporary bar staff, and then there's train tickets, hotel, how many rooms? Will she let him share hers? Probably not with Kenny there. So, one room with a double bed, one with two singles, and then he can shift in the night once the boy's dropped off. They'll look just like a proper little family. Perhaps he'll get Kenny a kite. They can kick a ball, paddle in the sea, and the kid can scoff candy floss and ice-cream till it comes out of his ears. And when the moment's right he'll grab Doll's hand and pop the question and he won't take no for an answer. He needs a ring though, something to slip on that finger. He eyes Mrs M.'s sparkler – but that would never fit his Doll.

'Can you sit still?' she says. 'No, on second thoughts move a bit and I'll start again. Turn your face this way a bit – that's it.'

How much is he going to get per time? Should have got that straight from the start: first rule of business, agree the terms. Odd business this though, not actual graft. But it is taking time, it is a job, and it deserves a decent hourly rate.

On the jaw the skin's thick, scraped clean with a razor; higher on the cheek the texture's finer, a slight trace of white scar, a faint freckle here and there, and then the transition to the metal. Whoever painted this was an artist; it's an exquisite piece of work. She sketches the arms of the specs – clear glass, it appears, an ingenious way to hold the mask on. Makes him look clever too. But he's aged since it was made. In his real eye socket the skin is thin and shadowed and there are lines, and at the corner of his eye a deep spray of crow's feet. He's caught the sun a bit too, so the colour is not quite matched. The eyebrow is painted like the real one but there are hairs emerging from behind it; the bony ridge retains some follicles.

'Move, please,' she says. 'Have a good wriggle, then look at me straight on.'

A mistake. It's unsettling to have him focused on her; she begins to feel self-conscious, unable to lose herself in detail. 'No. Look over there.' She indicates somewhere over her right shoulder, turns the page, selects a harder pencil and begins again, this time picking out the thinning hair pushed back from his forehead. How old is he? Thirty-seven? Forty, even? Or perhaps not quite; the war aged people. Yet her own skin is perfect, creamy, flawless. Like her mother's, they say, who had not a single line on her face when she died at thirty-six. Clem could almost wish for a flaw, a scar – something to show for all she's seen, for Ralph's death, for Powell's.

'All right?' Vince says.

'Move a little that way. That's it.'

Concentrate. Just the eyes this time: first, the real eye, the char-coal rim around the silvery grey, the pupil small, the lashes sandy, the pinkish lid, slight droop of the skin beneath the brow, the neat brown hairs; the simulacrum so faithfully painted to match in colour, the dreamy far-off gaze of it. Powell's gaze in the pigment – impossible but true. There he is. Powell. Steadfast, loving, everlastingly distant.

The pencil drops.

'One minute.' She scrabbles for it at her feet, face filling with blood as she stoops, notices a cigarette burn on the green rug. Stop this foolishness. Up she sits. He returns to the pose. On the side of the nose is a tiny sliver of shadow where the prosthesis isn't quite snug against the skin. Her eyes are drawn to it, drawn into the darkness. No. Return to the eye: the lashes, tiny fragments of wire, some damaged, the smoother skin around it, the eyebrow with its minute feathered brushstrokes.

'Have a rest,' she says. 'You're doing well.' He gets up and stalks about, yawns and stretches while she examines her work. Good. Curiously, the prosthesis appears more real in her sketch than the rest of his live face. Oh . . . powerfully it comes to her again: she wants to see behind it. She wants, needs, to really see it, see *him*. Vincent Fortune. She needs to touch the place, like a blind person, run her fingertips over the skin. She needs to draw it, make it her own.

He's looking at her oddly. A noble man, so noble in his cheerfulness, the way he tries against the odds. Look at him. He worked his way up through his regiment, only to get spat out the other end, disfigured, everything lost: looks, wife, livelihood. Her heart overflows with tenderness. Not only for Mr Fortune, but for all the damaged people. And for myself, she thinks, with my perfect skin, my blasted heart. I need to see him.

There's quiet for a moment. Her breath is constricted.

'You all right?' he says at last.

'Would you consider removing the . . . ?' Her hand goes to her own left eye and she sees him stiffen, confusion like a cloud across his face. 'It would make a marvellous companion piece.'

'I'd sooner not if it's all the same to you,' he says stiffly.

'It would help me,' she says. 'Please.'

He watches her, mouth a little open. She sees his tongue lick the centre of his bottom lip. 'Help you?' he says, and is there now a sort of cunning, a calculation?

'To see you . . . to see you as you are.'

'How'd that help? You'll be wanting me to strip off next!'

She says nothing. The pencil's pinched tight between her fingers. All the strings of all her muscles are taut as bowstrings as if the pencil could fly like an arrow and pierce his heart.

He waits for her to speak and she closes her eyes as she tries to make sense of what she wants: 'You see, my wound's invisible.'

'Aren't you the lucky one?' he says bitterly.

'No, listen. It's in here.' She makes a fist to press against her breastbone. 'But yours is . . . well, if I saw it, if I . . . I think if I drew it, made it *mine*, it would help me.'

He walks around the tiny room, creaking the boards. 'What's in it for me?' he says finally.

'I'll pay more,' she says.

'How much.'

'I don't know – *more*.'

He turns away from her, regards his own face in the mirror above the mantelpiece. She watches him from behind, catches the tremble of tension. When he speaks he sounds muffled. 'I've never even seen myself like that,' he says.

'You don't ever look in the mirror without it?'

She can't imagine that. In her bedroom, in the bathroom, in the mirror in the hall, her face is her own companion. She searches for a flaw, for a sign that she's alive; she sits in front of the mirror brushing and brushing her hair . . . Oh, Powell, the day he washed her hair at the beginning of the life she should be leading. A tear slides from her eye and though her practice is not to cry in front of *anyone*, she lets the tears fall. They drop on the paper; strange that they are transparent, one could almost expect them to be red.

She shudders. Perhaps in another version of life, I *am* living with Powell in Canada; perhaps we ride horses on the ranch with our little Aida; perhaps we have another by now; perhaps I'm happy there, and this is only a dream, the shadow side. A wicked, wicked thought comes to her: that she'd give this up in an instant, this life – yes, even Edgar – if that could be true.

He sits beside her on the bed and puts an arm around her shoulders. 'There, there,' he says awkwardly.

193

'Please,' she says. He puts a hand on the base of her neck and the sensation is enormously comforting. Her eyelids close. Didn't Powell's hand rest on her neck like that? *Powell, Powell.* She feels the hand tighten and lift and knead and her mouth opens and his mouth is on hers – there's a hesitation as he waits for her reaction – and she receives the kiss in a way she's received no kiss since Powell's.

'This what you want?' he says.

'Don't speak,' she murmurs, eyes shut fast, breath coming fast. It's as if flames are flickering over her lower body, an irresistible urge, and when he lays her down, when he pulls up her dress it's Powell, and, oh, how her breath comes fast and how he enters her, and she's in Canada and happy with him out on the prairie in the fresh, fresh air, galloping, oh, and galloping and galloping, and something happens that she's never known – a complete extinction, an enormous soft explosion. Oh, please, let it never end, and she's hanging onto him, onto Powell, for dear life, as if she's sinking – until it fades and she's aware of the sound of breath, a crash outside like the dropping of a dustbin lid. She keeps her eyes closed because when she opens them she'll have to know what she has done.

'All right?' he says. Rough, common English voice.

They are lying side by side on the shiny green coverlet. A fly buzzes near the ceiling. She pulls down her skirt. He sits up with his back to her, lifts his hands to remove the prosthesis, turns and lies down with his face only inches from her own. Her fingers lift to touch him; he flinches but doesn't prevent her. The socket is a cup of puckered scar, knotted yellow in places, purple in others – rough, bristly, smooth, shiny, ridged. A landscape in miniature.

Something happens in her heart or in her soul or in what she doesn't know, some giving way. So this is it. This is all it is. She kisses him softly right where his eye should be, and to her amazement she sees a tear rise from a tiny fissure. There's no eye but still, a functioning tear duct. With a feeling of enormous tenderness, of completion, she cradles his head and they are held in a moment like that until abruptly he pulls back.

He twists away, pulls himself upright and replaces the prosthesis, adjusts his clothing, tucks in his shirt. 'That what you wanted?' he says. 'Satisfied?'

She stares up at him, pulls her knees to her chest and leans back against the headboard. She has no words. The tenderness in her is gone, reaching like tendrils of ivy in the sudden absence of a tree. In a moment perhaps there will be shame – but now she's numb and glowing and the shock of his words, his aggressive stance, is too much, too staggering a transition.

'Time I was off,' he says. 'I reckon a bit more for that, don't you? I reckon fifty should cover it.'

Her mouth opens.

'Fifty to be sent to me care of the Wild Man.'

She presses the back of her head against the headboard, cold liquid seeping between her legs. Of course it was not Powell, of course not. She looks at her own hands and up at his painted eye, which is only a painted eye.

'I'll give you till Friday,' he says. 'And if not, well, I don't reckon Dr Everett's going to be too impressed.'

She can only stare.

'See, there's witnesses to us coming up here. The landlady for starters. I'll get her to have a look at the state of the bed after you've gone.'

He puts on his jacket and his hat, checks himself in the mirror and leaves the room. Perhaps an hour ticks past before she can move. She gets up from the bed, tidies herself, gathers her pencils and sketchbook, stows everything in her bag. Her hair's a mess. She screws it up and pins on her hat. Her cheeks are hot, scarlet. She smooths the bedspread and goes downstairs to pay the landlady.

24

Hot, so hot, the sun striking up from the pavement as she fled, heels hammering, past the Post Office, the flowers, hair escaping from her hat. She paused to tidy herself outside Mrs Fletcher's Hairdressing Parlour. The door stood open; it looked cool in there, and she could see no customers.

Her feet took her inside and her voice said to the girl beside the till, 'I'd like a bob. Might you have time now?'

'I'll ask madam.' The girl gave her a queer look and flitted through a curtain to the back of the shop. Clem sat down heavily. Don't think yet, don't think. She remembered the months in bed after Edgar, the way the world ticked on without her, the beautiful blur. That lovely softness you get from Veronal. A dose now – oh, how that would soothe, make it all float away.

Mrs Fletcher, a young woman, her own dark hair short and Marcel waved, agreed to cut Clem's hair, once she'd been reassured that Dr Everett had consented. 'We've no end of trouble with hubbies coming in raging on about us robbing them of their wives' crowning glories and such and such.' She laughed as she removed Clem's hat and lifted the tangled hair between her hands. 'You sure you want it *all* off?'

'A short bob.'

'You could sell this – it'd make a marvellous wig.'

'You're welcome to it.'

'Thanks very much, I'm sure.'

Over Clem's shoulder, Mrs Fletcher tilted her head in the mirror. 'I reckon it'll suit you. Maisie, wash madam's hair for me,' she instructed the girl. As the warm water poured over her scalp, Clem gritted her teeth, driving Powell from her mind. Oh, but it had felt like Powell; in her *heart* it had been Powell.

As Maisie combed out the wet strands, Clem gazed at her own face, cheeks flushed, eyes like painted eyes, unfocused. And then came Mrs Fletcher, snapping her scissors, the soft scrunch of the blades through thick hanks, the gradual sensation of lightness. Now every scrap of hair that Powell had touched was gone.

'Want a nice wave?' Mrs Fletcher asked, but Clem shook her head, liking the thick blunt ends of the straight hair that touched her jaw. It appeared darker than before, almost light brown with silvery lights. And when she walked out, she felt that she'd shed something heavy and soiled. Though it was difficult to keep her hat on. New hats would be required for this new style. New hats and dresses too.

Money – a clutch in her stomach – money for hats, for frocks, of course, she'd need money. But fifty pounds? No, don't think about that now.

Hale did a comical double-take when, as arranged, he picked her up, but ventured no comment. The church bell chimed three times as they drove away. Dennis would still be in surgery and she hoped to be able to get into the house and up the stairs, to wash, to change, to collect herself, before he came up for tea and the inevitable argument. But it was a *fait accompli*; hair cannot be uncut. Until tonight when she soothed him in the way he liked – the thought of that sent a bolt of shame through her. But she should have to. And once again she should have to ask for money.

Oh, what that man said about witnesses! Despicable creature. It was like something from a penny dreadful. And the mean, knowing expression of the landlady, eyes sharp with judgement, lips pursed tight. Oh, what had she done? It was as if she was waking, coming to: hot and shorn, a scarlet woman. Keep your eyes open, she told herself, for when she blinked there was the dim green room, the rumpled bed, the naked face. What had she done? A married woman. There was no excuse. No Powell. Powell was gone. This was real life. And what happened she had let happen. She did. It was no one else's fault. And what happened next she must . . . somehow she must orchestrate it so that Dennis should never know. Nor Harri, nor Edgar. All must be kept safe and innocent of her . . . slip.

The car drew up outside the house and, quietly, Clem let herself in, hung up her hat, made for the stairs but . . .

'Surprise!' crowed Harri, jumping out into the hall followed by the twins. Clem shrieked and then Harri shrieked, and the girls shrieked. 'My God!' said Harri.

'Auntie Clem?' said one of the twins uncertainly, and the two of them stood staring up at her with their round hazel eyes.

'What on earth are *you* doing here?' Clem said – fearfully rude, she knew. But, *Harri,* here!

Harri tweaked Clem's hair. 'What does Dennis think?'

'I've only just had it done.'

Mrs Hale came hurrying into the hall. 'Whatever's the matter?'

Harri was laughing now. 'Oh, it's all right, Halesy. We frightened each other half to death! Look at Clemmie's hair!'

Clem stood and let them look. In the hallstand mirror she could see herself: smaller-headed it seemed, sleek, her face sharper, satisfyingly different.

'Is it pretty?' asked a twin doubtfully.

'Goodness gracious me,' said Mrs Hale. 'I'd have walked straight past you in the street, madam.'

'*Madam!*' Harri laughed. 'Honestly! Halesy, bring us some tea and buns and milk for the children, do. And perhaps some bread and butter? Oh, I can't wait to see Dennis's face!'

'It'll be half an hour before the doctor's ready for his tea.'

'You can always refresh the pot,' Harri said. 'Go on,' she wangled childishly.

'Just this once then,' Mrs Hale said, dimpling.

'Isn't she a lamb?' Harri said.

Edgar came staggering out into the hall, and before he could see her Clem fled upstairs. Quick, quick, quick. She stripped off her frock; there were pale prickly hairs all down her camisole, inside too. In the bathroom she scrubbed between her legs and under her arms with a soapy flannel, splashed her face with cold water and then put on one of her cooler dresses – cream shantung, shin-length, loose over her stomach and hips. Certainly she needed new dresses now, jackets; most of her clothes were old-fashioned, they would not suit her hair. An idea began to form . . . she *would* get the money and all *would* be well.

When she entered the sitting room Edgar stared at her wide-eyed, and when she stretched her arms out, backed away.

'It's still Mama,' Harri said. 'Oh, bless his heart, he doesn't know you!' She was gleeful and envious, circling Clem as if she was an exhibit. 'I'm getting mine done,' she said. 'Only I'll have to lose a bit of weight. You look so young and' – she giggled – 'rather like a boy.'

Clem ran her fingers through the hair, enjoying the way it swung back into place and the cool lightness about her neck.

'I bet you D.'ll say, "You look like a flapper"! I bet you a shilling. Deal?'

The usually tidy room was strewn with bricks and a tin spinning top and some bright wooden threading beads escaping from their string.

'So what brings you here?' Clem winced at her own formality. 'Oh, sorry, you know what I mean.'

Harri was fingering a tail of her own bushy hair that tumbled as usual from a messy bun. She looked flushed and matronly in her antiquated blouse and skirt, the latter splashed with paint. Her hands seamed with it too. 'Oh, I don't know. I do miss the place and I shall want the girls to feel at home here as they grow up.' She giggled. 'Fancy Mrs Hale calling you madam!'

'I don't give a fig what she calls me,' said Clem.

'It's what she called Mum, but it seems so . . .' She threw up her hands. 'Anyway, *you* haven't been to see *us* for an age.' Harri jutted out her lip like a sulky child. 'And the twinnies wanted to see Eddie, and I just thought, if the mountain won't come to Mohammed.'

'Actually I had thought of coming to you today but . . .' Clem touched her hair. 'This happened instead.'

Harri sat on the sofa and Claris – was it? Yes, the larger twin – clambered onto her lap. 'And . . . I have been rather sneaky,' Harri said, a smile dancing in her eyes.

'How?'

Edgar had made his way over to Clem and stood unsteadily looking up at her, a finger in his dribbly mouth.

'Touch.' Clem put her head down to him. He reached out and poked not her hair but her cheek, and as his bright brown eyes met hers, something happened in her chest, a sensation like the twang of a rubber band, and she lifted him onto her lap, rubbed her face in his soft hair. Had she really thought she'd give him up, for an imagined life, this real, warm, solid boy?

Watching, Harri said nothing, but nodded, as if satisfied.

Now that she held him, Clem didn't want to let him go. It was comforting; here she was, back with her family, where she should be and everything was all right. Everything was going to be all right.

Mrs Hale rumbled in with the tea trolley. 'I'll brew another pot when the doctor's ready,' she said.

'Thanks most awfully, Halesy,' Harri said.

'Dinah wants to know if she should take the children up to the nursery?' Mrs Hale said.

'No,' said Harri. 'It's nice having them with us, isn't it, Clem? Let her have an hour off.'

'She can help me in the kitchen then,' Mrs Hale said. 'You know what they say about idle hands.' She went out and they could hear her calling Dinah.

Clem set Edgar down, and they laughed at the way he tottered across the room and sat with a thump on his bottom. Phyllis began teaching him how to build a tower with bricks, Claris cuddled on Harri's lap, the sun flowed through the window through the vase of white roses, shining on the children's heads, and all was well – just for a moment, a moment of balance, the way a drip can hang on a tap for a very long time before it falls.

'Was it something I said?' Harri asked.

Clem shook her head. 'I'm sorry. I've been busy . . . oh, nothing really. Dennis will be so pleased you're here. As I am, of course.'

'Don't worry. I'm not about to move back in.'

Clem rose to pour milk into beakers for the children. 'There's going to be such a mess!' she said, handing out fingers of bread and butter. She popped a piece into her own mouth, realising that she was ravenous. And after all, it was nice to have Harri here, to have a busy, sunny room to preside over, and it would help not to be alone when Dennis came in and saw her hair.

'How sneaky?' she said.

Harri grinned. 'Well, you see, I telephoned Mrs Hale and got the date of Dennis's golf club dinner.'

'Mmm?' The cake was cherry. Clem cut them each a slice and poured the tea.

'And I knew you wouldn't be going, so I made my dastardly plans.'

'What dastardly plans?' Clem took a bite of cake, squashing a glacé cherry between her teeth.

'I've invited Gwen.'

Clem stopped chewing.

'Oh, don't fret. It's all arranged. Mrs Hale's in on it. A ladies' dinner. We're having plaice, beef tournedos and apple snow. Don't look at me like that!'

Clem managed to swallow. 'Why are *you* so keen on seeing Gwen?'

'Why aren't you? She's your friend, isn't she?'

'Yes, but . . . you don't really know her, do you?'

'I'd like to. Bumped into her in Seckford the other day and we got plotting!'

Clem sipped her tea, too hot; it scalded the roof of her mouth.

'And Dinah's happy to have the girls in the nursery tonight. Worked out beautifully as Mildred wanted to visit an aunt who's about to pop off – sadly.' She paused for a moment to look sad, then grinned. 'So I'll be in my old room.'

'Dastardly all right,' Clem managed.

The door opened and Dennis came in. 'Well, well, well, if it isn't the bad penny!' He strode over to Harri and kissed the top of her head, ruffled Claris's hair. 'Good to have you back. That tea still . . .' He turned to Clem and his jaw dropped.

Harri sniggered.

'Good God,' said Dennis.

'Isn't it nice?' Harri said.

'You might have discussed it with me, darling,' he said stiffly.

'Don't be antediluvian,' said Harri. 'It's *her* hair.'

'She looks like a flapper.'

Harri snorted. 'See?' she said, holding out her hand to Clem. 'One shilling, please.'

Dennis stood at the mantelpiece and lit himself a cigarette.

'Oh yes, since you offer,' said Harri and, grumpily, he lit one for her.

Clem said nothing though she would have liked one too, would have liked something to do with her fingers. Instead she squashed crumbs onto her plate, licked them off her fingertips.

Mrs Hale came in with a fresh pot of tea. 'Any more bread and butter, or might you fancy a crumpet, doctor?'

'Everything's in order, thank you,' Clem said when Dennis failed to respond, and Mrs Hale withdrew.

'We'll discuss it later.' Dennis turned, frowning, rammed a piece of bread and butter into his mouth and perched on the arm of the sofa. 'Really,' he said, surveying the buttery smears, 'wouldn't it be prudent for the children to eat in the nursery?'

Clem started as the jack-in-the-box let out a sudden raucous squawk and Phyllis and Edgar crowed with laughter.

'Busy surgery?' she said.

He nodded curtly.

'Oh Lord. Don't sulk Dennis,' said Harri. 'I swear he can sulk for England – remember that time you had your fishing rod confiscated, D.? Face like fizz for a fortnight! And of course he sulked the entire time you were away, Clem.'

Edgar got up and walked a few precarious steps, unbalanced by the top he was holding. 'Good boy,' Dennis said, flicking Clem a dangerous look before he leant over and span the top for him.

Clem watched them, and listened to Dennis and Harri have a tiresome squabble, watched the bright flashing tin of the spinning toy, felt her heart beat, her lungs inflate and deflate, the passage of tea down her gullet – the cake she could not stomach now. Gwen! And still with the feeling of Powell inside her – *not* Powell – tightening, almost aching. And now Gwen arriving, who might so easily mention him. No way to stop her coming. Might she fake an illness?

The sunshine through the window lent everything a glittery provisional air, flashing on Dennis's teeth, the surface of his tea, the burnish on his shoes, the spinning top, on hair and the greasy sheen of butter on the children's chins.

She jumped up. 'Excuse me just one moment.' She closed the door behind her. From the leatherbound address book on the hall table she found the number Gwen had scrawled on her last visit. Tentatively she lifted the receiver, leaned into the round transmitter and waited for the operator's voice to emerge through the crackle. In the sitting room she could hear the babble of children, the drone of Dennis, and then a mocking laugh from Harri.

'Felixstowe 322, please,' she said, as clearly as she dared. There was a long hissing silence. Clem stood hunched like a thief in her own hall; she caught sight of herself, thin-faced and furtive, in the mirror.

'Putting you through,' said the operator, and then came Gwen's strident voice. 'Yes?'

'It's Clementine,' said Clem.

'I was about to set off.'

'Glad I caught you then. About this evening, we'll have to postpone, I'm afraid – tummy bugs all round.'

'Oh? Harri only telephoned this morning, she was all right then.'

'A sudden thing. I'm so sorry.'

The silence crackled with disbelief.

'Gwen?' said Clem.

'Get well soon,' Gwen said, and there was a click.

Clem put the receiver down and turned to see Mrs Hale regarding her quizzically.

'It turns out that Miss Carslake won't be coming this evening after all,' Clem said, 'so dinner for just the two of us, please.'

'Very good, madam,' said Mrs Hale.

Clem hurried up the stairs. She went into her studio with its new blue walls and pressed her forehead against the cool glass of the window. Green and grey out there and she could hear the cooing of a wood pigeon. Her little studio arranged for her by Dennis and never used, not yet. The sketches, the sketches of Mr Fortune: should she destroy them? They would be evidence certainly, but maybe evidence that her intentions were pure? It was about art, and that was all. No one could prove the other thing, the unplanned thing, the bad, bad thing.

But fifty pounds, where on earth could she get fifty pounds? Pounds, pounds, pounds . . . her head began to pound. That wretched man, nothing but a low-class crook.

Might she, quite simply, call his bluff?

25

F RIDAY AFTERNOON VINCE sits at the kitchen table filling in his coupon. It's cosy, what with the kettle coming to a boil and Doll beating some cake batter, bosoms jiggling away under her checked pinny. Like him, she's got a ciggie pinched between her lips. Companionable, that's what you'd call it.

'I've been having a think,' she says.

'God preserve us!'

'Now, Vince, none of your nonsense.'

'What then?'

'What you were saying, about a trip . . . well, I reckon that's not such a bad idea.'

'Oh?' He can hardly credit his own flaming ears.

'Can't be for long, mind,' she says, 'what with this place. But a night away, why not? Kenny hasn't had a holiday since God knows when, poor little tyke.'

'Hmm.' He stares at his coupon, sprinkled with ash now, and fills in some draws – no idea what he's putting. 'Whit weekend?' he suggests.

She dips a finger in the batter and licks it. 'Too busy, it'll have to be midweek – p'raps a Tuesday and Wednesday, what do you reckon?'

'Done,' he says. He's messed up the pools now, can hardly focus.

She pours the batter into a tin, slides it into the oven, then stands with her back to it, pinkie burrowing into her ear.

'You sure you can get someone in?' she says, 'Someone reliable to do, say, two dinnertimes and a night.'

'Or two nights?'

'I wouldn't be able to relax.'

'Just the one then. Walton-on-the-Naze?' he says. 'Ever been?'

'I shall have to think about a new hat,' she says, voice spiked with excitement. 'Wait till I tell Kenny!'

'Let me get it all booked up first, eh?' he says.

'You robbed a bank or something?' she says.

He taps the side of his nose. 'Let me worry about that side of things.'

Nothing from Mrs M. this morning though, he's waiting for the second post.

'Get that cake out in half an hour, will you, dear?' Doll says. And she goes upstairs to tidy herself before catching the bus to fetch Kenny.

He can't believe it. He's *done* it. She wouldn't have said yes if she wasn't serious about him, would she? She wouldn't call him 'dear' like that. So, Mrs M. He doodles two round shocked eyes on the margin of his ruined coupon. Shan't need a win anyway when she pays up. Last thing he expected was a fuck. But she was up for it. He'd have thought she'd be frigid but she surprised him there. You wouldn't think she had it in her – till he put it in her! He sniggers. Grinds out his cig. Still, she weren't a patch on Doll. Useful leverage though: play his cards right and she must be good for a couple of hundred. Connie, landlady at the Crown, she's witness to the goings-on if need be. Yesterday he dropped in for a pint and had a good old chinwag with her. Started out frosty as hell but he unfroze her, spun her a line, and turns out she's got a brother who'll run the Wild Man while they're away, so two birds with one stone. Not bad.

Once he's got the cash he'll be off down that station seeing about tickets; then there's the hotel too. Just think of Doll in that hotel room, all his for the night, undressing . . . He'll help her unlace her stays, those silky pink ribbons.

He hears the letter flap, goes through. A letter for Doll, but that's it. He paces round the empty bar, all ship-shape, ready for five when the first few drinkers turn up. On an afternoon like this they'll carry their pints out front for a breath of air. Sun shining through the stained glass. Here's an idea, a bloody brainwave more like! Why not set up a proper beer garden with tables and chairs? Make a feature of it – flower beds and that, appeal to families out for lunch, a better class of clientele. Dolly'll love it. He'll save it up for when he's got her away on the Naze. In their own little bubble they'll be, a bubble he'll fill with dreams. If he doesn't bring her home with a ring on her finger then . . . he doesn't know what.

The smell of baking drifts through; won't be done yet. Strategy, strategy, get it right. He gets a duster and goes over the bar, rubbing at the brass trim. So. Cash required pronto. She's had a few days with no result. Time to put the frighteners on.

Harri was kneeling at her little border weeding, Mildred perched on a stool by the sandpit supervising the children. Clem sat on a dragged-out kitchen chair with her sketchbook in her lap; she'd caught the curved and chubby children's limbs in play, their smiles and grumps, but now let her pencil go, felt lazy, warm, numb. *Stay numb, stay numb.* So glad to be away from the Beeches this afternoon though soon Hale would arrive to fetch her. They were having the Huberts – old friends of Dennis – for dinner, bound to be one long yawn.

'Look at the state of them!' Harri laughed at the sun-flushed, sandy children.

Clem smiled. Edgar's chin was stippled with the stuff, which looked incongruously like stubble on his manly little face.

'Nearly bathtime, methinks,' Harri said.

'I'll get the water on.' Mildred stood and went inside.

Harri knelt by the sandpit and accepted the handful of sand Edgar solemnly offered. 'Thank you, that looks delicious!' She pretended to eat it. 'Yummy!'

'Don't encourage him!' said Clem.

'Heard from Gwen?' Harri asked.

Caught off-guard, Clem paused, ran her pencil over the sketched curve of Edgar's cheek, added an eyelash. 'Not a dicky bird. I expect she's busy.'

'Still, it was odd of her – rather rude actually – simply not to turn up.'

'Oh, Gwen does what she pleases,' Clem said vaguely. 'It's what she's like.'

'Still.'

'At least it brought *you* to the Beeches. You'll come again?'

'I expect so.' Harri began to speak but her voice seemed to fade, along with the sounds of the children. From the river came a distant hooting from a barge, and though there was no breeze, the leaves on the aspen shivered and shushed.

'I say, are you quite all right, Clemmie?'

Clem blinked. It was only the Veronal; she'd begged Dennis for a draught last night, which had caused her to sleep deeply and numbly – dreams, yes, but jumbled and indistinct. It did render one a bit dazed next day, a little distracted.

'Well, I'm glad you live with a doctor,' Harri was saying, 'or else I'd recommend you see one. You looked all gone out there for a mo'.' She stood and brushed her skirt, peered at the children playing peacefully for once. And then she turned and said, unnervingly, 'No Aida this afternoon? I thought you'd be haring off to see her.'

'It's *Ada*,' Clem said and slapped shut her sketchbook. 'Actually I *shall* have to fly as soon as Hale turns up – we're having the Huberts.'

'Oh Lord! How screamingly tedious.' Harri pushed back the strands of hair that clung to her neck and Clem glimpsed patches of damp beneath the arms of her silky dress. 'Old Hubie was sweet on *me* once, you know.'

Clem managed a laugh. 'Never!'

'Not that he dared approach me himself. It all came through Dennis. "You could do worse," he said. "Worse than a boring bally banker?" I said!'

'Shall we get these children washed?' Clem scooped the protesting Edgar from the sandpit and carried him into the house, where, after the sun, the dimness made her reel.

As soon as the car drew up at the Beeches, Mrs Hale scurried out to greet them. 'That Dinah! I said she was to be back by five o'clock. I'm sorry, madam. I'll take the little lambkin, shall I?'

Edgar had fallen asleep on the drive, numbing her arm, and with some relief Clem handed him over. 'Bless his little heart,' said Mrs Hale, then as she turned to go into the house, 'I'll have her guts for garters when she gets back, don't you fret. I don't know what's come over her lately, I really don't.'

Clem followed her in, removed her hat, smoothed down the new hair, and started for the stairs, hoping for a few moments alone, but Dennis stepped out into the hall, glass in hand. 'Darling? Only just back? The Huberts are coming, had you forgotten?' He caught her arm and examined her. 'You look quite flushed. Been having fun?'

'Splendid! Sunshine, children and so on.' She pulled herself free. 'I need to wash, dress—'

'Oh, come and have a drink first.'

'But I need—'

'Doctor's orders!'

She followed him into the sitting room, scented with lilac from a vase of fat white blooms, with tobacco, with polish. For the first time this year no fire had been set, and sunshine slanted in, making it almost intolerably hot.

Dennis poured her a glass of sherry. 'Now, I have a bone to pick with you.' He looked at her sternly. 'I had a telephone call today,' he said, handing her the drink. She sank down on an armchair, a sudden hard throbbing in her chest, eyes on the gold-etched sherry glass, waiting for the sword, the drip, the heavens to fall.

'A curious thing,' he said. 'Your friend telephoned.'

Clem watched the shiver of the straw-coloured sherry – a little storm, storm in a sherry glass – bit her lip, feeling the danger of a panicky laugh.

'Hoped we were all quite recovered from a tummy bug.'

She took a sip and gave a little snort. 'Oh dear.' She smiled. 'I know it was naughty, darling, but Harri invited her last night and I just couldn't bear it so I told a teensy white lie.'

He shook his finger at her, mock cross. 'Naughty indeed,' he said. 'But your secret's safe with me.' He raised his eyebrows and gazed at her with amusement.

'What did you say?'

'That you were quite recovered and had gone out for a breath of air.'

'Thank you, darling.' She smoothed her skirt and her fingers went to the edge of her hair, just where it brushed her chin.

'What a tangled web we weave,' he said, and his innocence almost slayed her. His eyes were so like Edgar's, like Harri's; the Everetts were a different breed with their dark hair, high colouring and the bright chestnut of their irises. A breed apart from pale, fair, attenuated people like herself, like Powell, like . . . others.

'You're an angel.' She finished the sherry, put down the glass and perched on the arm of his chair. 'You do like my hair then?'

'Hmm, actually yes, though it kills me to admit it.'

She leaned and smiled into his face. 'You see, by cutting it I've presented myself with a problem,' she said.

He drew back his head, eyebrows raised.

'Surely even you can see that I need a new wardrobe—'

'My God!' he laughed out loud. 'You impudent child! You deprive me of your crowning glory and now I've got to pay for it with the latest fashions?'

She leant over him, touched his lips with her finger. This unusual gesture of affection made him glow though he still affected grumpiness.

'Don't think I don't know what you're up to, you minx! How much is this going to set me back?'

She took a breath. 'I thought a hundred pounds.'

'What!' he spluttered.

'I won't spend it all at once. I'll budget to replace my clothes as needs be. I'm in desperate need, for instance, of hats, and a good hat costs a fortune. And a dress or two for the summer, a light coat . . . and of course there are shoes, and I dare say I'll get some bits for Edgar and for the twins too.'

He sighed out a long breath.

'If not a hundred, perhaps eighty, or seventy? You don't want your little wife looking dowdy, surely? All the lovely female patients . . . Oh, I've seen them coming out of the surgery. I'm sure they're all devoted to you.' She pulled a face. 'I want to look at least as à la mode as they do.'

'Poppycock! As if I notice what they're wearing! And as for you, you baggage, you'd look exquisite in a hessian sack.'

'But Dennis—'

'Well, it hasn't escaped me that it's your birthday soon. Perhaps we could discuss this in the bedroom later . . .'

As he walked his fingers along her thigh she smiled, heart teetering lopsidedly beneath its cargo of shame.

In the hall she met Mrs Hale, coming down the stairs in a fluster. 'Dinah's still not back,' she said. 'Linda's seeing to Edgar's tea. I must get on with creaming my onions, ma'am. I hope that's all right?'

'Perfectly fine, Mrs Hale,' Clem said. 'I'm sure there'll be a perfectly good explanation.'

She went upstairs, paused to look into the nursery where freckly Linda was trying to persuade Edgar to take a spoonful of something. His lips were sealed, head straining away from the spoon. 'Perhaps just give him his milk?' she suggested, almost tempted to go in and take over, lift him from his high chair – he was beginning to love her, he *was* – but she must get changed before the guests arrived.

From the landing windows the sun shone warmly, watery shadows of the beeches swaying on the walls and ceiling. She gazed out at the trees, the luscious freshness of their leaves, saw a squirrel flow along a branch, the fluttering of some tiny bird. Home. This home was so lovely, she was thinking, when, glancing down, she noticed Dinah hurrying in – Dinah with a young chap, no, not so young. Her circulation seemed to stop, the breath solidify in her lungs, as she saw that the tall man in the wide-brimmed hat, bidding Dinah farewell now, was Mr Fortune.

26

Dear Mr Fortune, I enclose fifty pounds. That is the end to the matter. Do not come near my house again or I shall call the police.

SHE SIGNED HER name, then stopped, screwed up the note. *How stupid!* But what about the letters she'd sent before? If he wanted to ruin her he could do so in an instant. But if that was his plan, well, she still had *his*, which proved the way he'd wheedled for money, begged one might say, if one were to be uncharitable. And look where being charitable got one! She knelt and opened the sewing box, felt under the cotton reels for the flimsy sheaf of paper. Soon she'd throw them on the fire, but not until this beastly business was over and done with.

She paced the room. A loose floorboard caused the piano to sound each time she stepped on it. *Blackmail.* If there were to be a sordid trial, it would be the end: the end of her marriage, the end of everything she could imagine . . . There went the piano again, a sonorous groan. Outside the window birds snip-snip-snipped as if unpicking a wrong seam.

Last night she'd earned her money. Though fifty pounds was as far as Dennis would stretch. He'd been tickled when she demanded the money immediately but, long-sufferingly, hauled himself up to fetch it for her. 'My own dear little harlot.'

Into the envelope she folded five ten-pound notes. She'd wouldn't leave it in the hall but deliver it to the postbox herself, and that, surely, would be the end of the whole shameful matter. It had been rainy earlier, but it seemed that as soon as the letter had gone into the box, the sky broke open, sun glinting on all the wetness till her eyes stung. As she reached home Clem saw Dinah setting out with Edgar in the pram and hurried to catch her up.

'Perhaps I might tag along?'

'Course, ma'am.' Dinah seemed a little startled. Clem swallowed, darted a sideways look at her face. What did she know? Had Mr Fortune said anything?

'Hello, darling,' she said to the child, who was lying on his back, clutching a wooden fire engine and staring blankly at the inside of his white sunshade.

Dinah frowned at Clem's shoes. 'Shame to spoil them in the puddles though, ma'am.'

'Oh, they don't matter,' said Clem, glancing down at the old blue suede.

They set off along the pavement, all lumped up by tree roots so that the pram jolted. Birds fluted and the air was fresh with leaf and blossom and sweetness. Dinah seemed perfectly natural in her attitude. The letter was posted. And that was that. Wasn't it? Her heart could lift. *Lift heart, lift.*

The road was quiet but for the slow clopping of a horse, the squeak of a bicycle brake, but as they were about to cross the road, a motorcycle thundered past, setting Clem's heart hammering.

Crowing with excitement, Edgar sat up in his pram. 'Mama!' He pointed with a stubby finger, surprised to see her there. He looked far too manly and heavy-browed for his white sun hat and the frilly parasol.

'Yes, it's Mama,' said Dinah. 'Aren't you the lucky little man? Who ought to be asleep? Never mind, ma'am, the walk will send him off.'

She leaned over the handle to talk soothing nonsense to Edgar. When they crossed the road and set off down a lane, Clem dropped back a little. Ridiculous to get such a fright from a motorcycle! They were ten a penny these days; even Gwen had one apparently. Wouldn't she just! Bluebells just finishing between the trees and such a froth of flowers in the verge – cowslips, campions, huge pink clovers, Queen Anne's Lace – all abuzz with bees and flies. It was all over and done with now, the wretched man paid off. A blue butterfly paused on a buttercup, ludicrously pretty, lifted and was gone.

Perhaps Dinah had been right about the shoes. The suede was darkened already by drips and the soles were so thin she could feel every stone.

'Don't they, madam?' said Dinah.

'I'm sorry, Dinah. What was that?'

'I was telling Eddie all about the birdies,' Dinah said, 'how they build nests in the trees. Look, there's a blackie.'

'Do you really think he understands?' Clem looked at Edgar's bright eyes, the red cheeks, the clear dribble running down his chin as he gnawed his fire engine.

'You'd be surprised what they understand,' Dinah said. 'With my little brothers, I'd swear they understood every word long before they could speak.'

Clem nodded. 'And he's a clever little chap.'

'Oh, he's clever all right.' Dinah chucked him under the chin, adding, 'Though there'll be hell to pay if we don't get him off. I'll have to serenade him if you can put up with it, ma'am?'

'Of course.'

Dinah proceeded to sing, 'One, two three, four, five, once I caught a fish alive,' but Edgar stayed very much awake, pointing around him, saying, 'dat'.

'I expect it's the excitement of having Mama along,' Dinah said.

They stopped at the bottom of the slope where a deep, clear brook flowed over stones.

'Violets!' Clem exclaimed, stooping to touch the secretive petals.

'When he's a big boy he'll be able to fish for sticklebacks here,' said Dinah.

Clem took a deep breath. 'Have you got found yourself a young man?'

'Not a regular young man,' Dinah said.

'No one?'

'No one you might call special.'

Clem gritted her teeth. *No one you might call special.* They came to a place where the overarching trees made a tunnel of the lane; flakes of light drifted down through the thick leaf shadow.

'Goodness, I've never been along here. Isn't that odd?' said Clem, voice ringing falsely bright.

'Well, you don't have much call to be traipsing about, do you, ma'am? Oh, just look at the state of your shoes!'

'Only I thought I saw you with someone yesterday evening,' Clem said, wincing as a stone bit through her sole. Sharp spots of light danced in her eyes. 'When you were so late back.'

Dinah winced. 'I'm sorry, ma'am, lost track of the time. He had a watch on but it must have been slow. Won't happen again, ma'am. Mrs Hale gave me a proper row.'

'Who was this fellow?'

'Just a chap I've seen once or twice,' Dinah said. 'An older chap.'

Clem's gloves were moist with perspiration. She watched her muddy shoes on the stony ground for several steps before she asked, 'And what's his name?'

'Harris, like me. Isn't that funny?' Dinah giggled. 'He was right forward about it too. He said that once we was married, I shouldn't have to change my name!'

The sun vivid on green, yellow, pink, blue made curious patterns before Clem's eyes and Dinah chattered on as they turned towards home, about Mr so-called Harris and how brave he was – 'what with his nasty old war wound and all'.

That nasty old wound, that secret, ridged and ruined place: one tear rising clear like a spring.

'Are you all right, ma'am?'

'Just the heat.' Clem snapped her attention back. 'How did you meet him?'

Dinah told her how he'd just happened to be outside one day, asked directions. 'Funnily enough, it was on this very walk!'

A squirrel frisked across the path before them and flowed silently up a tree.

'Look, Dinah,' Clem said. 'I'm going to ask something of you.'

The girl inclined her head.

'You see, I happen to know something of your Mr Harris.'

'He's hardly *my* Mr Harris!'

They turned a bend. A thrush was thrilling out its song and a wood pigeon coo-cooed.

'I'm afraid,' Clem said, 'that I don't think he's a . . . a suitable person for you to see.'

'Not suitable?' Dinah stopped and looked up at her, puzzlement in her eyes. 'Whyever not? How do you know him? He never said.'

He never said.

Clem touched Dinah's arm. 'Don't you worry about that. Suffice it to say, I'd rather you didn't see him again, not while you're in our employ.'

Dinah made a shocked little sound and then fell silent.

They walked without speaking until the lane turned uphill and brought them from the shadow of the trees into a brilliant, hot shaft of sun where the rapidly drying puddles steamed and glinted.

'How are your family? Your father's lungs?' Clem asked, worried by Dinah's unusual muteness.

'Tolerable.'

'You know I wouldn't usually dream of interfering. It's for your own good.'

Dinah shrugged.

'And we do value you so much.'

More silence.

'I think you said your sister's getting married soon?' Clem tried.

'Next month,' Dinah said shortly. 'I've already asked for the afternoon off.'

'Take the whole day.'

Dinah peeped sideways at her. 'Oh . . . well, thank you, ma'am.'

'You see I only want the best for you.'

Edgar's eyes had closed. 'At last,' Dinah said. She stopped the pram to tuck the coverlet under his legs, and when he stirred began to push the pram more swiftly, singing, 'Go to sleep, my baby, close your pretty eyes,' in her thin voice.

'I do hope you understand?' Clem asked, once Edgar had succumbed and Dinah had slowed her pace.

'Any rate, it's not as if I'm all *that* gone on him,' Dinah said. 'Tell you the truth, he's a bit of a queer fish. And *old*.'

'Perhaps you'll meet a nice young chap at the wedding,' Clem said.

'Well, there is Martin, my sister's Bill's second cousin,' Dinah said.

'There you are then!' Clem's head was aching, her shoes were sodden, and she was hot, thirsty, glad to be nearing home. But when they emerged onto the main road, she noticed a motorcycle parked opposite the Beeches; beside it, a tall figure.

Dinah had paused to adjust the sunshade and when she saw him she gasped. 'Oh cripes, ma'am, talk of the devil. I'm so sorry. If you was to hold the pram for a minute, I'll run ahead and tell him to scarper, shall I?'

Gripping the pram, Clem watched Dinah run along the road. As Mr Fortune listened to whatever she was saying, he gazed past her at Clem, before slowly donning his goggles and helmet. He mounted the motorcycle, swerved round in the road and rode past, lifting his hand as he went.

'Well, that's him sent packing,' Dinah said.

'What did you say?'

'Just that he should clear off and not bother coming back.'

'Good girl.' Clem said, and then she grasped Dinah's arm. 'Thank you for being so equable.'

'Equable!' Dinah laughed. 'Well, no one's ever called me that before.'

Clem paused. 'And there's no need to go talking about this to Mrs Hale, or anyone.'

Dinah regarded her curiously then shrugged. 'If you say so. Well, I'd better get his Lordship settled down properly.' And she pushed the pram over the gravel and round into the back garden.

In the green shadow of the beech trees Clem stood, clenching and unclenching her fists.

27

'I'LL LEAVE YOU to settle in then,' says the thin man with the drip on the end of his nose. 'No shoes on the beds, please.'

'Bloomin' cheek!' says Doll as soon as he's gone. She pulls back the nets to peer out. 'Shame we've not got a sea view.' They stand looking out onto the yard at the back where, unfortunately, a Jack Russell chooses that moment to lift his leg against a dustbin.

'Nice enough room though,' Vince says, surveying the small, lumpy double bed, the black wardrobe and dressing table made for somewhere more palatial, the shiny red paint on the walls. Doll turns away but he catches her face in the dressing-table mirror: disappointment written all over it. Could've laid out extra for a sea view, could've chosen a better-class hotel come to that, but fifty quid only goes so far. There's the wedding to fork out for next.

'And we'll be out and about most of the time any rate,' he says.

She runs her finger along the mantelpiece, rearranges the china ashtray, shaped like a fig leaf, on its lacy doily.

'Let's have another butcher's at the boys' room,' she says, and they all troop back to the narrow single with its iron bunks that remind Vince of his old barracks.

'Can I have the top one?' Kenny clambers up the ladder.

'Course you can,' Doll says. 'Vince doesn't mind, do you, dear?'

'We'll be snug as two bugs in here,' Vince says. What time will the nipper be asleep? The real fun will have to wait till then. Strategy: tire him out good and proper, exercise, fresh air, then he'll sleep like a top. They'll have tea early, get Kenny settled, then downstairs to the bar for a quiet drink or three. And once he's got her well oiled, that's when he'll pop the question. The ring sits in his pocket in its tidy little box. Nineteen shillings and eleven pence it set him back – thin gold-plated band and big sparkly diamond (well, paste) but it looks the genuine article. A real knuckleduster. Get that on her finger and he's home and dry.

By the time he's unpacked and hung his clean shirt on the back of the door, Doll's powdered her nose and Kenny's lined up his lead soldiers on the windowsill, it's gone noon. A cold mist has rolled in since they arrived, and he's shivering in his blazer and boater. Doll's in a straw hat too, shiny yellow with a red ribbon. The plan was for the three of them to sit on the front eating fish and chips out of newspaper, but it's too cold so they go into a café where he orders fish and chips, peas, bread and butter and a pot of tea. As he pays – an arm and a leg – the woman behind the till grimaces sympathetically at his face. He'd forgotten; he'd only gone and forgotten, what with all that's on his mind. He feels himself colour up. Silly cow. She's on a hiding to nothing if she expects a tip now.

But come on, buck up! After all, here they are, a proper little family on holiday, anyone'd think that. They've got the window seat and all, and they can peer through the steamy glass and watch the trippers go past as they tuck into their grub.

'Mind,' says Doll as Kenny splashes vinegar on the table.

'Shall I be mother?' Vince lifts the big brown teapot and pours them all a cup.

'Can I bathe after dinner?' Kenny asks.

'You'll catch your death,' says Doll.

'Wouldn't.'

'Shame about the weather,' Doll remarks. 'These chips are a bit soggy, don't you think?'

'Nice bit of fish though,' says Vince.

'What's the point of the seaside if I can't go in?'

'I do like a bit of rock eel,' she says, 'though the batter could have done with a minute or two more . . . That's enough.' She glares at Kenny who's heaping sugar into his tea. 'Oh, I do wonder how Arthur's getting on,' she says. 'I should have warned him about that dicky valve. He'll have opened up by now. Oh, Vince, do you think you should telephone and tell him?'

'Forget all about it,' he says. 'He's a pair of safe hands. Enjoy yourself. You'll be back soon enough.'

'Want to bathe,' Kenny says.

Doll belches into her hankie. 'Excuse me. We'll see, if the sun comes out. Say thank you to Mr Fortune for the nice dinner,' she adds. She's left half her chips, he notices.

'Ta,' says Kenny.

'Call of nature.' Doll gets up and lugs her great fat handbag into the Ladies'. Whatever has she got in there!

'How about a kickabout this afternoon?' says Vince. 'We can go to one of them shops along the front, buy ourselves a football.'

'But I want to swim.' Kenny tips salt into his hand and licks it off.

'I don't mind, but it's up to your mum.'

'I want to bathe, *then* buy a ball.' More salt, scattered all over the shop.

'I'd lay off that if I were you.'

'But you're not me, are you?' Kenny bangs down the salt cellar. 'Bathe, kickabout then an ice-cream. Double scoop.'

'A few manners wouldn't go amiss. A few pleases.'

'Please, please, please,' says Kenny. 'Is that enough of 'em?'

'It's enough of your cheek. I'd have given my eye teeth for a treat like this when I was a nipper,' Vince says.

'What are eye teeth?'

Vince can feel his spirits flagging, but here comes Doll, freshly rouged by the look of it and what with the new yellow hat and red ribbon, she looks a bit on the gaudy side, truth be told. But it's touching, that's what it is, her holiday gesture, getting into the spirit of it all. If only she'd stop carping on.

They step outside into the chilly mist, the moan of foghorns from far out at sea.

'Mr Fortune says I can go for a dip,' Kenny says.

'What I *said* was it was up to your mum.'

'Too cold, dearie.'

'Not fair.' Kenny stamps his foot and Vince's hand itches to give him what for, demonstrate some authority, but he doesn't dare. The three of them walk along the promenade in silence. He doesn't dare tuck Doll's arm under his either. Lined up at the sea wall is a row of wheelchairs: old soldiers draped in blankets, staring, those of them that aren't blind, out across the Channel at God knows what memories of carnage.

A poster catches Vince's eye. 'Tell you what, how about the flicks?' he says.

'And can I have an ice?'

Doll laughs indulgently. 'Of course you can. What a good idea, Vince.' She smiles properly for the first time since they got off the train. The film on first is a Buster Keaton, right up Kenny's street. Sitting close enough to Doll to feel the warmth of her thigh, he enjoys her laughter, and their hands brush together and linger a bit, he'd swear, when he leans in to light her cigarette. He spends most of the film gazing sideways at her, wondering what she'd do if he crept his arm along the back of the seat. The thought makes his lips twitch. The grey light from the screen ripples over her face, and now and then her hand goes to her hair, or she rustles in her bag for barley sugars, or she leans down to whisper to Kenny.

'Well, that was a treat,' she says, once they're out and blinking in the cold daylight. 'You liked that, didn't you, Kenny? Say thank you to Mr Fortune.'

'Ta.'

'What now?' Vince asks.

'Bathe.'

'Tell you what *I'd* like to do, Vince,' Doll says: 'is get back to that hotel for forty winks if you wouldn't mind keeping Kenny amused?'

'Can I go in the sea?'

'How many more times?'

Kenny sticks his lip out.

'There's a dance in the hotel tonight, did you notice?' she says. 'That's why I need my beauty sleep.' She smiles at him, a sparkle in her eyes. So that's her little game! Put him on hold till later. Flaming tease!

'As if *you* need beauty sleep,' he says, warming right through at the thought of her in his arms on the dance floor.

'You can wipe that look off your face if you want any more treats,' she says, and he flinches – though of course it's Kenny she means.

'Like what?' Kenny asks.

'Saving your strength, eh?' Vince says, ignoring the boy. 'Tell you the truth, I wouldn't mind forty winks myself.' He thinks of the shiny red room, the narrow double in which, soon, they'll be pressed so close together.

'Crazy golf!' shouts Kenny, seeing a sign. 'Can we play crazy golf?'

'Not my cup of tea,' Doll says. 'but Mr Fortune'll play with you, won't you, dear? Then we can meet up later for our tea.' She pats his arm. 'You be a good boy,' she says to Kenny and without so much as a by-your-leave saunters off.

'Come on then,' says Kenny, tugging at his sleeve.

They eat tea in the lounge with the other residents. Piles of sandwiches, hardboiled eggs and potted meat, sausage rolls, dainties and fancies of all sorts, a right old spread. Kenny wanders off and joins the children at another table.

'Well, isn't this nice?' Doll says. 'I had a proper kip this afternoon too. Thank you for that, dear, must've needed it.'

Vince helps himself to another sausage roll.

'You been down the Labour Exchange lately?' she asks, so out of the blue it takes his breath away.

He brushes pastry flakes from his knees. 'Nothing doing,' he says. 'What with this.' He taps his cheek, deliberately tugging at the strings in her soft old heart.

'But there's plenty you can do, Vince,' she says. 'Something behind the scenes – storeman, something in that line, maybe?'

His teeth grind through stodgy sausage meat. He swallows, takes a swig of tea, lights up a cig, without, for once, offering her one.

'I'm sorry, dear, I didn't mean . . .' Her face has flushed. Her hand comes out and touches his knee. 'And in any case, look how well you do behind the bar. Slap bang in the public eye. So brave of you, dear. I could recommend you for another bar job.'

His breath is too shallow. He can't sit there like this panting. He goes off to the lav. What's she up to, coming out with that at a time like this? He leans against the white tiles, avoids the mirror, pisses, buttons up. And then he gets it. Ha! She's pushing, of course. She's pushing him to show his hand, wants to know where she stands. High time they got this on a regular footing, course it is.

Play it cool for now though, Vincey. Hold your fire. The ring sits in its box, sparkling away in the dark. No, not sparkling; it takes light to sparkle. The moment he opens that box then the sparkling will begin.

By the time he gets back, Doll's chatting with the people at the next table. She introduces them: Tom and Netta Earnshaw with their kiddies, a girl and a boy. The boy and Kenny are comparing soldiers. This wasn't the plan. No one else figured in that, but Doll and Netta seem to have hit it off, and that'll cheer her up. Vince and Tom manage a word or two about the football, about the news. Tom calls Kenny 'your nipper' and Vince tenses, waiting for Doll to contradict him, but she either doesn't hear or doesn't mind.

Nasty moment though, when the little girl cringes away from him. She snuggles up to her mum but keeps staring with round eyes, till her mum ticks her off.

'Show 'em some tricks,' Kenny says.

'Yes, go on, Vince, dear,' presses Doll. And he has them spellbound with his matchbox trick, the dancing hankie and the vanishing penny. He wins over the little girl by fishing it out from behind her ear and Kenny looks proud as punch. 'He's going to teach me,' he boasts.

'Can you vanish yourself?' says the girl.

'Still working on that one!' says Vince and they all laugh, and Doll nudges him fondly. They smile at each other and he relaxes.

You don't smile at a person like that, you don't nudge them, you don't go away with them to the seaside, if you don't mean business.

There's a big kerfuffle as the band arrive, trooping through the restaurant and into the bar to set up for tonight with their great black instrument cases, the name painted on the drum in silver: *Pendulum Swing Band*. Though the sun's nowhere near the yard-arm, Vince and Tom go through to the bar to get some drinks in. Tom and Vince give the staff a hand rolling back the carpet to reveal the dance floor.

Kenny and the Earnshaw lad come rushing through to skid about on the parquet – nice to see Kenny with a smile on his face at last. And it'll tire him out good and proper. The band start tuning up, blowing on their trombones, clarinets and so on. A long time since Vince's danced – a bit rusty – but no doubt it'll come back to him, and steering her round the floor, and afterwards back up them stairs . . . he can hardly wait.

28

A T EIGHT O'CLOCK Doll finally emerges from her 'boudoir', all done up to the nines, L'Heure Bleue wafting everywhere. She shall have another bottle of that for Christmas or her birthday – don't even know when that is! So much to learn about each other still, and a lifetime to do it.

'You'll keep Kenny company, won't you, dear?' she says, not quite meeting his eye.

'Hold your horses,' he says. 'I'm coming down with you.' But he's still to change his shirt; been listening for the bathroom, and every time he hears the door someone else nips in there before him. Wants a good a wash before he dons his clean shirt and runs a razor over his chin. Has to look his best for the occasion.

'I said I'd have a drink with Netta,' she says. 'Tom's settling theirs down.'

'Women swanning off to the bar while the men do the donkey-work? What's the world coming to?'

'Well, it *is* my holiday,' she says.

'Mine too,' he points out. 'And Kenny knows we'll only be down them stairs.'

'Still, in a strange place, I'd rather not leave him. What if he wants something? What if he gets scared?'

Vince takes a deep breath. 'I'll be down directly he's nodded off then.'

She hesitates, puts a hand on his arm. 'Tell you what, Vince, if you don't fancy a dance that's fine. You could stop up here, keep an ear out for Kenny, read the paper.'

'Why shouldn't I fancy a dance?' he says, staring at her red lips and cheeks, her brassy piled-up hair. She says nothing, just goes off downstairs, leaving him stood there in the corridor. As if he wouldn't want to dance with her! Why shouldn't he? This is the big finale of the trip – whatever's got into her? Just being a good mum is all it is, he tells himself, that's all it is. Treats that little toerag as if he's bone bloody china.

Finally he manages to get into the bathroom and catches sight of himself in the glass. Stares at the painted eye. Christ, he forgot all about it for most of today. Why does she have to go reminding him? He's still got his feet, hasn't he? You can hear the band starting up from here, a swing tune. He'll show her who likes to dance.

He goes back into the room, where Kenny's on the top bunk, cross-legged in his pyjamas. 'Mum said we could play cards till I'm tired,' he says.

'Did she now?'

'Crazy eights?'

Vince lights himself a cigarette. 'One game.'

'Hey, crazy golf, now crazy eights!' Kenny kneels up. 'Crazy day!' He deals the cards. Vince lets the kid win the first hand, but after that gets on a winning streak he can't resist. Seems like a good omen. The band's really swinging now, you can feel the vibration through the floorboards.

Vince shuffles the cards and runs through his tricks, fooling

Kenny every time, though he can feel his fingers fumbling, needs to brush up a bit.

'*Could* you make a person vanish?' Kenny asks.

Vince snorts, thinking of a certain Ted Chamberlain, but the head of a German boy – wide blue eyes – suddenly shoves itself into his mind; a head on top of shoulders one second, blown off the next.

Maybe it's the barrack-like bunks where he stood and played cards, back then; come to think of it, did tricks on the blankets, just like this.

'Bet you could if you tried,' Kenny says.

'Mr Sandman on his way yet?'

'Mr Sandman!' Kenny gathers and deals the cards. 'I'm not a baby.'

'One more hand,' says Vince, 'then I'll go down and tell your mum you dropped off. Play along and there's a bob in it for you.'

'But Mum said you'd be stopping up here with me.'

Those flaming drums thumping up through the floor, getting him all in a jitter. 'Shouldn't you rather have a shilling all to yourself?'

'Two bob?'

'You little shark! Not a word to your mum and I'll make it one and six.'

Kenny considers. 'All right then,' he says. 'But best of three first.'

Downstairs, the music's louder, ragtime now. At the bar, people are yelling above the noise; it's rammed in there and he can't spot Doll or anyone. The floor's a crush of dancers. He cranes his neck, trying to get a glimpse of Doll's hair or her flowery shoulders in among the melee, but he can't see, what with the smoke, the pulsating spots of light from the mirror ball. No sign of her so he shoves his way through to the bar. Can't stick being in a crowd like this. The racket's properly getting on his wick. That drumbeat – thumpa-thumpa-thumpa – right through his vitals. And where the hell's Doll?

They're dancing American-style, legs and arms flying, those who know the steps; others are just shuffling round. Well, he'll be in that category, him and Doll no doubt. At last he gets a flash of her hair. She's on the dance floor, found herself a partner. Well, of course, that's Doll for you. But his heart stops, actually goes and bloody well stops when he sees who her partner is.

The fog has come in thick now. He had to get out of there and walk it off. Rage roars through him as he strides along the prom smoking ciggie after ciggie, grinding them out, cupping his hand round the flame for a tiny flash of warmth – a tiny flash of warmth that's all he asked of her, the cow, the fucking cow. Did she plan it? Did she? Did she invite him here? 'I'll get that mug to stay upstairs with Kenny,' did she say that to him? You can't even see the sea in this fog but you can hear it, sighing away, saying *ooh dear, ooh dear, ooh dear.*

He'd like to walk all bloody night. Walk right out of this, this life, but you can't. Too much invested, you can't give up yet, Vince. Pull yourself together. He's half a mind to walk straight into that cold sea; in this fog no one would spot him. Walk in and finish it all. Then she'd feel bad. She'd surely feel bad as hell that she's gone and done him such a terrible wrong.

He goes down steps from the prom and walks towards the sea. Soon he's in the dark. You can just make out glimmery bits of wave. Smell of salt, taste of it in his mouth. How could she? He steps back, realising he's come right to the soft bit before the water starts.

Maybe it wasn't her fault though. Don't go jumping to conclusions, Vincey. Perhaps she didn't ask Chamberlain to come? Maybe Arthur told him where they'd gone? He should at least allow her to explain. Yes, get back and let her explain, go back and get warm at least. Brass monkey weather it is, with that bloody wet fog getting everywhere, cold drips running down his face, his neck and the prosthesis like an icy blade against the side of his nose.

But when he gets back they're still dancing. He comes across Netta and Tom in the bar and they give him such a funny look he can't stand it and goes up the stairs, into her room. He fingers her stuff, her undies, a stocking. He winds it round his hand, tight silk, unwinds it, lays it back across the chair where it dangles like leg skin. He dabs L'Heure Bleue on his wrist, lies on the bed, lights a cig, hearing the band – oh, it gets to him, it does, that kind of music, grates on his nerves. Surely she wouldn't have planned it? Surely she's not that much of a bitch?

It's just coincidence Ted turning up, she'll say, and as long as she says it, cares enough to say it, then that'll do, that'll have to do. He'll save the ring till one night when they're home, one of them nights when she's tired and good-tempered, when they have one of their little moments, that's what he'll do. His eyes close. He'll wait and sort it out, sort it out and

you put your head up and get a bullet through the brow, the eye, you turn your head you get it through the ear, straight in one and out the other, that happened to Griffiths, sharing a smoke and a snigger then there he was, still a smile, a cock-eyed wink, tin hat intact, and all his brains spilled in the mud with the rain pouring down, just the same cold rain that was clean at least, the only clean thing landing on the mud that was as much animal as mineral, snot, spit, shit, piss, blood, brains, fingers, spikes of bone and gobs of flesh, rats big as terriers, crows and what have you, worms, maggots, beetles, fleas, lice. Mud that's animal enough to move on its own so you're hardly shocked when it sometimes gathers and rises up into a man. That was the day he shot the stupidly brave Hun lad, looked right into his clear blue eyes and shot his head off, boom, gone. A day of endless rain, endless strafing, third day of rain, heavy fire with hardly a let-up, not more than a wink of sleep, then Griffiths bought it and no time even to cover him up. Jerry at it tooth and nail. He knew they were going to get him, every fibre said keep your head down, but keeping your head down meant seeing Griffiths, and now he was gone it was up to Sergeant Fortune to set an example and up went his head and for a moment it was still and his vision roved over the apron of tangled wire. Reload, reload, he cried, ducking down to clip the cartridges into the rifle and up again, seeing movement from Jerry's line only a football pitch away it seemed. Fire, fire, fire, but his eyes were on the wire in which capered a lad, Mount, was it? There he was stuck in a stiff dance, held up, a leg lifted as if he was prancing, head thrown back and tin hat caught on the wire behind him like a bowl, like a nest, like a bloody bird bath spilling rain. Too much noise, you couldn't get your thoughts in order, solid noise that knocked you off your feet, a giant's kitchen being smashed, pans clattering, plates, a tin of cutlery being shook beside your ear, inside your head and the rain, the rain. Reload, someone said. Him? Reload, and he really couldn't think in all the rumbling and he put his head above the parapet and there was the lad Mount doing his rain dance, the last thing his two eyes ever saw and

'Vince!' He starts, stares, opens his eye. His eye can't see that side – what's happening, what's happened? What the hell? And there's a woman looking down and it's dry underneath him, not wet but dry. 'What's up with you?' she's saying. 'What you doing in here?'

And he sits up and his heart is beating hard enough to make his tie flap and his breath won't come.

'You're in a right old state,' she says, more kindly. 'Bad dream? I just popped up to see how you and Kenny was getting on.'

He rises from the bed and it's as if he's rising from the trench, caked in mud. As if he's made of mud. He stands unsteadily. Without a word, he leaves the room. No slithery duckboards. The floor is dry under his stockinged feet. He runs his hand along the solid wall. The sound is only drums and wailing saxophone, not guns and shells. Blank as man can possibly be, he goes and lies down on the narrow bottom bunk.

29

'WHAT'S THE MATTER, dear? Cat got your tongue?' Doll's at the cooker frying chops. He hadn't said any more than the necessary on the journey back, what with Kenny there. She kept shooting him nervous looks across the carriage, and tried to draw him out once or twice: offered him sandwiches and barley sugars, tried to include him in a game of I Spy.

They'd got back to the Wild Man before the end of dinnertime, and she was straight behind the bar, greeting the regulars as if she'd been away weeks instead of only a day and a half. Soon as they'd closed up she'd paid Arthur off and gone round clearing the bar. Finding fault, of course, with how he'd done things, but chuffed that the place was still standing. And now there was that gap between dinnertime and the evening trade and she was cooking their tea, as if nothing had changed.

'Perhaps you could set the table, dear? Call Kenny down?'

Treating him just like a hubby. What does she do that for, if it doesn't mean anything? He looks at her shabby slippers, stout shins in wrinkled stockings, the flowers on the housecoat she wears to protect her dress. She's hardly the Queen of bloody Sheba.

'Come on, Vince,' she says. 'You've hardly said a word all day.'

He allows his gaze to reach her face, all creased with concern. 'Did you ask him to come?'

Her face stiffens and she turns back to prod the chops. 'Who?' she says and he could nearly laugh.

'Saw you on the dance floor.'

She uses a fork to test the potatoes, lowers the gas flame. 'Oh, you mean Ted,' she says, and gives a tinny laugh. Facing him, she folds her arms, and out it comes, all in a rush. 'Oh, Vince, I was as taken aback as what you were. I said to him, I says, "What are you doing, turning up like a bad penny?"'

Vince watches her face carefully. 'And what did he say?'

'Oh, some claptrap. Don't remember.'

'How did he know where you were?'

She glances anxiously at the sizzling chops. 'Reckon Arthur must have said. He's the only one knew where we was.' She slides open the table drawer and sets to rattling cutlery onto the table. 'You don't honestly think I planned it, Vince?'

The sound of cutlery sets his teeth on edge. He should help but sits watching her put out the tablemats with their seaside scenes – ha – and arrange the knives and forks in their three places. Three places like a tidy little family.

'Be a dear and call Kenny,' she says, 'or the chops'll be like leather.'

He clumps up the stairs. In the murk of his soul there's a gleam of light. Ted *could* have got it out of Arthur right enough. It could be true. The bastard, throwing a fucking great spanner in the works. Well, he'll have to be dealt with. Lying in his bunk last night he plotted murder, could have done it, mad enough to get up and smash the bastard in the face and keep on smashing till there was nothing left. He imagined hitting Doll too, shocking her, making her see – but he's never raised his hand to a woman, not about to start now. And Doll, oh, Doll, he's gone on her, he really is. It's love like he never imagined.

But Chamberlain will have to be got out of the way. Last night he went through the ways: gun, poison, knife, throttling. But then the face of that boy, the blue-eyed Hun, rose up. He'd killed others at the Front – par for the course – but they were further away, they were the enemy, only Huns. That boy was the only one he'd looked in the eye.

Cold-blooded murder wasn't in him.

'Teatime, Kenny,' he calls and waits to hear the boy coming before he trudges back down the stairs into the smell of frying meat. There must be another way to get Ted out of the way, something that stops short of murder.

Green grapes in a dish. With her softest pencil Clem cross-hatched, darkest where the fruit skin met the curve of the plate, the glaze reflecting the window, the shine of the brass light fittings where the sun cast . . . The lead snapped and she sighed. Pressing too hard. And it was not, in any case, a successful sketch.

She could go out. It was fine enough. Early June, peerlessly blue and sunny, how contrary to stay inside. A new concern was buzzing like a bluebottle on the edge of her attention but she swatted it away, pushed her pencil into the sharpener, revolved its little brass handle, watched the curling peels of paint-fringed wood emerge.

Out for a walk, perhaps, with Dinah again? Or why not take Edgar herself? The idea appealed. In stouter shoes she'd manage that walk through the trees, the green arch across the road, the sparkling brook. The new lead snapped in the sharpener, damn it. She began again, more carefully this time until the pencil emerged with a perfectly sharpened point.

There came a tapping at the door and Dinah's anxious face appeared.

'Everything all right?'

'Oh, ma'am, I'm sorry. I don't know what to do.' Dinah closed the door behind her and stood fidgeting, almost flinching, as she spoke. 'He's outside, that Mr Harris is! He came to the door bold as brass and luckily it was me what answered it. I was just getting the pram ready and Mrs Hale's out the back and—'

'And?' Clem pressed the pencil point into her fingertip.

'He says he wants to have a word with you. Oh, I'm so sorry, ma'am, bringing this on you.'

Clem stood and said, in a perfectly level voice, 'I'm sure it's not your fault, Dinah. He's outside, you say?'

'He said to say he'll wait for you across the road and that you'll know what it's about. I could get Mr Hale to see him off, ma'am, but I thought I should let you know first.'

Clem managed to manufacture a laugh, and even a yawn. 'I wonder what nonsense this could be?' She shook her head. 'Do you know, I think I'll go out there myself directly and see what it's all about.'

'Are you sure you should, ma'am? Oh, there's Eddie.' And indeed, there came Edgar's imperious cry.

'You get back to the nursery. And not a word, please, to anyone.'

'But, ma'am?' Dinah wrung her hands.

'Off you go.'

Downstairs, Clem donned her hat, jacket and gloves and stepped into the sunshine. No sign of Vincent until she reached the end of the drive. There he stood, across the road, in helmet and goggles, beside his motorcycle. No one else about. It was absolutely still and quiet, as if the morning itself was holding its breath.

As she crossed the road she hissed, 'How *dare* you come here! I can't be seen talking to you here.'

'Get on the bike then,' he said.

A small panting woman pushing a heftier version in a bath chair approached. The longer Clem stood there, the more people would see, would wonder, would gossip. Dinah might come out; she might be watching, might alert the Hales.

Vincent mounted the motorcycle, jerked his head towards the pillion. 'Get your leg over then,' he said, and sniggered.

She looked round. Could she? There was no real choice so she lifted her leg – difficult in her narrow skirt, it caused the material to rise almost to her knees – and settled herself awkwardly on the saddle. He pushed down with his foot and the whole contraption roared into life. Terrified by the sudden speed, she clung to him, eyes shut as her hat whipped off, hair blowing back from her brow. As they rounded bends they seemed to lean so close to the ground they were sure to tip: was this to be it then? Perhaps she was to perish in an accident with Vincent and it would all come out anyway, the whole sorry, squalid story.

After a while she dared to open her eyes and watch the green blossom-speckled hedges and verges stream by. The air was cool on her cheeks, the speed, when one became accustomed, almost thrilling.

The engine stuttered as they slowed and pulled up outside a mean little inn, beside a village green. Vincent climbed off and held out his hand, which she took only for momentary support as she got down and straightened her skirt. Hatless! She ran her fingers through her tangled hair. Her body vibrated with the memory of the engine, her legs weak, unsteady.

But she pulled herself up straight and addressed him as his class dictated. 'How *dare* you come to my house like that?' she said. 'How *dare* you put me in that position?'

In a leisurely manner, Vincent removed his helmet and goggles, readjusted his glasses in his wing mirror, and said, 'What you want's a drink.'

'What if Dinah's alerted my husband?' she said, 'Have you thought of that? They may well have called the police by now.'

'She's a good little girl is Dinah. Anyway, you came of your own accord, didn't you?'

He strode towards the pub's entrance. Hatless, bagless, hair awry, she could look nowhere but the ground as she followed him through the threshold. What kind of woman must she appear?

He showed her into a mercifully empty room – sawdust on the floor, the fug of last night's smoke feebly pierced by sunbeams – and went to fetch the drinks. Perching on a rickety chair, she removed her gloves, balled them on her lap, stretched her fingers, stared at the gaps between.

'Lemonade shandy, refreshing on a day like this,' he said, returning with two glasses. He'd bought himself a pint, a smaller glass for her. He pulled out a chair and seated himself opposite her, running his hand through his sandy hair. A damp lock had fallen between the lens of his specs and the false eye, which made her blink, though naturally he couldn't feel it. He offered her a cigarette, and as she leaned in for a light the table tipped, spilling a little shandy.

'Mr Fortune.'

'Vince, for Christ's sake! Not as if we're strangers!'

'Mr Fortune.' She cleared her throat and looked at him levelly. 'You said if I gave you the money, that would be the end of it. So what's this all about?' She drew on the cigarette. 'You do realise this could be construed as blackmail?'

'Just one more little thing,' he said, smiling rather impudently. She felt nothing about him now, she realised, nothing but impatience. Now that she'd seen behind the mask, touched it and sketched it, the tension was gone. There was nothing more from him that she needed or wanted – save an end to this nonsense.

'I simply cannot get you any more money,' she said. 'That's it. The limit of what I can do for you.'

He nodded. 'Understood.'

'So?'

'It's not cash I'm after.'

Surely he didn't think she'd go to bed with him again! Really, it was preposterous!

'What then?' She waited, tapping ash from her cigarette.

'I want you to play a part.'

She took a sip of the shandy, cool in her parched throat, and swallowed before she raised her eyes to him. 'A *part*?'

He nodded, pushed his hair back from his perspiring brow, and then, as if becoming suddenly aware of it, lifted the hair away from his painted eye. As she listened to him explain what he wanted her to do, her skin crawled with humiliation. Though of course she would not have gone with him again – not now that she was in her right mind – it was humiliating to know that he didn't want her like that. And what he *did* want, what he *did* say, was almost too preposterous to credit. *Risible*.

His 'plan', as he put it, was for her to visit the Wild Man at a specified time and to 'make up', to a 'certain gent' in front of a 'certain lady'. That was it. How killingly funny! Surely he could see how foolish he appeared as, so seriously, he unfolded this plan? It was hard to keep a straight face.

'You don't have to go getting up to any funny business,' he went on. 'All you have to do is flutter your lashes at him, get him to buy you a drink, just make sure the lady in question sees. You could ask him to drive you home. He's got a nice motor, by the way.'

She sipped shandy, dabbed her lips with her gloves. 'Do you mind telling me why?'

He ground out his cigarette. 'So, what d'you say?'

'What if I were to say no?'

Leaning back in his chair, he gazed at the ceiling, mouthing smoke rings. She tore her eyes from the wound on his neck and noticed how dusty her shoes were. She stretched out a foot, rotated the ankle.

'You want an end to this business?' he said, stubbing out his cigarette, making the wretched table wobble.

'What guarantee,' she asked, 'do I have that this would be the end of it?'

'I'm not a bad bloke,' he said. 'I know that's hard to swallow what with . . . well . . .' He raised an eyebrow and his mouth twitched. He reached out and took her hand and, with absurd sincerity, said, 'Do this last thing and I give you my word, my word of honour, you'll not see hide nor hair of me again.'

'Honour!' She snatched back her hand.

'You have my word.'

She snorted and shook her head. Her cigarette had gone out. She left it in the ashtray. 'I don't know,' she said. 'I need to give it some consideration. But my more immediate problem is what on earth I'm going to tell Dinah about today.'

'Say what you want.'

'Will you take me home now, please? At least limit the damage.'

He nodded. 'So, are you saying yes?'

'I'll say you took me to visit an old friend,' Clem decided, and with utter futility, considering she was about to experience the motorcycle again, smoothed her hair with her fingers. 'Someone from the war.' Ada, of course, good old Ada.

'I'll drop you a note with the date,' he said.

'I shall want your word that you won't contact Dinah again.'

He nodded. 'As it happens, I've got bigger fish to fry.' And unaccountably he laughed.

30

THE SOUND OF breathing woke Clem from a tense and flustered dream – of what? – the threads dissolving in the sound of huffing and puffing. Her eyes opened. There was Dennis, naked but for his socks and suspenders, doing his daily dozen, touching his toes, up and down, labouring away in a miasma of coal tar and Bay Rum. She quelled a surge of irritation. Really! Why did he insist on these performances when he knew perfectly well that she preferred him not to? The dream, what was it? A wire of anxiety tightened in her stomach. And then a twist of the wire as it came back to her: Vincent and his ludicrous scheme.

She was to await instructions. Instructions!

At least she'd got away with the outing. Vincent had dropped her off out of sight, and she'd entered the house and chatted to Mrs Hale quite naturally about the glorious day. She attributed the loss of her hat to 'a stray gust' – and caught the disbelief in the housekeeper's eyes, for it had unfortunately been a remarkably windless day – and then turned the talk to domestic matters. Dennis had never even known she'd been out. But she had not yet faced Dinah.

Dennis noticed that her eyes were open. 'Happy Birthday!' he said, pumping his arms, contorting his trunk one way and the other. She sat up, leant back on the pillows, dazed. She'd forgotten!

Forgotten her own birthday. She brought a smile to her face as she regarded this man who was her husband. Despite his exercise regime his belly was beginning to dome under its black curly pelt. Eventually he would achieve the seal shape of his father. He took a brush in each hand to sweep his thick mane into wings on his brow, separated by an immaculate parting. Clapping the brushes back together, he splashed Brilliantine into each palm and slicked it through his hair till it shone like patent leather.

'Now, my darling,' he said. 'You've had an extortionate sum for clothes and so on, but you might still find something else on the breakfast table.'

'Oh, Dennis, you shouldn't have.' Her heart turned painfully over.

'Nothing's too much for my little girl,' he said. 'And later on there's to be another surprise.'

A jar of alarm. 'Surprise?'

'Wait and see.' He wagged a finger. 'Sorry I can't be here this evening . . . but I'll certainly be back to take you to bed.' He grinned, eyebrows lifting, and bent down to kiss her lingeringly, his skin newly shaved and soft. He stood up, almost frighteningly glossy and gleaming, a healthy, vigorous, righteous man buttoning his white shirt, stepping into trousers, deftly tucking in the shirt-tails.

'Twenty-four,' she said faintly. 'How fearfully ancient.'

'You'll always be a girl to me.'

Her eyes closed.

'Happy Birthday, madam,' said Mrs Hale as she put the toast and tea on the table. 'Can I tempt to you an egg?'

'This is perfectly splendid, thank you,' Clem said, surveying the table. No cheap envelope beside her plate. But there, propped against a vase of irises, a card and a small beribboned box.

'Do you know anything about a surprise, Mrs Hale?' she asked.

The housekeeper smiled, finger to her lips. 'I'm sure I don't know what you mean, madam!'

Once Mrs Hale had left the room Clem poured Darjeeling into the pretty yellow cup. Dennis's breakfast had been cleared away but there was the faint smell of bloater in the air, a spot of coffee on the damask.

Once he'd gone downstairs this morning, she'd peered out of the window to see if anyone was lurking. But of course there wasn't; that was absurd. And on her way down, she'd put her head into the nursery where Dinah was changing Edgar's napkin, and the girl's manner had seemed perfectly ordinary. Still, it would be necessary to have a word with her today, clear things up. The wire was tightening inside. No call for it though, really. Everything was all right. The tea perfect, neither too weak nor too strong; the sun shining; it was her birthday. Pull yourself together, Clementine.

The card showed a posy of violets; the gift was a fine long string of pearls. She ran them slowly through her fingers. Pearls are made from irritation but so pretty, almost *innocent*, she thought. Unlike herself. How shoddy she felt as she ran them through her fingers, how undeserving of Dennis's kindness.

After breakfast she had Hale drive her to town where she took a solitary walk through the churchyard, lingering near the mossy graves. Oh, the day was hotter even than yesterday, close and muggy. She dawdled in the shade, wandered amongst headstones. Speedwell and daisies spattered the grass between the graves. Stooping, she ran her finger over the lichen-encrusted words on a tilting stone:

Kind of heart and clear of conscience,
Beloved by her family and all who knew her.
Missed on earth, welcomed in Heaven.

A lovely tribute. But could this lady, who died sixty years ago, this Sophia Smythe, really have been so saintly? *Clear of conscience.* How light that would feel, and how delightful. A white butterfly rested on the gravestone, where, also, she noticed, crawled a ladybird. *Fly away home, your house is on fire, and your children all gone.* She poked the glossy little creature with her finger, gently, but it stayed put. An old man, church warden perhaps, hailed and approached her, but she hurried away.

Still no message when she got home.

'I've had the most lovely walk,' she made sure to say to Mrs Hale, and she'd mention it to Dennis over luncheon. There was no flurry or fluster, nothing to make her heart clamour – so why would it not let up? She took coffee in the dining room and settled there to sketch the irises; took out her colour box to attempt the indigo hue, but once again she could not concentrate. Each ring of the doorbell or the telephone branched electrically through her veins.

Unannounced, in the afternoon Harri and the twins arrived in a great noisy hoo-ha. Clem went out to the hall where Mrs Hale, bursting with pleasure, was ushering them in.

'Happy Birthday!' Harri – wearing a ridiculously capacious straw hat – cried. 'Now, girls . . .' She lifted her finger like a conductor and the three of them began a noisy and approximate rendition of 'Happy Birthday' before they were even properly through the door.

'Thank you, children, so very clever,' Clem said. The muscles in her shoulders dropped a little, the wire slackened. This was the surprise of course: Harri and the children turning up, this was all it was.

'What beautiful singing,' Clem said to the girls, and, 'Oh!' as Harri whipped off her hat to reveal her newly bobbed hair.

'Well, *you* look so ripping, I couldn't resist,' Harri said. 'What do you think?'

'You appear . . . ' Clem hesitated, 'utterly different.'

'*Good* different?'

Harri's hair had been cut into a fringe, high – and not perfectly evenly – across her brow, and the rest of it stood out round her head like a fierce black helmet, within which her face looked small, her eyes enormous, her complexion rosy and clear. Her head was like a child's, a page boy's, affixed to a chunky woman's torso.

'Well, *I* think it looks a proper treat, Miss,' said Mrs Hale.

'Divine,' said Clem.

'Stan's sister did it last night.' Harri twisted to look at herself in the hallstand mirror and giggled. 'You should have seen the great piles of hair on the carpet! Like shearing a sheep, she said! She did the girls too.'

The twins' hair was so fair and wispy it was hard to see the difference, but Clem admired and stroked their heads, kissed their hot red cheeks, and they hurled themselves at her shouting, 'Auntie Clem, Auntie Clem.' This simple, animal affection surprised and touched her.

'Where's Eddie?'

'Napping – Dinah will bring him down directly he's awake.'

'That child could nap for England,' said Mrs Hale. 'Good little chap he is. So like his daddy.'

'Oh Lord, Mrs Hale, that's the last thing we want!' Harri said.

Clem took her arm and they went into the sitting room.

'Oh, what a glorious room this is with the sun shining in,' Harri exclaimed. 'I always forget. How simply luxurious to have all this space.' She stretched out her arms and spun, her grubby dress floating from her shins. 'You get used to being all cramped up in the cottage. Not that I don't love it,' she added quickly. 'It's all we need, isn't it, Clarry?' Lifting the child, she went to the mantelpiece. 'Look darling, this is Grandpapa's best clock. Look at the horses.' And she whinnied.

'Want Eddie,' the child insisted.

'I'll run up and see if he's awake.' Clem hurried upstairs and opened the nursery door. The curtains were drawn and the sun shone pinkly through; it was stiflingly dim and hot.

'Oh, ma'am, he's still asleep.' Dinah rose from a chair where she, perhaps, had also been napping. 'I could wake him, but there'd be ructions,' she warned.

'It's all right,' said Clem. 'I'll take some toys down for the twins. The Noah's Ark, perhaps.' It was on the floor and she crouched to scoop the animals inside.

Dinah knelt down to help.

'Look,' said Clem. 'Perhaps I should explain the queer situation with Mr Harris.'

'No need,' Dinah said stiffly.

'Well, yes, I rather think there is.'

Dinah reached for a giraffe. There was a faint skim of perspiration on her face and a sweaty smell; it really was unbearably close in the room.

'Is the window open?' Clem asked.

'Yes, only there's not a breath of a breeze.' Dinah hesitated. 'I did think it queer, if you don't mind me saying.'

'Mr Harris is certainly a curious fellow,' Clem said. 'I knew him in the war, you see, the field hospital in France. I ran into him by chance and he's become fixed on some ridiculous notion that I might help him – financially. Actually, he's been making rather a nuisance of himself.'

'Is *that* why he's been after me?' Dinah said indignantly. 'He did keep asking about you, come to think of it.'

'I expect so.'

'Ruddy cheek!' Dinah's voice had risen, and she flinched and glanced at the cot where Edgar was beginning to stir. 'Begging your pardon, ma'am.'

'And you see there's a third person, someone we both knew in France,' Clem went on. 'A lady – an invalid – and he, Mr Fortune that is, came yesterday to ask me to visit her. A lady called Mrs Gray, Ada, rather a sad case.'

Dinah's brow furrowed. She was pairing the animals – two elephants, two ostriches, two snakes – before dropping them in the ark. 'And he took you? Not on his motorbike?'

Clem nodded.

'What was it like?'

'Well, Ada was—'

'No. I mean the ride, ma'am?'

Clem allowed a conspiratorial smile. 'Actually, it was rather thrilling.'

Dinah's eyes widened and they both laughed. 'You'd never catch me on one of them,' she said. 'It's not natural, the speed they go!'

Edgar gave a sudden yell and Dinah jumped up. 'All right, little man.' She lifted him from his cot. 'All right, duckie, all right. Well, at any rate I won't be seeing Mr Harris again,' she said. 'Just let him show his face and I'll give him what for.' Edgar was writhing in her arms, rubbing his eyes, curls standing out like black bubbles around his head.

'No need to mention this to anyone else,' said Clem.

'Understood, ma'am.' Dinah hitched Edgar higher on her hip. 'I'll get his lordship changed and bring him down directly.'

'Thank you, Dinah.' Clem picked up the Noah's Ark and bore it back downstairs.

On the trolley beside the teapot and the fingers of bread and butter was smooth white cake. Dennis came up from the surgery and, scooping a twin under each arm, kissed their cheeks. 'Is this Claris, and this Phyllis?' he asked, deliberately getting it wrong and making them giggle.

'Bugger me!' He did a double take over Harri's hair.

'Dennis!' Clem nodded towards the children. 'But doesn't it look marvellous?' Smiling, she handed him a cup of tea.

'What's wrong with hair all of a sudden? It's a woman's—'

'If you say crowning glory,' said Harri, 'I'll scream.'

He pursed his lips.

Harri snorted. 'So, what time are you going out?'

'Can't wait to see the back of me?'

'That's about the size of it.'

'Harri!' Clem laughed, suddenly full of affection for her family, her home.

'Directly after late surgery. I ask you, hounded out of my own house!' He pulled a long-suffering face. 'Monstrous regiment of women,' he muttered.

'Simply monstrous.' Harri stuck out her tongue and crossed her eyes.

'Oh, you two,' Clem said. 'Anyway, we're hardly a regiment!' She caught a conspiratorial look flicking between them. 'What?'

'Surprise.' Harri tapped her nose.

With a sudden dip of the heart Clem guessed. 'I bet it's Gwen,' she said. 'Is it?'

'Oh, you wretch!'

'Clever girl,' said Dennis.

'Well, now you've guessed,' said Harri, 'I might as well tell all. We're to have a dinner, just us ladies – Mrs Hale's pushing the boat out. I chose the menu, I hope it's all right. Oysters, plaice, jellied capon with Russian salad, lemon soufflé, and Dennis has got some terrifically special Champagne.'

'Two bottles,' Dennis confirmed. 'But do leave some for me. Sorry I won't be there.'

'Well, you'd be a sore thumb at a ladies' dinner,' Harri pointed out. 'Oh, Clem! Now it's out in the open, why don't you invite Ada?'

'Ada?' said Dennis.

'Clem's mysterious pal.'

'Far too short notice,' said Clem, 'and in any case she's not . . . she really wouldn't . . . no.' The bright brown eyes of her husband and sister-in-law were searchlights on her face. Heat flooded her face as she crouched down to help Phyllis open the doors of the ark and tip all the animals out.

'Ada?' Dennis asked again.

'Just someone I used to know,' Clem mumbled. 'Elephant! Giraffe! What does a giraffe say?'

Phyllis looked at her nonplussed.

'What does it say?' Clem appealed to Dennis.

'Haven't the foggiest,' he said, frowning.

In the hall the telephone rang and Mrs Hale duly put her head round the door. 'Doctor, you're wanted.'

Dinah came in with a grizzling Edgar dressed in a sailor suit, hair wet from an attempted flattening. 'Back tooth,' she said.

Sighing, Dennis ruffled Edgar's hair and followed Mrs Hale and Dinah out.

'Well, fortunately,' said Harri, 'I have my magic necklace.' She lifted the amber beads over her head and handed them to Edgar who began to gnaw.

31

H ARRI SPRAWLED IN an armchair smoking a black Sobranie. Despite open windows, the room was oppressive, thick with smoke and the scent of roses and Harri's queer woody perfume. Clem wore her loosest primrose-yellow frock, arms bare, new pearls warm against the skin of her throat.

'So pretty,' Harri had said earlier, fingering them. 'He's got a good eye, you have to give him that.'

She'd rescued her amber beads from Edgar and wore them with an outfit fashioned from oriental scarves. With black kohl round her eyes she looked distinctly Bohemian and, perhaps, just the slightest bit cracked. Dennis had teased her on his way out, calling her an Egyptian, calling her affected. In return, she blew him an exuberant raspberry.

Clem regarded her now with a surge of fondness. 'I'm so glad you're here, Harri.'

'Goodness! Well, *réciproqué*, of course.' Harri kissed the tips of her fingers and blew. 'It *is* good to be back in the bosom, so to speak. Oh!' She jumped up as the roar of an engine and the spit of gravel heralded Gwen's arrival. Clem's stomach clenched. But it was only Gwen, good old Gwen. It would be all right. As long as there was no talk of *before*, it would be all right.

Gwen strode into the sitting room, dressed in jodhpur breeches, unwinding a long white scarf. Harri flung herself at Gwen in an embrace so enthusiastic it made Captain, who'd loped in behind her, growl and bare his teeth.

'It's all right, Cap.' Gwen patted Harri as if she herself were a dog.

'What a surprise,' Clem tried but Harri giggled as Clem put up her face for a kiss.

'She'd already guessed, the Hun!'

Gwen divested herself of a jacket, took from her bag a flat wrapped gift that could only be a record, and they went back into the sitting room.

'Half an hour, Halesy?' Harri called over her shoulder. 'We'll have some of your Melba toast with our sherry – or shall we start with the fizz, Clem? Oh, do let's.'

Captain flopped down in a lozenge of sunshine and Gwen sat on the sofa, stretching out her long legs. In her loose white silk shirt, she looked fresh and rather dashing.

'No gippy tummies this time?' She quirked her eyebrows at Clem.

'What's that?' said Harri.

'Nothing,' said Gwen.

'No Avis?' Clem said, pleading with her eyes for Gwen not to give her away.

'Gone, said Gwen, firmly enough to close the matter. 'And many happy returns,' she added, presenting the gift.

'You shouldn't have!' Clem peeled off the paper and read: 'ABC Original Dixieland Jazz Band. I don't believe I've heard of them.'

Harri snatched the record and set it on the gramophone. They listened for a moment to the jaunty ragtime. 'It simply forces one to dance, don't you think?' said Harri, and began to do so, causing Captain to growl warningly.

Mrs Hale came in with the Champagne and glasses and a stack of toasts, thin and crisp as autumn leaves, and set them down. 'Quite the party already!' she said.

'Come on, Halesy!' Harri grabbed her and tried to make her dance, which made Captain bark so loudly that Gwen had to grab his collar and sink to her knees to restrain him, and that coupled with watching Mrs Hale's stout body trying to keep up the pace and her face its dignity, made Clem laugh till the tears came.

Eventually Mrs Hale extricated herself and escaped, shaking her head, as the record wound down.

'After dinner, let's push back the furniture,' said Harri. 'Oh, we could really have done with a fourth, couldn't we? Two couples, well, *so-called* couples. I wanted to ask Ada – oh, I suppose *you'll* know her?' She looked, apparently guilelessly, at Gwen. 'Clem's friend from France – Red Cross, wasn't she?'

Clem turned her back to pour the Champagne. 'I don't believe Gwen ever had the pleasure.'

'When was this?' Gwen asked.

'Come on now,' Clem said, turning back to them with a painfully artificial heartiness. 'It's my birthday. No raking over old coals, if you don't mind.'

Gwen raised her glass, and they chinked and sipped and crunched toast and the subject was bypassed and the topic of conversation remained light and general. It was going to be all right. Clem began to relax as she swallowed the prickly Champagne too fast and felt it go, deliciously, directly to her head.

Throughout the iced oysters with brown bread and butter, the stuffed rolled plaice and the capon in aspic, Harri quizzed Gwen about her suffragist activities, fascinated by her escapades on

Felixstowe golf course – stories Clem had often heard. On several occasions Gwen and her comrades had raided the links, replacing the flags with purple ones, even using vitriol to burn the words *Votes for Women* and *Justice Before Sport* into the turf of the greens. On her wrist Gwen had a small raised scar, the result of an acid burn, which she displayed with some pride. On the final attack on the course, they'd been arrested, taken before a magistrate and sentenced to a week in prison.

'Heavenly!' exclaimed Harri.

'Don't be silly,' said Clem.

'What's it like in there?' Harri asked.

Gwen snorted. 'Well, heavenly's hardly the word I'd choose! Of course, it was an ordeal,' she added modestly. She was feeding titbits to Captain, who sat under the table with his head in her lap.

'How brave,' Harri said. 'Did you go on hunger strike?'

Gwen leaned forward to fill Harri's glass and her own. Clem's was still brimming. She was beginning to feel rather excluded from what seemed to be a mutual fascination between Harri and Gwen – or, at least, fascination on Harri's part and a rather nauseating gratification on Gwen's – and, come to think of it, she was feeling slightly queasy. A headache coming on, too much Champers too quickly. Uncharitable thoughts churned through her head though she smiled and nodded agreeably. Of course Gwen was admirable, heroic even, but heavens above, hadn't one heard enough about the antics of the suffragettes?

Mrs Hale came in to clear the plates. 'I'm sorry, madam, but little Edgar's beside himself and Dinah's run ragged up there what with the three of them. Linda's off and I'm up to my eyes.'

'Oh blast,' said Harri. 'I really should have brought Mildred, shouldn't I? I'll go up.'

'No,' said Clem. 'I'll go.'

'But it's your birthday,' Harri objected.

'I insist.' Clem stood and folded her napkin. 'Serve the pudding, Mrs Hale. I can catch up.' Clem went up the stairs, which seemed to go on for ever. Her head was woozy, legs soggy – she could hear Edgar wailing. She was glad to be away from the table, but would sooner lie on her cool bed in the quiet than tackle a struggling infant. Still, she went into the nursery to help and was able to give Edgar his bottle while Dinah tried to settle the twins head to toe in a camp bed. Dinah seemed quite natural, with no lingering awkwardness after this morning's conversation. Edgar, having calmed down, lay across Clem's lap sucking sporadically at his empty bottle, eyes glazed, twisting a finger in his curls.

'Good boy,' she murmured. Her eyes closed as Dinah sang, over and over, 'Wink and blink, and nod one night,' and she felt herself beginning to drift. She woke to feel the weight being lifted from her lap.

'I'll put him down, ma'am,' whispered Dinah.

'You're doing a sterling job,' Clem said as she crept out. She went into the bathroom to wash her face in cool water, and carried a glass into the bedroom to mix some powders for her head. From below she could hear Harri and Gwen moving through into the sitting room, the clink of plates as Mrs Hale cleared.

On her way down, she could not help but be drawn to the landing window. The sky was flushed, and though it was not dark there was a star already showing above the branches. Below the trees she glimpsed a figure – male, tall, slim – and clutched at the thick velvet curtain to steady herself.

Music pounded from below. Down the stairs she crept – a howl of laughter from the sitting room – and when she caught sight of herself in the hall mirror, her face was flushed, the new pearls gleaming as if wet against her skin. Silently she opened the door and stepped out into the cooler air.

Gwen's motorcycle and sidecar were parked by the steps. Clem went down and towards the tree, the gravel sharp through the soles of her silk slippers. Out on the road she heard an engine snarling away. There was no one there now, only the sound of the receding engine. Had there been someone there? In the dappling shadows one could easily be mistaken.

A blackbird sang from high up in the branches and there was the shifting in the leaves of some creature, bird or squirrel. She stood beneath the tree, breathing in its deep green scent, and then pressed her brow against its cool bark.

'Hello? Hello?' Hale came crunching towards her. 'Oh, it's you, ma'am. What are you doing out here? The missus saw the open door and—'

'It's perfectly all right, thank you,' said Clem. 'Just enjoying a breath of air. So muggy, isn't it?'

'It's close all right,' he said. 'What we want's a good old storm.'

'Quite.'

When she entered the sitting room she was not at first noticed. The music had changed now, to something slower, and the women were dancing; Harri's dark head against the breast of Gwen's white shirt, Gwen's hand low on Harri's back. Gwen's eyes were closed and the look on her face, serene and blissful, sent a fright through Clem.

'Now,' she said loudly. 'Shall we play a game?'

The two jumped apart.

'A game?' Harri's eyes were starry.

Something blared through Clem like a trumpet. Not jealousy?

Gwen gave her a lazy smile. 'I always like a game. What do you suggest?'

Gwen had left and both Dinah and Clem gone up to bed by the time Dennis returned. Clem, who'd been creaming her face, climbed into bed and waited nervously. One more thing, and it was over. All over. He was tipsy, she could tell, the way he was bumping about.

'Oh, good show, still awake...' he said, coming through the door. 'I thought you'd still be at it, thought I'd be coming home to an orgy of sapphists and suffragettes and Bolshies!'

'That *would* have made a good party!' she said.

He laughed and shook his finger at her. 'Just you wait, little girl.'

She took a deep breath. First must come the confession.

He launched himself at the bed, reached for her. 'I've got a bone to pick with you,' he said.

'What?'

'You were supposed to leave me some Champers,' he said. 'That cost me nearly a guinea.'

'Sounds like you've had quite sufficient.'

'Pretty.' He fingered the pearls, kissed the side of her neck, bristles tickling. 'Come on, lie down.'

She took a deep breath. 'No, please wait,' she said. 'There's something I must say.'

'Nothing to do with that Gwen, I hope!' He lifted himself on one elbow. 'Have you been naughty?' His fingers walked up her thigh and she caught and stopped them.

'Not naughty so much as... careless. I'm afraid you're going to be frightfully cross.'

'Never.' He fought his fingers free, pushed up her nightdress.

'Wait!' she said sharply. 'Please!'

'Can't I be frightfully cross later?' he groaned before hauling himself up to sit beside her. 'Go on then.'

'The money you gave me . . .'

'The fifty pounds. What of it?' An ominous timbre had entered his voice.

She took a deep breath and there was a genuine tremble in her own. 'I'm so sorry but it got lost.'

'*Got lost?*' From the dining room came the distant silly chitter of the carriage clock. '*Got lost?*' he repeated. And then came the deeper reverberation of the grandfather in the hall, striking and striking the hour. 'And how, pray, did it "get lost"?'

'I went for a stroll this morning. It was in my pocket. I don't know what I was thinking – that perhaps I'd walk as far as the shops, but I didn't, of course, in this heat. I stopped in the church-yard for a rest, then I came home.'

'And?'

'It must have fallen out or else I was pickpocketed . . . Oh, darling, my heart simply stopped when I realised it was missing.'

She could hear him breathing, smell tooth powder, alcohol and Brilliantine. She put her hands over her face.

'You didn't mention it, at luncheon.'

'I hadn't realised then . . . Darling, I've been so afraid to tell you.'

'My God, that *is* careless!' His voice was raised. 'Do you realise how much that is? How many consultations?'

'I'm sorry.' She began to cry; real tears for poor Dennis who believed every word, tears for her own lying heart.

'I suppose it didn't occur to you to inform the police?'

She shook her head. 'Oh, Dennis . . .' She reached out to touch his hot bare chest.

He frowned, pulled her head roughly against him. She could feel the tickle of his chest hair against her cheek and his bristles on top of her head. She could feel the outraged beating of his heart.

'I'm so, so sorry,' she murmured.

'Well, I can't pretend I'm not upset,' he said. 'Fifty pounds, just like that! My God!'

'What can I do?'

'You can lie down,' he said. 'You careless child. Lie down and I'll show you what for.'

As he ram-raided her body, she stared over his shoulder at the jumping ceiling: done, done, done, done, done.

32

Tomorrow noon. The Crown. V.

CLEM ROSE FROM the breakfast table to throw the note into the hearth, but on such a warm day there was no fire. She turned round and round uselessly, foot catching on the fringe of the rug, screwing the note in her fist. The raging cheek of him! No word since the ludicrous conversation in that squalid pub and she'd really begun to hope – even to believe – that he'd come to his senses.

She sat down and regarded the breakfast paraphernalia. Though her stomach was scrunched as tight as the note, she must eat. She gazed blankly at the irises, on their last day, indeed past it, petals softened and pendulous. From below came Dennis's voice, steady and reassuring against the querulous tone of a female patient. She spread toast with butter. Beside her plate, the note unfurled like an opening flower.

She was so nearly in the clear now. Just this one thing. And what a pathetically queer thing! One afternoon of play-acting and then it would all be over. Really? He'd certainly *seemed* sincere though with that class of person can one ever really know?

She spread honey onto the toast. Through the window came the trudge of feet on gravel, the ring of the bell, a busy surgery. An evil summer cold was doing the rounds, and going straight to the lungs of the elderly and the infirm, especially those fellows still suffering from the effects of mustard gas, Dennis told her. Each contagion did for another swathe of those.

Her cooling tea had grown a grey skin and as she tried a sip, bile rose in her throat. No, no, no, don't allow *that* thought.

'He's over there.' The landlady nodded towards their usual nook.

Vincent stood aside to let Clem in and, rather self-consciously, she squeezed past him. 'So?' she said.

'Brandy?'

She requested lemonade. Don't risk any clouding of the mind. As he stood at the bar, she noticed that the landlady was cordial with him, friendly even, and guessed he'd been cultivating her. His witness, of course. But it was going to be all right. She glanced around at the other clientele: a man perched on a barstool with a sheepdog at his feet, another lunching on a pie. No one taking a scrap of notice.

Vincent was soon back, offering her a cigarette, and when she shook her head, he lit his own, drew on it and leaned back, observing her.

The smell of the smoke brought a rush of sourness to her mouth and she sipped her lemonade. 'So?'

He looked tired, his fingers nicotine-stained, his nails ragged. 'This one last thing and then I'll vanish.' Pinching the cigarette in the corner of his mouth, he picked up a beermat, folded it between his hands, and opened them on emptiness. 'Like so.'

She smiled faintly at his trick.

'If not . . .' he went on, 'well, that's your lookout. I might just book a consultation with a certain doctor. I might just tell tales to a certain nursemaid. There's lots of things I might have a mind to do.' The beermat appeared back on the table.

'There's no need to be unpleasant, Vincent.'

He grimaced ironically.

'I mean, even if I had a mind to, how could I?' she reasoned. 'To be away for an evening. What's my husband going to think? I'm already skating on thin ice . . .'

He shrugged, exhaled smoke.

'And in any event, I don't know if I could convincingly "make up", as you put it, to a perfect stranger.' Though as she spoke she was shocked by a base little thrill at the idea of being *forced* to do so. There was a class of women who could perfectly well do it, did it – and far more – every day, she was well aware of that. Women fashioned of the same stuff as herself.

'Nothing would *happen*,' he said. 'It's smoke and mirrors, a charade.'

'A charade,' she repeated. Through the door came Giles Hubert. What was *he* doing here? She shrank down in her chair. 'Saw the little woman in the Crown,' he might say to Dennis, if he caught sight of her. And then what?

She picked up the beermat and examined it. Perfectly ordinary, a little soft at the edges, advertising Green King. A charade, Vincent called it. That made it sound harmless enough. 'Do I have your word of honour that this would be the end?'

Vincent nodded.

'Swear on the Bible?' she said.

'Got one in your handbag, have you?' Vincent smirked.

'All right,' Clem said. 'Swear on the life of whoever you care about most in the world.'

'I swear,' he said, and she saw how his knuckles whitened.

She fiddled with the beermat. 'Who would I be deceiving and why?'

'Just a certain party,' he said, 'that's all you need to know.'

She sipped the lemonade, wriggled her thumbnail between layers of cardboard and began to peel the beermat apart. 'How can you be sure it would work? What, for instance, if he wasn't taken with me?'

'You don't need to worry about that.' Vincent twisted sideways so that he could cross his long legs and she shifted in order to stay hidden.

'He'll think I'm a tart.'

He narrowed his eye. 'Would it matter?'

'It would matter to me!'

The door opened and Giles stood to greet the woman who entered, a woman who was not his wife. Clem was shocked, and then she almost laughed – as if she was in a position to judge! As she peered over Vincent's shoulder, the two shook hands before the landlady showed them upstairs.

'You'd never see hide nor hair of him again,' Vincent was saying. 'Spin him any claptrap you like. Ask him to buy you a drink, sit close beside him, use your imagination. Just make sure the lady sees.'

'If I'm to go along with this . . . this *charade*,' she said, 'it's only fair you tell me what it's all *for*.'

He lit a new Capstan from the stub of the other, inhaled and slowly blew out the smoke. 'Fair do's. This lady, she's the landlady of the Wild Man, and she and yours truly, we're like this.' He crossed two fingers. 'But someone else's got his beady eye on her and I don't want her head turned. I just want her to see what he's made of, that's all. Harmless, really.'

She refrained from laughing. It was like a trashy romance! Of course what else could one expect from one of his ilk? Though up above – maybe in that same green room – conducting his own tawdry affair, was boring, worthy Giles Hubert, who, at dinner, had seemed so devoted to his boring, worthy wife.

'Was it *her* life you swore on?' she asked. 'This landlady?'

He nodded and said, with unnecessary fervour, 'I did. I swear on her life.'

'However it turns out?'

'I *swear*.'

' "On her life" – say it,' she insisted, feeling pleasure in her power.

'On her life. And my own.'

'Even if it doesn't work? If I do my bit, that's it?'

'I swear.'

They sat in silence.

'All I want's for her to see that the sun doesn't shine out of his . . .' He cleared his throat. 'Then she'll come to her senses.'

'And when do you propose this pantomime take place?'

'Friday.'

'This Friday!'

He nodded.

She peeled the sides of the mat apart and laid them both face up. Two identical green faces looking in opposite directions. Covertly she watched Vincent smoke. All the money he'd had out of her, all the fear and fright and yet . . . still she couldn't hate him. Poor man, with all he'd been through. And he had – hadn't he? – helped her come to some sort of peace within herself. Came to mind the salt of that tear rising so purely, so queerly, from its duct.

'He always turns up of a Friday,' he was saying. 'Creature of habit.'

An idea was glimmering into life. It so happened that Dennis had his fortnightly game of bridge this Friday. She might make an excuse to be out – a Red Cross meeting in Felixstowe, say – and she could stay the night with Gwen. Dennis was invariably at the golf course on Saturday mornings. Afterwards, if she showed any interest, he'd talk about his round till kingdom come and probably never think to ask what she'd been up to. And if he *were* curious, the thought of Gwen would be a distraction. She could make something up.

She picked up her gloves. 'And this will really be the end of it?'

'I swore, didn't I? You have my word.'

'Then, Vincent, I shall take you at your word.'

33

I T'S A DEVIL of a job getting away. Kegs to change, dicky pipe
to see to, and then Kenny grazes his knee and wants patching
up, and all the while Doll's upstairs primping – the smell of singed
hair drifting down. Not a word about Chamberlain since the holiday but the trouble she's going to with them curling irons speaks
volumes. You could almost feel sorry for her, going to so much
trouble.

Eventually he makes his escape, sets off on the Norton, heart in
mouth. Strategy's immaculate but you can't control the other players, that's what bothers him. Must be what it's like directing a
moving picture, worrying whether all the players can carry it off.
Doll's got to fall for it, of course, *and* Chamberlain. Unlikely he
won't; he's a ladies man after all, eyes popping out of his head at
almost anything between sixteen and forty. So why – Vince acceler-
ates – why the hell does he have to go after Doll, just when Vince's
getting his feet properly under the table?

This reward is *due* to him. After the war, the shit, the sacrifice –
and it was sacrifice, it was heroism. If he hadn't put his head over
the parapet on that day, at that minute, he might have got away
with it. He could still have both eyes, be back at Mostyn's Mustards,
working his way up to the board, no doubt, so yes, this is his due all
right. He's due the pub, due Doll, due a position that befits him.

Coasting a bend, he steers to miss a grey shape, skids, begins to slide, rights himself – not too bad, not too bad – sees an old lurcher limping away, head down. Could have killed it, could have killed himself, but no, it's all right. Take it as a warning though. Deep breaths. Keep steady, Vincey boy.

With more care he drives towards the station. And there she is, large as life, though looking a bit on the seedy side – white face, dark shadows round her eyes.

'Under the weather?' he says.

She just gazes at him, eyes like water. Nervous, of course, she's bound to be, only natural.

'Here.' He hands her his spare helmet. She looks round, but it's quiet; just the odd dog walker taking not a blind bit of notice. She removes her hat, puts it in her bag, which he stows in the pannier as she straps on the helmet. And then they're off, taking it slowly, taking it carefully. Softly, softly, catchee monkey.

He drives round the back and ushers her into the outhouse. Had the forethought to put a chair in there, a cushion and – brainwave! – a mirror on a hook behind the door so she can tidy herself. He wonders now about fetching some of Doll's pots of this and that, and some scent, to liven her up a bit, but – they don't like to be criticised, women, he knows that much – doesn't dare.

'All right? All set?'

She's wearing grey gloves, clenched tightly together on her lap. Through the thin cloth you can see the shape of her rings. 'Take your rings off?' he suggests. 'Best if he thinks you're single.'

She nods and begins removing her left glove.

'Well then, I'll leave you to it,' he says. 'When it's time I'll give you the nod.'

He'll have to trust she comes out of herself; she looks about as seductive as a draper's dummy at the moment. He has an idea – she wants perking up, of course!

He shuts the door on her, hurries across the yard and into the back, through into the bar. Ted's not yet arrived. What if he doesn't? It's still early, but he always comes on a Friday, regular as clockwork. He must, he has to.

'Where the heck have you been?' says Doll.

'Man about a dog.' He gives her his sideways smile – good side, of course, which usually does the trick – but she only frowns.

'I don't know what you did with that keg, but it's clogged, wants seeing to.'

'Straight away, ma'am.' He does a mock salute.

'Oi!' She's seen him taking a brandy, but he's out of the door again, and she can't follow him, not with customers waiting.

He nips across the yard, opens the outhouse door. There she sits, stiff as a poker in the gloom. 'Get this down you,' he says. 'And for pity's sake cheer up a bit. It's a lark!'

Grinning, he shuts the door. A lark! He takes himself aback sometimes, he really does. A proper card they used to call him, with his jokes and his conjuring tricks. That side of him got smashed by the war, that and how he's been treated since. But once he's set up, back will come the jokes. He'll stand behind that bar and have them in stitches, night after night.

In the cellar he fixes the problem with the keg, comes up out of the hatch to find Kenny poking in the larder. 'What are you after?' he says. 'You've had your tea.'

'I'm a growing boy,' Kenny says, cutting a hunk of cheese.

Normally Vince'd want to clip his ear for that – growing boy indeed, I'll give you growing boy. Once he's married, officially the stepfather, he'll come down like a ton of bricks, knock some manners into the kid – but not yet.

He returns to the bar, into the thick of it.

'All sorted, Doll,' he says and she gives him a grateful nod.

His eyes keep flicking to the clock, not half past yet. He catches Doll doing the same. He's got a fizzing in his chest, pours lights instead of bitters, darks instead of lights, 'Don't know what's got into me,' he says. They're all used to him by now, the regular punters; whether they know how deep in it with Doll he is or not, he's no idea, but there's likely gossip. He hopes there's gossip. They must wish they were in his shoes – look at her! She's laughing and joking now in the amputees' corner. Sinclair, or whatever his name is, is in his bath chair, the two fat stumps of his thighs under a rug and his eyes staring straight at her bosoms, which, fair do's, are right in his eyeline. He'll never get his hands on them though, poor sod.

Right on the dot, Ted waltzes in as if he owns the place. Vince looks up from the pump. Christ he's got his ice-cream seller's jacket on, straw hat, moustache gleaming like a pair of brass handles. He waves at Doll who only nods, but she tenses, Vince notices, holds herself a little straighter, pats the back of her hair.

'Steady on,' says the punter as beer overflows the glass.

Ted makes for the bar. Vince is ready for him, 'Pint of the usual?' he says affably.

'What I ought to do is bring a tankard of my own, hang it behind the bar,' Chamberlain says. There's someone at his usual seat, so he stands, gets out his pipe.

'Busy this evening,' Vince remarks. 'It's the sunshine brings them out. How's business for you?' He'll let him get settled, get the first drink inside him.

Chamberlain's mouth purses and he wobbles his hand from side to side. 'Not an easy time,' he says, 'what with the strikes and all. A load of Bolsheviks in the works if you ask me. Just got to hold me nerve.'

Vince nods sympathetically. The two men at the end of the bar bang down their glasses and leave, and Chamberlain claims his usual perch. Good, good, so far. That's one duck lined up. Doll stops to have a word with him. Vince watches the gobbling way his lips go at the pipe, the yellow teeth, fat neck. Whatever does she see in him? Answer's obvious, Vincey-boy: spondulix, it's all about spondulix.

Doll comes back behind the bar. 'Just popping up to make sure Kenny's doing his—'

'Homework,' Vince supplies. 'You leave that to me.'

He goes out to the backyard where the sun's still shining, crosses to the outhouse door and steps in. She's just where he left her, clutching the empty brandy glass, maybe not quite so stiff.

'Come in the front door straight into the bar,' he says. 'He's sitting at the end. You can't miss him, jacket like a blooming deckchair.'

He shuts the door and stands with his back against it. Christ, if he's jittery, how must she be feeling? He opens the door again. 'Chin up,' he says, 'do this and we're square.'

She nods once and he closes the door, legs it across the yard and back inside.

34

SHE OPENED THE door and, blinking in the brightness, walked round to the front of the Wild Man. A long pretty pub, Suffolk pink, with window boxes of white geraniums and pansies. Rather a pleasant place. With the brandy and the lingering effects of last night's Veronal, she felt daring, detached, almost peaceful, as she adjusted her hat and stepped inside. The place was certainly a cut about the Crown, clean and cheerful with bright yellow paint and gleaming brass.

From behind the bar, Vincent nodded expressionlessly towards a portly man in a garish striped blazer, puffing away at his pipe. 'Act the damsel in distress,' he'd told her earlier. 'He'll be eating out of your hand in no time, you watch.'

And so she approached the man. One or two people looked up. Unusual for a woman of her class to enter a public bar alone, that's all it was. No one knew her – she glanced around to make sure. Just a couple of old men yarning away and a corner full of wounded veterans playing cards and dominos. The landlady was chatting with them, laughing about something. She was a gaudy, big-beamed common type, rouged and powdered. *Vincent's* landlady? *Really?*

Clem stood close beside the man, who turned at once, eyes flicking down her body. 'Excuse me,' she said, 'I'm in rather a predicament. I wonder if perhaps you might help?'

'Well, well,' he said, puffing at his pipe, regarding her through baggy eyes as he let out the smoke. 'Never let it be said that Teddy Chamberlain failed a damsel in distress. What's the problem?'

She pressed her lips together to stop the laugh that tried to bubble up. How oddly easy this was! 'Well, you see,' she said, 'someone dropped me off and we had a disagreement and now he's driven away.'

He guffawed. 'Driven away! Left you high and dry, has he?'

She looked ruefully at him through her lashes.

'Allow me to buy you a drink?' he said.

'Oh, that would be so kind of you. Mr Chamberlain, is it? I've had to walk for simply miles.'

'Teddy to my friends.'

'Anna Chance,' said Clem. She'd chosen the name as she sat waiting in the outhouse.

'Delighted, Miss Chance. Anna, if I may?' He took her hand in his plump, moist one and squeezed as he gestured to the landlady, but it was Vincent who came to serve them, almost barging the landlady out of the way.

'What can I get you?'

'The usual for *moi*, and for the lady?'

'A lemonade would be simply divine.' She was beginning to enjoy herself.

'This cad who left you stranded . . .' began Mr Chamberlain.

'Not really a cad – my brother.' This she had not planned to say, should not have said, bringing poor dear Ralph to her mind as it did. But *no*: concentrate. Stay here. Get through this.

'Some brother!' said Mr Chamberlain.

Clem blinked. 'He hasn't been the same since . . . well, he came back from France in one piece, thank heavens,' she improvised, 'but his mind . . . He forgets things, you see. He stopped the car for me to jump out and open a farm gate and then simply drove off. So I'm quite stranded.'

'Thought you said you'd quarrelled?' He scratched his chin.

'Well, naturally, we're always quarrelling! Cat and dog.'

He let his eyes rest on her lips, slid them once more down her body. 'Don't you worry, dearie,' he said. 'We'll have a nice little drink together and then we'll see if I can't drive you home.'

'Oh, would you really? How simply saintly,' she said, wondering if she might be going too far.

But he didn't seem to think so. 'Take a pew.' He patted the high stool beside him and she obeyed. 'So where am I taking you, Anna? Pretty name. Palindrome.'

'Oh yes!' She was surprised one of his ilk should have the wit to think such a thing – and immediately ashamed of her snobbishness. Feeling Vincent's scrutiny, she kept her smile going unnaturally long. 'Felixstowe.'

'Nice town, first-class resort,' he said ruminatively. 'Used to go to the shows at the Pavilion before the war. Marvellous spectacle. And to bathe when I was a nipper. In a rush, are you?'

'Well, I shouldn't like to be *too* late. My brother will be home by now, you see, and they'll all be wondering what's become of me.'

The landlady was giving her an abrasive look, and from behind her smirked Vincent, evidently pleased with her performance.

'What do you do for a living, Mr Chamberlain?' Clem asked.

'Teddy, I insist. We're all friends here.'

'Teddy.' She made herself look at his brassy moustache, his salami-mottled cheeks, his watery blue eyes.

'I'm in motors,' he began, and as he talked exhaustively about the trade, she kept gazing at him, wondering how long she must continue. Was it going to be enough, this devoted gazing?

The landlady had come to stand nearby, polishing glasses, quite clearly eavesdropping. Clem risked a glance at Vincent, who gave a single encouraging nod and got on with mixing a drink.

'Mrs Pepper, Miss Chance.' Mr Chamberlain broke off quite suddenly to do his introduction.

'Delighted,' said Clem, smiling at the older woman who returned the smile, but tightly.

'Good evening.'

'Isn't it a heavenly evening?' Clem said, and watched dents darken between Mrs Pepper's eyes. She'd applied too much colour to her brows and cheeks, but her face was kindly, actually rather lovely. 'Mr Chamberlain . . . sorry, Ted' – Clem smiled at him coquettishly – 'has come to my rescue. Isn't he a brick? He's going to drive me home.'

'Is he indeed?'

'Don't you worry, my dear. I'll be back,' he said as Mrs Pepper turned away, plucking empty glasses from a table.

Mr Chamberlain was relighting his pipe. 'You don't mind?' he said, lifting it in her direction.

'Oh no, I adore the smell of pipe smoke,' she said, and that set him off on a diatribe about types of tobacco, and the superiority, in his consideration, of Granger Rough Cut, which really was, he guffawed throatily, 'a cut above'.

'I don't suppose you might have a cigarette?' she asked.

'Funnily enough, I do,' he said. 'I like a gasper for a change.'

She took her holder from her bag and leaned close as he lit the cigarette, steadying herself with a hand lightly on his arm, which seemed to quiver at her touch. But at the first inhalation she felt dizzy, reminded of her condition, and she held it away from her.

Mr Fortune had been right. This wasn't difficult. All she had to do was look at him, simper a bit, say, *yes, yes, oh, really?* Mr

Chamberlain was playing along almost as if conscious of the charade, which seemed to be working in so far as it was making the landlady cross, but which might, she reflected, actually work in *his* favour and backfire entirely on Vincent.

'Well, let's get you home then,' said Mr Chamberlain at last, hauling himself off the stool and straightening his jacket.

'Too kind of you,' she said.

'Just one moment,' said Mr Chamberlain as they reached the door. He went back to speak to Mrs Pepper but she pointedly struck up a conversation with someone else and ignored him. Clem caught Vincent's eye and a corner of his mouth quirked upwards. Soon be over, soon be over. She felt in her pocket for her rings . . . there was her wedding band but she couldn't feel the engagement ring. Her gloved fingers scrabbled; she tried her other pocket, and then began to delve in her bag.

'Come along then,' said Mr Chamberlain. Still rummaging in her bag, she followed him outside.

'Here she is,' he said, sweeping a hand in the direction of his motor, a shiny red and black vehicle with its soft top rolled down. 'Four cylinders,' he was saying, patting the car proprietorially, 'nippy little girl, forty miles per hour . . .'

Must have dropped it in the outhouse! She could not possibly go home without her ring. 'I'm sorry,' she said, 'I must . . .' What, what? 'Something I need . . .' And she fled round the side of the pub, across the yard to the outhouse. Only as she flung open the door did she realise that he was behind her.

'I see,' he said. 'Like that, is it? Well, this is a turn-up for the books!' He pushed her inside, one hand drawing her against him as he elbowed shut the door.

'No,' she said. 'No, you misunderstand. I've lost something.'

His moustache was damp on the back of her neck. 'Get off,' she said and twisted away, catching sight of a glint under the chair as she turned. She crouched down, reached under the chair and grabbed the ring.

He was leaning against the door. 'However did you lose something in here?' he said slowly. 'Thought you came in from the road?'

She could think of no plausible explanation, she could think of absolutely nothing. Lemonade, bitterly mixed with bile, rose in the back of her throat.

'I do believe you've been playing me,' he murmured, 'and now here we are. Look at us, alone in a dark place – what should we do? I'm not short of a bob or two if that's your game.' He lunged at her and she thumped her fist into his belly but he only laughed. 'No little tart gets the better of me.'

As his hand went down to lift her skirt, she brought her knee violently up between his legs. With a groan he let her go and crumpled to the ground. She pulled open the door and ran out, but what could she do, dishevelled as she was? She would have to go back into the bar, get Vincent out to deal with this. She straightened her clothes, her hat, and took off her left glove to restore her rings. She'd simply have to walk back in and ask Vincent to take her to Felixstowe, or to telephone for a cab.

Vincent emerged round the side of the building. 'What the hell?' he was saying. 'What's happened? His car's still there. What's up? Where is he?'

Clem nodded at the outhouse. Vince stood motionless, staring at Clem, before he went to open the door.

Mr Chamberlain was staggering to his feet. 'Fortune,' he grunted. 'Help me up, will you? That mad bitch . . .'

Clem cast around. Should she begin to walk, simply walk away? But it was miles.

Vincent had helped Mr Chamberlain out and now he stood, bent over, hands on knees, panting.

'Let's get you back inside,' Vincent said. 'A brandy on the house.' He shook his head at Clem, glaring questioningly.

'I'm sorry,' she mouthed, grimacing.

In answer Vincent threw his hands apart, and Clem winced, realising that Mr Chamberlain had witnessed this communication. Slowly the man stood upright, restored his hat, looking from one to the other. His skin had gone a peculiar chalk blue and his jaunty jacket was soiled.

'I see,' he said.

'Brandy on the house,' Vincent repeated. 'A double, do you?'

'Think I'm beginning to get the picture—'

'I'm sorry,' Clem said to Vincent, 'but he tried to—'

'Shut up,' snapped Vincent.

'A nice little plot cooked up between the two of you, eh?' said Mr Chamberlain. 'What's the game, eh? Now, let me see . . . get this little tart to chat me up in front of Doll?'

'Show you up in your true colours,' said Vincent. 'And it did, didn't it?'

'He tried to . . . molest me,' Clem said.

'You led me in there, you fucking tease.' Spittle flew from Mr Chamberlain's mouth.

'I didn't,' said Clem to Vincent. 'I didn't mean him to follow.'

Vincent was opening and closing his fists. 'Come on, Ted,' he said at last. 'Let me buy you a drink and then I'll take this . . . lady home.'

'Please,' said Clem.

'Doll's sorry for you, you do know that?' Mr Chamberlain said slowly, eyeing Vincent. 'If you could be a fly on the wall during some of our little *tête-à-têtes*.'

Vincent stood motionless, hands hanging loosely at his sides, as Chamberlain continued. 'I've said to her often, Doll, I've said, why don't you send him packing? Sponging off you, putting the customers off their drinks.'

Vincent moved not a muscle.

'That's enough,' Clem said weakly.

'Ugly tin mug. Christ, who wants to be faced with that when they come out for a pint?'

He began backing away from the dangerous stillness of Vincent, but seemed unable to stop himself blurting. 'But she's soft as putty, isn't she? She says, "Oh, I haven't the heart. Wait till he's got a job. He's making himself quite useful about the place in the meantime." The hash you made of that decorating! Hopping mad she was!'

Vincent stepped forward, drew back his fist and aimed a cracking punch at Mr Chamberlain's jaw. The man clamped his hand against it but didn't seem able to stop. 'You at the Naze!' he crowed. 'Thought you'd sweep her off her feet, did you? You know what she said? She said, "You come along too, Teddy. I shan't be able to bear him, the creepy way he looks at me."'

Vincent smashed his fist into Mr Chamberlain's face again, and this time he fought back and the two of them fell, heavy and grunting, to wrestle on the ground.

There was nothing else for it. Clem ran back into the pub. Mrs Pepper looked up, puzzled. 'Come quickly,' Clem said. 'There's a fight. You must come.'

'Just a tick, dear,' Doll said to the man she'd been talking to, and hurried outside with Clem.

'Pack it in, the pair of you!' she shouted when she saw the two men tangling on the ground. 'Good God in heaven, what's going on?'

Vincent was on top. His tin eye had slid round the side of his head to reveal the awful angry landscape. Mr Chamberlain was bleeding from the nose.

'I shall throw a bucket of water over the pair of you,' shrieked Doll.

Vincent pulled away, got up, stood with his back to them adjusting his face. His breath was coming hard; you could see his ribs expanding and contracting, the ridges of his vertebrae even through his shirt. A couple of men had come out and were making their way across. 'Everything all right, Doll? Need a hand?'

'Show's over,' said Mrs Pepper. 'Go back inside.'

'Help me, Doll,' said Mr Chamberlain, and, throwing a filthy look at Vincent and Clem, Doll took Mr Chamberlain's arm and escorted him back inside the pub.

Clem shut her eyes for the ride to Felixstowe, feeling the sweet summer air whip against her face, cool on her silk-stockinged shins. She went with the swaying, deep to the left, deep to the right, as the engine roared; twice as fast it seemed as on the earlier journey and she clung on tight, arms round Vincent's waist, cheek pressed against his back.

Eventually he stopped and she opened her eyes. They were at the top of the Spa Gardens. Still light, of course, nearly the longest day. The sea sparkled pinkly opalescent; the trees and bushes were beginning to gather darkness between their leaves.

'Well,' Vincent said. His specs were bent and the eye sat askew, some of the scar visible. His mouth was a flat, grim line.

'I must sit down,' she said and, with unsteady legs, went to the nearest bench. Stiffly he sat beside her.

A man with a white cane tapped past. 'Evening,' he said, sensing their presence.

'Good evening,' Clem said, Vincent not a word.

'So?' he said after an uncomfortable few moments.

'I did my best,' Clem began and she explained what had happened. He listened, lips pressed together, cradling his right hand, knuckles bruised and swollen, in his left. 'I'm sorry,' she finished, 'but he would have—'

'All right. I get it.'

They sat in silence. Swallows were swooping and there was the seaside smell of petals and salt; the breeze from the sea was getting up and she shivered. Vincent, who had been gazing out to sea as she spoke, turned to look at her. He held his hand against his prosthesis, trying to make it straight. 'You all right then?'

'Well, I . . . stopped him.'

Astonishing her, Vincent sniggered. 'You stopped him all right. He wants stopping. He wants stopping once and for all.' His voice was raw and harsh, increasing her shiveriness. Were they swallows or bats?

'So, it's over?' said Clem.

He was silent. Distantly you could hear the shushing of the sea, or perhaps it was the breeze in the shrubbery.

'I'm sorry it went wrong,' she said, and she meant it. She did feel sorry, sorry for this man with his ludicrous scheme, this poor, poor soul. She felt an instinct to touch him before she left, to kiss his cheek, but she refrained, stepped back. After all, one doesn't want to risk encouragement.

'Time I went,' Clem said. 'I'm staying with a friend, and she'll be wondering . . .'

'Want a lift?'

'No, thank you,' she said. 'It's not far. I'll be perfectly all right. Goodbye, Vincent.' And she stood and walked away.

35

WHEN CLEM WENT down to the kitchen in the morning there stood Gwen in paisley dressing gown and Turkish slippers, burning toast. The reek of it caught in Clem's throat. The kitchen table was a sprawl of newspapers, books, pamphlets, letters, an overflowing ashtray, a box of flea powder. How typical of Gwen to shun a char and do – or not do – for herself. Captain, flopped on his side on an army blanket, took up half the floor, adding his doggy smell to the infusion.

'Morning.' Gwen blinked at her. 'Feeling better? Sleep?'

Clem nodded though she hadn't slept for more than a few moments at a time, heartbeat scattering wildly as the farcical events of the evening played over and over in her mind, making her cringe, almost laugh, squirm. *Poor* Vincent. But as long as it was over, as long as it was really over, she could forget about it now.

'Tea . . . or Turkish coffee?' Gwen's peppery hair was flattened on one side, her cheek pillow-creased. From the stove the coffee pot began to gurgle out a tarry aroma.

'I'd rather milk,' Clem said, blanching.

'Milk, eh?' Gwen nodded as if a suspicion was confirmed.

Clem stepped over the dog's haunches to sit down.

'Here.' Gwen pushed things aside to make space on the table and put down a plate of blackened toast, guffawing at Clem's expression. 'Charcoal's tip-top for the bowels,' she said. 'But I can do fresh if you prefer?'

'Thanks. Don't trouble.' Clem sipped milk from a chipped cup, avoiding the chip. Last night she'd claimed a headache and gone straight to bed, thus postponing the inevitable inquisition, but now she was certain to be in for it.

But, 'I thought we might walk to the ferry this morning,' was all Gwen said. She poured thick coffee into a tiny orange lustre cup and lit a Gitane. 'You?'

Clem shook her head.

Gwen sat down, drew deeply on her cigarette and paused, closing her eyes to savour the taste. 'Ferry across, picnic lunch at Bawdsey?' she suggested on the smoky outbreath.

'Not feeling very well, I'm afraid.'

Gwen tilted her chair back till she was balancing on its back legs. 'So, *what* was it you were up to last night?'

Clem began to grope for an answer but the rich mixture of dog, Turkish coffee and French tobacco made her retch. Her hand flew to her mouth, and tears stood in her eyes. Captain hauled himself up and lumbered across to the table to scrutinise her.

'Sit,' Gwen said and fed him a toast crust. 'So, number two on the way, I gather?'

Clem flinched.

'Heard you vomiting in the night,' Gwen said. 'And you're the colour of a maggot.'

'Thanks,' Clem smiled weakly. 'Actually . . .'

'Actually?' Gwen shimmied forward on the chair and the dog laid his great head on her lap, eyes beseeching. 'Oh, look at him! You don't want this, do you?' She reached for Clem's toast and fed it to him bit by bit. Nauseously Clem watched the long pink tongue caressing Gwen's buttery, black-flecked fingers. 'Pleased?' Gwen said. 'Only you don't look it.'

Clem closed her eyes to prevent the tears but they squeezed through her lashes.

'Thought not.'

'I was so ill after Edgar.' The dog was watching her intently, brown eyes sharp beneath shaggy grey eyebrows.

'But that was after the business in France,' Gwen said. 'Entirely different circs. No reason for it to happen again.' She leaned over and patted Clem's hand. 'Chin up.'

'I'm not ready.'

'You'll get used to it. I imagine Dennis is cock-a-hoop?'

'Will be when I tell him.'

Gwen crowed. 'Call himself a doctor? *I* knew soon as look at you!'

'Well, I'm not hiding it from *you,* am I?'

Gwen pinched her cigarette between her lips and squinted against the smoke as she topped up her coffee. 'Like that, is it?'

'Not at all!' Clem protested, then gave up and shrugged. 'Yes, I suppose it is.'

'You don't want it?'

With her fist, Clem dashed away a tear. 'Oh, I don't know.' It was in her at that moment to tell Gwen about Vincent, about her whole ridiculous predicament. But what would that achieve apart from demonstrating to Gwen, once again, what a weak-minded ninny she was?

'Well, I do know of someone,' Gwen said. With a fingernail she delicately picked a crumb of sleep from her eye. 'But I'd advise against, dear. Risky business. And there's no reason for it, is there? You're healthy, married, not short of a bob or two.'

Clem couldn't speak for the sickness rising in her throat. Everything smelled foul: the dog, the coffee, the smoke, even the oilcloth tablecloth. She hadn't been so sick during her pregnancy with Edgar though she could hardly remember much of that. Returning from France so stunned she barely functioned, marrying Dennis in a blur, becoming pregnant; it seemed as if a distant shadow sister had lived through that.

Last night, lying in the narrow spare bed, it had come flooding back – the fright and joy of learning she was carrying Powell's child, his joy, and then the unspeakable, the unbearable end. Oh, now the door had come unlocked and there she was, the furled-up fern child small enough to curl into a walnut shell, into Gwen's tiny lustre coffee cup.

'Why not just buck up and get on with it?' Gwen was saying. 'Think yourself lucky. I can fetch you a pail if you want to vom?'

Clem put her hands over her face and leant over her lap. The dog put his great head close, sniffling her hair.

'Captain,' Gwen said indulgently, 'come here. Leave her be. Pail?'

Clem shook her head.

There came the wallop of the newspaper through the letter flap.

'Why don't you go back up?' Gwen said. 'Lie down for half an hour?'

Clem raised her head and looked about her. It was as if the kitchen was only lightly sketched over the interior of the hospital where Aida had left her. The chequered pattern red on white, tiles cold against her knees as she sank down, cold against her cheek as she gave herself up to the loss.

'Either go and lie down, dear, or buck yourself up, do,' said Gwen.

Clem swallowed hard, mustering herself back to the present.

'What about a walk?' Gwen said. 'Nothing wrong with you a breath of fresh air and a dose of common sense won't fix.'

Clem decided. 'I shall go home,' she said. If she went soon, there would be time to bathe and pull herself together before facing Dennis, who would be on the golf course by now. Or she might fake a headache, pretend sleep. If she could get her hands on the Veronal, she could *really* sleep, deeply sleep the day away.

Gwen fetched the paper. 'I'll drive you,' she said. 'Bet you've never been on a motorcycle?'

Clem gave a sickly smile.

'Either on the pillion or, if you'd rather, you can squeeze in the sidecar with Captain. I can hardly put *him* on the back!' She laughed and ruffled his head. 'But first, I'm going to finish the pot.' She poured coffee and sat down again, flapping open her newspaper.

'I'll go up and collect my things,' said Clem.

'There's hot water if you'd like to take a jug up.'

Upstairs in the tiny, cheerless, book-stacked bedroom, Clem poured water into a cracked and dusty bowl, washed and tidied herself, trying in vain to make her hair sit neatly. Would Powell have liked her hair like this? *Honey*, he used to call her, *honey*. Gazing at her wan face in the mirror she noticed a wretched spot starting on her chin, another symptom from her first pregnancy though not, as far as she recalled, with Edgar. *Edgar!* The name seized at her. What a terrible mother she was, she'd hardly thought of him at all.

The smell of a fresh Gitanes floated up the stairs, bringing back the nausea. How could she think straight with this unwanted start of life inside her? *Could* she bear to get rid of it? And if not, could she live with the lie that it was Dennis's?

Though, remember, Clem, it *could* be his.

*

Gwen looked up from her paper. 'Another female MP elected,' she remarked. 'Hoorah, that makes a grand total of three.' She snorted and stubbed out her cigarette. 'And more strikes – Tube workers, dockers. Good luck to them, I say. Anyway' – she stood up, yawned hugely, stretched till her vertebrae clicked – 'I'll get dressed. Let Captain out, will you?'

Clem opened the door onto the back garden, where a path wandered between overgrown bushes of laurel and bay, and dandelions and daisies fisted up between the paving stones. Captain ambled out to lift his leg against a bush.

Back inside, Clem idly ran her eyes over the newspaper: an advert for Bile Beans; another for Palmolive. She could not be bothered to read about strikes or politics, but her eye was caught by something at the foot of the page.

STOP PRESS

Local businessman run down outside the Wild Man Public House.
Further details in final edition.

She read it twice and sat down heavily. *No.* She put her thumbs between her teeth and bit hard, the pain igniting a spark inside her. It *could* be Mr Chamberlain. It *could.* Vincent so low last night, so quiet, so furious. There could have been an accident when he drove back. After all, look at how *she* met him; that accident comes back now – her blundering into the road, the swerve, the crash.

If she hadn't stepped out into the road at that precise moment, she never would have met Vincent. The thought sideswiped her and her hand flew to her abdomen; it seemed impossible that she might not have met him. It felt like destiny. Like, she snorted, fortune. But it *was* possible; any possibility is possible.

So – think, *think*. If it *were* Vincent and if he'd run down Mr Chamberlain then . . . what did it mean? What could it mean to her?

36

S OMEONE IN THE next cell, a drunk, sings, 'Oh, willow, tit-willow, titwillow!' – not a bad rendition; someone else yells at him to shut up. Vince sits on his bench staring at his knees. Ridges of bone stand out through the flannel; underneath the skin's scarred and rough. The biggest scar from when, as a nipper, he fell through Dad's cucumber frame. His own fault; they'd warned him he'd come a cropper and come a cropper he did. 'You could have cut yourself to flaming ribbons,' scolded Mum. Funny that coming back to him now, the way she knelt in front of him, blood on her lap, pressing back the flap of skin. The scar on his knee healed like a big sad mouth, and she'd pull her own mouth down whenever she noticed it. She died before the war, thank Christ, and she never had to see him ruined. His hand goes to his face, the plate bent so some of what's beneath must show, but at least he managed to hang onto it.

'On a tree by a river a little tom-tit sang, "Willow, titwillow, titwillow."'

'Shut your fucking cakehole,' comes the rough voice. 'Some of us are trying to kip.'

'Nuff of that now!' shouts a copper.

The walls are painted shiny yellow. Light from the corridor falls in dim stripes through the bars and onto the tin piss bucket. It's not cold – that's something – but there's a hell of a stink. The blanket, the floor, everything stinks of shit and piss and fear.

Will Doll be opening up as per usual today or will the police keep people away? Probably the body's been moved by now, lying in a morgue. *The body*. Still doesn't seem real.

After leaving Clementine in Felixstowe, he rode back fast, stopped off at a pub on the way for a few. Hadn't drunk much earlier, needing to keep a clear head, watching her flirting away like a proper pro – never thought she had it in her – and Ted falling for it hook, line and sinker. It could have worked, *it could have bloody worked*. It'd been going like clockwork. Doll was hopping mad with Ted, you could tell. After he and Clementine had waltzed out the door together, she went back behind the bar, face like thunder.

'What's up, Doll?' he said, all innocent, and she snapped, 'Nothing.'

It'd been hard to keep a straight face. He'd wanted to clap, to cheer, could hardly wait for closing, when, after Doll turfed out the barflies, they'd have a cosy drink together, have a good old heart-to-heart, agree what a flighty bastard that Ted Chamberlain had turned out to be. But then it all went so bleeding wrong. He puts his face in his hands and moans. In the fight he'd happily have throttled the fucker, squeezed the life out of his fat throat, but Doll had set them to rights. He's never seen her quite like that – blazing, magnificent, fearless. But the look she gave him afterwards, it turned his soul to dirt.

And later, when he got back from Felixstowe there stood Ted by the driver's door like a target for his front wheel and there was no thought, no choice. He accelerated and hit him full on – the face, the eyes comical as he saw the bike heading for him, no stopping, the soft impact, the whoomph and crack of a body felled, the scrape as the bike skidded across the car park. Wouldn't have cared if he'd killed himself and all, but he got off scot-free, hadn't so much as torn his trousers. There were witnesses, the police said, more than one, who all told the same story: he seemed deliberately to speed up towards the victim.

The door unlocks and an old duffer in a uniform comes in with a cup of gnat's piss and a slab of bread. 'Your legal rep's on his way,' he says. 'Get this down you first.'

He stands and watches as Vince slurps the tea. It tastes like some tea long ago, beach-hut tea brewed by Mum in a metal teapot. The bread's stale and he dips it in the liquid, realising he's famished, as famished as a kid just run out of the sea, cold and shivering, towards Mum holding out a towel, towards a cup of hot sweet milky tea.

' "Is it weakness of intellect, birdie?" I cried. "Or a rather tough worm in your little inside?" ' goes the singer.

The old policeman shrugs. 'Where'd you cop this?' He taps his own cheek.

'Somme, last push.'

The copper grunts in sympathy. 'Wife's nephew fell at Flanders.'

'Oh, willow, titwillow, titwillow!'

'Hey, mate, can't you shut that fucker up?' shouts the complainer.

The copper rubs his face wearily. 'Well, good luck to you, mate. Sounds like you're going to need it. I'll see if your rep's ready.'

Vince swallows the last of his tea as the legal man is ushered in. His face is soft and dented like a kiddie's toy, grey and furry, tiny wiry specs perched on his nose. 'How do,' he says, taking Vince's hand in his massive, spongy one. 'My name's Barry, John. Here to offer my services. Initial fee ten bob. Pretty pickle you've got your-self in here.'

He huffs himself down on the bench beside Vince. 'Hearing on Monday, just a formality you understand. You plead not guilty, of course. Anyone likely to bail you out?'

Vince shakes his head.

'Well, for now, if you just go through the events for me . . .' He takes a notebook from his pocket. His cuffs are frayed, grease spots on his lapels, surprising Vince. Still, he's probably bottom of the heap as far as legal men go. What more can he expect?

'I did it,' Vince says.

'Gracious me, don't go saying that!'

'I did it,' Vince repeats. 'I wanted him done for.'

Mr Barry makes a winded sound, puts a hand on Vince's arm and gives him a shake. 'Come on, man. Understand what's at stake, do you? Or do you *want* to swing for it?'

Does he? Vince wonders, and a great fatigue sweeps over him. Why not? What's he got to live for? Maybe he should just hang and get it over with?

'Every chance we can avoid that,' Mr Barry's saying. 'War service, NCO, I understand? That'll go down well. And what with this . . .' He indicates Vince's face. 'Unusual case too, death by motorcycle. I can possibly procure you Sir John Kingsley, someone of his ilk. Interesting case, possible question of setting a legal precedent and so on. You could go down in history – how does that strike you?'

Vincent stares at his knees.

'Come on, man, buck up.'

An officer walks past, jangling keys. He releases not the singer but the shouter: 'At least I've heard the last of that prick,' he shouts as he goes, and in response the singer starts up again: 'He sobbed and he sighed and a gurgle he gave, then he plunged himself into a billowy wave.'

297

Swing for it, Vince thinks, *swing*. Feels a tightening in his neck, a crack as it breaks. To go through all he went through in France then swing for an arse like Ted Chamberlain?

'And an echo arose from the suicide's grave, "Oh, willow, tit-willow, titwillow."'

'Mind putting a sock in it, old chap, for a moment or two?' calls Mr Barry and the singer is silenced.

'So, you reckon you could get me off?' Vince says.

'That's the spirit.'

'But there were enough people there saw what happened.'

Mr Barry chuckles. 'That's as maybe, but within the law, you'll find, if there's a will there's a way.' He scratches his head, examines his nails. 'It's all a matter of how one frames things, of course. Now, take me through your version of events. Any previous knowledge of the deceased?' He licks his pencil.

'He was a regular at the Wild Man, where I live, where I work,' Vince says. Whatever will Doll say to him putting it like that? It was never official lodgings, never official work. But it's the truth.

'And what occurred yesterday evening?'

'He waltzes into the pub, chats up some blonde—'

'A Miss Chance, apparently.'

Vince gawps. *Chance?* Recovers himself. 'Anyway, he chats her up in front of Doll, Mrs Pepper that is, the landlady.'

'Were he and Mrs Pepper on what we might call intimate terms?'

'No,' Vince says, 'never.' He takes a deep breath. 'Now me and Doll, *we* was.' Doll'll have his guts for garters for saying so, but it's the truth.

Mr Barry pulls his head back in surprise. '*You* and Mrs Pepper?'

Stung by his surprise, Vince goes on. 'Yes. We are.'

'On intimate terms?'

Vince nods. 'I get on well with the nipper and all. We'd talked of getting wed . . .' Maybe that's going too far.

'You were engaged?'

'No, but . . .'

'You had an understanding?'

'In a manner of speaking.'

'I see.' Mr Barry writes something in his notebook. 'Help me to understand something here, if you will. If Mrs Pepper and Mr Chamberlain were not in any way "close", why should he, as you put it, try to make her jealous?'

'See, I reckon he, Chamberlain, had taken a fancy to Doll – sorry, Mrs Pepper.'

'Despite the fact that it was *you* with whom Mrs Pepper had an understanding?'

'He wasn't to know, was he?'

'Was he not? I'm struggling to follow.'

'I reckon he was playing up in front of her with the blonde—'

Mr Barry raises his hand. 'Pure speculation.'

'See, he didn't know how close we was, me and Mrs Pepper,' Vince says, 'but I reckon he'd got wind of it. We had a holiday together – her, me and the kiddie – and he only goes and turns up. At Walton-on-the-bloody-Naze.'

Mr Barry frowns and sticks out a shiny bottom lip, jots something down. 'Let's return to events on the night in question. I believe that earlier that evening there was a fracas in front of the Wild Man. We have a witness.'

Vince looks up sharply.

'But your version, please.'

'Well, Chamberlain left with – Miss Chance, was it? – and that was the back of him as far as I was concerned.'

'So?'

'But then I goes out a bit later and there's his car and there he still is and we have words.'

'Words?'

'Well, we have a bit of a brawl, then Doll, Mrs Pepper, comes out and puts a stop to it. I go off then – hopping mad, I don't mind telling you.'

'What was the cause of the disagreement?'

But Vince can't think straight now.

Mr Barry sighs. 'I'm not quite following. But continue, please: where did you go?'

Vince hesitates, remembering the drive. Clementine clinging like a limpet. No sense implicating her, is there? She'd only go and bring up the money business. She'd be like a fish hook hauling up all sorts of muck.

'Rode around till I'd cooled off,' he says.

Mr Barry sighs. 'Letting that pass for the moment, take me through your version of events when you returned to the Wild Man at around half past ten.'

'I rode back into the car park, quite dark it was by then. Chamberlain standing near his car.'

'Anyone else there?'

'Not that I saw.'

'And what happened then – as far as you want the jury to know, of course?'

Vince swallows, clears his throat. 'All right. As I rode into the car park he stepped forward as if he wanted to stop me, and I swerved but I hit him. That's it.'

'Ah, let me get this straight. It was getting dark. Impaired visibility, I imagine? And with your restricted sight.' He indicates Vince's missing eye. 'Excellent. And he, Mr Chamberlain – probably inebriated by that time – stepped into the path of your vehicle?'

Vincent looks at Mr Barry's serious, hairy face. It's a farce, that's what it is. Mr Barry's making up a story and all he has to do is go along with it. And it could be true. It could have been like that.

'If you say so,' he says. 'That's about the size of it.'

'Now, about the earlier scuffle, you'll have to come up with some sound reason for that. I suppose Miss Chance was there?'

'P'raps. Couldn't swear.'

'If Mr Chamberlain left the premises with her, she must have been. She might well be key.' He tapped his pencil on his teeth. 'A list of witnesses is being drawn up – I imagine she'll be among them.'

Mr Barry stays a few more minutes compiling a list of character witnesses. Doll the main one, of course, but who knows what's going on in her head now? Regimental names, they'll go down well, a few local tradesmen he's had dealings with. Sir fucking Mostyn. Eventually Mr Barry hauls himself to his feet, smooths his twill trousers over thick thighs.

'Quick hearing on Monday morning. Apart from "Not Guilty", you won't have to say a word. But in the meantime think, man, fill in any holes in your story. One could wish you hadn't volunteered guilt on arrest, but that can probably be explained away. Shock and so on.' He crushes Vince's hand. 'Keep your spirits up. Every chance here, every chance. Sergeant Bright?' he calls and the man comes, keys jangling, to let him out and the singer starts up again: 'Though I probably shall not exclaim as I die, "Oh, willow, titwillow, titwillow."'

Vince lies on his back, staring at the greasy ceiling. The thud of the body against the wheel, the weight of it. Killed a man. Meant it too. Killed men at the Front, of course, but that was different, not personal. Though the blue eyes of the young Hun will never leave him. He curls his knees up to his chest and groans.

37

GWEN'S MOTORBIKE CRUNCHED to a halt on the gravel. Clem unfolded herself from the sidecar, brushed the dog hairs and drool from her sleeve, eyes darting to the front door, the windows. No one.

'Care to come in?' *Oh, please, please say no. To be alone . . . only to be alone . . .*

Captain leapt from the sidecar and began a series of elaborate stretches, before swaggering across to the steps to lift his leg.

Gwen, in breeches and leather helmet, remained astride the bike. Raising her goggles, she watched the dog, smiling indulgently. 'No, thanks. Rather think I might call in on Harri,' she said. 'Always good value, isn't she?'

Clem stiffened.

'Don't object, do you?'

'Ten to one she'll be with Stanley's family,' Clem said. 'She often takes the twins there on Saturdays; the girls adore their grandpa.' Even to her own ears her voice rang false and too insistent.

'Nothing to stop me trying,' Gwen said. 'Is there?'

'No, no, of course not,' Clem said quickly. 'By all means do call. She'd love to see you. Of course she would.' She flushed under the scrutiny of Gwen's gaze. How was she able always to see straight through one?

'Well, thanks most awfully for everything.' Clem stepped closer to kiss Gwen's cheek. 'You're a good chum.'

Gwen accepted the kiss, cleared her throat and pointed to the sidecar. 'Rightio. Captain, in.' She waited for the dog to lollop back inside, where he sat looking haughtily ahead.

'Look,' Clem said, 'if you *do* see Harri, please don't say anything . . .' She indicated her abdomen.

Gwen gave her a withering look, and then her eyes shifted and she looked past Clem, lifting her hand. 'Hello there,' she said as Dennis appeared, golf club in hand.

'Miss Carslake.' He shook Gwen's hand before putting a proprietorial arm round Clem's shoulder. 'This is a surprise, darling. Thought you were out for the day?'

'Feeling seedy so Gwen brought me home,' Clem said, refusing to meet Gwen's eyes. 'Thought you'd be on the course by now.'

'Couldn't get a bally tee before twelve. Been practising swings in the garden.' He brandished his club. 'Heard you arrive.' He patted the glossy black wheel arch of the motorcycle. 'I say, rather a beauty, isn't she?'

'Isn't she just?' Gwen's eyes rested on Clem, who flinched.

'In the sidecar, I hope?' Dennis said. 'Wouldn't like to see you riding pillion in that outfit!'

'Naturally.' Clem smoothed her grey skirt, the skin of her legs remembering the fast silk of the air last night.

'You do look peaky, darling,' Dennis remarked. 'Inside for you, *toute de suite*. Miss Carslake? I expect Mrs Hale's got coffee on the go.'

Gwen shook her head. 'Decent of you, but no, thanks.'

'Well then, let's get you inside, old thing.' Dennis steered Clem towards the steps. 'Thanks for giving her dinner,' he said to Gwen.

'But . . .' Gwen began and then stopped. 'A pleasure,' she said, narrowing her eyes at Clem.

Dennis glanced frowningly between the two of them. 'Come along, Clementine.'

Gwen snapped down her goggles, lifted her hand, kicked at the starter of her bike and roared away.

Dennis followed Clem into the hall. 'What was all that about?' Her heart pounded dangerously as she scanned the hall for a note, a message. But there would be none. It was over. *Over.*

'Whatever do you mean?' She turned to him, ran her finger along a pattern on the chest of his Fair Isle pullover: brown, red, fawn, brown, red, fawn. 'Go and have your coffee, darling, do,' she said.

He removed her hat and smoothed her hair, rather tenderly. She closed her eyes to avoid the close scrutiny of his gaze. If Vincent were involved in the accident at the Wild Man he might be in custody, might at this very moment be giving her name. Might she be counted as a witness? Might the police call to question her?

'What's going on in there?' He touched her brow.

'I've a wretched head coming on,' she said. 'I rather think a bath.' As she mounted the stairs, she was aware of his eyes on her back and kept her step firm, head erect until she was in the bedroom, where she allowed herself to collapse backwards onto the stiff cretonne bedspread.

Genuine tendrils of headache began to creep from the back of her neck to meet around her brow and she closed her eyes. So much had happened in the past twenty-four hours, so many questions were battering, and she was so tired that her brain simply gave up. She lay numb and dazed, drifting into unconsciousness.

*

And then she was awake, Dennis looming.

'You look as if you've crash-landed, darling!' he was saying. 'I've had Mrs Hale draw your bath.' She struggled upright. 'You silly child, letting yourself get so exhausted.'

'I'm all right,' she said.

'Hmm. I've got to run now but presently' – he wagged his finger at her – 'I *shall* want to know what you got up to last night.'

She smiled weakly.

'Miss Carslake seemed taken aback when I mentioned dinner,' he said. 'I take it you *were* there?'

'Oh, Dennis, do call her Gwen, for goodness' sake. Of course I was there! Telephone her if you don't believe me!'

His smile was strange, uneasy, perhaps; his bright brown eyes searched hers. The first clock began to chime and she jumped.

'A bag of nerves,' he said. 'Anyway, toodle-pip for now. Proper rest after your bath now, Mrs Everett. Doctor's orders. I'll have Mrs Hale bring up a tray.'

He bent to kiss her brow, bristles already emerging since his morning shave, sandpapery against her skin. She reached up and caught his hand. 'Might I have a few drops of Veronal, darling? Just to help me settle?'

He shook his head. 'A good bath and forty winks is all you need.'

'Please?' She grasped his hand.

He sighed, left the room and returned with a glass. She sat up and swallowed the contents, feeling relief already although it would take a while to reach the fuzzy place she craved. 'You're too kind to me,' she said.

He looked so pleased it nearly broke her heart.

Once she'd heard the engine of the car dwindling down the drive she got up and, squinting against the headache that sparkled around the edges of everything, took the scrap of paper scrawled with a name and a number in Gwen's spiky hand from her pocket and slid it in a dressing-table drawer amongst her stockings and undergarments.

From the bathroom she could hear Edgar and Dinah in the nursery. 'One, two, buckle my shoe,' Dinah was reciting, and there was the faint rhythmic creak of the rocking horse. She undressed and allowed her body to sink into the warm water, bath salts gritty under her behind. She let her head hang back; the water soothing, gurgling in her ears to drown the nursery sounds. And then she sat up and reached for the soap, stroked suds under her arms, round her neck, over her breasts, all slippery and pinked from the heat. Her belly was flat still; hipbones cusped like the ends of the cradle. Inside curled a tiny *it*, with no idea who it was, with no idea of anything at all. If it were to be stopped now, it would never be and never know and would that be so terrible?

She got out of the bath too fast and, dizzied, knelt on the rag rug by the tub until the spell had passed. Now she could hear only the dim murmur of Dinah's voice. Bed, she really did feel like bed, like sleeping for weeks. But what if the police came? She was too tired now to think of anything, any story, anything to explain . . . It would have to be the truth. The dangerous, preposterous truth, which might spell the end of it all for her: this marriage, this household, this life.

Beside the bed was a tray with cold chicken and salad, bread and butter, a glass of water, but she couldn't contemplate a mouthful. She folded back the bedspread and the blankets and slid between the smooth, cool sheets. She closed her eyes, waiting for sleep to take her, but, oh, it was like a bloody war in there: battalions of worries, great battering skirmishes. She tried behind her closed lids to create some order, at least to sort and list the enemies, but every thought sent shocks right through her as if the bed itself was quaking. Until at last the Veronal did its work and sleep, blessed sleep, rose like the brown water of the river, drowning her thoughts as it closed over her face.

When she opened her eyes the light had changed and she could hear Dennis singing in the bath. His clothes were folded on a chair; the lunch tray had gone. Soon he came padding in, wet-haired, towel round his waist. 'You've had a proper rest,' he said. 'That'll do you a power of good, darling. Why not stay put? Dinner on a tray?'

She lay gazing at him as if from underwater as he towelled his hair with ludicrous vigour and strode about naked, gathering his clothes. How must it feel to have such hairy skin? Damp curls everywhere – though not all men had so much body hair. And certainly not women. Did Gwen go to Harri's? Perhaps they'd spent the day together.

'No, I'll get up,' she said, swimming herself to the surface. 'I want to see Edgar before bedtime.'

'Good show, darling. Oh, by the way' – in shirt and socks he sat down, bouncing the mattress – 'there was a murder last night at a pub near here! Rather marvellously called the Wild Man.'

She sank back against the pillows.

'Practically our own doorstep! Some chap ran another down – deliberate, they're saying – some sort of love rivals. A *crime passionnel*. Thrilling, what? You expect these things in gay Paree, or even London. But here! Good Lord, whatever next!' He laughed. 'Old Bloomingdale was full of it. Certified the death, of course, that being his patch. Think I'll get Hale to run out for the local rag.

Get the latest, eh?' He pulled on his trousers, arranged his braces. 'Take your time, darling. Let's have a sherry, shall we, and then the infant shall come down and entertain us?'

Clem's face felt papery, her smile a feeble pencil line. 'Shan't be long,' she said.

Dennis was pouring sherry as she entered the sitting room. On the low table by his chair lay the evening paper. She snapped her eyes away from it.

'What have you got there?' She squatted beside Edgar who was trundling a wooden train on the floor.

'Choo-choo.' He lifted and waved the engine.

She made a whistling train sound and he grinned, teeth gleaming in his miniature Dennis mouth. There was not a fleck of her in him as far as she could see. Dennis to a tee. He would grow into a handsome man. She ruffled his soft hair.

'Not sure about this "choo-choo" nonsense,' Dennis said. 'What's wrong with "train"?'

'It's the way Dinah goes on. It does no harm.'

'He'll have to learn to speak properly one day – why not start now?' He drank half his sherry and topped it up again.

'Give him a chance, darling! Actually, I've been meaning to say, Dinah is such a good girl, I thought I'd like to reward her.'

'Mmm?'

'Put up her wages a little?'

Dennis shrugged, handing her a glass of sherry. 'You're the boss in that department.' He raised his glass. 'Chin-chin.'

'How was your game?' she asked, keeping her eyes away from the paper though every muscle strained to look. The sherry tasted wrong – this wretched condition. She sipped, letting it pool on her tongue before swallowing, closed her eyes to feel it snaking hotly down her gullet.

'Best draw a veil over the first five holes,' he said, 'but then' – he rubbed his hands – 'blow it all, what do I do on the sixth but score a birdie! Wiped the smile off Bloomingdale's face, I can tell you.' He proceeded to take her through his game, stroke by stroke, as she watched Edgar drag his train about. Absent-mindedly, Dennis picked him up as he spoke, and the boy tugged at his moustache.

'Ouch, none of that now.' He put Edgar down and the boy toddled across to the newspaper, gleefully to scrunch and tear.

Clem knelt to extricate it from him, but it was a page concerning the Suffolk Show that was in her hand: sketch of a Clydesdale and a list of prize-winning fowl. Edgar began to grizzle. 'There, there,' Clem said. 'Let's play with the choo-choo.'

As if conjured by the nursery word, Dinah appeared. 'Should I take him up, ma'am? He's getting fractious, bless him.'

Clem nodded. 'Thank you.'

'You see?' Clem said when she'd gone. 'She's a treasure. She shall have an extra shilling a month.'

'Won't we need to up the Hale's wages too then? We don't want to start a general strike!'

They were quiet for a moment, listening to Edgar's wails receding up the stairs and then appeasement being reached on the landing.

'Well, why *not* give them all a rise?'

Dennis shook his head. 'You're too sweet, darling,' he said, and a darkening happened in her heart. She rose to put a record on the gramophone, choosing an operatic aria at random. Dennis lit a cigarette and leaned back his head, wagged his foot.

The smell of the cigarette was making her feel queasy. There were white roses in a vase on the piano, she'd arranged them the other day – oh, only yesterday! It felt like weeks. She buried her nose in their crumpled petals, swayed to the warbling soprano until the record crackled and stopped.

'Play something?' Dennis said. 'You scarcely play at all lately.'

'So out of practice. And still rather a head,' she said.

'Poor darling. Come and sit down.'

Clem obeyed, reaching for her needlework box where several stockings waited to be darned. Dennis picked up the newspaper and rattled the pages back into order, muttering, 'Wretched infant.' There was silence but for the ticking of the clock and the rustling of paper until Dennis said, 'By George.' Abruptly he lowered the paper and stared at her.

'What is it?'

'This so called Wild Man murder business.'

Goosepimples rose on her hot arms as the stocking slithered to the floor.

'Listen to this.' He read with incredulity in his voice. 'Police are searching for a female witness, a "mystery blonde" – a Miss Anna Chance – but she's proved untraceable. Obviously a false name. Apparently she was seen with the victim earlier in the evening. Description . . .' He stopped and looked at her over the top of the paper, then shook it, a puzzled expression on his face as he contin-ued to read: 'A lady of refined appearance, judged to be in her early twenties, slim, fair bobbed hair, grey outfit, yellow cloche hat . . . Police are appealing for help in tracing this young woman who may be an important witness.'

He raised his head and stared at her, and it broke over her like a great wave that she should tell him, just let it all out. Oh, and *what* a relief it would be even if he sent her packing. Even if that were to be the very end of this life, in this house, with these people.

As she opened her mouth, Mrs Hale tapped on the door and put her head inside. 'Soup's on the table. I've done you a cold one, seeing as it's such a scorcher, a nice Vichyssoise.'

'Thank you, Mrs Hale,' said Dennis. 'We'll be there in five minutes.'

Mrs Hale darted her eyes between them. 'I'll hold back the entrecôte then, shall I?'

Dennis nodded and waited till Mrs Hale, with obvious reluctance, had withdrawn. 'So?'

Clem manufactured a laugh. 'Darling! Whatever are you suggesting?'

He stared. 'I couldn't have described you better myself.'

Laughter like chips of glass.

'The clothing?'

'Fashionable colours,' she said, 'and those hats are ten a penny. Really, Dennis! You aren't seriously thinking?'

'Refined appearance . . . fair, short hair . . .'

'Half the women in England have had their hair bobbed,' said her voice.

Frowning, Dennis lit a cigarette from the end of his last one. 'And last night?' he added. 'Miss Carslake—'

'Call her Gwen, you silly old stuffed shirt,' she teased desperately.

'That moment of hesitation when you mentioned dinner? And you rushing off to Felixstowe like that, and staying the night when Hale could perfectly well have come and fetched you? You must admit, it does look rather fishy, darling.'

Clem met his eyes, startled to realise that he was afraid. She took a deep breath and a decision made itself inside her. 'I was feeling nostalgic for my old town,' she said quietly, 'for a particular reason.' She stopped and blinked, eyes brimming. 'Gwen's such a good old chum, and we were going to go walking around all the old haunts before I told you . . . and then I felt too ghastly for dinner.'

She glanced up at his handsome, credulous face, and then down at her abdomen. 'You see, I think . . .'

Dennis put down his cigarette, came to her and knelt by her chair. 'You think?' His eyes were bright and questioning.

'I'm not sure yet, but—'

'Oh, my sweet, my clever little girl.' He jumped up. 'Ha! This is marvellous, Clemmie, this is simply ripping!'

'*If* it's so.'

'How late?'

'Two weeks, getting on for three.'

'Any other symptoms?'

'The usual things.'

'Darling.' He bent down and kissed her lips and then stood again, kicked at the newspaper and shouted out a laugh. 'And to think I thought . . . !'

'I can't believe it.' She made her voice a little cross. 'To think that of me! You really are a perfect buffoon.'

'I am, aren't I!' Almost bouncing on the balls of his feet, he calculated on his fingers. 'March or April – a spring lamb!' Pacing around the room, waving his cigarette, he began to speculate about the sex of the child, how Edgar would react to the news. 'I see your point *re* a pay rise for young Dinah now,' he said.

'I didn't like to speak of it. You see, I've been rather afraid . . .'

'No, no.' He sat on the arm of her chair and took her hand. 'You were unwell last time but now you're well. No reason to think it will recur. We'll take such care of you, darling, wrap you in cotton wool. I do love you so.'

'Yes,' she said, smiling up at him. 'But do you know, I *am* feeling a bit shabby – think I might go up.'

'Of course,' he said. 'I'll see to a tray for you, bring it up myself.' He shooed her away, and as he went to stub out his cigarette he stopped, eyes snagged by the newspaper and, in the mantel mirror, she caught a slide of unease behind his smile.

Upstairs she undressed once more, put on a fresh nightdress and stood by the window, open to let in the sluggish air. The weather would surely break tonight – a swarm of storm bugs were clustering on the glass. She took the scrap of paper with Gwen's handwriting from the drawer, tore it into minute scraps and scattered them in the grate. The telephone rang and she jumped as if she'd been shot.

Dennis came in with a tray: Vichyssoise, bread and butter, a glass of white wine, a dish of wobbly pink shape. 'In you get,' he said.

'What was it?'

He inclined his head.

'The telephone?'

'Oh, nothing you need worry your silly noddle about.'

She forced breath into her lungs and made a smile come into her voice. 'Go down and have your own dinner, darling,' she said. 'You must be famished.'

He went to the window and gazed out for a moment, fidgeting and clearing his throat. 'I did however make a telephone call myself,' he said, back still turned.

She held herself utterly still.

'I spoke to Miss C. – to Gwen. And we agreed that you were at home last night, feeling poorly due to your condition. As it happens, the Hales were off and I'm certain Daisy would verify should it became necessary.' He turned and approached her. 'You dined alone and were snug as a bug in bed when I got home from bridge. Understand?'

'But—'

He lifted a finger. 'Just in case there were to be any nonsense with police and so on with this . . . rather coincidental description.'

Clem's eyes rested on the cold green surface of the soup where floated a dust of pepper.

'Understand?'

She nodded, unable to raise her eyes to his. Sweat was crawling in her hair.

'Now eat up and let's forget all this silliness, eh?'

Obediently she lifted her spoon and dipped it in the soup.

'I love you, you know that,' he said.

She looked up. 'Oh, Dennis . . . I should tell you—'

'No.' He almost shouted it, and she started, splashing soup on the tray. His hair had flopped over his eyes, and in his expression once again she glimpsed fear. A fly was buzzing in the room now like a tiny drill. Pushing his hair back, Dennis softened his voice: 'Least said soonest mendest, eh?'

'Yes, darling.' The fly tried to settle on her wine glass and she batted it away.

'Best foot forward then?' He bent and kissed her head. 'Eat up, that's the ticket.'

She listened to him descend the stairs, heard a blackbird singing, the dim bang of a door somewhere in the house. The fly had settled on the pink shape and she watched its progress, the way it gorged itself then stopped to rub its forelegs together as if washing its hands, the iridescent sheen of its wings.

She lifted the tray, put it on the floor – let the fly make merry – and paced the room, hand to her mouth, unable fully to grasp what had just happened. Dennis was prepared to overlook this? Prepared not to know? She'd thought him so straightforward, or she'd believed him to be, but this . . .

Her eyes in the mirror were unfamiliar – the pale grey inked away, shadows beneath them. The spot on her chin. She looked flawed. And that was right, that was correct, that was some satisfaction. She was flawed. Nothing was flawless. She sat at the dressing table and gazed, angled the side mirrors to catch her profile. She picked up her brush and pulled it through her short hair. Last night people had seen this face in the Wild Man, but no one knew her. Unless Vincent spoke up how could they possibly trace her?

He might speak up though, he might.

The telephone rang again and fear jolted through her like an electric shock. She climbed back into bed, pulled the sheet to her chin. The fly lifted into her eyeline, snarled around the room, settled back on the tray and went quiet. She need not fear, she told herself. If Vincent hadn't spoken yet, the chances were that he would not. If he did, there were the letters to prove the blackmail; it would not go well for him.

And Dennis would protect her, dear Dennis, prepared – it seemed – to lie for her. Queerly this made her respect him more, *like* him more. And there was the baby to consider now, of course. Dennis was quite right. They must look forward, only forward.

She slept badly, woke late. Dennis had already gone down, and with her newly heightened sense of smell she detected bacon and coffee in the distance. There had been a storm in the night and she'd lain and listened to the grumble of thunder, which reminded her of shelling at the Front, and – because it was not that, because it didn't mean a flood of ghastly injuries to treat – it had seemed delightfully innocent, somehow *pure*. Now the air was fresh. She stood and stretched, pulled back the curtain and inhaled the smell of wet grass and roses, listened to the fluting of a thrush.

On impulse, she knelt to retrieve her old sketchbook from the bottom drawer of the wardrobe and with it, it seemed – or perhaps it was only fancy – came the smell of war, of cordite and gangrene. Dennis was right that she should burn it, but first, crouching on the floor, she leafed through pages of dead and dying boys to stop at a sketch of Powell. The best likeness, the most successful portrait she had ever achieved: the face of her one true love, wide silver eyes with pewter rims, dimple in his left cheek, mouth always on the edge of smiling, as if he saw the joke of the world and was trying to suppress his laughter. He was nothing like Vincent, really, nothing like him at all.

And he was gone.

The locks in the doors in her head were sprung; it must come together, all the contents of all the rooms. It was all one life, one *her*. This was it. There was no Clem in Canada. No Powell. All she had was here. Holding her breath, she lifted a finger to face it, to open the one page she'd never been able to look at. A moan came from her as she saw again the tiny thing, her own homunculus, a sprig of a creature curled as if to fit into a walnut shell. No, it was larger than she remembered – more of a hen's egg – or had she merely enlarged it in the drawing? Face tight as a bud, fingers, toes, ribs and bumpy vertebrae: tiny, tiny Aida.

Gwen had not wanted to leave the 'result', as she'd called it, with Clem on that day, but Clem had begged and Gwen had given her half an hour and, crouching on the bathroom floor, she'd used her pencil to catch, to keep, at least in graphite, Powell's child.

The telephone rang and Clem jumped. She closed the sketchbook and shoved it back into the wardrobe. She must learn not to react so to every call; after all, living in a doctor's house there were so many. She took a deep breath, determinedly slowing her heartbeat.

She must bathe, she must dress and breakfast, perhaps get Hale to drive her and Edgar to Harri's. Yes, that's what she'd do. Continue as normal, that was the way. Perhaps she might tell Harri about the baby? The thought carried her hand to her belly. She recalled once more the sketch of Aida, and, with a marvellous rush of understanding, it came to her that the child was back. Clever thing, clever girl. Aida had found her way back.

She stood listening to the sounds of the house – her house, her home, her precious life – palm resting on the cradle of her pelvis. Please let this be, she murmured, please allow me this and I will be content.

38

UNDER A THIN blanket he tosses and turns, hips and shoulders aching from the cold hard bench. Not more than a wink of sleep at a time, just a scrap of dream. Funny how Mum and Dad have got into his dreams lately; just now there was a woman, Mum or Doll, stroking his face and he was whole. Two eyes, he could feel them moving, blinking; he could see both sides of everything.

In this cell the green tiles shine like stagnant water, black stuff between them making a pattern; the ceiling has cracks like roads to follow to nowhere. Three days now, and all that time the buzz of the electric globe, the bleak light. What he'd do for a bit of darkness to have some proper shut-eye, a bit of softness, a clean sheet.

It's never quiet. You might get a few minutes, then someone shouts or a door bangs, and everything echoes: footsteps, voices, slams and jangles.

He's in a cell alone today and that's a blessing.

Breakfast comes, bread and tea, and then Mr Barry turns up.

He comes in huffing and puffing, and Vince stands, a bit of a lift in his heart. What's Doll said, what's Mostyn?

'How're you keeping?' Mr Barry extends his hand.

'Tolerable. Hardly the Ritz, is it?'

'Seen worse,' he says. 'Least it's cool. It's a scorcher out there today. Mind if I take a pew?' He lifts his coat-tails, lowers himself onto the bunk, shuffles his arse about. 'Come to update you on progress, a few questions and so on.'

'Seen Doll?' Vince asks.

Mr Barry pulls out a handkerchief to blow his nose, folds it carefully and stows it back in his pocket before he replies. 'Ah . . . that, yes. Mrs Pepper . . . now, rather a disappointment, I'm sorry to say. Might be that we have to look elsewhere for our principal character witness.'

Vince can feel the meat of himself shrink against his bones. 'What's she said?'

'And rather the same story with Sir Mostyn, I'm afraid.'

'What's *he* said?'

'Full of praise for how you *were*, but says last time he saw you he thought you were, shall we say, disturbed. We can call him, of course, to vouch for you in the past, but what we need is someone more recent to give you a character reference.'

Vince traps his arms under his armpits, breathes in and out, getting himself under control. 'So what's she said then, Doll?'

Mr Barry takes out his notebook. 'She seemed aghast, if I may say, at the idea that you were, so to speak, betrothed. "First I've heard of it" were her precise words.'

'I never . . .' Vince almost wails.

'Her story is that she put you up when you were down on your luck and you did a bit of work in the bar for board and lodgings.' He flips the page and reads: '"He never was a permanent fixture." And, most injuriously to the case, she says she got the idea that you had previous knowledge of Miss Chance – looks passing between the two of you and so on. And she says Chamberlain told her the same thing, thought you'd cooked up some scheme between you.'

'We never!'

'Quite sure of that, Mr Fortune?'

Vince nods, heart thumping him in the ribs. 'Told you, never seen her before.'

'You must know how damning it'll be for you if it turns out otherwise? Best come clean now.' Mr Barry takes out his hand-kerchief and blows again, pressing a finger against each nostril.

Quiet for a moment, and then Vince blurts: 'Doll really say we were never together?'

Mr Barry folds his handkerchief, returns it to his pocket, then takes out and glances at his watch. 'Certainly she implied so.'

'We even went on holiday – her, me and the kiddie.'

'Ah yes, I did put that to her. She said it was all above board, separate rooms. I've spoken to the hotel manager. It seems also that your Mrs Pepper was witnessed dancing "into the small hours" with a chap that evening, a chap who happens to go by the name of Edward Chamberlain.'

Mr Barry looks at him significantly and waits, riffling the pages of his notebook with a long thumbnail.

Within himself Vince can feel a change of heart as definite as a change of weather. 'He weren't invited,' he says. 'He just turned up.'

Mr Barry clucked his tongue. 'This is not going well, Mr Fortune. You can surely see my problem? First, on arrest, you admit your guilt. You said' – he opened his notebook again – '"I did it. I wanted him done for." And to clarify, you added: "I rode at him on purpose." And you see, now we have a motive – the green eyed-monster, as you put it yourself. I'm not saying there's no hope, but . . . well . . .'

'Doll really made out we was never intimate?'

Mr Barry sniffed, wobbled his head from side to side. 'Ah, she might not have said *never*, but she was certainly scandalised at the suggestion.' He sniffed. 'I wonder . . . puts herself about a bit, does she? The jury never react well to that. I wonder if sexual provocation might be some sort of defence, deliberately playing you off against each other?'

'No,' Vince says. 'No, that's not right, that's not what I said.'

'A love triangle. I imagine we can dredge up some racy stuff about Mrs Pepper. Any other men you know of? Money changing hands?'

'It's not *her* on trial!'

'Not as such, but . . .' Mr Barry flicks through the pages of his notebook, chuntering under his breath as he thinks.

Vince is hot, clammy. He's not having her name dragged through the mud. Even if she did deny him. Not his Dolly. She's got her reasons, her name to keep clean. Dolly humiliated – he can't have that. And if he was to go down this line, ruining her reputation, upsetting Kenny, he might avoid the noose, but what then? If he doesn't swing, he's in for a long stretch by the sound of it. A stretch of this: walls damp, skin damp, whole place stinking. Christ, he'd rather be back in the trenches taking his chances. And when he's served his time and they let him out – then what? That thought is like stepping off a cliff.

Christ, he could do with a smoke now. 'All right. I did it,' he says quietly. 'It's all on me.'

'Now, now,' Mr Barry says. 'No call for that.'

'No, I mean it. Straight up. I did it.'

Mr Barry shakes his head. 'Haven't got time for this now.' He hauls himself to his feet, bangs on the door, signal to the screw. In an undertone he says, 'You don't want to throw your life away, do you, old chap? Not after serving your country. Officer, weren't you?' He shakes Vince's hand in his moist one. 'Throw all that away for one moment of madness? Think about it: war hero, throw in the shell shock for good measure. Perfect defence in the making.' He raises an eyebrow at Vince. 'When you've come to your senses you ask for me, Mr Fortune. But don't leave it too long.'

Once he's gone Vince pisses in the bucket then, rolled up in the blanket, lies back on the bench, pressing his itching head against the hardness of the wall. Swing for it. The words shoot through him . . . yet if he offers no defence, it'll happen. And he won't have to think. No more thinking. It's like a weight lifting if he can see past it, past the actual moment . . . The weight of his life, money, face, work, love. It's all too bloody hard.

After

39

November 1920

FLAT ON HIS back on his bench, Vince watches the glass grille of his cell. The condemned cell. Pete and Bob arrived a while ago to take over from the night shift. Two men watching him twenty-four hours a day in case he tries to top himself. Waste of bleeding time that is. Why not let him, and save themselves the bother?

Apart from the lack of privacy, can't grumble. Since the sentence they've treated him like royalty – if royalty was banged up in a cell, as royalty sometimes was back in the day. Warm blankets and a proper pillow, food worth eating, even a paper now and then. Bob's the only one of the lot of them he really gets along with. They look at the horses together, study the form, gas about the football and the state of the world: the strikes, unemployment, poverty, the massive fucking mess of the country after all the bright hopes. Touch on nothing personal though, beyond a swap of war stories. Bob sent home after the first Somme, gas damage to his lungs, and true enough he does wheeze like a bloody great steam organ starting up.

When they're chatting Vince sometimes forgets where he is and what he's waiting for. Sometimes, flat out, staring at the changing squares of light, he imagines he's free; at a race say, listening to the drum of hooves, with all the lucky sods out there – a few quid in their pockets, a girl on their arm dolled up for the day, or the prospect of finding one, a good cold pint of ale.

But at least he doesn't have it weighing on him any more: the rest of his life. He never needs to earn another penny. Like flaming royalty!

'Can you vanish yourself?' that little girl asked in the hotel. And so did Kenny. All his tricks: the floating handkerchief, flying thimble and the rest. When he was a nipper he made himself a vanisher out of a biscuit tin with a secret compartment to disappear all manner of objects into. Always put on a show of a Christmas afternoon, mystified his mum and dad. Once he was invited to a kiddies' party to do his conjuring, but one saw straight through the trick, made him a laughing stock. Still, what he wouldn't do for a vanisher now, a bloody great vanisher, to step right into.

There's a bang on the door and Bob opens it to bring in his tray: a rasher of bacon, hunk of bread, tea, a couple of fags.

'Get that down you.' He puts the tray on the bench.

'Last breakfast,' Vincent says.

Bob blanches. 'Now, now, son. Light?' Vince leans towards the flame and draws down the smoke. This time tomorrow he won't be smoking.

'Guvnor says any last requests? Within reason, of course.'

Vince has been ready for this question and there's only the one thing he wants. 'Mrs Pepper . . . I'd like to see Doll.' His voice goes croaky on her name.

'She said no before,' Bob points out.

And it's true, but this is different, surely? This is his last whole day; it isn't possible to take it in, not really. His live mind can't imagine being dead. How can he really believe that they'll take him from the cell and hang him by the neck?

'Try,' he says, drawing so hard on the cigarette he can see it shrivel. Slow down, slow down. He sips the tea.

'You could have a drink,' Bob says. 'Whisky? Pint? Bit of beef-steak? Saucy mag? Or is there anyone else, any family?'

'Only Doll,' Vince says. 'See, if I could make my peace with her, then . . .'

Bob sighs wheezily. 'I'll see what I can do.' He goes to the door and summons another screw, gives him the message.

Later, Vince is taken for a handcuffed walk along dim corridors to a small room where the prison doctor is to check him over.

'Waste of bleeding time,' Vince says, trying to keep it light. He looks at Bob, but his eyes are on his boots and no one's smiling. The doctor's short, neck pudgy and chafed against his wing collar, eyes bloodshot. He's in worse shape than Vince, that's for sure. Bob stands beside the door, silent and switched off, and a spotty assistant with bum fluff on his chin stands to attention beside the desk.

'Lift your shirt,' says the doctor, and when Vince does so, presses the cold metal of his stethoscope against his chest. 'Deep breath.'

When he's finished he scribbles a note.

'Fighting fit, am I?' Vince says.

'Step against the chart now. Evans . . .'

The assistant steps forward and ushers Vince back against the wall, and he feels something touch the crown of his head. 'Five foot eleven and nine-twelfths,' Evans says. And the doctor writes this down. 'Please step on the scales now. We'll have that, if you please.' He holds out his hand for the prosthesis.

Vince freezes.

'We need the weight exact.'

'But—'

'Rules is rules. Wigs, specs, wooden legs, everything extraneous off.' His palm remains outstretched. 'And you hardly need it now, do you?'

That he might lose his face has not occurred to Vince. He pinches the arms of the specs between his fingers. 'No . . . please,' he says. What if Doll says yes? What if she turns up? He couldn't face her without it – how could he? 'Please,' he says.

'I'll get it off him,' Evans says, taking a step forward, but the doctor shakes his head.

'But you can't wear it for . . .' The doctor pauses.

Vince stares at him.

'There's a hood,' the doctor explains. 'It won't make a difference, on or off. Your face will be hidden.'

'All right, but . . .' Vince cannot let go of the arms of the specs, the thin metal biting his fingers; the rest of him has gone cold and rigid as metal too. 'Let me keep it till then. Please.'

The doctor harrumphs, shrugs, makes up his mind. 'Can't weigh more than a couple of ounces. I'll calculate. Step on the scales.'

Feeling a plunge inside, Vince hesitates, as if the scales them-selves are dangerous.

'Look lively,' the doctor says, and Evans nudges Vince towards the steel contraption. He takes a breath as he steps up. It rattles and the needle flickers, eventually settles. 'Ten stone, five pounds and three-eighths of an ounce,' says Evans, and the doctor writes it down.

'To calculate the drop,' Evans says helpfully.

'Now, now, Evans, no need for that,' the doctor says. He looks, for the first time, into Vince's face as if he is still a live human being. 'We do want it all to go smoothly, you understand. Best for all parties concerned.'

Vince steps off the scales and the rattling starts again. He turns and sees the needle settle back on zero. The drop.

'Finished here,' the doctor says to Bob, who's been standing silently beside the door. 'You can keep it till the end,' he says to Vince, indicating the same area of his face. 'I'll have a word with the governor.' He extends his hand. 'Goodbye,' he says.

'Ta,' Vince says and lets the doctor shake his hand; this little man looking up at him, a little man who can go out into whatever weather is happening outside and home to his missus no doubt. His hand is small and damp. One of the last hands I'll touch, thinks Vince. None of this seems real. The doctor will see him tomorrow, see him afterwards, certify him dead. Rum old job, listening to a man's chest one day, shaking his hand; certifying his death the next, ticking a box on a form. You must have to have a heart like bloody granite.

Cuffing him, Bob takes him back to the cell. When he's back in his cell Vince lies down, staring at the ceiling. God, bring Doll, he pleads silently. Please, God, bring Doll, please, God, make her come.

After months of doing next to nothing there's no bloody peace today. First off, the chaplain arrives and tries to get him to pray, but he can't pray, can't even make a show of it. This bloke is young, feels sorry for Vince, and he can't have that: someone not long out of short trousers pitying him, too young even to have served, all gawky limbs and startled eyes, like some kind of animal, a hare or fawn. Bob and Pete sit at their bench pretending to mind their own business. What a job, sitting on their arses all day. No job for a real man.

'No, ta,' says Vince. 'Not a believer.'

'But you'll find, Mr Fortune, prayer to be the greatest comfort in this, your hour of need.'

'Just get my girl to visit,' he says. 'That's all the comfort I want. Just put in a word, will you, with the governor, or go higher up if you need to?' He indicates heaven with his eyes and finds a laugh – or something like a laugh – burbling out, and it's a rum old feeling after such a time.

The chaplain shakes his head. He's clutching a Bible, looks crestfallen. 'I'll see what I can do. If you change your mind, I can be summoned right up to the last' – he hesitates, flushes – 'the last . . .'

'Moment?' Vince supplies. 'I'll bear it in mind.'

'God bless,' the chaplain says, taking Vince's hand and bowing his head in a moment of silent prayer before he's let out of the cell. Vince imagines him bolting off down the corridor. He'll be there tomorrow, waiting for a change of heart, praying for Vince, if not actually with him. Well, perhaps that's some sort of comfort.

In the afternoon there's a knock on the door, another screw comes in and Bob leaves, saying nothing. Surely he wouldn't go off without saying goodbye? His shift ends soon; the other two will be here, the ones who barely say a word, even to each other. Surely Bob wouldn't leave like that? He's a pal, the last pal Vince's likely to have; the thought is shrivelling. Maybe he should have gone along with Mr Barry. Is it too late now? He could ask . . . but the thought of it makes him tired. What would face him if he did get off? Years banged up? And if not, turfed straight out into the world where no one wants him, job prospects zero, chance of love the same. He'd probably end up topping himself anyway, might as well get it done for free.

When Bob returns there's a grin on his face. 'Well, surprise, surprise,' he says.

He can't take it in at first. 'What?'

'She's here.'

'Who?'

'Blimey!' Bob raises his eyebrows at Pete, who snorts. 'Who do you think? The Queen of bleeding Sheba?'

Vince stares.

'Mrs Pepper,' Bob confirms.

All the air's squeezed out of Vince's lungs; can't catch his breath.

'She's waiting,' Bob says. 'Ten minutes you've got. No touching. No funny business, or visit curtailed pronto. Got that?'

Vince can't speak.

'Got that?' Bob repeats.

Vince nods. Bob cuffs him and raps on the door for it to be unlocked. The awkward jerky walk, can't get in step with Bob, heart beating right up in his bloody throat. Months since he's seen her, not since that last day in court when the judge set the black square on his wig and sentenced him to death. It was all so solemn, like a play, and it seemed nothing to do with him at all. He'd wanted the reassurance of catching Doll's eye but her face stayed turned away, hidden by the brim of her hat. And now she's come to see him! She would, of course she would, big-hearted Doll, of course she bloody would.

She's already sitting at the table when Bob uncuffs him. She's wearing her best alpaca suit – green, a little shiny, hideous, really, the one she wore to give her evidence in court – and a dark hat that does nothing for her. Looks like she's put on weight and her cheeks are rouged too bright – but, still, it's her, it's her. She's only gone and come!

Bob stands against the wall; the other screw lurks with a face like a wet weekend – well, don't look at *his* face, look at *Doll's*.

She doesn't lift her eyes till he's sitting opposite. Three foot of wooden table between them and, oh, how he yearns to touch her. Words aren't coming and there's only ten minutes. Christ, he can smell her, the mothball smell of her suit, a trace of L'Heure Bleue. That'll still be the same bottle; she ekes it out, dabs a bit in her elbow creases, on her wrists, behind her ears, only on special occasions. Pulse points she calls them. It's an honour that she's put it on today, for him.

'Well,' she says at last. 'How are you, Vince?'

'I'm all right,' he says. 'Well looked after, grub and that.'

She nods. 'Well, that's good.'

There's no clock but still he can hear the seconds ticking away.

'It's good of you to come,' he says.

'I wasn't sure,' she says, 'but then I thought, well, Doll, you might be sorry tomorrow if you don't.' She looks aghast at herself for saying, he supposes, 'tomorrow'.

'I wanted to tell you, Doll . . . I wanted to say . . . thank you . . . and I'm sorry.'

'No need, dear.'

'And I wanted to say . . .' He steels himself; this is the only chance he'll get. 'I wanted to say how I've loved you.' He darts a look at the guards but neither alters his expression.

She adjusts the rim of her awful hat. There's the creak of Bob's boot as he shifts, and from far away the slamming of a door.

'What's it like out there?' he says.

'Drizzle,' she says. 'Leaves coming off all over the shop.'

'Well, it's that time of year.'

They lapse into silence. He stares at her face, drinking in the heavy, smudgy lids, the eyes with their smile lines all round though she's not smiling now, her soft cheeks. It's murder to be so near and not be able to touch.

'How's Kenny?' he asks.

'He's fine, dear.'

'Getting on all right at school?'

She nods and clears her throat. Vince can sense Bob shifting, impatient for them, he shouldn't wonder. As if he's read Vince's mind Bob says, 'Five minutes, Mrs Pepper, then I shall have to remove the prisoner.'

Doll looks up at Vince, for the first time really looks at him. 'I shan't open up tomorrow,' she says quickly.

Something inside Vince lurches – the drop, the thought of that drop.

'That's good of you, Doll,' he says. 'That means a lot.'

'Out of respect.'

'Good of you.'

'I had to tell the truth, dear,' she says, leaning towards him, a plea in her eyes. She wants to be forgiven.

'Course you did,' he says.

She's fiddling with her buttons. He hears her stomach gurgle. She always had a noisy tum; he remembers the warmth of it, the luxury of her big soft body in the bed. That was true, those times – not many, but more than once, she gave herself to him, and no one can say that's not true.

'How's business been?' he says, despairing. He doesn't care about the fucking business, but gratefully she tells him about the pub, how customers flocked in after the accident – bless her kind heart for calling it an accident – to have a good gawp at the place, but now it's levelled off.

'Time to say your farewells,' said Bob. 'Got to stick to timings, governor's orders.'

'Would you have married me?' Vince says quickly. 'If it wasn't for . . . everything.'

She presses her lips together. Lie, he wills her, *lie*. But there's a fight going on inside her between kindness and truth, he can see it, and truth wins – of course it does, she's honest to a fault.

'I told you before, dear, I'll not be tying the knot again. Why should I?'

'Would you have married Ted?' he says childishly, feels Bob's attention sharpen.

'Come on now,' he says. 'Time for fond farewells.'

But Doll ignores him, snorts and shakes her head. 'Not in a million years! What do you take me for?' She laughs, herself at last, if just for a moment, and relief flows through him. 'I always said I've got my own business, my Kenny, why should I want to tie myself to a man?'

'Love?' he says.

Bob has stepped behind him, clears his throat.

She wrinkles her nose and her eyes go soft. 'I only loved the once, you know that. I married him, he died fighting for his country. No one could ever fill his shoes.' She tilts her head and smiles. 'It's nice of you to say you loved me though, dear. A bit of love never goes amiss, does it?'

'Time's up,' says Bob. 'I'm sorry, Mrs Pepper. Someone will come for you presently. Please wait here.'

'But I did have a soft spot for you, dear – you do know that, don't you?'

Vince stands, and before he can be stopped he leans across the table and grasps Doll's head, her hat between his hands, and pulls her towards him, kisses her hard on the mouth. And they grab him – of course they do – wrestle his arms behind him, cuff him; and all the time she watches, her open mouth a blur now, and he's taken away, and on his lips a taste of her lipstick and on his hands something sticky. She must've touched up her hat with that black stuff from the chemist's, she must've touched up her hat specially for him.

All the clocks in their various places strike five, then six, then seven. She pretends to sleep as Dennis gets out of bed, yawns and stretches, slides and creaks into his clothes and goes downstairs humming. *Humming*. But, of course, he doesn't know what day it is, is not aware.

And what will *he* be doing now? Vincent. She should have gone to see him. But it was impossible. How would it have seemed? And to get herself involved at this stage would have been foolish, if not dangerous. But she does wish Vincent knew about the child. It might be a comfort for him – or perhaps quite the reverse.

And in any case it could be Dennis's baby, it *could* be. To all intents and purposes, it will be.

As soon as he's safely downstairs she gets up and pulls on her dressing gown, catching sight of her silhouette in the dressing-table mirror, the marvellous mound of her growing belly.

One more look at Vincent, while he's still here. She slides the sketchbooks she hasn't touched for months from their hiding place in the wardrobe and sits on the bed, leafing through the pages until she reaches, first, the portraits of Powell and then the studies of Vincent – the different versions of his head – and though her fingertips are icy she feels a flush rise to her cheeks, to her breasts, as she remembers how that day ended.

Oh, the eye, the painted eye, the way she managed to capture that – the love shining from it, love that's got nothing to do with Vincent Fortune, of course, but *her* love, reflecting back from that painted surface; her love for Powell so strangely returned, almost as if, yes, absurd though it is, she can allow herself to think it, as if he'd returned to her – his ghost, his essence – returned to her briefly through another man. Before she was able to let him go.

One by one she tears the sheets from the sketchbooks – all the portraits of Powell and all of Vincent – and begins to fold.

He wakes and the grille is black. The electric light casts a dim grey-ish light. The two guards are strangers; shame he couldn't have had Bob here at the end, a friendly face. It can't be more than an hour. And then it will stop. He can feel the beating of his heart; it doesn't know what's coming. He feels sorry for his good old heart that's beat since before he was born, beat faithfully through everything, through Mum's death when he thought it would break, through thrashings and kissing, through quiet times on the riverbank wait-ing for a fish, in the trenches, on the battlefield, quietly in his sleep, like the clappers in Doll's bed: his poor, faithful, unsuspecting heart. He cups a hand to his chest – it's not his poor heart's fault, is it? He thinks of Doll, the love of his life. She put on her precious last drops of L'Heure Bleue for him, she touched up her hat, she's not opening up today, a Friday, out of respect – a Friday, too, that'll cost her a pretty penny. That must be a sort of love, mustn't it? A soft spot is a sort of love.

If they'd had a child together at least it would be part of him left behind, a little kiddie to keep on living for him. A girl it would have been, he's sure of it, a little sister for Kenny. Oh, how Doll would've loved a girl. Vince's blood going round in her veins, her own heart, which was part of him, beating on till God knows when, into the next century if she was lucky. And whatever would the world be like by then?

If there had been a kiddie though, then he wouldn't be letting this happen. He'd have had to stay alive for her. He can almost see her – very beautiful she'd grow up to be, a credit to Doll, and she'd look after her mum when she was old. But, oh, this is rubbish, rubbish, rubbish. He hears footsteps approaching and he and the two screws all look towards to the door.

They let him keep his face for the last walk, cuffed to a stranger each side, all out of step, lurching along. It's a long walk and two flights of stairs up. He's cold. One of the guards, a stranger, smells medicinal. Neither of them say anything, not one friendly word. Then they come to a door with a little group of men standing outside. The doctor, the chaplain, three more. The door's opened and he's taken into an empty room. A room with a small dark window – not quite dark, the first grey of dawn – the glass glittering with raindrops.

'Hands behind your back if you will, Mr Fortune,' someone says, and it comes to Vince that he could lash out. He could go down fighting. But his hands, icy and damp, go obediently behind him and he feels a strap tighten round his wrists. With his hands pulled back like that, his heart's a fist punching against his chest and his breath begins to come in gasps. He can stop this. Can he, can he, is it too late now? Is it too late? Something in him begins to fight against himself, but he keeps it down, keeps it in. Oh Christ, but he needs to piss now.

There's a door in the wall opposite, and now they're leading him through it into a small chamber in the middle of which is a trapdoor and chalked on the centre, where the two flaps join together, the shape of two feet. Behind the trapdoor is a lever; above the trapdoor a noose. One of the men lifts off the prosthesis, a pug-nosed man whose green eyes linger on the scar. Bare-faced, Vince finds himself struggling as they take him onto the trapdoor, strap his feet together. He's not ready, not ready. Maybe he should have tried to pray, maybe he does wants to pray. He wants to piss, he says so, he want to piss, he wants to pray, he wants to . . .

'Make it easy for yourself,' one of the men says in his ear, that bad smell. Another has man stepped into the room, Vince senses, and he tries to turn, but as he does, the hood goes over his head – whiteness – and he thinks of the vanisher, of stepping in – now you see me, now you don't – and there's something round the neck, hard under his left ear, heart going like the clappers, breath all hot against the cotton, can't get his breath . . . Wait, wait, white, white, all he can see is

40

PULLING A SHAWL around her shoulders, she pressed her warm forehead against the glass. The sky was just beginning to lighten though there was still a litter of leftover stars, a rag of cloud wiping the grimy moon. And they began, the clocks all out of time, to strike the hour. She closed her eyes.

And so it was eight o'clock, and then eight o'clock had passed.

On the branch outside was the dark shape of a blackbird, absolutely still, then lifting and vanishing into the blue-black. Stepping backwards till the bed caught her behind her knees, she allowed herself to fall flat on her back. Gone. But within her belly, a kick of life.

She had Hale drop her at the top of Harri's lane and waited for the growl of the engine to fade away, leaving her with the sound of dripping from a privet hedge – and otherwise silence. It was a still day. No sun, the sky was a heavy sodden grey and in the air hung the breath of rotting leaves, a faint sweet tang from the brewery.

Later she'd visit Harri – and no doubt find Gwen ensconced beside the fire. There was Christmas to discuss, but for now she turned away, and threaded down the lanes towards the river. In her arms was a hessian bag, borrowed from the pantry, filled with a light yet bulky load. Through the boatyard she went, passing a man in goggles working with a blowtorch, vivid orange sparks splashing the ground. Other boats, swaddled in tarpaulins, slumbered.

She let herself out of the yard, through a gate and onto the river path alongside the brown sluggish water moving patiently, inexorably seaward. Strands of the weed that clung to landing posts drifted like clotted hair. She stood in the raw, chill river's breath.

A chap with a whippet passed by, nodded, eyed her curiously. It must look queer for a woman to be lurking there alone on such a disagreeable day.

A heron stood motionless only a yard or so away, shoulders hunched in an attitude of resignation. She stepped closer, and with a reproachful look it hauled itself into the air and lumbered away, across the river towards the far bank with its huddle of Scots pines feathered black against the sky.

No one to see. She crouched and opened the bag, revealing a rustle of folded paper boats, on which glimpses of Powell and of Vincent were visible in different planes: an eye here, a finger, an ear. One by one, she lifted these fragile craft and set them on the brown water, watched them sail off on the rush, sometimes tangling in weed or lodging against a landing post before they were washed free. She waited till each one was out of sight before she launched the next. The last one she raised to her lips before she set it on the water, holding her breath until it vanished on the tide.

And then, a little light-headed from crouching, she straightened up, took Vincent's notes from her pocket, tore them into tiny shreds and scattered them on the water, smiling at a hapless duck which, supposing the paper to be bread, snapped its beak amongst the scraps.

How the children would have loved to see the boats. Well, she'd make more. She'd teach the twins, help them with the folding, and on a sunny day in spring, they'd come down here to launch them.

She remembered the last time she'd walked along here, with Harri and Gwen and the children. Gwen's gauche attempts to be jolly and aunt-like had been- quite killingly cringeworthy, and poor Captain had loped along looking most put out. But it was nice that they were happy, Harri and Gwen, though downright peculiar – typical of Harri, as Dennis said – not to simply find herself a solid chap and settle down like any normal woman.

He seemed to have stopped finding the idea of sapphists in the least titillating since Harri had 'joined the brigade' and that was a relief. And there had been no further mention of Harri moving to the Beeches. Still, she'd be there for Christmas, and Gwen too, no doubt, and all the children, and Dennis, of course. She didn't love him the way she'd loved Powell, but in quite another way – a daily way, a calm and grateful way. Yes, she loved him well enough.

And, of course, next Christmas, there would be another to love. As she stood, hand on belly, watching the brown flow of the tide, she felt a surge of movement inside. The boats were gone. Powell was gone. Vincent was gone. But the child was certainly there, growing and kicking. A girl, oh, let it be a girl, *please* – let it be Aida.

A watery sun penetrated the army-blanket cloud, casting leaden gleams on the tide, and she turned away – it really was a chilly day – and hurried towards the warmth of Harri's.

ACKNOWLEDGEMENTS

With thanks to Andrew Greig, Jane Rogers, Tracey Emerson, Bill Hamilton, Moira Forsyth and Alison Rae for their careful reading and invaluable input and advice.

www.sandstonepress.com

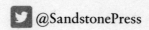 facebook.com/SandstonePress/

@SandstonePress